REEL LIFE

A NOVEL

JACKIE TOWNSEND

Copyright © 2012 Jackie Townsend

ISBN: 0983791503
ISBN-13: 9780983791508
Library of Congress Control Number: 2011911574

rp Ripetta Press, New York, New York

For my dad

REEL LIFE

C H A P T E R   1

The Wizard of OZ

July, 2003

The movie had started. The psychic was reading Dorothy's future in a crystal ball, and Betty felt a strong inward pull in her womb, a sense of life giving her another chance, a way forward. She looked around her. Her oldest, Sam, was stretched out on the floor so close to the TV screen that the images illuminated his face; her youngest, Nick, was curled against her, sucking his thumb and blue blankie at the same time; the missing rebel, her middle child, Clay, was in the basement battling it out on PlayStation's Lord of the Rings. These moments with her children were what made sense, Betty thought, resting her eyes shut.

Then the banging started up again. "Mom!" Sam screamed, and she opened her eyes. "Tell Dad to stop hammering. I can't hear!"

"You don't need to yell," she responded calmly.

Dave, her husband, was upstairs repairing the A/C. It had almost been a relief returning home from California to find him immersed in a busted condenser, the upstairs flooded. To be so consumed moving furniture and airing out the carpet with fans that she had no time to dwell on the fact that her little escape to California was over, that Monday Betty would go back to work, and Dave would begin his job search. That their lives would continue on the same.

A ferocious wind knocked and banged. "Go out and find your dream," said the psychic to Dorothy in the face of that black, ominous tornado swirling in the distance. He was frantically boarding up his trailer and urging Dorothy on her way, and Betty reminded herself that things could never be the same. Sweating now, she unstuck herself from Nick, got up, and went to shut the window. Better to keep the stifling July air out than in, she decided.

"What does that mean, Mommy?" Nick said urgently, popping his thumb from his mouth. "To find your dream?"

She turned toward him quickly, intent on his odd question and the sight of Dave standing in the shadow of the kitchen light with the dirty filter. He was half smiling at Nick's question, also waiting for Betty's answer, and they held eyes for the first time that day, perhaps for the first time in weeks, since she'd told him she was pregnant and he hadn't said a word, not so much as a word.

She looked back at Nick, wanting to say something meaningful, something real, something the opposite of what her own mother might say. "It means you need to find what makes you happy," she settled on finally, as Dave pounded back up the stairs in search of his own dream. Or what she thought was his dream: to fix up this run-down farmhouse where he could have a workshop and studio to craft his furniture. He would make a living off his art. He would do what he loved. She wasn't sure whose dream it had been. It was all so convoluted, now.

She went back to the task of shutting the window, which wouldn't budge. A waft of hot, muggy air hit her face and she gave up. She came back to the couch and stuck herself back to Nick, who'd been mulling on Betty's answer. She gazed down at his angelic face, thinking about her own dreams and what had become of them. Because here she was, thirty-nine years old, planted on a Power Ranger bedspread before the TV with bowls of buttered popcorn and peanut M&Ms, and dressed in one of the terrycloth robes her mother still sent her every year at Christmas. It was her dream to have a family, to be the mother her own mother wasn't. She pushed her hand through Nick's long curls, wondering if that dream was possible now.

"Like candy," Nick blurted out.

Betty stifled her regrets. She'd almost forgotten the question, but looked at him and laughed nonetheless. "Exactly, like candy."

"I love you, Mommy," he said, with such stabbing innocence that Betty blushed.

"I love you too," she said, never feeling anything truer, more powerful in her life. Betty, too, had looked up at her mother with such adoration once. She had asked her mother a similar question about dreams. The answer was long forgotten now, but surely, knowing her mother, it wasn't grounded in any reality. And Betty so much needed to face her own reality: this pregnancy. It was only now starting to sink in. "Vasectomies aren't foolproof," she'd told Dave. He'd accepted that answer apparently. "I'm giving up the workshop," were his only words regarding the subject days later. "I'm going to get a nine-to-five job because with a new baby we can't survive on one salary anymore."

My salary, Betty had wanted to remind him.

Her stomach grumbled and turned over. Glenda, the Good Witch, was waving Dorothy off on her journey with that shrill voice and glossy smile. It always gave Betty the creeps. Nick must have sensed her discomfort. He moved off the couch and sprawled onto his stomach next to Sam, who was still engrossed in the film. The sight sent Betty back to when she and her sister, Jamie, lay sprawled out side by side before this same film. Jamie was always so absorbed, anxiously waiting the end so that she could discover, once again, that it was all just a dream and then jump up and point out to Betty which Oz character corresponded to the ones in Dorothy's Kansas life because this was the part—when everything returned to black and white—that Betty stopped paying attention. Betty preferred to believe that Dorothy and her friends experienced all those crazy things in Oz. Otherwise she felt cheated out of two hours and forty-five minutes. But Jamie liked to boast that she could see right through facades, particularly Betty's. This pregnancy had put an end to their plans for Betty to be Jamie's surrogate. "It was an accident," Betty had told Jamie when they were together in California. Her sister didn't say much, but her expression was painfully clear. She didn't want to know anything more about it. If only Jamie had probed Betty then, in that moment, even just a little, maybe Betty would have told her everything she'd come to feel about her life with Dave. Maybe she wouldn't feel so trapped now. But Jamie didn't probe. As always, she just left.

Dorothy was clicking her heals now.

Could the movie be over already? Betty fixed her gaze on the glittery red shoes and asked herself, "Did I really put everyone's dreams at stake?" Then she closed her eyes to block out any possible answer. In fact she seriously considered turning off the TV now, before Dorothy got back to Kansas. But then she saw Clay out the corner of her eye pretending not to watch from the hallway. And Sam and Nick were both still riveted. It wouldn't be fair to them to turn it off now. And as for herself, could she really live on in a dream like that? When this baby grew up and asked Betty questions about his or her origins, would she tell the truth? Would she tell Dave the truth?

** 1972 **

Their mother loved old movies, especially those big song and dance extravaganzas, the ones where the girl always meets her prince. *The Wizard of Oz* didn't exactly fit this happy-ending formula, but the girls were enamored by it and so their mother did everything in her power when it aired on TV each year to make the evening special, dreamlike, an evening with her babies in Oz. Though they weren't babies anymore, Betty nine and Jamie eight. But babies fit better into their mother's need for organization and structure, skills that transferred over from her job at L.A. Unified where she created custom learning programs; babies will be content if contained inside a playpen with toys and stuffed animals just like students will be productive if they have a dedicated, clean workspace with sharp pencils and good light.

"We didn't have TV when I was a young girl," their mother was saying, attacking their red manes with baby shampoo. Same bath, same pigtails, same hair bows—they were a year apart, but their mother liked to think of them as twins; in fact, if she could turn them into one being, she would. "On Saturday nights I'd ride the Red Cable Car down Hollywood Boulevard to see whatever film was playing. I didn't have any siblings, and my parents, well…" She drew a blank for a long moment before settling on, "Movies were my escape."

Betty didn't want pigtails. She wanted her hair loose, free, and dark like her mother's. She wanted her mother's olive skin. In fact, the girls looked nothing like their mother, something she often compensated for by dressing them in outfits identical to hers. For movie nights in front of the TV they all wore terry cloth robes that zipped up the front. Each year she'd present them with a new set just for the occasion. Tonight it was yellow with red trim. "When I was a young girl, people got dressed up to go to the movies," she'd say, as if they were all prancing around in ball gowns. Then their mother would go and retrieve, rather ceremoniously, her Mary Jane shoes from the closet, those she wore as a young girl to see the premier of *State Fair* at Grauman's Chinese Theater. Betty, as the eldest, got the honors, and just seeing the glossy patent shoes on Betty's feet always made their mother light up like a Christmas tree. But this year Betty was struggling to get them on. "Your feet look like stuffed sausages," Jamie announced, plucking a shoe off Betty's foot and sliding it on her own like Cinderella did the glass slipper.

"Mom!" Betty blurted out, before biting her tongue because her mother was already staring at her like she was a distant relative. "Mom's giving them to me," Betty, steadying her voice, kindly reminded her sister, who's expression said that she knew better, and they both turned now and searched their mother's face for the answer. But their mother's gaze remained on the shoes—one, then the other. "Aren't they just the most precious things." Silence.

They were waiting. She sighed, for she hated choosing. "Well, certainly Jamie should have a turn."

No, she shouldn't, Betty wanted to cry, pulling off the other shoe as if glad to share. For Betty knew how her mom reacted to crying, how she reacted to negative feedback in general: she crawled upstairs into her bed. Things had to go perfectly. Loud noises or bad words would be like throwing water at that witch in the movie. So Betty kept quiet, vowing that Jamie would get hers later. She wasn't sure exactly how, but then she wasn't sure how Dorothy actually made it home from Oz either, even though Betty had seen the movie three times now. Apparently if you wished for something enough, it just happened.

Downstairs in the living room, their mother had laid out their rainbow bedspreads, plus Betty's dolls and Jamie's stuffed horse, all cozy before the TV, where Betty and Jamie were settled now. It was a sparkling new, sixteen-inch color Panasonic that their mom had surprised them with in celebration of her promotion. One-to-One, the teaching program their mother had developed for adults going back to high school was going district wide. The Certificate of Outstanding Achievement was already framed and hanging on the living room wall. Now the girls could watch Oz in Technicolor, and their mother could watch the girls in her own colorful reflection. Their dad, on the other hand, seemed less than thrilled about it. The TV was something she'd done without his consent. There was a din going on in the kitchen about it now, about her promotion, Betty couldn't help hearing. Like who would put dinner on the table now that her hours and commute into downtown would be longer. But their mom had already lined up one of her student aides to baby sit; she'd filled the freezer with frozen pizzas and Tater Tots; and the kids were old enough to make their own lunches. She had an organized answer to each one of his concerns except the main one, the one that he could never seem to articulate. Finally she just said, "We need the extra money, Tom." And with that there was a long and bitter silence, and then the popcorn exploded out of the pan.

The girls looked at each other. They'd been lying on their stomachs with chins propped on hands, waiting for their father who had instructed them not to touch the TV until he was present. But the way things were going…they decided in a silent exchange that they couldn't wait.

A guitar string broke, or so it sounded. A small white dot appeared center screen and exploded into zebra lines, and stayed zebra lines as Jamie frantically tried other channels. Their mom came in carrying the bowls of popcorn, but stopped short when she saw the fuzzy screen.

"It'll be OK Mom," they both instinctively blurted out, as their dad limped into the room just behind her. "I specifically asked you girls not to touch the TV." As a family therapist, he liked to sing his words when he was angry so that he wouldn't sound angry. But it was the *you girls* part that stung Betty, because, technically, it was Jamie who'd defied his authority. But no matter who did what, they were always *you girls*. Sure they both had the same Raggedy Ann hair, but they were two different people. Didn't anybody see that? Betty searched her mother's face for acknowledgement, but she seemed lost inside that box, unable to fathom it not working, something going wrong after all her efforts to make it just right.

"I told you," Jamie said, as the images suddenly came into focus, life got its color back, and their mom sighed with relief.

Their dad moved behind the set and began fiddling with the antenna anyway; sure he could make the picture better.

"Dad!" Betty and Jamie yelled in unison.

"Just one minute girls."

Someone exhaled.

Their dad was notorious for unfixing things that didn't need fixing in the first place.

"Dad move, it's starting!"

"Oh all right," he sighed, letting out a long slow hiss like he was contemplating the futility of his entire life's efforts. He stumbled back around the couch behind where their mother had taken an unsettled seat, and they all watched like that for a while, stiffly, until Judy Garland broke out into song about that rainbow and the dreams on the other end of it, and their father started whistling patronizingly along, as if to remind them about what once lay on the other side of his rainbow. Handsome and talented is how their mother, in rare moments, would describe him as an actor. They had met when he was playing King Lear in summer stock in L.A., so he could be something of a snob about film actors, and he carried a particular disdain for Judy Garland and her big, wide, red mouth. This was the part in the movie where he clucked, made faces, and teetered himself down the back bedroom hallway, which he did now, all laborious and noisy. Like the Tin Man, their dad was perpetually poised to fall over. When their mom was pregnant with Betty, he fell from a stage ladder and crushed his ankle into a million tiny pieces. His role as Horatio in Hamlet was cut short so that he could spend six months in the hospital with no medical insurance. He was still there when their mother went into labor, their stays overlapping and their bills exponentially mounting. That's when he gave up acting and began studying to be a family therapist. That's when their mom, who'd been choreographing theater productions pro bono for her alma mater, went back to school for her teaching credential. Basically, as it seemed to Betty, all her parents' hopes and dreams ended once she was born, and she'd always wanted to ask her mother if what happened was Betty's fault.

"O, what a rogue and peasant slave am I." They heard their father say from where he stood with his ear at the bedroom door of his elusive, overachieving, thirteen-year old son—eighth grade class president, debate team captain, honor roll…

The storm had come, Dorothy's house was swirling in the air, and their mom motioned for the girls to come up with her on the couch. There was always that natural hesitation, then Betty took one of her dolls, Jamie her horse, and, as much as they might not have wanted to, they curled back up into the babies their mother still wished she had nestled on either side of her. When Dorothy's house crashed down, they all took refuge in the still and silent aftermath, for they were in OZ now. And for a while it did feel dreamlike, all those funny little people in their colorful little world. Until Dorothy, after all that fanfare, came upon the frightening realization that she was winding down that yellow road, alone, and their mom released her grip with a *well-then* sigh. This was the part where, for her, the movie ended, and she made a move to go. "What was your dream Mom?" Betty quickly asked.

She seemed surprised by the question. "Well my beautiful babies of course. I couldn't dream of anything more." She got up.

"But what would you ask the wizard for, if you could?" Jamie added, and their mother frowned. Then she blinked a few times. Finally she just sat back down. "Well, I'm certainly doing things I never dreamed I would. I never would have thought I would be reporting directly to the school board." She pulled her knees to her chest.

"When I was a young girl, at night when my parents' drinking was at its worst…" She paused. "I would go for long walks to the top of the hill in Hollywood where we lived, and there I would stay for hours dancing around under the twinkling lights." An idea struck her, and she released her knees. "All my girlfriends wanted to be movie stars, but I wanted to be Jeannie Crain. I wanted to be a dancer."

Jamie sat up. "That's what I want to be!"

"No one's asking you," Betty said.

Their mom continued, not hearing them. "But I was alone a lot when I was young. I guess what I ultimately dreamed about was having you kids. I thought if I had lots of children around I would never be alone again."

It sounded better the first time she said it.

"I'm never getting married and I'm never having kids," Jamie said flatly.

It was an idiotic thing to say, Betty was sure, and she shared a knowing look with her mom, a perfect knowing look, and it was in this look that Betty saw her own dream, both clear and colorful like the Emerald City she and her mother were floating towards now. "I…am the King…of the forrrrrrrest…st..st..st," said the Lion, working on his courage. They'd made it inside the City's doors, and Betty was reminded of how much she disliked the place—surreal and freaky—Dorothy and crew parading around, getting all buffed and puffed in preparation for seeing the Wizard, rehearsing what they were going to ask for—the Lion strutting around with that rug as a cape and the inverted flowerpot as a crown. "I…am the king… of the forrrrrrrest…st..st..st." Only this time it wasn't the Lion, it was her father's baritone voice bursting forth from somewhere. "What makes a king out of a slave?" He was lurching into the living room now. "Courage," he said. "What makes the flag on the mast to wave?" He paused. "Courage." The rest came quickly, perfect pitch and timing. "What makes the elephant charge his tusk in the misty mist, or the dusky dusk? What makes the muskrat guard his musk?" Another pause. "Courage." It went on like that, each time "courage" increasing in vigor until the finale: low, steady, bedeviling, "What have they got that I ain't got?"

"Courage, Dad," Jamie said flatly.

Applause loomed.

The intermission came on.

Their mom began clearing the empty bowls, and their father shuffled back down the bedroom hall. Jamie hopped up and began pirouetting around the dining table, and their mom had no choice but to pause and watch, her smile growing more distant and faint with each perfectly executed twirl until she just disappeared altogether. Betty wished that her sister would pirouette right through the pane glass window, a vision she imagined now, turning back to face the frozen screen and thinking that she might be too old to see the enchantment anymore. She was almost ten, practically a teenager herself.

Part II began. Betty could hear the soles of those shoes twist and tap against the kitchen linoleum as Jamie made her dramatic return. There was one rather hard landing, then—howls of pain— and Betty whipped around to see her sister crumpled on the floor clutching her ankle. It was an image Betty stared at for a good minute, thinking it's not the pane glass but this might just do. She turned back at the screen and let another minute pass, until the flying monkeys plucked Dorothy into the air and her sister's howls reduced to whimpers; no doubt she was just angling for attention that wouldn't be forthcoming, for their Mom was predictably MIA, and their father was now lecturing Steven in his room. Their bitter monotones seeped through the wall as Betty made her way into the kitchen at last, in the casual guise of retrieving the popcorn bowls their mother had failed to bring back. It was tough to remain unaffected, though, upon closer sight of her sister. "Hold on." Betty hurried to Steven's room and got her dad, who went sweaty and pale and seething upon site of his younger daughter sprawled on the kitchen floor. Where's your mother!" he demanded, his eternal question, and proceeded to limp to the bottom of the stairs and summon her.

Steven made a rare appearance at this moment, if only for the intrigue and fascination, for there was a balloon now where Jamie's ankle had once been. He began debating out loud, logically and methodically, what to do with the shoe, whether they should take it off or leave it on, and if they were going to take it off how to do so. Their dad joined in, which meant an argument, a forced sense of command. Betty went and retrieved some scissors at Steven's muffled side request, the sight of which sent Jamie into spasms. In the background, Dorothy doused the Wicked Witch with water. She began melting, shrilling, and on queue their mom appeared at the top of the stairs, groggy and disheveled. They all stared at her for an interminable minute, until at last she clicked into gear and came hurrying down the stairs.

Here's where the crisis became almost comforting: when the witch melted into vapor, their mom's eyes got their focus back, and all arguing subsided. Ice, towels, and insurance cards appeared at once, their dad remaining soothing and calm. "Everything's going to be all right," he said over and over to Jamie in the tone he'd developed to hypnotize his patients. Even Steven stepped it up. He went and found their dad's car keys and wallet so they wouldn't have to spend an hour looking for them. Their mom had already called ahead to the hospital and packed Jamie's bag, "just in case," and at once they were out the door.

"Ding dong the witch is dead, the witch is dead, the witch is dead…" Betty moved in closer to the TV and assured herself that everything would be all right, because now Dorothy had the broomstick; she and her friends could go back to the Wizard and Dorothy could go home. She covered one eye. Dorothy and crew were making their way towards the Wizard's great hall. They were shaking and trembling and clutching the broomstick. She covered the other eye. She wasn't frightened she assured herself, imagining the Wizard's enlarged, disembodied head. She just didn't want to see the silly man behind the shower curtain. He didn't make sense.

Gun fire, trampling hooves, a train whistle; Betty uncovered her eyes. Steven had switched the channel to the *Wild West* in an attempt, said he, to ease her fright. She fell mute with him on the couch and tried to do just that, until their mother returned an hour later. Jamie would be OK, she reported with a forced smile. She had a slight fracture, and would have an operation tomorrow to set it; their dad was spending the night at the hospital. She then turned and stared so absently at the TV, and for so long, that Betty wondered if she realized they were no longer in OZ. "My baby," she cooed, sitting down next to Betty and pulling her in close.

"Jamie's the baby, Mom," Betty corrected her.

"I know, but you're my baby too." She spoke dreamily, from far away, like Glenda the Good Witch ascending in her bubble. Then all of a sudden the bubble popped and she turned to Betty, "You were so brave tonight."

Steven chuckled at the TV.

"Jamie is really lucky to have a sister like you."

Betty averted her gaze from her mother.

"I never had a sister. At least one I know of…" Betty's mom had been adopted, and it wasn't unusual for her to wonder out loud about a sister or half-sister she might not know about. "Sisters," she said, as if the word itself were divinity, life's universal force. "They're so important, Betty, especially when you get older. You and Jamie will always need to be there for each other."

Betty looked down at her lap, wondering if she should tell her mother about how she'd wished for Jamie to get hurt, and that, like with Dorothy, her wish had come true. But then she somehow knew that her mother didn't want to hear the truth, or wouldn't hear it even if Betty did tell her. There was a new, larger bubble around them now, around she and her mother both. "You're my special daughter."

This was not the first time her mother had told her this. Now she wanted to ask her mother what, exactly, made her so special. Was it volleyball? Talented, was how the coach described Betty's play after their last game. Was this what her mother was referring to? Whatever it was, something didn't feel right, Betty realized, here inside her mother's bubble. In fact nothing did, not even the next day when they all went to visit Jamie in the hospital. She and Steven were too young to go inside, so they waved at Jamie from the window. Glenda and Tin Man were at her side. She was holding up her brand-new paper doll set for Betty to see, and Betty wanted to smile back, knew that she should, but all she could think about was what Glenda had said about them being sisters: they would always need to be there for each other. What Betty was starting to wonder was why.

C H A P T E R   2

A STAR is BORN

July, 2003

It was just past three a.m. now, tomorrow afternoon in Thailand, or something like that. Jamie couldn't sleep. She wasn't sure if she should, so she stared out the window into space. Sixteen hours, direct flight, L.A. to Bangkok, where her husband had taken a sabbatical from life. Going on six weeks now since she'd seen him. She hadn't even bothered to go home to New York first to pick up a few things she might need. After seeing Betty at their dad's in California, in all her fourth-pregnancy glory, Jamie couldn't imagine stepping inside their empty Manhattan loft, hearing the creaks in the old wood floors, noticing the missing family photos or treasured trinkets they'd never kept out, feeling the dry, lifeless air because they didn't even own a plant. They had wanted it that way. She had wanted it that way.

The plane hit some bumps, and she gripped the armrest with one hand, while waving the steward over for more champagne with the other. Turbulence never used to bother her, but it had been two years since she had flown, and alcohol seemed to help. A movie would help. She extended her seat back and perused the on-demand selection, an odd collection of American classics she was surprised to see: John Wayne, Cary Grant...James Mason in A Star is Born, *which she selected, though with a sigh because she'd seen the tragic love story of Esther and Norman in so many different versions.*

This one, the '54 remake with Judy Garland, starts with famous Norman blind drunk and fumbling up his performance on stage. Later, drunker, he discovers Esther singing in a dingy nightclub and becomes mesmerized by her voice. A star she will be, he decides right there and then, and she falls desperately in love with him, and he with her. Her insecurities fall away in the face of this love, and she does in fact become a star. "He made me believe in myself," Esther says, and Jamie closed her eyes thinking of her own husband and how years ago she might have scoffed at that romantic notion, back when Jamie considered flying like walking and work her life. All this before CADnet, the start-up she'd given up everything to go and work for, went bankrupt. "So do something different," her husband had said to her after the shareholders had finally settled out of court a year later. She was free to go back to work then, yet she'd felt paralyzed, unmotivated, not to mention guilty. "Write poetry, be a garbage truck driver, I just want you to be happy."

A shriek rippled through the plane then, startling and haunting Jamie at once because of its sneeze-laugh quality. She peeked around the dimmed cabin. Passengers slept to the droning jet propulsion, screens flashed here and there; she faced forward again, unsettled because in fact she had asked him for something that she thought might make her happy. And he'd said, no.

It was a year ago, hosting a dinner party for Roberto's friends, now their friends, a scene Jamie liked to refer to as a gathering of the UN, with Europe, Asia, and Southeast Asia represented. Sure, Jamie had traveled overseas during her tenure as an engineer, then partner at BCC Engineering, but she had only been a visitor. She had no idea what it meant to live in another country, or to adopt a nationality, and certainly not an American one. Though Roberto, in no uncertain terms, had made it clear to her that he was not American, would never be American, even though he'd lived in this country for the same number of years he hadn't. A mixture of Thai and Italian, he'd grown up all over the world.

Still, eighteen years in the U.S. was a milestone that the dinner guests, many of whom had similar backgrounds, were toasting to that night. Roberto pretended to be proud, but Jamie could sense his uncertainty, a longing he would never admit to. Certainly he was tense. Tomorrow the company he worked for, Delphiant, would announce two thousand more layoffs. "I'm ready to lay myself off," Roberto had warned her that morning. Five years was enough. This was not what he pictured himself doing—the way he'd started out, with some friends from Stanford all working for themselves. Under the name of CS Partners, they built software using rapid development tools and prided themselves on remaining small, high-end, and tightly focused. Five years later they merged with a competitor and formed RAPID to meet surging market demand, then not much later RAPID was purchased by Delphiant, and suddenly Roberto was working for a Fortune 500 company managing a department of five hundred, soon-to-be two hundred and fifty, after this third round of layoffs tomorrow.

"You mean quit?" Her voice had been shaky, for she was not working, her CADnet options were worthless, their Schwab account was dwindling, and they had the mortgage on this loft. How would they survive! She screamed this silently, then immediately despised herself for being that kind of person.

Consequently that night she'd had too much to drink. For Jamie that meant the California girl in her came out, the brash voice and direct remarks. Someone's wife had asked her why she and Roberto, nine years together, six of them married, pushing late-thirties, didn't have kids. Jamie told her she couldn't have kids. The room went quiet, and Roberto got up and started clearing glasses. She didn't care anymore. The conversation had grown stale anyway. She, Roberto, their guests, they'd all been contributors in different ways, to the nineties technology boom-turned-bust. Tonight it was about whose stock options were worth the least. Hers were, of course, and why they continued to discuss this she had no idea.

Anyway it had put her in a mood, and then she caught her reflection in the snow-frosted window after their guests had left and she was cleaning up. Her mascara was smeared, her hair hung half out of its clip; she looked haggard, a mess. She gathered some empty glasses from the coffee table and brought them back to the sink where Roberto was packing up the leftover risotto, suddenly tired of everything in her life, particularly all the nothing conversations they'd had about kids. "Shouldn't we be doing something else at night?"

"Like what?" he said, and she didn't immediately answer because he knew "like what."

"Like putting kids to bed," she said finally.

"Why would someone want to do that?"

"Someone—you mean the rest of the world."

"I'm not the rest of the world."

For a long time she looked at him not looking at her. "So you don't ever think about it?"

No, he did not think about it.

"Not even about regrets? Suddenly you're fifty and feel like you're missing something?"

"I won't."

"How do you know?"

"I know!"

"Why are you yelling?"

"I'm not yelling!"

She sat down at the kitchen island then. This was no longer about kids. "I don't want you to be alone in the end."

"I won't give up our life."

She had no response to that.

He put the risotto in the fridge, turned, and looked at her. "You knew this about me, Jamie."

Perhaps she had, did. She wasn't really sure anymore, what she knew versus what she remembered.

"We could at least see a fertility specialist, consider the options." What she hadn't told him, beyond the discovery of her infertility, the news of which he'd taken rather well, was that according to her gynecolo-

gist they had few options. "We don't have to actually do anything." She didn't bring up Betty's offer to be her surrogate, that she was already doing something. "It can't hurt."

"What part of the word 'no' don't you understand?"

She'd not expected such an outright rejection. Her eyes narrowed. "So what you're saying is that if I want a kid, I'll have to leave you?"

"Yes."

He was back at the sink washing the stockpot, his back to her. She watched him work, carefully and methodically. "Is it because it wouldn't be mine?"

He slammed the pot in the sink. "I'm not going to have this discussion with you now, Jamie." She let out a gasp as he marched towards the bedroom.

"When fucking when then!" She screamed this so unexpectedly loud that dust trickled off the brick wall and an utter darkness swept over her, as if fifteen years of indifference about kids had finally eaten through her insides, as if she were twenty-one again and the cancer was all her fault.

He paused at the bedroom door. It seemed like he wanted to say something.

She didn't wait for him to. She got her purse and left.

His face when she got home the next morning…She couldn't bear the image of it. "Why didn't you answer your cell phone?" he'd said. He was sitting on the couch where he had been up all night worrying. "I didn't know where you were, Jamie." She just stood there, her heart in her throat, wishing he could hate her sometimes, as she could hate him. But all she saw was hurt in his eyes and a vow that had been broken.

She squeezed the bridge of her nose with her fingers. Even here on this plane, almost a year later, she could feel the warmth of him, that strong desire she had for him as they sat there on the couch holding each other. He made no apologies. Not for that night, not for resigning from Delphiant three months later, not for going to Thailand on sabbatical with or without her, and certainly not for something that had happened long before they'd met. He knew what he wanted and what he didn't. She knew this about him *she reminded herself: that it was possible he might return to the country of his birth; that one day the American/non-American scale might tip in the other direction. What she hadn't known was how vast that ocean would be, how far the journey was to the end... or the beginning. The beginning or the end, would she ever stop wondering? Because here she was again, hurtling through space and time to be with him and find out.*

That shriek again. Jamie looked around the cabin, this time finding the source: an oversized woman up ahead in 5b watching the same movie as Jamie, only she wasn't laughing she was crying. Jamie blinked a few times, slowly, before resigning that the woman was Vivi, her stepmother, transported here from another life along with the movie, apparently, if only to torment Jamie with memories. It was a disconnected thought, one she instantly shook from her head. Then she changed the channel before she too succumbed, for she knew this part of the movie by heart anyway, the part where it becomes clear Norman isn't going to be the man Esther wants him to be, and, still, she can't stop loving him.

** 1976 **

Her full name was Vivian Capari. She and her two daughters moved in down the street the same week Betty and Jamie's mom moved out. Vivi was a plump, blond, sassy woman with a high-pitched, earth-shattering laugh. Migraine headaches and mysterious ailments kept her housebound mostly, so she insisted her daughters' friends, the mailman, and random passers-by stop in for chats and general company. After only a few weeks, the neighbors were lining up to sit at her kitchen table, seeking advice like she was some kind of healer.

Because it was so rare for Vivi to leave the house, it was no small event for her to march down her new, palm-tree-lined suburban block in her thin yellow housedress to meet the neighbors that had yet to introduce themselves.

"Vivi's here," the voice bellowed, as if it was the answer to all Betty and Jamie's problems. The front gate slammed behind her, sending Betty and Jamie scrambling off the couch as if they'd been caught. Three months ago they had curfews and chores. Three months ago soaps were off limits. Now this episode of *Family Feud* they were watching was simply a warm up to *Ryan's Hope, All My Children,* and *One Life to Live.*

"Hello," Vivi called again, peeking through the front window.

Betty got the door while Jamie fled to the kitchen and watched from a safe distance her sister being enfolded into the woman's flesh. "You must be Betty," she squealed.

Jamie thought of stepping back into the garage but Vivi was already pulling Betty past Richard Dawson and right for her. "And you must be Jamie." Her hands went to her cheeks. "Why look at that gorgeous red hair." Her eyes went back to Betty. "Both of you. Just gorgeous." Then she laughed a hearty, blistering laugh and pulled both of them into her arms. At school Jamie was referred to as carrot top. So this fresh daisy scented woman was either lying or blind or both.

"And now I see why," Vivi said, letting go. Her eyes were devouring a picture on the wall by the kitchen—their dad in *Hamlet*, Jamie explained.

"Fabulous," Vivi exclaimed after a moment of utter silence. Then she perused the surroundings. On the kitchen counter was an open bag of Lays Potato Chips next to a bowl of half-eaten onion dip. The soggy remains of Steven's Captain Crunch and a piece of their dad's peanut-buttered toast lay on the kitchen table. Last night's disastrous crock-pot attempt was soaking in the sink atop a pan burned with pizza crust. "Your mother at home?"

"She's at work," Jamie said, which wasn't exactly a lie.

"That so," Vivi smiled.

"And where's that handsome brother of yours?"

Betty and Jamie stared at her blankly. Steven was a senior in high school. They had no idea where he was. More strange was that she seemed to know him.

"Then you can come home with me right now and meet my girls. They're twelve and thirteen, the same ages as you two. You'll all be friends!" She turned towards the front door like their fates had already been decided.

"I've got ballet class," Jamie lied.

You stay here, good idea, was her sister's expression. They were still in sweats and t-shirts, after all, and Betty seemed unsure about her hair, her sister's hair.

"Well, not exactly class," Jamie added (Vivi's gaze was like truth serum). In fact, she'd been missing class lately; getting there had become too complicated given the new joint-custody schedule. Her mom couldn't seem to get home from work in time, and her Dad, when he could rearrange his schedule and shuttle Jamie there between patients, was always harried and sweating and late. "But I was going to practice."

"I bet you're fabulous," Vivi announced, shuffling Jamie and Betty out the door.

They squinted down the block of A-frame tract homes with front yards the size of postage stamps and backyards a connected alley. The sun was making its way through the late morning haze, what Southern Californians called June gloom though to Jamie and Betty it meant *Ryan's Hope* was starting. To Vivi it meant sunstroke and she stepped up her waddle. She was more nimble than she appeared and in minutes they were inside her house, which, to Jamie's surprise, was exactly like her own, only totally different. Not muted. Vivi's walls were sky blue instead of taupe and decorated with seductive oil paintings instead of faded family photos. Tomatoes simmered in a pot on the stove, and no bowls of chips or candy or diet sodas cluttered the counter, just an array of vitamin bottles. One read: Zinc.

Vivi led them directly to the kitchen table, which had already drawn a small crowd: Masa, Vivi's older daughter, and Keith, Steven's best friend and Betty's volleyball coach. And then there was Steven, who had just arrived from his summer job at the Department of Parks and Recreation. Vivi greeted him with a cackle-hug like she'd known him for years. "You didn't tell me your sisters were just dolls."

Steven shot a wink their way. "I didn't want them to upstage me."

"And that red!" Masa pawed at Betty's hair. "You're so lucky."

Betty tucked an errant curl behind her ear, fleeting her gaze away from Masa's enviously long and gorgeous chocolate mane, and Jamie shared her sister's pain. It had been their mother's idea; with a new life and hair style all her own, she'd convinced Jamie and Betty to get shag hair cuts like hers for the summer. Only their shag cuts didn't turn out like Karen Carpenter's or their mother's for that matter: theirs puffed and curled.

"What happened to you, Steven?" Masa prodded, and Betty clarified that their mom and dad didn't have red hair either.

"Then where did that gorgeous color come from?" Vivi was dying to know.

"The milkman?" Steven offered, something they'd always made fun of, now didn't seem so funny.

"Our mom was adopted," Jamie blurted out, as if that might solve the mystery.

"Go ahead, Jamie," Steven said dryly. "Give away the family secrets."

Keith, coming to Jamie's rescue, asked her if she was coming out for the V-ball team this year. "We could really use her," he assured Betty who smiled faintly and mumbled something about Jamie trying out if she wanted, which Jamie interpreted to mean, don't even think about it. So she told Keith that she was dedicated to ballet and wouldn't have time. But Keith had moved on to Masa now, asking her the same question, though Masa didn't hear him because she was engaged with Steven on the other side of her, going on coyly about some big decision he was making. Steven slid back in his chair and glanced away from his sisters who had now turned at him, confused. The "decision" was related to Jill, his girlfriend, and whether he should break up with her before going to Harvard in the fall. Apparently, he'd been seeking council from Vivi's kitchen table for days now. This, six months after bringing Jill home to meet his family after just one date acting like she was going be the mother of his children, literally, right then and there on the couch. But then he'd been like that with all his girlfriends. "I say dump her," Jamie said, only because she knew it would get a laugh, which it did.

"Kit!" Vivi hollered to the ceiling. "Masa, where's your sister?"

"In her room reading as always." Masa smiled at Betty as if her mother only ever embarrassed her and she got up from the table with no notice of Keith's infatuated gaze, as if she had no idea how striking she was at thirteen-going-on-twenty. She whispered something into Betty's ear to which Betty laughed falsely in response. Her sister looked antsy to leave, Jamie noticed, which was weird because it was usually Jamie who preferred the isolation of home. It couldn't have been Keith's seeming attraction to Masa that caused Betty's eyes to glaze over; Jamie knew that Betty didn't like Keith in that way. There was a natural law about red heads: if you were one you weren't attracted to one. Keith's hair was strawberry, but still, it was like dating someone from your own family.

Vivi beckoned Jamie to follow her to the bedroom Masa and Kit shared, the same room seven houses down that Betty and Jamie shared. Only Betty had divided theirs in two with a strip of masking tape after the news of their parents' split, the split that she and Betty had yet to discuss or acknowledge. Perhaps the announcement was still too raw, the day itself a blur of hot and sweltering images: the silent car ride out to the Valley to see their parents' therapist; their parents' low, detached words in that room with a black-bearded stranger; dull yellow light; Jamie's legs sticking to the vinyl couch; Betty's legs sticking to her legs; Steven biting his tongue in silent frustration because he was missing his Leadership meeting for this; their mother's confession about another man; their father's silent convulsions; Betty fixing her eyes on her lap.

But it was the "other man" part that Jamie was stuck on and that no one had spoken of since. It was so out of the blue and muddled with everything else, not to mention their joke about the milkman. She had no idea what it meant. She had wanted to ask Betty, but when they got home that day Betty went to their room and immediately stuffed all her clothes in a garbage bag. "Mom said I could live with her," she was saying, throwing in her stuffed gorilla and knotting the bag shut. Jamie sat mute on her bed, fighting off what seemed natural, which was to pack a bag too because where Betty was going, she would go. Jamie couldn't imagine it otherwise. But what she couldn't imagine more was her father here alone without either of them. So she sat still and watched Betty drag that garbage bag to the living room where their dad sat slouched in a chair at the dining table. Jamie could hear the bitterness through her father's muffled voice, then Betty shuffling back. After she'd dumped out the contents of her bag on the floor, she pulled a roll of masking tape from her pocket, and, as if the divorce was all Jamie's fault, split the room in two by running a line of tape across the floor.

"Kit," Vivi called, barging into her daughter's bedroom. "Why don't you come out and be social like I asked you?"

Kit was stretched out on her bed reading *Moby Dick*. "Hi, Mom," she said in jittery, nervous tones. She stood up from the bed, tripped on her shoe, and tumbled onto the bright yellow carpet. "Oops," she said, giggling and straightening her glasses.

"I'm afraid my daughter's the worst klutz." Vivi shook her head as she walked away, leaving Jamie there, uncomfortably shy and biting her lip. Where Masa's features were bronzed and glamorous, her younger sister's were pale and gangly; her blond hair was dirty, and she looked like she'd be blind without those glasses. Vivi stuck her head back in to remind Kit to invite Jamie to see *A Star Is Born* with them that night. She offered to call Jamie's mom to get the OK. "I'll call her," Jamie yelped because in that instant she remembered that it was "Mom's night" tonight, the night that would officially commence the back and forth. Their mom was picking them up at their dad's after work and driving them over to her new apartment where she planned to serve a special dinner to honor the occasion. Jamie was dreading it, petrified that the *other man* might be there, petrified that after she got back to their dad's, he would certainly ask her if the *other man* had been there, and she would have to lie. Or better yet, don't go to her mother's at all. Never go over there. That's what she'd tell her, right now, over the phone. "I'm sure my mom will be fine with it," Jamie added, tucking her arms into her t-shirt.

"Great," Vivi said. "We'll leave at six."

"Barbra Streisand is one of the few things my mom will leave the house for," Kit said after her mom had left.

"My mom has all her albums," Jamie responded, confiding that she'd never seen an R-rated movie. Kit said that she'd seen *Jaws* in Minnesota, and since they'd moved to the beach she hadn't been in the ocean once. Jamie smiled even though she wasn't listening. She'd gotten distracted by a collage of magazine photos posted over Masa's lace chiffon bed.

"She's a model for Elite," Kit said flatly. Then she pointed to some napkin sketches tucked into the wood frame of the bureau mirror. "And an artist." Kit sort of giggled because Jamie's mouth was hanging open. Jamie shut it, confused and surprised that Kit wasn't the slightest bit jealous of Masa, like Kit had already figured something out about older sisters that Jamie hadn't figured out yet. And with that they both laughed and couldn't stop, like it was all there was left to do, until Masa flew through the door dragging Betty in her wake.

From under the bed, Masa retrieved a large portfolio and began flipping through the pages that Betty pretended to admire. Jamie told Masa she looked amazing, and asked what it was like to wear all that makeup, and Masa asked Jamie if she wanted to try. Of course she did, until she saw Betty's expression and declined, stifling her disappointment. It seemed that her sister could never feel the way Jamie wanted or expected or needed her to feel. The one time Jamie fit in, it seemed Betty wanted to fit out.

Masa slid off her blouse and bra and searched for an alternative outfit. "Did you call your mom yet about the movie?" Her pointy boobs were dangling in Betty's face.

"We're supposed to have dinner at *home* tonight," Betty reminded Jamie, emphasizing the word home to mean not really home but their new and improved, alternative home, the one she still hoped to move into. It had not been a formal pact—them keeping silent about their parents' split—but that's what happened. And now they were just waiting for it to disappear.

Masa gave Kit a makeover while continuing her pleas to Betty about coming to the movie so that she wouldn't have to be out with Vivi and Kit alone. Betty finally caved. Jamie imagined that even Betty, with her solid eighth grade social standing, couldn't afford to snub an invitation from an Elite model.

Masa showed Betty and Jamie to her parents' bedroom so they could call their mom. After Masa left and shut the door, Betty went to the side table and picked up the phone. Jamie shadowed her, noticing an oxygen tank at the foot of the bed and the table littered with prescription pill bottles. A large painting hung over the headboard: a laughing Vivi laying half exposed amongst her sheets.

"Creepy," Betty said, staring at the picture and dialing.

"I think it's cool," Jamie said, examining it closer and seeing Masa's initials.

"Did you hear the way Vivi talks about Masa, like she was some kind of goddess or something?"

"Well, isn't she?"

Betty glared past Jamie and cleared her throat into the receiver. "May I speak with Mrs. Waterson?" It was a moment before their mom got on and Betty proceeded to explain that she had a volleyball practice that evening that she'd forgotten about, and Jamie was going with her because she was thinking about trying out for the team. It was an impressive lie, Jamie thought because their mother had never stepped foot inside a gymnasium and had absolutely no idea about Betty's practice schedule.

"What'd she say?" Jamie said after Betty hung up.

"Fine."

"Fine?"

"In fact she said it was great, you trying out for the team."

Jamie frowned bitterly, holding back an emotion that stung her eyes. Had her mother completely forgotten about her younger daughter's dedication to ballet? That she wanted to be a ballerina? "Why didn't you just tell her the truth? She doesn't care what we do."

"She's the one that's suffering, Jamie."

"Then why does Dad sit alone at the table every night crying into his cold coffee while she's moved on to a whole new life?"

"She couldn't live with him," Betty said, like she was their mom's best friend and confidant.

"You're just pissed because you couldn't live with her."

"Dad wouldn't let me."

"Are you sure about that?"

Betty headed for the door.

"What about *him*? Maybe you can't live with her because of *him*."

Betty paused.

Jamie swallowed. "Did you even know about him?" Her voice was trembling.

Betty dropped her shoulders and turned around. "You were there too, Jamie. Don't you remember?"

"Remember what?" Jamie sat on the bed. She was trying desperately not to cry.

"He came over, Jamie."

"When? Who?"

"Gary, that night, after Mom had been crying for days. She made me call him to come get her."

"Was Dad there?"

"She said that she was going to die if I didn't."

"Is she sick?" Jamie asked, after a pause.

Betty made out like that question was stupid.

Silence ensued. Jamie thought she could hear dust settling on the pill bottles, among the silk sheets, and deep into the wall-to-wall carpet.

"This place is weird," Betty said finally, glancing around. "I want to go home."

Jamie looked around as well. She wanted to go home too—Dad's, Mom's, she didn't care anymore as long as Betty stopped looking at her like that, with those homesick eyes that reflected her own.

But it was too late. The door flung open, and Masa with her wide sultry smile said, "I have to tell you something," and dragged Betty off to her room. Jamie followed, guiltily and wondering how she could get them out of going to the movie, but she came up blank. Then Steven poked his head in to shoot them goodbyes (as if that were normal) before he went off to some activity with a long name to be followed by his fateful date with Jill. "You're not really going to break up with her, are you Steven?" Betty asked, almost too casually and reminding Jamie of how much her sister adored Jill. Where Steven would head straight to his room when he returned home from school, Jill might linger and chat with Betty about volleyball (Jill played on the high school team), Betty's friends, what high school was like. For Jamie it was a painful reminder that Betty liked the idea of a sister, just not Jamie as that sister.

"Of course I'm not going to break up with her," he said, to Betty's utter relief. "I'm going to spin it around until she has no choice but to break up with me." He winked at them and left. Betty, mouth agape, followed him to the front door. But he was already off before she could say whatever it was she'd wanted to say, Jamie didn't know.

At six, counseling hour was up, and the kitchen table was cleared. Vivi threw on a housecoat over her housedress, grabbed a large box of tissues, and drove them to Mann's Theater in her white Chevy with red vinyl interior.

The man who sold them their tickets flashed Vivi a discriminating look when he saw the thirteen and under girls hiding behind her wide girth as she bought the tickets. "They're going to see sex at some point," she said loudly, and the girls all blushed. "Better they see it with me."

They sat in order of Vivi, Jamie, Kit, Masa, Betty and shared an oversized box of popcorn and cokes. Vivi passed out the tissues, warning everyone that they'd need them later. She blew her nose as the lights dimmed, and the song "Evergreen" seeped into the theater like weeping gas. A lump hit Jamie's throat as the emptiness she'd felt earlier with Betty in Vivi's room came stinging back in her eyes. Barbra did that to her. She tried to push it back, but it was no use. Every Barbra Streisand movie Jamie had ever seen had been with her mother and Betty. Not even Vivi's loud, high-pitched laugh could change that. The whole audience was laughing at some-thing Barbra had said, but Vivi's shrieks carried over them all, and Masa nudged her mother to stop. Jamie and Kit scrunched down in their seats. The rest of the movie remained like that, a rollercoaster ride, Vivi in the front car singing, cackling, covering her daughter's eyes or sobbing. It finished with Norman rolling his red Ferrari off a barren desert road. Vivi wept and wept, while her daughters wept in smaller proportions until all of their weeping consumed the theater, which was also weeping. Jamie stifled her own sobs, sobs for everything that she didn't understand. Why couldn't Esther and Norman just be happy together? They loved each other. It was all so complicated and made no sense, and it made Jamie go back to pondering the question about this *other man* in her mother's life. And then she just felt disgusted, so disgusted that she vowed never to be burdened by love, or worse, grow to depend on it like their mother had now. She would give up ballet and make her own way doing something else. Her thoughts circled and spun as she won-dered what that something could be. Something finite, something she could control. In her grief she glanced over at her sister sitting motionless, misty eyed but tearless, that ever elusive glisten.

After the movie Vivi insisted that they buy the album, which they purchased at Tower Records on the way home. It was nine p.m. when they got back to Vivi's house. Their mom wouldn't have returned Betty and Jamie to their dad's until ten, so they had no choice but to stay longer. Vivi put on the album and removed the plastic from the couches. Kit and Jamie sat in the love seat with the lyrics page, singing along until Vivi told Kit she was tone deaf. Jamie giggled only because Kit giggled, and because what her mother had said was absolutely true: the girl couldn't hold a tune whatsoever. Jamie though, Vivi exclaimed, had a wonderful voice. Surely Vivi was just being nice; still, Jamie ran a hand through her hair and sang louder.

Halfway through the third song there was a knock on the door, which Vivi hurried to get like she was expecting someone. Jamie couldn't see who it was, but when she heard the deep, heart-stopping voice, her eyes went wild at Betty.

"I've been hoping to meet you Tom," Vivi said, opening up her arms and letting their father stumble into her embrace. "Sorry I didn't come over earlier, but you got my message today then?"

"Yes, thank you," he said, ducking through the doorframe and stepping awkwardly into the room.

"It's been a busy week getting our bearings," she went on. "I finally had the chance to meet your girls today. They're absolutely fabulous."

Fabulous. Jamie pondered the word that didn't sound right.

Vivi led Tom over to the couch and sent Masa off to get him a glass of water.

"Mom said it was OK," Jamie blurted out before her dad could speak.

"I took your girls to see *A Star is Born* tonight," Vivi clarified.

There was a long pause while Tom gazed fondly if not awkwardly at his girls. "And your mother was OK with that?"

"We called Mom at work," Betty said.

Masa returned with Tom's water. He took a sip and then fumbled to set the glass on the coffee table. "It was your mom's night tonight," he managed finally, a tremble in his voice. "And I'm not sure I approve of her passing off her duties without checking with me first."

Masa's eyes popped open. "Her night?"

Betty was already on her feet. "We should probably be going, Dad."

Tom shifted in his seat and wiped his brow. "I suppose the girls told you," he said to Vivi, who sat attentive beside him.

"Told us what?" Masa said.

"It's no big deal *really*," Jamie inserted, lunging at her dad and pulling at his sleeve to stand up. But Tom wouldn't budge; he had everyone's attention and that's all he ever wanted. The room went silent in wait. Kit glanced at Jamie.

"Their mother left me." Beads of sweat sprung from his forehead. "Twenty years and she…" His voice shook and his chest filled.

"Dad," Betty demanded. "Can we go?"

"Masa asked and I'm going to tell her," he replied sternly, and Betty's face turned red. She glared at the floor while Jamie jabbed a fingernail into her thigh.

"I asked their mother what she wanted," Tom went on. "She said she wanted more, but then she couldn't tell me more of what."

"More?" Masa was curious to know.

Vivi turned to her daughter, "Another man, dear." Then to Tom, "And my goodness, you need something stronger to drink."

It was hard to tell whose face was redder, Jamie's or Betty's. Their dad looked momentarily liberated, but then smiled through his teeth and said, "No thanks. I should get my girls home." He was about to get up but then abruptly stopped to pinch the bridge of his nose underneath his glasses. After a moment his shoulders began heaving. This is how their father cried, in big cracks, like the world was breaking open.

The room fell mortifyingly silent. Kit and Masa looked shocked, not so much from the news as from the sight of this broad, towering, fifty-year old man with a doctorate in family therapy breaking down before them. And then they did something entirely unexpected and unacceptable. They went over to Tom and each put an arm around him. "It's OK, Tom," they uttered in unison. "It'll get better, Tom," they said with all the sincerity and earnestness Betty and Jamie could never muster, Betty now staring out the window and Jamie busy figuring out how she could crawl under the couch.

"Go ahead and cry, Tom," Vivi soothed. "Get it out. We've all done a lot of crying tonight, haven't we girls." All three of them were gathered around Tom now. Masa was holding out a box of tissues, and Tom took one as his crying subsided. Then he heaved a few more times, a crescendo of sorts, before he stood up and apologized. Betty and Jamie pushed their father out the front door, but Vivi ran after them with the album. "Take it girls. It's yours." Jamie grabbed it before their father could make a comment about Barbra's big frizzy head on the cover (if he disliked Judy, he detested Barbra). "When I want it I can borrow it," Vivi said. They were neighbors now, after all.

Two nights later the girls went over to their mom's new apartment for the first time. It was a cardboard box with faux furniture and plastic plants and a Formica kitchen with a half stove; but all Betty noticed was the missing extra bedroom. "It's a pullout," their mom exclaimed with all the gaiety she could muster as she stripped off the cushions from the living room couch. But at a petite five two and dressed in heels and work clothes, their mother couldn't yank the thing open. Jamie, awash in her newfound determination to remove herself from this familial mess (not to mention relief that the *other man* was not present), stepped in and did the demonstration. She stretched out on the mattress that unfolded like a letter trying desperately to make it appear comfortable and stay open when all it wanted to do was fold back up. Their mom added how nice it would be when it was all fixed up with pretty sheets and pillows. They could all shop for them on their next weekend with her.

They ate dinner at the small glass dining table fixed with paper party goods, Marie Callender's takeout, and a present arranged on each of their heart-shaped plates. Each gift was wrapped in gold paper with different colored bows. Betty got movie tickets to *A Star is Born* and Jamie got the album. The show was at seven so they needed to hurry. Betty and Jamie didn't look at each other. In fact after that night, they stopped looking at each other ever. They couldn't; it was all just too embarrassing.

CHAPTER 3

Little Darlings

August, 2003

Betty hung up after her conversation with her mom feeling entirely frustrated. Mom had rattled on about Jamie and how happy she sounded being with Roberto in some breathtaking seaside on the Gulf of Thailand. The words "really" and "happy" and "breathtaking" were repeated a few times with a manic, forced gaiety, one to which Betty refused to respond because she knew her sister better than that. Jamie would never let on to a sense of happiness.

"I know," Betty had responded to her mother rather defensively, when in fact she still knew nothing directly of Jamie's whereabouts after she left California in such a dramatic huff. Betty (having no idea Roberto was in Thailand at the time) just assumed that her sister had gone back to New York, where Betty had since left her two, very casual voice mail messages. No drama. "Just checking in," she'd said, making it easy for her sister to return the calls, but Jamie had not returned the calls. And although Betty refused to harbor any ill will towards her sister, given the circumstances of their last parting, she knew this was wrong. Her sister, in their entire lifetime together, as distant as they'd ever been, had never failed to return Betty's call. It may have been a few days later, but she'd call.

"It's amazing how far she's come," her mother had gushed. "I mean look at her now."

"Mmmm." Betty braced for the recitation she knew was coming.

"Remember how low she was? She had to practically crawl her way out of the bottom of a barrel. I mean she was near death Betty." A deep, heavy sigh. "I'll never forget when they wheeled her through those double doors into surgery. There was nothing I could do. I've never felt so helpless as a mother." She filled the air with a rather large, ceremonious pause then, as if Betty might offer her sympathy, when in fact Betty could only feel her own helplessness, as a daughter because wasn't Jamie's cancer, like, a million years ago. Wasn't it time Betty unburdened her own problems on her mother, her guilt and sadness and worries about this baby, her marriage? But she knew she couldn't. Her mother would only latch desperately on to them, as she had with Jamie's illness, and turn it into her tragedy; or worse, relate Betty's transgression to her own before wrapping it all up in a decorative box and sealing it tight with a pretty bow.

No thank you, Betty thought, her mother now on another track, having barely taken a breath. The woman operated in two states of being: up and down. Today, clearly, she was up. Richard must be living up to her princely expectation. Richard, her fiancé—they'd recently gotten engaged, and Betty wanted to be truly happy for her mother. She'd struggled for so many years after her second husband, Gary, left her. She was going on now about the extension she was building on the house so that Richard could have his space. "You know, for all that man stuff he likes to do because when Richard enters a room, the space is filled! I'm still blown away by this relationship, that at this stage in life, I could finally find real love. You know my career has always been my life…and you kids of course…but love and passion are what I've always wanted." Her mother paused so that Betty could speak. But Betty was thinking about that movie she'd seen a million years ago, the one about adolescence. Tatum O'Neal's character had wanted a romantic love so badly that she manufactured one. Betty couldn't help thinking that her mother had done the same. Only her mother was not a hormonal girl of fifteen, nor was *she about to lose her virginity. She was a Los Angeles City Councilwoman. Betty shook her head, for she could never reconcile the woman in this position with the woman who was her mother.*

She inserted her own news then, her plans to have a home birth. She'd been doing some research and begun interviewing midwives, and…"That sounds lovely dear," her mom interjected, making some excuse about a critically important commission meeting she had to prepare for, and getting off the phone. Betty could have told her mother it was a beautiful fall day in the Maryland suburbs, when in fact it was August—hot, muggy, the Potomac a mosquito infested swamp—and her mom wouldn't have heard a thing.

Betty picked up her birthing book, repositioned herself on her bed, and tried to relax. Her mother's un-motherliness always seemed to elicit in Betty a newfound determination to prove her own motherliness. She turned to the page she'd dog-eared, the chapter on water births. Even though she was thirty-nine, she considered herself a strong case for a home birth. All three of her previous labors had been easy, in hospitals, with no drugs and only a few pushes. She held this secret notion that her body was made for childbearing. Physically, emotionally and mentally, her whole being seemed to thrive on it.

She re-read the passage she'd highlighted earlier. Water births empower couples to "give birth," and not to "be delivered." That sounded so right to Betty. It was her body after all; her child, her labor, and so why couldn't she assume more responsibility for it? Just thinking of the doctor not listening to her in those heated moments got her riled even now, and she knew Dave felt the same way. Though he'd been by her side through each birth, at some point during the process he would seem to disappear. He was there physically, but after being barked at by one too many nurses, he could only sit there holding Betty's hand with that look of futility in his eyes. This home birth was for him too. He would hand craft the birthing tub himself. He would become engaged in the life growing inside her. This could be their new beginning.

She set her book on the nightstand and went down the hall to check on the kids. Clay was twisted up and turned backwards on the bottom bunk.

Sam's arm dangled off the top. She was relieved to see Nick, on the toddler bed, asleep at last.

She stood there listening to the cacophony of their breaths. Nick's stood out, clogged and heavy from his bout of crying; he had wanted his daddy to sing him a bedtime song. Betty had tried to explain to him that his daddy wouldn't be home until after he was long asleep. He asked why, and she told him that Daddy worked nights now; he asked why, and she sighed and told him that she'd already told him a million times why; and Clay said, rather mockingly for a seven year old, that they needed the extra money; and Nick asked why, and she bit her tongue and said "because," probably too sharply. She tucked Sam's arm in, switched off the hall light, and crept downstairs.

She went to the battered green couch in the living room and puffed up the cushions. They'd had this thing forever. The thought left her standing there hugging a pillow and contemplating turning forty and still living paycheck to paycheck. The thought had become part of her, as had the thought about finding a career that re-inspired her, as had the thought about forgetting that thought and moving on to a new, hopefully better thought, like this baby being a girl.

She was moving again. Feeling antsy, like she needed to talk to Jamie, like she needed to tell someone. For a while she let herself believe that her sister would simply show up on her doorstep like she'd always done. Now Betty wondered if that wasn't Glenda's spell talking: "sisters are always there for each other." Betty got the sense that this time Jamie wasn't going to be there for her, unless Betty directly asked her to be, which was the hardest thing of all: she and Jamie didn't ask each other for things.

She climbed back up the stairs to write her sister an e-mail. The computer was in her sewing room now. She sat at the desk, pushed aside a stack of bills, and looked around her. This used to be her favorite room in the house, where she could come and sit in the rocker Dave had made her and knit or sew or work on a pattern for hours on the weekends, while Clay slept in his crib. Now it was also an office, storage space, and soon-to-be-nursery. The iolite curtains were torn from when Nick swung on them after he'd seen the movie Tarzan. The pine tree had grown over again. She had thought it the right move, to leave D.C. for the country.

She opened a new e-mail, thought for a minute, and then started typing. This was perhaps Jamie's last chance to see life enter the world. She had not been at any of Betty's other births; work or timing or something had always gotten in the way. It didn't seem right or fair for her sister to miss that, Betty wrote. She paused then, admitting that her need went deeper. "As seasoned as I am," she typed on, "everything about this pregnancy feels different. I feel an undercurrent of uncertainty that I've never felt before as a mother. Perhaps you can't stop me from failing, but what I know is that you'll try, which is why I want you to come. Whether you've been there for me or not, Jamie, it feels as if you always have been.

"This baby feels, to me, like closure; on what I don't know…or perhaps the life out there I'm not living. My sabbatical from the museum starts next month. I've saved enough vacation, and with maternity leave I'll get six months pay. After almost twenty years, if all goes well with Dave's new job, I will at last be able to quit for good." Betty paused again there, deciding to leave out the part about his employer being Home Depot. Jamie already thought Dave was irresponsible. She had a hard spot for Dave that Betty thought unfair. He was a devoted father, and he supported Betty's wishes whatever they were. Even now he'd love this baby, no questions asked. And with that Betty closed her eyes, took in a deep breath, and continued. "This is my time, Jamie. I want to enjoy this pregnancy, this birth, this baby. I want to take time off to figure out what I'll do next. I know I'll always need to work—have to—as did our mother, but please don't say I'm like her. You know I've always wanted to start my own clothing business. Maybe I will. But what I'm trying to say is that maybe this baby can be closure for you too, for us."

She sat back and pondered the words she knew she would have to erase. The screensaver came on after a minute, her image reflecting off the screen. It morphed into Jamie's—Betty would recognize those piercing eyes anywhere. "There is no closure!" her sister would have said to Betty's last sentence. Her *sister's words from years ago stung Betty hard even now. Little Darlings, the name of that silly Tatum O'Neal movie, popped into Betty's mind, the movie her mother had managed, with her dreamy love-struck voice, to resurrect from Betty's memory. She craved food just thinking about it and in a minute she was downstairs hunting through the pantry for peanut butter. She spread a heaping portion on a slice of bread and scarfed it down as if she were feeding not herself, not this baby, but Jamie, her sister, who was out there, God knew where, starving herself as she liked to do in her adolescence while nagging Betty about eating too much, not suffering enough, as if suffering were a competition. Betty had suffered back then, silently and like every other adolescent with an absent mother. She was suffering now. If that's what her sister wanted to hear from her then fine, Betty would admit it. Maybe she was like their mother. Maybe she, too, had fabricated her love for Dave, would continue to fabricate her love for Dave. Betty wasn't sure anymore. She no longer knew what was real. She only knew that suffering was a competition no one wins.*

** 1980 **

They went on the "Lose Ten Pounds in Seven Days Diet" together. Jamie had read about it in *Seventeen* magazine and showed the article to Betty, suggesting they do it together, as if it were normal for them to do things together, as if they'd ever done anything together beside fight over toiletries in the bathroom. Still…Betty considered April's party coming up next Saturday night, her crush on Rich, and the possibility of squeezing into those size eight jeans. Sure, Betty at last agreed, figuring that it might not hurt to shed a few pounds though she had never felt herself to be particularly fat. Before Betty knew it, a schedule had been posted on the bathroom door with each starting weight logged in: Betty 135; Jamie an-already-thin-for-their-five-foot-eight-height 120. The strategy was simple: mix two Slim Fast packets with water and ice in a blender—vanilla for Jamie, chocolate for Betty—for breakfast, lunch, and dinner.

It actually tasted good, Betty thought, the first morning she gulped down her breakfast under the gaze of Jamie's policing eyes.

"You girls want me to fix you something to eat?" Their father, bent over the railing at the top of the stairs, was disheveled and wrapped in the tattered blue robe their mother had bought him many Christmases ago. His attempt to see them off to school was always futile; to see them at all was a challenge because he worked evenings counseling couples. Then he'd stay up until two a.m. watching Sid Caesar or Mel Brooks, anything that might possibly make him howl with laughter. And God forbid *Young Frankenstein* was on. Their dad had a laugh like he was gasping for air that could be heard clear down to Vivi's house, so she liked to tease. Anyway, he was not a morning person. "How bout an omelet?"

No. Bye. Slam.

They liked to think they were doing him a favor.

Later that day, in class, that omelet sounded pretty good. Betty could barely concentrate; when she wasn't daydreaming about Rich, she was anticipating her next meal in the form of a shake, one she liked to imagine was from McDonald's. When the noon bell rang, she hurried to her locker and drank lunch from the thermos Jamie had prepared for her. Then she headed to the gym to turn in her stat sheets from Friday night's game.

Rich was practicing free throws with his teammates when Betty entered the gym. Their eyes caught and it was all she could do to remain cool. He didn't look like the typical high school jock. His build was stocky and buff, but his face was boyish, freckly, unassuming. He may have even blushed when Betty caught him missing his free throw. According to April he didn't date girls outside his church.

Betty crossed the court and handed the stat sheets to Assistant Coach Mitchell. He studied them as Rich cruised up with a ball under his arm. "How'd I do coach?" His skin was glossy with sweat.

"Triple double," Coach said.

"That's it?" He frowned at Betty. "Are you sure you counted right?" He smiled to show her that he was kidding.

Betty blushed, tongue-tied. She could only watch as he turned and dribbled back onto the court. She headed for the exit fighting a smile, but by the time she made it outside, her braces were showing. That was the most Rich had ever said to her. The diet must be working.

She passed Jamie and Kit sitting on a bench just outside the gym. Through their friendship Jamie had managed to get Kit to come to school on a regular basis rather than feign the migraines or other illnesses she'd inherited from her mother. Kit compromised by wearing black and dying her hair purple. Her sister, in turn, seemed to be exploring her own style lately. She'd started blow-drying her hair and wearing makeup, and today she wore Betty's hand-sewn tapered sweatpants…and without asking, Betty noted with a touch of anger. But she let it go, and, in a friendly mood, headed over. She stopped when she saw Ron, April's younger brother, walk up and take a seat next to Jamie. Ron was a math geek according to April, but he had April's good looks and nice, approachable smile. They were probably theorizing about advanced algebra, Betty figured, changing paths and heading for the quad. The band on her waist felt loose already.

The next morning Betty woke up charged. She had survived twenty-four hours on the diet and as a result lost two pounds. "One-thirty-three," she announced with amazement. Jamie stepped on the scale next. "One-eighteen," she said, unimpressed.

By lunch Betty felt malnourished and faint. April caught Betty just as she was sucking down the last traces of her Slim Fast and begged Betty to come with her to the gym. April wanted to chat with Coach Mitchell about this week's game schedule, though her flirty eyes said she had another motive.

The gym hushed when April walked in; even Coach Mitchell grew awkward. April had that affect on guys. She wasn't just pretty, but friendly in a genuine, hypnotic way. Field hockey, flag team, class secretary, no click was excluded. Betty and she had become friends all because of this stats job that Betty was lucky to get. A ton of other girls would have killed for it. But conveniently Coach Mitchell, aka Keith, Betty's ex-volleyball coach and their brother's best friend from high school, still liked to do Betty favors. Plus April had strawberry hair like Coach's, and she liked to call the three of them Club Red.

April and Coach Mitchell exchanged some information about the schedule. Three years ago Keith was the team's star player. After graduating he played at USC until he got injured and lost his scholarship. Now he was finishing his degree at Long Beach State and coaching part-time. But even with the new mustache, whistle, and all-coach attitude, he still couldn't keep the girls from flirting with him. All the girls except Betty that is, who kept an eye on Rich presently knocking down free throws, five in a row before he dribbled over.

"Coming to my party, Rich?" April asked, nudging Betty in the side. Rich spun the ball on his index finger and didn't answer.

"You never come to my parties."

"They're past my bedtime."

"Bring Coach with you. He'll make sure you get home in time for bed."

Rich looked at Coach, who wasn't listening. "What do you think, Coach. You going to April's party?"

He grunted, "Yeah, right," and stepped onto the court.

"How about as a chaperone," April called after him, while Betty stood there hopeful, so hopeful that when she got home that afternoon she hit the cupboard searching for something tiny that she could eat to stabilize her nerves. She perused the faux wood pantry, which contained a plethora of junk food items to choose from. Since Betty had started driving over a year ago, their dad, still single, lonely, and generally miserable, left the grocery shopping up to her and Jamie. Hostess Ding Dongs, Pop Tarts, Tater Tots, Captain Crunch, all viable options on which Betty needed to decide in a hurry before Jamie came home. Her stomach growled, and then she remembered Vivi's lasagna in the fridge. Vivi had been bringing over a platter once a week ever since their father began using his hypnosis techniques on her migraine headaches. Betty got a fork, removed the foil, breathed in the flavors, changed her mind, shoved the platter back in the fridge, and bolted from the kitchen.

The next morning she lay in her bed feeling the flatness of her belly and imagining that lasagna sliding down her throat. When her mouth began watering, she exchanged the lasagna image with one of herself in the size eight jeans pressed up against Rich in some dark corner of April's party. But just as the tingling moved from her mouth into her thighs, Jamie's alarm blared and her sister, who never snoozed, switched on the light. Betty followed Jamie to the bathroom, feeling dizzy as she stepped on the scale and weighed in at one-thirty-one. When she saw her sister's weight, one-sixteen, she suggested, very carefully, "Maybe we should at least eat an apple or something." In fact, she was satisfied with her own accomplishment and, if it were up to her, she'd call it quits right there. But all she got from Jamie was an empty stare. "A piece of toast?"

Jamie's look grew mean and no more was said.

But by lunch, after drinking her shake at her locker, Betty was glad Jamie hadn't let her cheat. Perhaps her stomach was shrinking and she was getting mildly used to the hunger torture. Or was it her social status, which seemed to have suddenly elevated, keeping her going? For instance, she was heading through the quad under her protective air of pretense, when April suddenly called out to her from a crowd of cool seniors, before running over to tell Betty that she had talked to Rich again, and he'd agreed to come to the party, but only if Betty was coming. Was Betty coming? Betty, not sure she'd heard April right, glanced around and tried to keep her heart from exploding. "I'm coming," she said at last. Then those seniors came over to corral April for a road trip to In-N-Out Burger. "Come too," April pleaded at Betty, who was thrown off guard. It was an important moment; this was a crowd that Betty, with her steely braces and size-ten attire, didn't normally hang out with. She wasn't necessarily out. She was the starting setter for the V-ball team and had her own solid core group of athletic friends. That did provide her with some status after all. But she wasn't in either. At a size eight, clearly things were going to be different, and she'd have to thank Jamie one day for this moment, some day long from now when her sister no longer hated her for eating the double-double-with-cheese that she was about to eat.

The next morning Betty weighed in at one-thirty. Even with the In-N-Out Burger, she'd lost an additional pound and her pants felt loose enough. But Jamie, who had lost another two pounds, seemed concerned about Betty only loosing one. "Yeah, but five pounds," Betty countered, "That's pretty good." No, that was not pretty good, her sister's face said. She seemed more determined than ever. That's when Betty realized that no matter how much weight she lost it would never be enough for her sister. So forget it, I'm done, Betty's mind told the mirror as she brushed on mascara. She'd never be able to please Jamie. She didn't want to please Jamie. A minute went by with thoughts like this before it occurred to Betty, seeing her sister's lingering shadow in the doorway through the mirror, that perhaps Betty didn't always have a choice. She might have even said something sisterly right then had their dad not come limping towards them, half asleep and asking if anybody needed a ride. It was thirty minutes by bus along the ocean to their high school.

"Yes!" Jamie yelped. She hated the bus.

Betty hated her dad's crappy van. "No thanks," she said, unable to stand the thought of her friends catching her in it, not to mention the thirty minutes of their father's Columbo-like inquiries about their mother and *that man*. What was there to say that wouldn't infuriate him? That Gary owned a thirty-foot cruiser? That he and her mom lived in one of those brand-new condos on the Marina where he kept it docked? That Betty had been the maid of honor at their wedding? That she didn't know exactly what Gary did for a living, but that they had a lot in common (those would be her mom's words)? That he always offered Betty rides to wherever she needed to go? That he was teaching her to drive a stick? That aside from his GTI, he also owned an antique Corvette? That their mom wasn't always there when Betty and Jamie went over for "Mom nights"— Tuesdays and Thursdays—because her One-to-One program was being matriculated to other districts? Last Tuesday she was in San Diego, and tonight she was in Sacramento. And since tonight Jamie wasn't around either, working part-time for a typing service to save money to buy a car, Gary drove Betty to an empty parking lot near the marina and gave her driving lessons. Afterwards he took her to Marie Callender's for dinner and let her sip from his beer. And instead of dropping Betty back at their dad's that night, he simply handed her the keys to his just washed and polished black GTI, which he wasn't using this weekend. Take it he had said, and she almost died.

The next morning, Friday, Betty covertly poured her breakfast shake out in the sink when Jamie wasn't looking and then feigned puzzlement when the scale showed she hadn't lost any more weight. And it wasn't just Marie Callender's; since that In-N-Out burger, she'd had a slice of pizza, a bagel and cream cheese, and some of

April's fries. Did alcohol count? Betty was already dreaming of the Doritos she'd stashed in her locker when Jamie stepped on the scale. The dial settled on one-twelve, which is when Betty instinctively blurted out, "OK Jamie, that's enough. You've lost enough weight."

"But I've only lost eight pounds. I've got two more to go."

"It's Friday," Betty paused. She could feel her voice shaking. "We've been on the diet for five days. It's not healthy."

Doom washed over he sister's face. "I'm only doing this for you."

Betty was shocked. "Don't do it for me."

"Why not? You said you wanted to lose the weight. We said we were going to do this together."

Betty stared down at the scale. "I know."

Saturday morning Betty was up early trying on blouses. Thankfully their dad was already at work, made evident by the distant sound of a Crockpot gurgling. Jamie slept until noon—the less time awake, the less time she spent hungry, she had said, weighing herself in at one-ten. Her sweats were hanging off her hips as she shuffled around the house sapped of energy. Mostly she just lay on the couch in front of the TV. Kit called a bunch of times, but Jamie didn't feel like going out that night. Big surprise, Betty thought, sensing her sister in one of her especially fun, Saturday night moods. And though Betty wanted to be concerned, she knew her sister wouldn't listen to anything she had to say.

It was four p.m., so she still had five more hours to go until the party. "Let's go to the movies," she announced out of the blue. Jamie loved the movies because she didn't have to socialize, she could dress like a slob, it was dark, and it killed a good two hours of dead space. It was something they could do together without really being together, and not even Jamie could turn down popcorn, which was like eating air if you ordered it without butter.

Betty went to the kitchen and returned with the Calendar Section of the *L.A. Times*. She ran her finger along possible selections at the Mann. *The Goodbye Girl* they'd seen last weekend with their mom. Betty was dying to see *The Blue Lagoon*, but it was rated R. *Private Benjamin*, seen it. They finally settled on a six-thirty showing of *Little Darlings* at AMC. Betty got ready for the party, figuring she'd drop off Jamie after the movie and then head straight over. She showered, blow-dried her hair, did her make-up, threw on a white long-sleeved blouse, and then at last slipped on her size eight jeans. It was a stretch, but she managed to get them buttoned.

Even Jamie made an effort. She put on 501s and a tank top and brushed her eyelashes and hair, all of which Betty made sure not to notice. Her sister hated being noticed.

"It stinks of Gary's hair jell," Jamie said, climbing into the GTI. Then she eyed the stick shift. "Are you sure you know how to drive this thing?"

Betty didn't answer. She was hungry and trying to concentrate, sweating by the time they arrived, thinking surely that she at least deserved a large Coke. But as Betty slowed her pace past the greasy fumes of the concession stand, Jamie marched straight into the theater. It was the first time Betty wondered if something else might be going on with her sister. She'd recently made some big announcement about giving up ballet to focus on her studies. Could that be it? Or was this diet simply affecting her brain.

The theater was packed. They took seats next to a teenage couple alternately devouring each other and a box of Juju Bees. The surfers behind them were throwing popcorn around, which was making Betty salivate. Jamie, however, sat slouched and impervious, even after the movie started and the cheerleaders in the front row whistled at Matt Dillon and Betty joined in (she had a hell of a finger whistle), Jamie just sat there still. During the movie, Betty would glance at her every so often, but it was as if she'd been transported somewhere else. Betty couldn't imagine what was so engaging about two girls at summer camp competing to lose their virginity, though, it did put the embarrassing topic right out there in front of them. Betty was a virgin, and she was pretty sure her sister was too. They were equals in that department—an awkward, somewhat irritating thought. So in the movie, Betty let Matt Dillon become Rich, which was easy because he kind of looked like Rich, or had his same body type anyway, white skin and cut muscles. Rich's eyes were light blue though. Betty imagined she'd be staring into them soon, tonight to be exact, and she revisited the feeling that had passed between them the other day. Her body invisibly trembled, and a feeling came over her she couldn't quite identify; she had this overwhelming sense that she would marry Rich. And with that notion came others: like the fact that Rich was Catholic like Betty's mother, who'd been a virgin when she married their dad. Would Betty be a virgin when she married Rich? Would Rich ask this of her?

Perhaps her mother would have the answer to these questions.

And then the movie ended, rather abruptly, Betty thought. She wasn't even sure who had won the bet. She turned to Jamie, wanting to make a connection, the kind one needs at the end of a film when reality returns in the form of deserted tubs of popcorn and smashed boxes of Junior Mints. But her sister seemed intent on studying the credits. Betty stood up, but still Jamie searched the fine print. Betty waited one more impatient minute and then escaped with all the other horny teenagers plowing towards the exit. Whatever her sister was searching for back there was beyond Betty…would always, it seemed, be beyond Betty.

She waited for Jamie by the dreaded candy counter, lightheaded from the glare and nauseous from the smell of hotdog grease. Finally Jamie appeared, last out, her hands shoved in her pockets, her face a red, puffy mess.

Betty followed her outside, concerned. It was dark now, and the air had that warm, lonely feel to it from the Santa Ana winds. "The movie was good," Betty offered, catching up with Jamie at the car.

"Yeah," Jamie murmured, climbing into her seat.

Betty took the short cut home, turning off PCH onto a side street that curved along the jetty and over a tiny bridge. "I didn't like the ending though," Betty added, rolling down her window, an innate response to the expanse of ocean sliding beside them now. Jamie rolled down hers too, with a curt reply, "The ending was the whole point." Then she flipped open the glove compartment.

"I just thought," Betty hesitated. "It was weird that they didn't have more closure between the girl and…you know…Matt Dillon's character."

"What closure? There is no closure." In her hand were Gary's Marlboro Reds, and she pushed in the lighter knob.

"I was just saying…I guess I needed something more…"

"Maybe there is nothing more." There was a pause while Jamie lit the cigarette and it registered on Betty what her sister was doing. "Does Gary know you're smoking his cigarettes?"

She blew smoke out the window. "He buys me beers too."

Betty frowned, then scoffed. "Hardly."

"Kit and me, before he drops us off sometimes, he'll pick us up a six-pack."

Betty narrowed her eyes against the smoke and tried desperately not to feel burned, because of all her sister's faults making shit up wasn't one of them. It became suffocating, her mother's absence, and when KROQ started playing The Cure, Betty cranked up the volume to block it out. *Whenever I'm alone with you …you make me feel like I am home again…*

And then they were home. Again, and Betty slid the gear into neutral.

The porch light was on, and a pale yellow glow seeped through the front gate.

"I'm going over to April's party now," she felt the need to remind her sister, who'd thrown her cigarette out the window but didn't follow suit. She sat there staring straight ahead.

Another minute of that and Betty switched off the ignition and asked her sister what the hell her problem was. "You've been moping all day, and now you're…" She grabbed the steering wheel. "Something in that movie must have really scared you."

Her words hit a nerve, as Betty knew they would, and she didn't have to look to see her sister's eyes swell. She still wouldn't speak though, and so Betty had no choice but to muster up some sisterly cheer. "Why don't you come with me to the party?" It felt like someone else had said it.

The street lamps hummed.

"April won't mind. She's pretty cool."

Otherwise it was silent.

"Well?"

"No."

"Why not?"

"Because I don't want to."

Betty gave her sister one last hard stare, and then turned away to discover their dad teetering towards them, barefoot in his work slacks, his face livid. Betty restarted the engine and Jamie jumped out, crossing in front of the headlights as their dad trembled and cursed to the world about that car, that fucking car, HIS fucking car!

"Dad, STOP IT!" Jamie screamed rather violently, and he did stop. She had an affect on their father in a way Betty didn't. Jamie would put up with his tears. All Betty could do was drive off; she had no need to see him cry. In second gear it took a while to get momentum. Then she ripped it into fourth, then fifth; it wasn't until she crossed the border into Sunset Beach that she downshifted into third, then second, expertly, as if she'd been driving a stick her whole life.

April lived in a one-story suburban row house halfway between the beach and school. Cars were clustered at odd angles in front of her driveway, but Betty didn't see Rich's hatchback among them. She could hear music blaring and the din of drunken voices as she approached, feeling so out of place, for she wasn't a surfer or a cheerleader, nor thin or beautiful. She wasn't even on the honor roll. She drew in a deep breath and went in.

Her V-ball friends were at a party elsewhere, and she didn't immediately recognize anyone she felt comfortable talking to, including Masa, who was entwined with her boyfriend, also a model, on the couch. The two of them looked like they just shot the cover of *Surf* magazine. It wasn't that Masa wasn't friendly, Betty assured herself, now sidestepping them, just absent, untouchable, oblivious. No one else was near them either.

Betty squeezed past some bodies to get into the kitchen. No sign of Rich or April, but there was Kit in the corner talking with April's brother, Ron. "Where's Jamie?" Kit yelled to her over the blaring music, the ends of her dark purplish hair dangling inside her drink. "She's at home," Betty yelled back. It hadn't occurred to Betty that Kit and Jamie had been invited. "Do you know where April is?"

Ron tilted his head at the bedroom hallway.

"Thanks," Betty said, heading in that direction. It took her some maneuvering through more bodies to get to April's room, where she was slightly shocked to find Coach Mitchell seated on the canopy bed surrounded by April and her friends from Flag. Betty blinked into the far too bright florescent light, what made everything so obvious, particularly Coach, dressed in kakis and a blue polo with the collar flipped up. He was laughing at something April had said, but quickly straightened up when April waved in Betty.

"What are you doing here, Keith?" It was Kit, stumbling in behind Betty and, in her own goofy obliviousness, alerting everyone to the elephant in the room.

Coach stood up awkwardly. "I was just asking myself the same question."

"He's chaperoning," April slurred. "Speaking of which…" She eyed Betty and asked Coach, "Where's Rich?"

Blood rushed to Betty's face.

"He didn't have such a great game last night." Coach spoke cautiously, a fleeting look at Betty. "And at practice today I heard him and a couple of the guys talking about a dance at his church."

"Do you think you'll make it to State this year, Coach?" Betty cleared her throat and said. She was trying with everything she had to smile.

Coach responded and Betty listened with all the intensity she could muster, her mind spiraling downward as Coach went on about the season. It seemed to take his mind off the fact that his being here was against school policy. For Betty it gave her something to grasp onto instead of shame, disappointment, and the fact that she was fat and unwilling to do anything about it. Coach's voice drummed between her ears, as did the voices of April's friends, which all operated at beats faster than her own. In a corner she saw Kit and April chatting like best friends. Apparently it was April's brother, Ron, who'd invited Jamie and Kit to the party. Betty went to search for a bathroom.

After she'd stared at herself in the mirror for a long senseless while, people banging on the door, she pulled herself together and headed into the backyard for some air. April was there, surrounded by guys. Betty went to the keg and filled a plastic cup with beer, sure that if April saw her she'd wave Betty over. But April didn't see her, so Betty just stood there awkwardly, considering going home. Now would be the time. Then she thought about home, that bitter, motherless house, her sister morbidly locked up in her room for no other reason, it seemed to Betty, than to make Betty feel guilty. Guilty of what! Jamie's the one who got everything she wanted. Betty got riled even now, thinking of how Jamie had automatically gotten Steven's room after he left for college, when in fact Betty may have wanted it. Betty thought of her brother now, back east, a place that didn't exist in Betty's reality. For Christmas he had given Betty a sweatshirt from Wellesley, Jamie one from MIT, and both of them Student Aid Application Forms; her sister had already filled hers out, while Betty hadn't even thought of college. She took a big swig of her beer, gagging down the foam and ignoring the taste, which she hated. She forced herself to drink more, each gulp counteracting the pain of Rich's absence.

By the time her plastic cup was empty, her jeans felt tight and Coach Mitchell was cruising over. Apparently the girls who were flirting with him earlier had turned their attentions elsewhere, and Betty felt sorry for him. Keith had always been nice to her family, so she grabbed his empty cup and refilled it with beer. He grabbed hers and did the same, and the two of them made camp there. They joked about that big crush he used to have on Masa, he laughing at himself and Betty laughing with him. She was too drunk to know how long they stood there. All she knew was that being with Keith felt close to home.

At some point the crowd cleared out and she started to sway. Keith helped her find a bathroom, and then waited outside while she peed, for forever it seemed. When she came out, she saw Kit and Ron pressed up against a wall, kissing. Was this the same Kit with the thick glasses and greasy hair? Something Jamie had said about Ron a few weeks back tried to cut through the haze of Betty's intoxication. It wasn't so much *what* she had said as much as *how* she had said it. She'd practically choked on his name, but Jamie was always so purposefully unaffected that Betty didn't read anything into it then. Now Betty wondered if she had simply missed everything!

Keith led Betty back to the kitchen and poured them two tequila shots. They toasted something...the beach, which was just a few blocks away, and the next thing Betty knew that's exactly where they were, sitting in the GTI watching the light shimmer off the low-breaking waves. They talked for a while—it could have been all night, it could have been ten minutes. Keith said that he'd always thought Betty was cute and that Rich was an idiot for not asking her out, which took Betty by surprise. She became mortified all over again at the thought that everyone knew about her crush. She blinked away the sting, and then they were in the back seat and he was pulling her onto him. She didn't have the energy to resist...she didn't know that she wanted to resist. She heard waves crashing. He tasted like the beach.

* * *

She had to focus hard not to let the gate slam behind her, and then palm the stucco wall as she passed through the courtyard where she found the front door to be locked. They didn't keep keys because they never locked the door, in theory anyway. The alternative was to climb through the kitchen window, which in sober circumstances wasn't difficult. There was a bar counter that lined the outside sill, and all she had to do was push herself up onto it. It took a while, but she finally got the window open and was able to crawl in over the sink and slide her feet to the floor. It was dark, and the room was spinning. She stood there waiting for it to stop. When it finally did, a hole shot through her stomach, or so it felt, and she began furiously opening and closing cupboards. A bag of Lays was the first thing she grabbed and ripped open, the salty chips washing away the stale taste of beer and Keith's mouth. His kisses had been powerful—her tongue was still throbbing—and there was a stickiness between her legs. She was trying hard not to sway.

"What are you doing?"

Betty spun around.

Jamie moved in out of the shadows, and Betty released her breath. Her chest was pounding and her ears were ringing. "I'm making a quesadilla," she said bitterly, after her mind caught up with her sister's question and ignoring the I-caught-you look on her face. She turned back to the open fridge, adding, "Because I'm starving, that's why," even though her sister hadn't said anything. But the holes were there, searing through Betty's back, forcing tears to her eyes. She grabbed tortillas, salsa, and a brick of orange cheese and slammed them on the counter. If anyone found out…if Rich found out, if Steven found out…it was too overwhelming to even acknowledge. She shut the fridge, got out a frying pan, poured in oil, turned on the stove, not necessarily in that order.

The room went still…Until the oil sizzled in the pan and Betty dropped in the tortilla and grated on the cheese, trying to keep focused. Had she even wanted to? Wasn't she supposed to be in love? Or did this mean that she was in love? "I think it's ready," Jamie said, to the rising smoke. She was in her habitual seat up on the counter to Betty's right. Betty wasn't sure when her sister had actually moved herself there, but there she suddenly was, and they were watching the cheese melt away the pain together just as they had always done. Betty folded the tortilla in half and flipped it over with a spatula. When it was done she slid it on a plate and cut it into slices, picked one up, gulped it down, picked up another one, gulped that down, picked up a third just as the first began to coat her stomach, at which point she paused. A feeling in her bones, what started as a tremor and grew into a full-blown quake. "For God's sake, Jamie, you've gotta eat something!"

There was a tremendous silence.

A standoff of sorts.

Then Jamie tucked her knees inside her shirt, picked up a slice, and ate it.

CHAPTER 4

THE EXORCIST

August, 2003

Roberto was staying at his father's seaside apartment. It was everything and nothing Jamie had expected. Forget jet lag, she was in a permanent stupor. She had come to Thailand only once before, six years ago, to meet Roberto's father, Giorgio, and, after one whimsical discussion over risotto in San Francisco, marry his son. It was Christmas then, and she and Roberto had all that dot.com money, on paper anyway. With Giorgio their only witness, they took their vows overlooking the Chao Phraya River at the Oriental Hotel in Bangkok, where they were staying for a few days before flying a puddle jumper off to some exclusive private island resort to recover in pampered style from another year of hard glorious work (they both agreed not to call it a honeymoon). But things were different now—neither of them employed, no anticipated millions. More important presently though, was that it was August, monsoon season, and her hair was an immediate disaster, Medusa-like in this thick balmy heat. And Giorgio didn't believe in air conditioning. Roberto had warned her about this…and that the shower barely spit water. After just one week, her face was a mess of freckles, her pores clogged with sweat. She didn't bother with shoes, going around in a sarong over her bikini, and she'd had to buy clothes off some street vendor.

Roberto had pushed together the two tiny twin beds in the guest room and cleared out the one pencil drawer in the bureau for her. At first breath she wasn't sure she could manage the awkward accommodations: the bathroom was the shower, the kitchen a stark, disinfected closet, the bedcover a thin sheet. But it was too hot to be cynical, and Roberto was so excited that she had finally come. Everything they'd been keeping from each other was out in the open now, and hopefully behind them. There was nowhere to go but forward, in this case outside onto the terrace, from where they could see the sea spread out for miles in all directions and a colossal statue of Buddha sitting majestically on a far-off cliff. Any discomfort she may have felt about her accommodations got lost in its bronzed, peaceful presence, and in the days to come she would often find herself just standing there staring at it.

Thailand, she decided, was more a state of being than a place.

Like all mornings, father and son took their coffee on the front balcony, the one facing south because it was shaded from the overbearing morning sun. The "coffee shop," as Giorgio called it, was a wooden bench nestled amongst potted plants and flowers. There was a pedestal table with room for one coffee cup, his. It was a shrine, of sorts, to himself and the inconsequential corner of life he now occupied. Fifteen years ago, rather abruptly, Giorgio retired from his prestigious post at ItalSteele because they had wanted to transfer him back to headquarters in Italy. Gone were the perks, the glamorous travel, the servants, the drivers. He moved to a seaside village called Hua Hin, opened a restaurant, and over the years grew into an isolated and lonely man; or so Jamie was discovering him to be during these past few days after not knowing her father-in-law at all in the course of her marriage to his son. Roberto had always treated his life in Thailand with his father as if it was his own precious secret. And, anyway, she'd been too busy with her career to come with him on his visits.

When Jamie joined them on the balcony this morning, Giorgio was particularly introspective, his body sagging from some great weight. He'd been gesticulating more than usual for this time of day, seated on the bench smoking his cigar, lamenting about some condo going up that would soon block his sea view. It was the latest infringement on his peace. Apparently the same harried construction disaster had happened to Bangkok; what had been paradise when he arrived thirty years ago was now an incongruous slew of dilapidated, smog-infested skyscrapers. The canals had dried up, the monkeys had fled, and the jungle was hacked up! Her father-in-law had such a thick Italian accent that Jamie had to smile when he spoke. He was tall, like his son, and while they both had the same Roman nose, they looked nothing like each other: Roberto with his silky almond eyes, brown hair, and supple skin; Giorgio carved and etched, his hair and skin bristly and white. He was proud of his physique, and he walked around the house shirtless and in his boxers, a gold chain hanging around his neck, that Toscano dangling from his lips.

Jamie turned back to face the shore. But to what condo was he referring? The view remained sublime, the shore empty and luminous with its lone fishing boat, some boys lazily casting out a net. She set her espresso cup on the balcony railing. She couldn't say she enjoyed the thimbleful of coffee she was served each morning, but she was adapting to living with less; that scalding hot Starbucks, the ice-cold martini, wine served at fifty-eight degrees—she had come to expect all those things. Now that they were gone, she found the new routine becoming a more natural part of her, listening to Giorgio and her husband pontificate in some version of Italian, Thai, and English, as the Gulf of Siam lapped below. If she was on the edge of reality or reason, she didn't know.

"Ah, but enough about the past," Giorgio reverted back to English as if to be sure that she, too, understood. "A man always remembers the past better than the present."

It was minutes before anyone spoke again, subdued by the rising heat and the weight of their private reflections. Would she, too, think the past better than the present when she reached Giorgio's age? Would Roberto? How awful that would be, she thought, turning back to face her husband. He was seated next to his father, eating from a plate of papaya, listening like he'd heard it all before. He gestured to Jamie to have some, but she was full from the pineapple he'd already fed her, still recovering from his intense gaze as she sucked each slice down, wanting her to enjoy every sense just as he did.

As if she could. It reminded her how far away she was from them and the past they shared. How little she understood of this place and what it meant to them. Until Jamie had agreed to join Roberto here (a decision that came to her rather abruptly only a week ago), Thailand had remained an image she viewed through the reflection in her husband's eyes. All those nights they spent lingering at their kitchen island over a bottle of wine, she lost in his musings about all the foreign places he had once lived with his father. But nothing could compare to the soft hue that bathed her husband's face when he spoke of the Thai house in the jungle by the river, the mango tree outside his window, the snakes he and his father would hunt in the backyard, weekends in a place called Hua Hin where he'd learned to play golf.

After morning coffee Roberto and Jamie lay at the pool by the sea with unopened books. At two o'clock, Roberto would head to Giorgio's restaurant where he was filling in as chef. The previous chef had disappeared without reason or warning (rumor had it he returned to his wife in Italy, though no one wanted to admit that because they all had wives in Italy or elsewhere).

She glanced over his shoulder. Salt *was the book he was reading.*

He glanced over her shoulder. Pol Pot?

She shrugged. "It was on your dad's night table."

"You went into his room?"

She buried her nose in the book. "The door was open."

He didn't ask what else she had found there. Like the picture of the Thai beauty on Giorgio's nightstand——Roberto's mother, Jamie knew, because her husband kept the same picture tucked away in his bureau at home. Not Giorgio's wife. Giorgio's wife lived in Italy with their two children, Roberto's half siblings about whom he knew little——just that they were older than him and had children of their own now.

"What was your father going on about this morning?" she finally asked.

Roberto narrowed his eyes, as if trying to remember.

"Don't pretend you don't know."

He looked past her for a moment, and then laid his head back. "He asked me what you are going to do next, now that the lawsuit is over."

The lawsuit was over a year ago," she said, with not a small amount of guilt: she was not achieving; she was living off her husband. And on top of that, chalk up another wasted year thanks to Betty.

"He asked if you were going back to BCC."

"BCC." She repeated the word, just to see how it sounded. Can one go back, she didn't ask. Do you want me to go back? "What did you tell him?"

"I said you don't know. I told him that one of your lead engineers wants you to start a consulting firm, but that you don't know." He looked at her. "Am I right?"

She sighed. She didn't know anything. Nothing was right. But he already knew that about her, which is why he didn't ask what would be the next logical question: if not BCC or the new firm, then where? What? It could all lead to that subject she'd already left him over. Left him and come back.

"I'm sure your father thinks I blew it leaving BCC."

"He thinks I blew it leaving Delphiant."

"Did he say that?"

"He doesn't have to." He turned on his side to face her. "He wasn't happy about me starting CS Partners after college either. He wanted me to go work for a big company, to have the kind of security that he'd had with ItalSteele. He's always had regrets about leaving the company when he did, turning down the position they'd offered him in Turin…giving up the house in Bangkok, the maid, the gardener, the cook, the driver."

"But he's done well with the restaurant."

"He could have been COO worldwide."

"Then why didn't he go back?"

A question he pondered, but only for a moment. "Apparently after thirty years in Asia, there is no going back. Wife or no wife, my father has always done what he wanted." He paused and looked at her pointedly. "I'm the living product of that."

Jamie searched his eyes now, as she had in the past, for some sign of the loss. But she could never find it, or them, for he hid all his losses so well.

"You have to understand, Jamie, my father is a conservative man who has worried incessantly his entire life about two things: his health, and his money. Here, he can live freely and like a king for nothing."

"But he shouldn't worry about us. You've done well. You deserve this."

"We've done well, Jamie. We deserve this."

That, she would not believe, and she cleared her throat. "Well, he should be proud of you."

"Of course he's happy I'm here. But you have to understand, he feels that sending me to the States was his greatest achievement. He'd been preparing me for this since I was born. He sent me to international schools and was relentless about my studies and not to mention golf practice…don't forget Tiger Woods is half Thai, too. My father didn't spend a hundred thousand dollars to send me to Stanford only to see me end up living in exile."

"Is this exile?"

He laid back and closed his eyes. "To me it's home."

She sat up on her elbows adjusting her eyes at the sea, for he'd once told her, with some ferocity, that he would never have a home. She didn't remind him of this now, struck by the fact that he was more at home here than any other place she'd seen him, driving on the opposite side of roads steaming in the aftermath of a crushing rain; the way he glided through these balmy, windswept rooms with that gentleness she'd discovered to be so natural to the Thais. "Farang farang," the ladies who swept their floors and made their beds and served at the restaurant might call out to him fondly. To which he might respond with an undecipherable Thai phrase, and they would cover their mouths and giggle. His Thai was rusty.

She narrowed her eyes at the sea because the faint idea that she should ask him something, something rather important, came to mind, like what he, too, might do next with his life, or if that concept of life existed any longer. They had agreed on three months here. That is what they'd loosely discussed. It was against her nature not to push him on this question; it was enough *to manage with her inertia, but his too? Though being a chef wasn't exactly inert. And cooking had always been Roberto's passion, being a chef an idle dream of his, a curiosity more than a future. But then that was back when she had a certain idea of what "future" meant: solid career=wealth=freedom=no worries. This was Giorgio's formula of life too…and look at him now do nothing but worry.*

She sat still like that for a while, listening to the waves and contemplating the sweat rolling down her stomach and dissolving into her towel. It felt like her internal drive was leaking out of her, and she couldn't afford to lose any more motivation. This sabbatical was supposed to refuel the drive she would need to move on from the surrogacy and get back on track. She was still a respected design engineer, and plenty of opportunities were out there. Drip, drip, drip. Her thighs burned. She looked up, noticing that the sun had again moved outside the confines of her umbrella. She sighed over at Roberto, who was on his back, arms over his head, thinking that they were both still young, after all, and certainly too young for retirement, let alone exile. "I'm starving," Jamie announced, as if she'd never been anything else.

There was something about Thailand that made her hunger animalistic. She often felt like she might die if she didn't eat something—a pile of rice in the shape of a bowl, or some Tom Yum, a spicy shrimp soup that only made her sweat more. Something about the oppressive air and the Thai chili peppers and the warm wine were so perfectly incongruous. She looked at Roberto, lying there next to her, half unconscious, bronzing before her eyes. He was clearly not ready for food; it was only eleven after all. So she sustained herself with images and scents of their commingled sweat, their entwined bodies, the heat of his flesh, all boundaries dissolved. None of this seemed rational. Something had taken possession of her, she decided, and she got up rather quickly. "I'm going to the water in search of a breeze or something." She started towards the shore without waiting for a response. Her thoughts and the burning hot sand quickened her stride, her one goal was feet in the water—everything else, all other previous goals, seemed childish and distant.

The relief was anticlimactic. The water was warm and murky, the sand eerily soft under foot, and crabs poked at her feet but she forged on, wading a long way out until the water almost reached her breasts. It took a while. She picked up a shell floating by, admiring its smooth, undefined shape before throwing it back into the water and turning back toward the shore because she sensed him approaching the sea to join her after all. From the jungle behind him rose the glass condo Giorgio spoke of. She wasn't sure if it was beautiful or not, any of this, all shades of gray: the sky, the sand, the murky sea through which she couldn't see her hands. Until she saw Roberto wading in, ever so slowly, as if the water was cold and not hot. He ran his fingers along the water's surface. She gazed at his disheveled figure, the slightly softening flesh around his waist, his brown hair sticking up; she sensed the jasmine in his sweat from twenty feet away and wondered if she was possibly too attracted to him, if their joined chemicals were addictive and controlling.

He dove under a small swell. Lured, she did the same, resurfacing by his side, the side of Me Firsts, where motherhood and families were forsaken for a life of this, to be loved selfishly, to be taken care of.

They treaded around each other even though the water was shallow enough to stand. Those dark brown eyes held hers and they didn't speak, didn't need to. She flipped on her back, staring at the burnt sky. He touched her breast.

After their swim he went to the restaurant. She rinsed off at an outdoor shower and, in some kind of trance, went for a walk along the shore. She'd only paced a few yards down the beach when she heard cries like those of seagulls. She looked up over the rocky sea wall and caught a cardboard sign that read Thai Massage 500 baht. The cries grew louder and then piercing, "Lady Lady. Lady want massage?" Dark arms and hands were waving at her from a shaded rocky inlet. She climbed up and they immediately folded her into their den. A half dozen Thai ladies, and not the usual gorgeously girlish Thais that worked as servers in restaurants and hotels, as the picture of Roberto's mother came to mind. These women were stolid, older, chaffed by the sun and their work. Two lay on massage tables asleep. The other three took care of Jamie, a curiosity more than a paying customer, a woman in need of healing. Nothing seemed urgent.

The largest woman sat Jamie on a table over a pot of warm water mixed with herbs, fruits, and spices. Gently she washed her feet with the brush. Then the woman lay Jamie face down on a bed of fresh sheets. A breeze sent an odd and rare chill up her spine. The woman was now on the table between Jamie's legs, massaging jasmine-infused oil into her back and torso and buttocks. Long strong strokes combined with points of pressure and Jamie's muscles at once relaxed. She closed her eyes and listened to the sea. The last thing she felt was a mist on her face. Then she fell asleep.

A heavy, deep sleep.

When she woke sometime later blinking at the sky (someone had turned her over onto her back), something was at once different. The sky, such a clear and perfect blue, she'd not seen it this color all week and she wondered if perhaps she'd been transported with the breeze into a different reality. She blinked again but the color did not fade, and the more she blinked the more startling it became, as did a rather sudden and astounding realization that she was going to be someone else. She sat up on her elbows, dazzled and bewildered—was it really possible to be someone else? She thought back to California, how she'd left with such clarity about who Betty was, and who Jamie was not: a mother. She was not going to be a mother. But coming to Thailand was about so much more than that, it was about the past being over, and yes in some ways she had known this, but only now, in this moment, did she feel the full force of it. Failure, a fear of which had always possessed her—unnaturally, she thought—had come—her career, her relationships—she failed all of it. But with its coming had come its going, and now she had nothing left, not even her fear anymore because for the first time since she could remember she wasn't scared. She felt exorcised, hollowed out, that smooth undefined shell that had floated by her earlier was now here, lying on this soft bed of orchid scented sheets, still and at peace and ready to be filled once again.

But with something else, and nothing she had wanted or expected.

All five ladies were standing over her now, partly amused, partly curious at her expression. The large one sat her up; another bowed her head and passed Jamie a cup of scalding hot lemon grass tea saying, of all things, that it was good for fertility. Another ran a comb through Jamie's hair, mesmerized by the red color. For a long time she worked through the knots, while Jamie sat still in the full and vibrant sense of her body. Then they placed a plastic bag filled with mangosteens in her hands and sent her back from where she came.

** 1984 **

Classes were in session, the halls of the Bio/Chem building deserted except for a male student approaching from the back entrance. A tall, gangly guy, Jamie immediately recognized him from her dorm, Jared somebody—she couldn't remember his last name—he reached the grade postings just before she did. He was one of those wiz kids, a freshman at sixteen, now eighteen and set to graduate. His shirt collar was tucked under, and his chords were tied around his waist with a rope. He might not have showered in a week, and Jamie wished he would hurry up and leave so she could search the board without being asphyxiated. Plus, she was in enough heart-thumping anxiety already in anticipation of the B she needed to pass the class. And perhaps Jared sensed her angst, for just then he turned around and fixed his eyes on hers, smiling—an eerie, chuckle kind of smile, as if he knew something about her that she didn't. Then he turned and walked off towards the back exit. Jamie watched him go, his body swaying and waggling as if he were drunk, or liberated by something.

She took a big breath of post-Jared air and ran her finger down the list, pausing at her grade, what became a blinding flash of white, before her lids closed slowly over her eyes, as if for good. Despair, inevitability, were the sensations that shook her core. And then she just stood there, humiliated, her heart sinking into her stomach. The sad part was she'd studied her ass off. In fact that's all she'd been doing since this whole college horror story began four months ago—Jamie, straight A student on partial scholarship to one of the top engineering colleges in the country, struggling to get Bs and Cs in her freshman core. No one else seemed like they were struggling, and she wiped a tear, subtly, in case Jared the prodigy was watching. But when she glanced down the hall he had already disappeared into a glare of white sun.

Why wasn't she born smart, the easy kind of smart, she lamented, fleeing back to her dorm, chin down, clutching her textbooks. Thankfully her roommate wasn't around so that Jamie could sit morbidly motionless, as she could do, on her bottom bunk without freaking anybody out. After a while she moved to the metal desk and opened her Differential Equations book to prepare for that final on Monday. She read the same equation five times before going over and opening her door like everyone else did on Friday afternoons so that friends could breeze in and out of each other's lives. She heard some girls from her sponsor group pass by on their way to a party, and Jamie rose in the fleeting thought of inviting herself to join them. But she sat back down possessed by another being now, one who hated her guts and whose emotion might suffocate her if she didn't do something. She dug a fingernail into her wrist, and when that didn't work, when the tears began falling and wouldn't stop, she did something she rarely did. She called Betty.

A girl answered the phone, sounding bothered. When Jamie heard the receiver bang against the wall, she considered hanging up. But then Betty got on and Jamie quickly made something up about Steven wanting to know what Betty wanted for Christmas. Gift giving negotiations between and among their disparate family members had become a holiday tradition. Betty, Jamie, and Steven would exchange many phone calls discussing who was giving what to whom, the logistics of Christmas morning with Dad, Christmas Eve with Mom and which James Bond flick they were going to see on what night. And when it came to gifts, Steven, who had returned from college and become instantly rich, it seemed, working for a real estate developer, spared no expense. So Jamie could tell Betty was thinking hard about her answer. She spouted out some options before deciding on a camera, then a sewing machine, no, the tall boots she'd seen in the Robinson's Catalog.

"Anything else?"

"No, I'm good."

"OK then."

"OK."

The line went silent.

"What are you doing tonight?"

A simple enough question, one Jamie couldn't answer. She slid against the wall down to the floor.

"It's Friday night, Jamie. You should go out."

"I have a Differential Equations final on Monday."

"So."

"It's just…you know…hard." Jamie palmed the phone and breathed. "The math I mean."

"Why don't you just come over?"

There was a silence.

"*The Exorcist* is showing at the Wash," Betty went on. "And I know of a party we could check out after."

It was what she was hoping her sister would say, but still the invitation, so casual and obvious, surprised her so much that she couldn't answer.

"Well?"

"I guess, OK."

Jamie didn't let herself think because if she did she'd think she was groveling, in need, and probably wouldn't go. She threw on a jean miniskirt and dug up a tank top that wasn't black or gray from the bottom of her drawer. She pinned up her hair with clips, dabbed some makeup over her swollen eyes, mascara for her lashes, and set out in the dry, dusk air for Betty's dorm.

Pitzer, Betty's college, was just a short, ivy-and-stone walk from Jamie's college, Harvey Mudd. Both were part of a group of small private colleges located in the foothills of the San Gabriel Mountains. The fact that she and Betty went to schools next to each other and two hours drive from home was in no way planned. While Harvey Mudd was ranked third in engineering, MIT had been Jamie's first choice. She had wanted to get as far away as possible from home, not because she hated home, but because she thought that the farther away one traveled to achieve something, the more successful they would be at achieving it. Her brother had gone to Harvard and now drove around Orange County in a Mercedes. Plus, she'd been wearing tank tops and flip flops all her life and the blizzards of the east seemed sufferably romantic. (To date Jamie had had little romance.) That C flashed before Jamie's eyes again and there was nothing romantic about that. Suddenly she was glad MIT had rejected her.

After checking in at the front desk, Jamie walked up four flights of steps and down the beer-stained carpeted hallway to Betty's room. Her door was open and Billy Joel was blaring from her stereo, but Betty wasn't there. Jamie helped herself to a Michelob Light from the miniature fridge and then perused the surroundings that felt all so familiar even though this was Jamie's first intimate look into her sister's college life. Her old black Singer sat on a tiny wood sewing table with its fang driving into what looked like a sleeve (to this day Betty still sewed her own clothes). The floppy gorilla Betty's had since childhood sat perched on a chair in the corner. It was dressed in Betty's high school volleyball jersey and wore a pin that said, "Betty for Senior Class Secretary." Jamie herself had thrown away everything from high school the minute it was over. But Betty saved everything down to that last yellow ribbon, not to mention those three-inch notebooks stacked on her shelf containing pictures that would trace Betty's life back to birth.

Betty rushed in then, wrapped in a towel, her hair dripping wet. "Who's this?" Jamie said, picking up one of the dozens of frames arranged on wood planks that served as shelves. Betty came over and examined the photo. Their greetings typically consisted of not greeting each other, as if their relationship was one long conversation and they were simply picking up where they'd left off.

The photo was a young girl, eight maybe. "That's my little sister."

"I thought I was your little sister."

"You know what I mean."

It was the Big Brothers Big Sisters of America program the colleges sponsored, the one Jamie hadn't even considered because she couldn't imagine disappointing someone like that. But Betty didn't think that way. Jamie set the frame back down and perused the other photos: Betty with her middle school friends; Betty with her V-ball team; Betty piled on top of her dorm sponsor group; Betty with Rich at her high school prom. Then there were the family photos: Jamie was still getting used to the idea of her dad seeing Vivi romantically, though she was happy for him. It was their mother and Gary's wedding picture that always made Jamie pause. Barefoot, their mother wore a beige iolite sundress and daisies in her hair. She was forty but looked eighteen in the photo—then again she always looked eighteen. Gary, her husband, looked like a rock star in white linen standing beside Jamie, seated with a paper plate of catered food on her lap, frowning. "God I look miserable."

"You were miserable," Betty said, over her shoulder.

"Well at least you look happy."

Betty stared at the picture. "I was oblivious. And fat. God, I hated myself back then." She turned away from the picture towards the mirror. "Where is Mom anyway? The season ends next week and she still hasn't come to one of my games."

"Well, if Dad might miss one…"

Betty gave her a weary look. Their dad didn't just come to Betty's games, he whooped and cheered and harassed the ref. Jamie knew this because she went to most of Betty's games too.

"She could at least come see my dorm room," Betty added, staring off for a moment, as if their mother's selective presence was still unfathomable to her. *This is not news Betty,* Jamie was about to remind her, but then Betty switched on her blow dryer and that was the end of that topic.

Nathan's picture got special placement on her sister's bedside table. He was alarmingly handsome, Jamie noted again, picking up the frame. "Where's Nathan tonight?"

"I told him I had to study," Betty said, hair flying, what was left of it—these days she wore it short and cropped behind her ears.

"Are you guys still a thing?"

"We're friends."

"I thought you really liked him."

"I did…do. Just not seriously…you know."

Jamie put down the photo and began searching Betty's makeup bag for something she could use but found her birth control pills instead.

"Yes, I'm on the pill," Betty answered before Jamie could ask.

Jamie didn't know why she was surprised. "I thought you said you and Nathan were just friends."

"We are." Betty spoke to the mirror, as if she were defending herself to herself. "Intimate friends."

"Oh," Jamie said, pretending that she didn't feel overwhelming stupid. Of course Betty was on the pill. Just because Jamie was a virgin didn't mean everybody else was.

Betty finished feathering her bangs, and by the time she was done, thirty minutes had flown by and Jamie had hardly noticed. Waiting for Betty was like breathing.

"Rich has been calling me," Betty said offhandedly, unplugging the dryer.

"High school Rich?"

"He wants to get back together." She came over and sat down on the edge of the bed, her skin moist from the heat. "I saw him at Thanksgiving. And we kind of…you know."

Jamie didn't know.

"Got together." Betty fondled a piece of blue cotton fabric next to her, what would ultimately become a team sweatshirt; there was already a pile of finished ones on her bed. "Nathan was getting so serious." She stood up and began rambling, something she does when she's nervous, about Rich and then Nathan and then the fact that she was sleeping with them both. Her eyes were glossy by the time she'd revealed this last tidbit of information, unsure if she'd meant to, but peeking at Jamie for a reaction none-the-less. Silence ensued, one Jamie was to fill, presumably, with some keen insight, and she desperately wanted to, for her sister was in rare need of advice. But Jamie's mind was still an undefined number of sexual episodes behind. She herself had embarrassingly little experience with guys. How had all this gone on without her ever knowing it?

"Which do you like better?"

Jamie looked up. Betty was at her jewelry box holding a dif-ferent earring up to each ear, the moment long gone, and it struck Jamie sadly that this was only the beginning, that Betty would go on to live many lives outside the realm of her younger sister. How naïve she had been all these years, believing that everything was happening to them both, at the same time, in parallel.

Betty slipped on the gold candelabras that Jamie had pointed to. They brought out the cerulean in her eyes, eyes that Jamie had always admired, though something was different about them tonight. Jamie wondered if it might be the birth control pills. Her sister looked flushed and borderline beautiful, cinching her white blouse over black jeans with a matching chain-link belt. Her plumpness was gone, and the gloss in her eyes revealed a vulnerability Jamie hadn't seen before. Or perhaps it was just the coke Betty was presently unveiling from a tiny folded piece of newspaper. "A friend gave it to me," she offered sheepishly.

Jamie stared dumbly at it. Then she retrieved a dollar bill from her back pocket and rolled it up as if she'd done it before thinking, whatever it takes. Betty cut the lines on an unused picture frame. It felt a little awkward, like making a new friend, but also so natural and old. "I'm thinking about transferring to UCLA," Jamie said off-handedly, washing the bitterness down with her beer.

Betty, about to do her line, paused.

"What am I doing at Harvey Mudd anyway? They're just a bunch of engineering geeks…"

Jamie felt Betty study her for a moment. Then she smirked and said, "You think I know what I'm doing here? I only came to Pitzer because they recruited me for volleyball. And who wouldn't have, the team sucks, we've lost every game this year." She paused and did her line. Jamie did a double take. It was true, Betty's team was last in their division three league, but still, she'd only ever known her sister to be resolutely positive.

"Plus Steven had that connection with the dean of admissions," Betty went on. "And Mom was all gung ho on the 'arts' program. But it's 'Liberal arts,' not art. I still kick myself for not applying to UCSB. They have a great fashion program there. That's art, to me anyway." She passed the bill back to Jamie. "I'm supposed to declare my major this semester, but I have no idea what I want to do." Her eyes, which had been fleeting about, now settled firmly on her younger sister. "At least you know what you want to do, Jamie."

Jamie, still bowled over by her sister's confessions, decided that yes, it was the coke talking. Still, listening to Betty, Jamie thought back to all those years of ballet and wondered, for the first time, if she did know what she wanted to do. When and why had she decided to give up ballet, for instance? She couldn't remember. Was it because she was no good at it? Or was it because she was afraid she was no good at it? Because afraid is how she felt now—of failing, of being singled out, of not being singled out, of something, everything. Where did this fear come from? And how the hell would she ever get rid of it?

They stuffed the rest of the six-pack into Betty's canvas book bag, and each grabbed a cotton sweatshirt from the pile on Betty's bed. They felt like the bad girls they'd never been, and in a good, amped up way, they left.

The Wash, a ruinous amphitheater overgrown with weeds and bramble, located on the southeast corner of campus, was a good distance from Betty's dorm. They had to hustle through Marston Quad and Walker Dorm and then cut across the track field. Beyond that it was a quarter mile of dirt and grass on which they ran with Jamie clutching the bag to her breasts so the beers wouldn't clink. They were laughing by the time they got there, for the coke had kicked in, and just like that, the night seemed full of potential.

The place was a party scene on Friday nights, starting with an open-air movie. Semicircles of crumbling cement steps wrapped around patches of grass where students stretched out on blankets. A portable movie screen was set up on the stage made uneven by years of seismic activity and looked like it might tip over at any moment. After paying their buck with a student ID, Jamie and Betty took seats on a high step and immediately twisted the caps off two beers. It was early December, the air dry and breezeless and thick with the smog that lived in these foothills. You felt it when you breathed in deep, or gasped as Jamie just had, too loud, because Betty was flashing her a discerning look. Jamie wasn't gasping at the air, however, but at the opening credits of *The Exorcist*, which had started. Apparently, they'd both forgotten about Jamie's little issue with horror movies. It's not my fault, Jamie always insisted, as she did now to Betty. For where were her parents when she sat home alone watching *The Blob* at so young an age? And where was Betty for that matter? Steven? Jamie's hands were over her eyes by the first scene, her thumbs plugging her ears by the second, and by the third she was half inside her sweatshirt. It was tiring and stressful. "Who goes up in the attic alone?" Jamie needed to know, watching through her fingers the movie mother creep up the attic steps to check out a noise. "At night, no flashlight, what the hell is she thinking?"

Betty didn't respond. She seemed more amused than affected.

"I just couldn't do it," Jamie winced. Then she contemplated her gutlessness. How would she ever succeed in life if she couldn't explore the dark? "What's happening now?" she asked Betty, still wanting to know, because as terrifying as it was, there was this need to know how horrifying it could all get. She twisted off the cap of another beer. It helped.

At some point Jamie's whole body was inside her sweatshirt, and her sister glanced at her and laughed. "Just watch the movie Jamie."

"Right." She relaxed her muscles and checked out the crowd. If people were cringing it was ceremonious, in fact mostly they were laughing, which is when it occurred to Jamie that this was probably their second or third viewings, and like the *Rocky Horror Picture Show*, they were screaming and acting out the lines for fun.

"Shit," Betty said low.

"You mean fuck." Jamie retorted. It seemed more appropriate for the occasion: green vile oozing from the possessed girl's mouth.

"No…I mean, shit, there's Nathan."

"Where?"

Betty tilted her head towards a particular patch of grass, where Nathan was kicked back on a blanket with some friends. "He can't see me here."

Jamie caught the back of his dark curly head, and was struck, again, by his looks. Plus, he'd been so nice to Jamie that one time she'd met him, quiet, unpretentious, and a hell of a lot sexier than Rich. "Well, we can't leave now." Jamie fixed her eyes back on the priest, who was in the middle of performing his exorcism, and forced herself to laugh and feign terror along with everyone else. *Laugh, and the horror won't seem so scary*—it seemed to be working, because after a while of carrying on like that everything seemed to turn sideways, surreal, and for the first time since freshman orientation, liberating and fun.

Betty on the other hand, was consumed by the sudden knowledge of Nathan's proximity and wanted to leave. "He thinks I'm studying," Betty chewed her lip. "I do NOT want him coming with us to the party."

Linda Blair's head-turning three-sixty was a bit anticlimactic. Nevertheless, the audience cheered and clapped, and in the din Jamie and Betty took the opportunity to flee, something they would have done unnoticed had Jamie not knocked over one of the five empty beer bottles at her feet just at the same time silence resumed in the theater after the priest threw the devil and himself out the window. Jamie and Betty froze while the pool of blood amassed around the priest's head, and the bottle clanked down the cement steps and onto the grass.

Nathan turned around to see who had caused the commotion. But Jamie and Betty had already bolted out the exit. They hit the grass running and didn't turn back. They ran until it hurt, until they couldn't think or breathe or remember any of the reasons that brought them here tonight. When they reached the track field, they abruptly stopped and bent over their knees, panting. They looked at each other, started laughing, and couldn't stop. Everything seemed so funny to Jamie suddenly, and she hadn't laughed like this in a long time, least of all with Betty. In fact she couldn't remember ever laughing with Betty like this. Like friends.

Their adrenaline was pumping now. After a pit stop behind a bush to pee, each taking turns guarding the other, they headed to Pomona where the coach of Betty's intramurals team was throwing a party with his suitemates.

When Betty and Jamie stumbled off the elevator onto the fourth floor, two guys from Betty's team, a balding Swede and a short guy with glasses, immediately welcomed her with a "Betty sandwich." She introduced them to Jamie before dragging her over to the keg where Bill, her coach, stood perched against a door drinking from a plastic red cup. He was barefoot, wearing jeans and a white t-shirt, and probably stoned. He gave Betty an "oh-hey" nod, and it was the way her eyes shimmered and her mouth curved a certain way that told Jamie what was really going on: Betty's quandary wasn't over sleeping with both Nathan and Rich, it was about her crush on this Bill guy, whom Jamie, just by the looks of him, instantly disliked. Perhaps it was his blond haired, blue-eyed nonchalance, or the way he just poured Betty a beer without bothering with Jamie. Or perhaps it was written in the cosmos somewhere: no man will ever be good enough for a woman's sister. But Jamie had liked Nathan, why couldn't Betty just like Nathan? And anyway, when had her sister become so popular with guys, Jamie wondered, pouring her own beer and drifting off to let Betty flirt with Bill.

At the quarters table now, the Swede shifted over so that Jamie could squeeze in and have a turn. She nailed her first glass and randomly jabbed her elbow at the guy to her right, who turned out to be a very, very cute guy she couldn't help noticing in her chemically induced haze. The guy gave her a sideways glance and downed his beer. She didn't glance back; instead she nailed the next five quarters before missing, if only to impress him, which apparently it did, at least enough for him to finally say something. "Are you Betty's sister?"

An eternal question that Jamie couldn't help but answer sarcastically, "How could you tell?"

He examined her. "Visiting then?"

"Sort of." She'd hold off on the geek label for tonight.

The quarter went around the table a few times before the cute guy hit her with a drink. A good sign, she thought, guzzling her beer. But then he stood up. Bad sign. Jamie tried not to stare at him making his way to the keg, hoping he'd be back, guessing that he wouldn't.

"Betty told me you go to Mudd?"

She turned. It was the short guy with glasses.

"So you knew him then?"

She looked at him, confused.

"The guy who jumped."

She pulled back slightly.

"You know that wiz kid." He turned to the table. "What's his name?"

"Jared Peterson," someone said as a quarter hit a glass.

Jamie set down her beer. The party was loud, but she heard him right.

"Guy gets a fucking B on some test, writes his parents a note, and jumps off the roof of Marston. Unbelievable."

Someone chuckled. "It *was* his first B."

A quarter hit a glass.

Jamie's head started spinning.

The cute guy was back, moving his lips but she couldn't hear him. Her mind was back inside the Bio/Chem building, her gaze looking into the empty white light of Jared's soul. His quirky, lost, indeterminate smile flashed before her. She hadn't even smiled back.

The room became a swirl. She stood up from the table and asked where the bathroom was. "Are you OK?" she heard the cute guy say. Air, she told him, and he took her to the balcony off his room. She had to clutch the railing in order to stay upright, the air tasted toxic, and she was completely wrecked. "Did you know him?" He sat down on the bed beside her, which is when she realized that she was on a bed, unsure how and when she'd made that transition. He repeated the question and she attempted to tell him no, she did not know him, but that she'd seen him that day, checking his test results and that must have been when…she stopped herself because her words sounded slurry and the cute guy was headed for the door. Her heart sank, but then he shut the door and returned and it rose again, fluttering, then pounding, and she leaned into him for support, perhaps, or for other reasons. His body felt hot, and all she wanted was to be in his arms. No, actually she wanted more than that; however blurred her sensations were, she didn't care. They started kissing, first slowly and then with their bodies wrapped around each other. They fell back on the bed and she felt his hands up her shirt and then her skirt, her own hands pushing into his jeans in an attempt to unbutton them, unsure about everything except the fact that she wanted no more of the things wrong with her, her fear and virginity in particular, which at this moment were one and the same and soon to be exorcised from her body. She couldn't believe it was happening at last.

Until he stopped abruptly and sat up.

She blinked at him. He seemed to be glancing anywhere but at her, and she got this horribly empty feeling, like she wasn't there, like she was missing, because if she wasn't mistaken, he looked, simply put, bored. "That was fun," he said, and walked out. Jamie sat there for a minute longer, discombobulated and stunned. A grimy, sleazy feeling seeped into her pours as she fumbled to straighten her shirt and untwist her skirt. She tried with everything she had not to sway on the way out.

She glanced around for Bill thinking that that's where she'd find Betty, but Bill had his arm wrapped around some blond now. The sight sent a flood of water to Jamie's mouth and she weaved her way to the elevator whose door slid magically open. She fell in. A hand caught the door just as it was about to close, and Jamie covered her mouth. "I'm going to be sick."

"Oh, God, hold on!" Betty kept the L pressed, as if that could make the elevator go faster. When they finally hit the lobby, Jamie ran for the exit and made it just in time to heave into the bushes. Betty held back her hair, chatting briefly with a few drunken friends who happened to pass by, until at last all that Jamie had left was heavy, sour air. She wanted to crawl up into a ball and die right there, but Betty dragged her back to her dorm room, clearing the fabrics off her bed just in time for Jamie to fall on top of it.

The ceiling was moving. "I got a C on my Bio/Chem final." She covered her eyes with her forearm.

"So."

"I needed a B to pass." She tasted tears, though in her inebriated state it felt like someone else was crying.

Betty slipped off one of Jamie's shoes. "So take the class over."

Jamie's mind floated on that a moment. She'd never quite considered that option before. "Maybe I can't make it here."

"Jamie, it's the first semester." Off with the other shoe.

She sat up on her elbows then, which probably wasn't a good idea. "A guy jumps off a building because of a B?"

"It's fucked up." Betty grabbed a pillow, her Pitzer blanket, and made camp on the floor.

Jamie turned onto her side. "I'd never do it," she said, wiping her cheek.

Betty yawned. "Do what?"

"Jump."

There was a pause. "I know."

They lay like that for a while, the room buzzing with their drunken silence. Jamie's mind was swirling through images and thoughts—the cute guy, Jared, Linda Blair's retching possessed face, the pool of blood seeping out from behind the priest's head and the fact that no priest was going to save Jamie from what possessed her. And since she wasn't a jumper, she was going to have to live with humiliation and fear, perhaps forever, all of which culminated into one horrifying and painful reality: "I'm nineteen and I've never been on a real date." She didn't know what she was saying anymore.

"Yes you have."

"No I haven't."

Betty sat up on an elbow and thought.

"See, you can't think of anyone."

"I'll think of someone, just give me a minute." Betty readjusted her blanket and lay back down. From the blackness came, "Don't transfer, Jamie. Stay here with me."

Jamie slid her leg off the bed and found solid ground with her foot. And just like that everything stopped moving, as if that was all Jamie had ever needed to hear.

Time passed. It could have been a minute or an hour.

"Charlie Tramwell," came out from beneath her sister's blanket.

There was some silence, and then Jamie sighed, half-uncon-scious, into her pillow. "That was in the fifth grade, Betty."

Her sister chuckled, and Jamie didn't remember anything after that.

CHAPTER 5
Blue Velvet

September, 2003

September had cooled the air, tinted the leaves orange, and brought a much needed respite from Betty's second trimester. The morning sickness had subsided, and her energy was back, in excess. She couldn't remember being this productive in her previous pregnancies. That morning she and Dave had met with Debbie, the midwife, and things had been a whirlwind ever since: soccer games, play dates, laundry, dinner, after which she'd sewed another baby blanket, done her birthing exercises, and taken a hot shower, all while Dave put the kids to bed. It was ten p.m., and here she was, wide awake at her computer, researching birthing tubs while humming along to the Grateful Dead song Dave was singing to the boys next door. He was better at getting them settled into their beds than she was. With her there would be pillow fights, giggles, and raucous laughter. But when Dave sang, the boys would lie in their beds and chill. She rested a hand on her belly and relaxed into the rhythm. Their voices grew softer, and then went silent, and she thought Dave might have fallen asleep on the floor in there, as he'd been doing lately. Until she heard the heavy weight of him pounding down the stairs, what felt like the whole house coming down with him.

She printed out the pages from the Internet she'd found, and went to find him. They'd barely seen each other since meeting with Debbie that morning, let alone had a chance to discuss anything. She wondered why she wasn't exhausted, why she still felt restless after a long day…a long week, in fact; work had been crazy too. She'd been preparing for the museum's annual auction fundraiser. This year they were expecting more than three hundred guests for a five-course meal, a peek at the new exhibits, and a chance to bid on a pair of Jackie Kennedy's gloves. It sounded exciting, and perhaps it was the first time she'd planned it…ten years ago. Now she felt more like a glorified assistant, and this event wasn't even in her job description. She took the project on initially as a favor to her boss thinking it would lead to other opportunities within the museum or exposure to the Met in New York. She was a manager now, in garment restoration, but she couldn't remember the last time she actually took a stitch to one of the First Lady's gowns or worked with the fabrics themselves. How had she gotten so far removed from what she loved doing?

Two months until her sabbatical. She counted every day.

She found Dave downstairs in the basement, no lights on, sitting on the couch watching the Home and Garden channel. Dave normally didn't watch TV, so she figured he was doing this for his job. Even though he didn't like Home Depot, they clearly liked him. He'd recently been moved to full-time days with salary and benefits, with weekends off now to work on the birthing tub, which she needed to discuss with him.

"This couch smells funky," she said, switching on the table light and sitting down next to him.

"Boys," was his delayed response, one he gave without looking at her.

She stared at the show with him for a minute. He put an arm over her shoulder and began massaging her neck, and she relaxed her head back. "So what did you think of our meeting with Debbie?"

He stopped rubbing.

"I thought the three of us had a good rapport going, no?"

He started rubbing again, this time barely scratching the surface of her skin. It felt more annoying than anything else. "Because you know, it's really important. I just thought she really knew what she was doing. You know Gracie had her baby with Debbie and loved her. She's gentle, yet tough."

"You mean gruff." He was still staring at the TV, where some guy was walking around knocking on walls looking for hidden openings.

"You don't like her?"

"I didn't say that." He pulled his arm away.

"Then what did you say?"

He batted his eyes at her. "I said she's great."

Betty ignored his tone and kept her eyes on the TV. "And she doesn't take any risks. If there's the slightest problem we go right to the hospital. Speaking of which, we need to get the tires on the GTI replaced."

"We don't need to get them replaced, Betty. What we need is a new spare."

"Whatever, let's just get it."

"We've got four months."

"And about the birthing tub…" She paused to clear her throat. "I'm thinking we could just buy one." She examined the papers in her hand, feeling the bitterness of his eyes upon her. She couldn't help herself. She was trying to be patient and understanding with him. She knew this wasn't easy on him. "I didn't say you couldn't build it," she quickly added. "Of course you can build it. I just didn't know…well…Debbie thinks that we could do a deep corner tub, one that would fit nicely in the master bath upstairs."

"So now Debbie's a carpenter?"

"She recommended this particular style," she said, handing him the Internet printouts. "Her other clients were really satisfied with it." She felt her adrenaline pumping as it had that morning, when she'd met with Debbie alone, before Dave had joined them. And it wasn't even about the water birth. She and Debbie had started idly discussing Betty's baby clothing business idea. Debbie had gotten all excited about some research she'd done. The trend in midwife births was reaching the higher income markets. The middle class was going green, and mother's not only wanted natural births, they wanted natural fabrics for their newborns' clothes.

Dave glanced at the sheets and set them aside. "We don't have two thousand dollars, Betty."

She was about to speak.

"And Sam needs braces."

She clenched her jaw. "I know Sam needs braces." Louder, "Of course I know Sam needs braces. And why can't you be positive for once, help me come up with a solution instead of immediately batting down the idea because we don't have the money!"

He smiled at her. "But we don't have the money."

She pulled her knees into her chest as her whole body contracted. "Home Depot has moved you to salary plus benefits, Dave, and after just one month. I told you they'd figure it out. You've got a college degree, for heaven's sake, and one year of law school under your belt. You did own your own furniture business." She didn't look at him after she'd said that. "It's just a matter of time, Dave. I told you to give it a chance."

Abruptly he switched the channel, found her show, and handed her the remote. "Here. This is what you want, right? Sex and the City?"

Neither spoke for a minute. The couple on the show was in the middle of a fight too, apparently. The actor who played Charlotte's husband Trey was the same guy in the movie Blue Velvet, a thought that struck Betty every time she saw this show; that and the fact that the actor had aged. That she'd aged.

"Look Betty, I said I'd make the silly tub. I want to make the tub. I'll make the tub, alright?"

She pulled her eyes from Trey to look at her husband with another imbedded thought. "But will you?" She felt horrible, yes, but part of her just wanted him to yell at her, scream at the top of his lungs, maybe even slap her because wasn't that what she deserved?

Instead he went to the metal cabinet against the wall and unlocked a drawer. He brought back the small bag of weed he kept there and began *rolling a joint on the coffee table. She watched him, going numb. Maybe this is what she deserved, to sit and watch her husband punish himself inside a chemically induced fog. She hadn't said anything about this recent indulgence of his. It's not like he had a problem, she assured herself. And he hadn't complained once about the rather demoralizing job she knew he had taken for her and the kids because she'd asked him to. She folded up the brochures. It was ten, and she felt her body becoming one with the couch. They'd talk about the tub tomorrow, she decided, picking up her knitting from the basket she kept there, a receiving blanket she'd been working on. Debbie had wanted her to try this new hemp yarn and she admitted she liked the feel of it. She looked up, her fingers on autopilot now. On screen Carrie and Miranda were in Barneys. Maybe Betty could sell these blankets at Barneys.*

Meanwhile Dave had licked the paper, rolled the joint, and twisted the ends. "You know they can't afford that stuff," he muttered, standing up.

She reached for the remote and turned up the volume.

He didn't move immediately. He stood staring at those women on screen he despised so. Sometimes Betty wished he could despise her. It was she who deserved his punishment, not the other way around. She couldn't keep the thought buried forever. Had she punished him in some unconscious way for getting a vasectomy without her consent after Nick was born? She'd been stunned by what he'd done, embarrassed and unwilling to tell anyone about it. But there was still a one percent chance that Dave could get her pregnant; vasectomies weren't fool proof—the words she'd said to Dave. She kept hearing them over and over. Could she believe it too? That this baby was Dave's because wouldn't it be so ironic? It's what she planned on telling him if he asked. But he didn't ask, he would never ask. Just like he would never leave her; he'd live in this crumbling down house forever, she feared, a prisoner of his own ideals of her, she a prisoner of her own guilt.

She reached up and touched his arm.

He took the joint outside.

** 1987 **

"Must we punish ourselves?" Betty asked the sky, when her sister insisted on seeing *Blue Velvet*. "Must every movie we see be dark and morbid?"

Betty had wanted to see *Moonstruck*, a chick flick, something to lift Jamie's spirits. But here they were, at what might be the last single screen theater in existence, and which also happened to be in walking distance from their dad's house where Betty, and now Jamie, had been camping out since college. One minute into the film and already they were faced with a severed off ear. Jeffrey, an unsuspecting college kid, just found the half moon of cartilage in the woods, bloody and crawling with gnats.

That ear, combined with the stench of grease and other unknown fluids imbedded in these old foam seats, made Betty want to crawl out of her skin. To distract herself she began to go over all the things she had to do before she left: finish packing; decide what she could fit in her GTI and what she should ship ahead UPS; get her car serviced; and map out her cross-country route. She had seven days to get to Washington, D.C., to start her new job as a garment restorer for the American History Museum. Steven had gotten her the interview through his D.C. connections. It was an entry-level position, but at this point she'd take anything to get away. Everything was set. If only Steven would call. He was supposed to be here.

Betty rubbed her temples and tried refocusing on the movie, though she seemed to have missed something. Jeffrey—intrigued, bored—Betty wasn't sure, was now searching for the person missing the ear. But how and why he'd come to be in the closet of this woman's apartment, this very disturbed woman slipping on the blue velvet dress, Betty had no idea. Hence the title, *Blue Velvet*, the only dot Betty could seem to connect in the film now thirty minutes in. And they weren't even at the good part yet, what began when a man barged in, a most disturbingly evil little man, and began terrorizing the blue velvet woman while a horrified Jeffrey watched on from between the slats in the closet door. Things quickly degenerated. Apparently the woman was this man's to sodomize and do with what he wished. Betty sunk lower into her seat, her brow furrowed deep into her temporal lobe. He had the woman in a chair now, her legs spread, and he began having some kind of demonic episode with her crotch, as if it were the devil in disguise of his mother, or vice versa; it made Betty sick. The woman rolled her head back and fluttered her blue-shadowed eye lids like she was getting some sick sort of pleasure from what the guy was doing, which wasn't entirely clear from Betty's view. "Mommy, Mommy," the man cried, which is when Betty released a sick laugh of her own, passed Jamie the popcorn, and headed for the bathroom.

She sat on the toilet and stared absently at the graffiti carved into the wood door. She had waited so long for something to happen to her, and here it was finally happening. She had a plan, at least until four days ago when the doctor discovered a tumor the size of a golf ball in her sister's colon. Now everything was all fucked up. Jamie was checking into the hospital for surgery the day after tomorrow, the same day Betty was scheduled to leave and before the biopsy results would return, most likely. It was too much to comprehend and Betty didn't know what to do. She had to believe things would be fine because otherwise she'd think it entirely unfair, and not so much for Jamie but for her. What a horrible, selfish thing to think.

Back in the theater, everything had dissolved into a blue haze. Betty, barely able to see, felt along the aisle seats before she found their row and sat down again. The sodomite—Frank was his name—and his derelict friends had Jeffrey in captivity now along with the woman. They were all jammed into Frank's car headed down some black barren road, towards hell Betty had to presume, and she sighed. She had no idea what was going on and was about to ask Jamie what she'd missed, but then realized Jamie wasn't there. Betty looked around, making sure she was in the right row. Their half-eaten tub of popcorn was still on the floor, and yes, Betty checked, it was as her sister insisted it to be, unbuttered.

After five minutes, her sister still missing, Betty got up and searched the theater. In the background Frank went on brutalizing, the sounds of which were so disturbing that by the time Betty got to the lobby, her face was clenched and she was palming her ears. In the welcoming light, she took deep breaths and glanced around. No Jamie. She checked the bathroom. Nothing. She couldn't get herself to go back inside the theater because certainly Frank was taking Jeffrey somewhere to torture and kill him, and she wanted to make sure the scene was over. So she bought some Peanut M&Ms at the concession stand and wandered around reading the poster board reviews. Finally she forced herself back inside, head down, thinking this completely ludicrous, which is when she slammed into Jamie coming up the isle.

"Where were you?"

"Where were you?"

Someone shushed them, and they fell into the first two empty seats they could find. As it turns out, Frank had not, in fact, killed Jeffrey. He'd kicked the shit out of him, and Jeffrey was in the hospital now having the flashbacks, if only to torture Betty, who now got to witness the gruesome beating she'd wanted to miss. When the screen warped and went black, Betty almost cheered.

It was pitch dark for a minute until someone went and got someone and the lights came on. There was a technical problem; would be just a few minutes. Betty pulled out the crumpled bag of M&Ms from her pocket. "Tonight is your last chance to eat before the surgery." Jamie, staring at the screen as if the movie were still playing, turned and blinked at the bag. "Thanks for the reminder," she said, extracting a single M&M, which she proceeded to chew slowly, as if doing so might dissolve some of the calories going into her body.

"What time does Jim arrive tomorrow?"

"I told him he didn't need to come."

Betty stifled a sigh. Her sister still refused to admit how much she cared for Jim. She could be so stubbornly dispassionate. "But he's coming."

"He's coming."

The film reel warped back on, flickered, then garbled to a halt again.

"That didn't sound good," someone behind them said.

Jamie hunkered down.

Betty cleared her throat. "Do you wonder how you got it?"

"Got what?"

Betty dulled her eyes. Her sister knew what.

"Too Much In-N-Out-Burger?"

"You don't eat fast food."

"Too much tequila?"

"…And other substances."

They glanced at each other.

"Why you and not me?"

"Maybe I'm being punished."

"Oh please. For what?"

"Do I need to go over it again? The tequila, the…"

Betty sighed.

Jamie sighed. "Then it's a mystery," she said. "Like the ear."

Betty shook her head. Then she chuckled, and the chuckle developed into a laugh, and she couldn't stop. Water streamed from her eyes while Jamie watched on with a flatly amused expression.

"Feel better?" Jamie said when Betty finally pulled it together and wiped her face. "Seriously, Jamie."

"Seriously, Betty."

They looked at each other seriously. Then Jamie looked down at her hands and said, "It's only been four days. I haven't had time to process it."

"The doctor wants me to get a colonoscopy when I get to D.C." Betty paused. "You know, just in case…"

"…It's hereditary…I know…sorry."

"That's *if* I go to D.C."

"You're going to D.C."

I'm staying no matter what, Betty wanted to say. "But you're not worried, are you?"

"Just about my bikini line." Jamie drew an imaginary line vertically along her pelvis indicating what would be her scar. When she looked up again her eyes were wet, and Betty had to look away. It was the first time she'd seen her sister show the slightest disbelief or fear about what was happening to her. The moment caught both of them off guard. "Do you think they're ever going to fix this thing?" Jamie cleared her throat.

"Hopefully not," Betty insisted. "Let's go. I need a drink."

"But what if I die? I'll never know how it ends."

Betty narrowed her eyes at Jamie for a long moment. Then she got up and walked out.

"Where are we going?" Jamie said, catching up with her outside.

"Wherever you want. It's your night."

"I thought it was yours."

"It *was* until you trumped me."

They wandered up Main Street considering their options. Aside from two surfers in stripped down wet suits eating at the window of Surf and Taco, few people were out. Friday, dusk, and the only sounds were the cry of seagulls circling the beach. Betty loved this time of day, the way the world hushed like the inside of a sea shell. She would miss it.

They decided on McHale's Tavern only because they'd never been in it. They used to pass the windowless establishment on their way to Grandmas Ice Cream when they were kids. The same sign was posted on the shut door, "NO ONE UNDER 21 ALLOWED." There was no sense of an outside once the door shut behind them. Over-forty men who'd seen too much sun sat slumped over the bar. A jukebox played Jimmy Buffet. Dull yellow light shone over a pool table in the back, all of which amounted to an atmosphere that said one thing: *people who grow up at the beach never leave the beach.*

She and Jamie took stools at the bar and began hurling peanut shells on the floor already littered with them. "Here's what I don't get," Betty began.

"I'm listening."

"Why didn't she leave?"

They held eyes a moment.

"The blue velvet woman I mean. It wasn't like Frank locked her in her apartment. She was free to go out, to sing at that nightclub. Why didn't she try to escape?"

"Maybe she liked being punished."

Betty pulled back slightly, and then thought better to just forget it. "I don't think this movie had a point."

"We're all fighting the evil in ourselves," Jamie offered after more disturbed thought. "That's why being punished sometimes feels good."

"And the ear? What happened with the ear?"

Even Jamie had to sigh. "I guess it would have been helpful to see the end."

They gave up on understanding the movie and ordered beers from the bartender. Then Betty went to the payphone to call Joel, who'd been bugging Betty all week about coming out with them tonight. They were celebrating something, after all, even if they couldn't figure out exactly what.

"I thought you guys broke up," Jamie said when Betty returned.

Betty took a sip of her beer. "I feel sorry for him. He's kind of lost right now, between jobs and with me leaving…"

"*Leaving* being the operative word."

Betty half-smiled.

"What will happen if you *don't* leave, Betty?"

"Nothing."

"Exactly. Nothing will happen. Don't you see!"

"Calm down there."

"And anyway, once this is all over I'm off to San Francisco. I'm gone. I can't fucking wait."

Me neither, Betty wanted to say, about her own departure.

With that they sipped their beers and imagined their respective futures far from the beach bums currently shimmying around them.

Joel sauntered in fifteen minutes later wearing that Bob's Big Boy smile of his. Betty beamed a smile back. She couldn't help herself; she had a soft spot for Joel's wholesome, hungry demeanor. His hair was thinning but the rest of him was full and strong. He'd been a football player in college and was a very physical person. Betty had met him at a party a year ago, and he swept her off her feet—literally threw her over his shoulder and held her there until she agreed to go out with him. He came over to them at the bar, gave them big hugs, and immediately ordered three kamikazes.

"To Jamie's golf ball." He raised his glass.

"To Betty's new life." Jamie raised hers.

Betty avoided their eyes and downed her shot. She was sure Joel didn't appreciate Jamie's comment, even though he'd been supportive of Betty's move. He wanted her to be happy he'd said. They were only twenty-two; their careers came first. But Joel had a jealous nature, and over the past few months he'd gotten worse. She knew he couldn't handle a long distance relationship. They'd already broken up and gotten back together twice, but her leaving town…that would certainly be the end of it.

After one more round of shots, Jamie and Betty hungry, they suggested Hennessey's down the street where they could order fries and bump into people their own age. But Joel wasn't ready to leave. He ordered another beer and guzzled it down while Jamie went to the restroom. Then he slapped Betty with a strong kiss. She pulled back. His blue eyes had turned dark, intense, like bullets awaiting a target, bullets Betty recognized, yet she convinced herself that tonight, given the circumstances, things would be different.

They dragged Joel from the bar and made their way down Main Street. He had an arm about each of their shoulders and kept saying how much he was going to miss them. Betty refrained from mentioning that one of them, perhaps both, might not be going anywhere.

Hennessey's was packed, no tables available, so they put their name in with the hostess and waited by the bar. It took Jamie a while to squeeze her way through the crowd and order three pints. On her way back someone shoved her elbow and spilled half of one of her beers onto her shirt. Joel reached over and grabbed the guy by the jacket and told him to apologize. The guy laughed, so Joel got in his face, and the two started going at it. Betty tried to reach out for Joel, to hold him back, but his Big Boy face had turned red with rage, and he was long past hearing her. The crowd was swaying and dispersing, and it wasn't long before the bouncer came over and took care of the situation by kicking Joel out of the bar.

Betty flashed a smile of apology at Jamie still juggling the three pints of beer, while inwardly she was cursing herself for letting Joel come tonight. Let him drive home drunk, she thought angrily. She was done with this crap. Then she chased him down the street, afraid he might do something stupid because he was inconsolable when he was in a rage. She caught up with him seated on a bus bench far down the block and had some time to calm him down before Jamie reached them. They got Joel in his car, and Betty drove the three of them back to their dad's place.

"It's just Joel being Joel," Betty assured her sister as she got out of the car. The look Jamie returned, *that's the problem*, was the same look she had for all of Betty's boyfriends. Betty stayed with Joel in the car while he sobered up. She didn't want him to come inside, she was sure her father was still up, and she didn't want him to see this side of Joel. Her dad adored Joel, unlike the other guys Betty had brought home, unlike perhaps even his own son. Joel is a real approachable guy, had been her dad's flabbergasted assessment, so wondrous was it that a young man might treat him with such simple, honest respect.

Betty looked over at Joel now, sitting limp in the passenger seat. "Look, Joel," she started.

"I don't know why I do that." He was holding back tears, she could tell. "I don't know what's wrong with me. You must hate me. You hate me, don't you?"

It was a scene they'd played out many times before. "There's nothing wrong with you Joel, and I don't hate you. How could you even say that?" She said all the positive things she could think of saying as he spiraled into a web of insecurity and self-loathing. All she wanted to do was get out of the car and go to bed. He asked her to come back to his place, but she told him she was exhausted and just wanted to sleep. He said that he understood, but when she moved to get out of the car, he grabbed her arm and held her back. His grip hurt, but she managed to wriggle out of it and push the car door open. He was out of his side in a flash and met her just before she started up the front walk, and when she didn't stop, he grabbed her by the arms and pinned her against the side of the house. "Please don't leave me, Betty. I don't know what I'll do without you."

She swallowed. Her arms were bruising under his force. "Look, Joel, we're both drunk. Let's talk tomorrow when we're sober. OK?" She kept her voice even and calm, not wanting him to sense her fear, and it seemed to work at first, as he loosened his grip, but as she turned to go, he grabbed her again and knocked her against the wall so hard that the back of her head whacked against the stucco. "Do you love me, Betty?"

Her eyes flashed open in disbelief. She felt something trickle down the back of her scalp, and then she heard the house door open. Joel let up, and she pushed through the front gate into the courtyard, shuddering when it slammed behind her, as it did automatically if you didn't guide it closed. It was like setting off a fire alarm, and Betty knew that she only had about thirty seconds before the engine came roaring. She pretended Jamie wasn't standing there at the open doorway, "Everything's fine," she told her sister, passing by with no eye contact just as their father came lumbering down the stairs, furious. "How many times have I told you girls not to let the gate slam?"

Betty and Jamie stood in place and didn't answer, which incensed him, and he moved quickly at them. His hair was messy, his face unshaven, he looked to be preparing to saying something commanding, fatherly, for this wasn't just about the gate; after all, his younger daughter was having surgery day after tomorrow, and his older was leaving town for good.

They waited, because deep down they did want to hear something fatherly.

But when he got to them he froze, predictably, and stared at them like they were creatures from another world. After some moments like that, he managed the obvious, "Have you girls been drinking?"

Betty, dulling her eyes, turned and headed towards her bedroom.

"I'm worried you're not taking any of this seriously, Betty."

"Taking what seriously?" She heard Jamie say, deadpan, behind her, and Betty walked faster now, biting her lip to keep from smiling.

After she closed the bedroom door she went to examine the back of her head in the full-length mirror. It was a small graze, really nothing at all, and she dabbed it with a tissue until it dried.

* * *

Jim arrived the next day. Betty kept herself busy packing, she wasn't sure if she was leaving, but organizing her things kept her sane and distracted her from her headache...and Joel's calls. She told her dad to tell him she wasn't home.

Her wardrobe she split into three piles: one for the drive, one for UPS, and one for Jamie. Whatever Jamie didn't want, which would be all of it, would go back into the UPS pile. Maybe one of her new roommates would want it. When that was done, she reminisced through her picture albums, yearbooks, and high school memorabilia for an indefinite period of time. Every so often a scene from *Blue Velvet* would pop into her head..."Mommy, Mommy," she'd hear Frank's words, then find herself staring off, disturbed.

Late that afternoon their dad and mom, along with Jim, took Jamie to the hospital to check in for surgery the next day. Their parents had been meeting daily to deal with all the arrangements. In moments of need, their mother was in her element: tireless, organized, overbearing...manipulative, modest, coy... her motto: whatever it took. She spent long hours on the phone getting all the insurance preapprovals, filling out the hospital forms, and getting referrals for second opinions from prominent community members. She bought Jamie a new robe, slippers, and toiletries bag and wrapped them in a box with a big bow. Their father signed things as she directed, though, as a therapist, he was more preoccupied by what Jamie might be feeling emotionally—none of these doctors care about *feelings*, he would say; we should be discussing her feelings. He was seeing Vivi romantically now, but he could still not mention their mother without trembling or choking up. Betty hated watching his disappointment and bitterness unfold all over again, so she avoided the hospital that night and went out with a few high school friends to say her goodbyes, for they were assuming she was still leaving the day after next.

When Betty did at last swing by the hospital, after she was sure her parents had gone home, Jamie, who had been given a sleeping pill, was already asleep, and Jim, stretched out beside her with his jacket and shoes still on, was also asleep. Betty stood there, waiting, though for what she couldn't say. Finally she just left. All this time she'd been wondering why she had to compromise her own plans, her own happiness, and her sister didn't even look sick.

Betty's mother wore jean overalls for the surgery that was supposed to take four hours—battle fatigues—normally you'd find her in work attire: slim skirt, blouse, and comfortable pumps. She was petite and pretty and young looking, obsessed with being young looking. But her birthday last week had taken its toll apparently. Today she looked her age: FIFTY, as she kept reminding everyone. "I'm fifty, and my daughter may have cancer." She wore no makeup, the gray in her hair was seeping through the auburn dye, and her skin sagged. She was now at the nurses station ordering some poor girl to get them coffee that was hot because the coffee from the machine in the waiting room was not hot enough at all. She'd get it herself, but she couldn't leave because her daughter, as we speak, was having LIFE THREATENING SURGERY.

Her husband Gary sat quietly in a corner with an issue of *Road and Track*. You might not even know he was there if he hadn't engaged Jim—seated next to him and clutching the book *Trump*—in idle conversation. In his own sordid way, when he wasn't prodding you with beers, Gary was an easygoing, unobtrusive person. He had that to contribute in this moment, at least. As opposed to Betty's father, who for whatever reason had taken a dislike to the man who had stolen his younger daughter's affections, perhaps even more than he disliked the man who had stolen his wife. He limped around the halls and practiced his relaxation breathing.

Steven, of course, was nowhere to be found.

"Where's Steven?" Betty's mom kept asking, like if Steven were here none of this would be happening.

"Mom, sit down," Betty pleaded.

Steven had taken leave from his real estate development firm to run Senator Gordon's California presidential campaign. He was finally doing what his family had always assumed he would do: public service. And though he lived in Orange County, he was currently with Gordon's team in Russia meeting with Gorbachev. When their mom finally managed to get hold of him and tell him the news, Steven promised to catch the next flight back. That was four days ago. No one had heard from him since.

Her mom, seated now, was staring down the hall at the double doors marked SURGERY. Everything had been organized and done, and now, without a specific task to do but wait, she was unraveling, Betty could sense—the slackened jaw, the dull, recessed eyes. "I remember when you girls were babies," she slumped against Betty and spoke in a soft thin voice. "You were such darling little babies."

"Jamie's going to be fine, Marie." It was their dad in his hypnotic tone. He'd come over and rested a hand on her shoulder. "Just breathe," he said, and to her credit, she did try it for a minute. Then she grabbed Betty's arm. "Dear, you need something to eat!"

Betty looked at her, then the wall clock. They had three more hours. "I'm not hungry, Mom."

"But when is the last time you ate, dear?"

Betty didn't respond, but that didn't matter; her mother was already dragging her down the hall towards the cafeteria.

"What we need is grease!" she exclaimed to the cashier, paying for their cheeseburgers. They took their trays to a table by the window. "Sometimes good old fashioned grease is just what the doctor ordered!" She took a ravenous bite, but when Betty didn't follow suit, her face soured. "You're not going to eat?"

Betty looked at her burger, and for perhaps too long because when she looked up again her mother's whole face had changed. If she had needed a new task, poof, suddenly she'd found one. "YOU, Betty." Her mother wiped her hands and leaned forward. "I haven't even asked how YOU'RE doing with all this." And then, after a moment of silence, she sighed and used a real voice, "How *are* you doing with all this?"

Betty blinked. Normally she would have said a simple "fine" to avoid, well, being disappointed by her mother's attempt to be motherly. Today she took in a deep jittery breath and said, "Joel is… well…he's scaring me, Mom."

Even her mother seemed surprised. "Joel?" Her eyes shifted back to her burger. "Joel's a lovely boy, Betty."

"Not always."

"Oh, certainly he is." She picked up her burger and took another bite.

"He's got a bad temper."

"Oh, this burger's terrible." She set it back down. "Don't eat it, Betty. Do you want me to get you something else, dear?"

Betty couldn't answer. Her mother was up and clearing the plates. "Well, whatever it is, dear, I'm sure you'll work it out."

A minute passed. Betty couldn't get herself to stand, and so her mother had no choice but to sit back down.

"I feel so guilty leaving Jamie like this." She paused. "But if I don't leave now, I'm afraid I'll never go."

A moment passed. Then her mother took Betty's hand in hers, warm. Betty wanted to let that warmth inside; she needed a mother's guidance. "D.C. is such a big step for you, dear. A wonderful and important step, and so I don't want you to even think about not going." She spoke with absolution. "Your sister will be fine. Whatever happens…your father and I will take care of things here."

There was some relief, of course, on Betty's part. Though if she could count on her mother for one thing this was it.

"You've got to take care of Betty, Betty."

Bittersweet relief, because that statement seemed to sap whatever energy her mother had left. "I wish I had the opportunities you girls have now." Her eyes receded. "In my era we got married and had babies." She fell into a state of quiet reflection here, what she did in times like this in order to draw upon a new energy and purpose, she would go back over all of her astonishing accomplishments, because what was life for, if not reflection. "I only got my teaching credential out of necessity. I had no expectation of becoming a principal, and who would have thought *One-to-One* would become such a huge success…and now…" She glanced around and lowered her voice. "I've been approached by the Learning Channel to produce one of their shows." She paused for Betty's wild laughter, like certainly she'd fooled everyone, like certainly this crazy mother of Betty didn't belong on camera.

"What's weird is that I was so desperate for a change in my career. I'd been doing Special Learning programs for so long, and then change just came. Producing is something I've always wanted to do. It takes me back to my roots as a dancer, a choreographer. I wasn't going to say anything about this *now*, of course. Of course it all means nothing in the bigger scheme of things…it all means shit." She giggled at the word "shit." It was like Jamie saying the word "shucks." Her mother rarely cussed and when she did it sounded, well, silly. "I just can't help sensing a new phase in my life approaching. Gary turns sixty-five next year and wants to retire and putter around on his boat, you know, like he likes to do." Her eyes went off somewhere. It was a good minute before they came back. "But I feel like I'm just starting my career. I'm too young to retire…Can you believe I'm fifty?" She didn't wait for a response. "I don't feel fifty."

And there it was, Betty thought, pulling back her hand. At last, her mother had sailed full circle. Jamie's surgery, Betty's departure, everything circled back to her: she was fifty and, if Betty read it right, what that whole speech came down to: her second marriage was in trouble. Not that her mother would ever admit this reality that seemed to hit her only now, for she looked as if the wind had just died from her sail, sinking, every so slowly, into her seat. Smaller and smaller—soon she wouldn't be there at all. "I'll have to thank Jamie later for such a lovely birthday present," she said from somewhere below the belly. "I'm kidding of course, but you know what I mean."

Betty stood up then. All at once she needed air, big heaping gulps of air. "I think I'll go back to Dad's and wait."

Her mother barely looked startled. "Well, of course. That's the best thing for you, dear. Go get some rest."

Betty didn't look back. She exploded out the exit doors onto a sunny July day. "Beach day," she said out loud. It felt cleansing, absolving and she said it again, "Beach Day," how she and Jamie would define a day like today. Not a weekday, not a school day, not a holiday, not a Saturday, but a Beach Day. And if a Beach Day happened to fall on the weekend, there was never a question of how one occupied their time or where one went: Betty with her gang of friends to the south side of the pier, Jamie with her obstinacy to the north.

Betty was headed there now, until she spotted Jim sitting on a bench reading his book on her way to her car and she paused to study him. This, after years of unknown crushes and unrequited heartbreaks, seemingly, was her sister's first boyfriend…and possibly Betty's first competition. Six foot five, not handsome, not ugly, kind of scarecrow looking. He and Jamie had been together for six months and yet Betty had only met him once, last month, at Jamie's graduation; Jim was in her class. Spotting Betty, he asked her with some amount of desperation where she was going and if he couldn't go with her. Betty drove him along Ocean Avenue towards the pier, feeling the need to unleash on him some burden in the depths of her, or pass it on anyway. He paid the five bucks to park in the beach lot, where they sat in the car watching the surfers. He was upset that he had to fly to San Francisco that night, but he had no choice because he was starting his new job the next morning. He hoped Jamie would wake up from the surgery before he left. Betty wanted to commiserate about having the same problem, but there hadn't been a pause. Jim went on about how he and Jamie met, about how much she had to adjust to the idea of holding his hand in public, about how much fun they had together, that Jamie was his best friend. He boasted about Jamie being BCC's first pick, about how driven she was in her career, about how she'd be making more money than he. He talked about their plans: how after she recovered, Jamie would join him in San Francisco and start her job. They were planning on moving in together, he said, just before choking up.

Betty stayed silent. Her sister had never mentioned moving in with Jim, but that was no surprise; Jamie kept her true feelings so apart from everything else. She didn't want Betty to know she was happy because then Betty wouldn't need to worry about her anymore, be responsible for her anymore. And Jamie needed that,

Betty knew. But that was about all she knew. And with that in mind, she started the engine and drove them the few blocks down Main Street to the Bay Theater. Jim didn't seem surprised, all he said was that Jamie loved David Lynch, which made Betty frown because of course she didn't know that either.

The movie had begun thirty minutes ago. They bought tickets and skipped the popcorn. When they reached the point in the film where Betty had left off, Jeffrey's flashbacks, Betty tried not to think or feel or worry about the point of the movie—she just watched and absorbed. In the end though, when the film reel stopped and that obnoxious light flooded the theater, she still didn't understand her sister any better. And as far as David Lynch was concerned, well, Betty wasn't going to go there. But she did find out why that woman in the blue velvet dress didn't try to escape: her son and husband, the man with the missing ear—they had been in Frank's captivity all that time. She was doing what she had to to keep the people she loved alive.

Their father was the only one in the waiting room when Betty and Jim returned. The surgery had gone well he told them. Jamie was resting in post op and hadn't been allowed visitors. They were able to get the tumor out by removing two inches of colon; no colostomy had been necessary, he was in relief to report. The biopsy results would be back in two days, her dad went on with relative composure, but when Betty asked where her mom was, he stammered and stuttered. "I tried to help her relax. I don't know why she won't listen…She was having an anxiety attack."

"What?"

"She went to see her doctor."

Betty closed her eyes on a vision of her mother's head sinking beneath her cheeseburger. *Don't you worry about a thing dear, your father and I will take care of things here.* "She wants you to call her," her dad was telling her now. Betty opened her eyes and steadied her gaze at his shirt collar. She had no response, for Betty knew that her mother had given everything she had, done everything she could, and she would not be back.

The doctor came up and said they could see Jamie now. Betty hurried in ahead of Jim and her dad, relieved that it was finally over, only the room was spinning when she got there; the floor tilted—something wasn't right. What she was seeing was not right: her sister—tubes sticking out of every orifice, her face gray, her neck stained yellow, all that slurping and slushing—she looked like a corpse, and Betty gasped. It was unreal, impossible; she turned and ran out.

With her dad trailing behind her, she ran into the first bathroom she could find, reached for the toilet, and threw up. Her dad held back her hair, there now. But she had nothing to throw up because she'd yet to eat today, which made it even worse—those retching, moaning heaves. When she was done she sat on the disinfected linoleum and leaned her back against the wall. "I'm not going to D.C.," she blurted out to her father, who'd been stroking her back and telling her to breathe, just breathe and you'll be all right.

I am breathing.

He went on, hypnotically, but all Betty heard was Glenda's words: "Sisters are always there for each other." At least now she understood why—because mothers weren't always. She leaned over and heaved one last time.

Jim was just leaving when Betty finally returned to Jamie's room. Her sister still wasn't awake and while he looked disappointed, there seemed to be a certain amount of relief in his step, his very quick, fleeing-like step down the hallway towards the elevators. Betty kept pace with him to his cab, listening to him go on about how horrible he felt about having to go. She said that she'd call him with the biopsy results, but then realized, after his cab took off that she didn't have his number. Jamie would have it, she reminded herself, watching the cab dissolve from sight, trying to suppress with all her might the very un-Betty-like feeling that neither she nor Jamie would ever see Jim again.

"How's Jamie doing?"

Betty spun around.

It was Joel, and she gasped. "What are you doing here?"

"I just wanted to know."

"I know. I know. I'm sorry, you just scared me." She released a breath. "The surgery went well."

"That's good news."

"We'll see I guess."

He came closer, sheepishly. "Betty, I'm sorry."

"No, I'm sorry," slipped out again, and then she thought, why? Why am I always so willing to be sorry? She looked up at Joel then, searchingly, for there must be a reason she was with Joel. Perhaps they were meant for each other in some inexplicable way. Perhaps she could help him become a better person, and, in return, Joel's big heart would always be hers. She gazed into his liquid eyes and wanted to believe this. But inside all she could feel was resignation, and her dreams being crushed. She said goodbye to Joel, told him she'd call him later, and then went home, took a shower, and forced food into her body.

By the time she came back, Jamie was awake and Steven was there, talking into the phone attached to Jamie's bedrail. A rush of relief washed over Betty, until her brother palmed the phone and mouthed, "When are you leaving for D.C.?" as if there had never been any question. She pretended she'd not heard that and went to Jamie's bedside where, she noticed, Jim's roses were already wilting on the side table, and though her sister's smile was faint, the irony was back in her eyes, there was color to her skin, and the stains were gone. The sucking and slurping sounds were still going, but her sister looked a million times better than dead.

The extra long chord afforded Steven room to pace around in passionate debate with whoever was on the other end. "Sorry, it's important," he mouthed to Betty after another five minutes had passed and he still wasn't off. "Get off the phone!" Betty barked, and then, stunned by her own ferociousness, stood there blinking into the reverberating silence. Even Steven looked startled, if only for a moment; fear was not an emotion in her brother's capacity. Still, she steadied her gaze on him until he did finally hang up. "You're worried about Jamie?" he scoffed, like where had Betty been these past six days. "Jamie will be fine." He motioned his eyes at the door. "It's Mom and Dad you got to worry about." He paused for Betty to laugh, to share with him in this wholly ironic moment, for as usual he'd cut right to the hard cold truth of the matter, but seeing Jamie with that tube down her throat made even pretending to laugh impossible. All she could do was swallow and take notice for the first time of her brother's goatee, his potbelly, the Birkenstocks… and that he didn't look like Steven.

In fact no one looked like themselves any longer.

Even herself she didn't recognize, loading up her car the next morning for her journey east. For a time she hadn't thought she would go—*Betty needs to take care of Betty*—but perhaps deep down she always knew she would.

C H A P T E R   6

sex, lies, and videotape

September, 2003

"And who is this someone else?" Roberto asked her facetiously.

She delayed her response. Everything seemed delayed in this heat. She had accompanied him on his round of golf that morning. They were walking up the eighth fairway, a long, wide stretch of grass carved out of the jungle, when she told him she thought she might be, in actuality, someone else. There was a deep, lush silence all around them. The three of them—Roberto, his caddie clothed from head to toe, and Jamie shading herself with an umbrella—might have been, in this infinite moment, the only people on earth.

"Buddhists believe that there is no 'you' or 'I,'" he explained, reminding her about the religion so pervasive in his native country. "We are everything."

The air was so thick she could scoop it with her hand. "So then I am you?"

He pulled out his seven-iron. "Perhaps."

She pulled out her video camera, an old eight-millimeter model that Roberto had as a child. Giorgio had found it so that she could tape Roberto's swing. She did so now. He struck the ball clean, and it flew in a sweeping arc through the air, landing five feet from the pin. "When I was a kid, I wanted to be on the Asian tour."

"I wanted to be a ballerina."

They walked towards his ball.

"It's interesting how your mind doesn't absorb information until its ready," she continued her existential train of thought. "I've read the Buddhist literature before, somewhere, some time ago. But I didn't get it until now, here."

"Get what?"

"That I'll never really find myself. That that's not the point."

They were on the green. Roberto went and lined up his putt. "Tamada," his caddie said. "Chai," Roberto responded, then missed the putt for birdie.

They walked to the ninth tee. A Thai was selling water and snacks from a thatched hut, and Roberto bought sticky rice with mango wrapped in a banana leaf. They sat on a shaded bench and devoured it together. "You're someone else too you know," she said. "You weren't, I didn't expect..." she couldn't finish. Nor did he push her to. She hadn't expected him to love her like this. "Save it for the monkeys," he said, and then pointed to the camera, "The battery I mean."

"This is the hole?" She scanned down each end of the fairway. He'd brought her here to see the monkeys that lived on this hole.

Roberto got up to the tee, and then hooked his drive left. The ball hit a tree and landed in the jungle. "You might want to edit that one out," he said. She continued videotaping him as he walked with his caddie towards where his ball had gone. His caddie clawed her way into a tangle of draping, giant-sized leaves. Roberto followed, cautioning Jamie to stay put because of the Cobras. At first she thought he was kidding, then she reminded herself where she was and heeded his advice. The Cobras were here first, after all, while this golf course, Thailand's first, came after thanks to The Brits, who carved it out along the railway they were building between Burma and Singapore. They needed their leisure, after all, Roberto had explained to her. The clubhouse was a Pagoda.

The caddie found Roberto's ball, and he punched it out with an eight iron. Jamie couldn't see him, but she saw the ball roll and stop thirty yards *before the green. Then, in a flash, a monkey ran towards it, grabbed it, and popped it in its mouth. "Did you see that?" she gasped. Roberto and his caddie had returned from the jungle, and they all watched for a short time. "It looks like he's going to eat it."*

"I told you," he said, walking on.

She turned on her video camera and hurried forward.

"Don't get too close."

The whole monkey village descended upon the ball then. There must have been a hundred of them, all shapes and sizes, jumping around screeching and throwing the ball and chasing it. The caddie waved a club at the largest monkey coming after the trash in her bag. It might have been frightening if it wasn't so fantastic. Jamie couldn't stop smiling, and taping.

"What, are you making a movie?" Roberto called out. He'd already putted out and was heading to the tenth hole.

She ran towards him, out of breath. "Maybe I will make a movie." She got in front of him and walked backward holding the camera up to her eye. "Rolling."

"First of all you're not holding it right." He stopped, pulled the camera from her hand, and held it up to his eye. "Like this," he said. Then he focused the lens and started taping her. "What will your movie be about?"

She continued walking backwards. "I don't know," she motioned around her. "This?"

"Ma no . . ." he said, putting on a thick Italian accent.

"You were the film minor. You tell me."

He pulled the camera from his eye and thought for a moment. "I don't know."

"Yes you do."

"All I know is that my protagonist would be as flawed as the Whiskey Priest in 'The Power and the Glory'."

"Go on."

"But he's got to have redeeming qualities." He'd stopped walking again. "He must be saved."

She felt something sensual pass from herself, through the camera he was pointing at her, to him. The air seemed even thicker. "And?"

"After that I don't know."

"You should write a script."

He thought about it, shrugged. "Someday, maybe."

His unusually pliable response surprised her. She looked at him differently—at everything differently—and hoped that he could someday write a screenplay. In Thailand things like this didn't seem so impossible.

He was pointing behind her. She turned to see a thick black cloud heading their way. He put the camera in the bag, grabbed her hand, and led her to shelter in a nearby rain cubby. A minute later it came pouring down. They sat on the covered bench and waited for the sheets to pass, as if right through them. She felt drenched, and yet she wasn't even wet.

"It's gone by so fast," she said.

He didn't need to respond. He knew she was referring to the shrinking number of weeks they had left in Thailand before their scheduled departure. But time seemed so irrelevant now, here, where the water poured off the leaves as if from buckets. The sight took hold of her with such intensity that Roberto had to nudge her back to life, and she looked at him blankly, wondering if she'd entered some kind of altered state or if, in fact, she was alive for the first time. These past few months, consumed in monsoons, basil, and garlic seeping through her pores, exhaust and tobacco flowing through her lungs, she'd been experiencing a strange and new heightening of her senses. The Gulf was no longer gray but a smoky blue, the Buddha out her window not bronzed but golden.

Her body had changed. The giggling Thai ladies had cleaned out Jamie's insides with papaya and lemongrass, kneaded curves and soft tissue into her brittle, bony limbs. She'd been freed of that slouch, the one she'd developed after years of sitting hunched over her computer. And she was stronger from doing yoga daily. In the mornings while Roberto worked out at the gym, Jamie would lay her mat to face the Buddha and did sun salutations until the sun did eventually shine, if only in her mind.

In the afternoons when Roberto and Giorgio were at the restaurant, when the world would go quiet, Jamie would laze by the empty pool or wander along the shore, reading from the volumes of Graham Greene and Joseph Conrad she'd been sneaking from Giorgio's bedroom. Roberto had read all of them by the time he was twenty, but Jamie hadn't read a novel since she was about the same age. They would spend late nights discussing them; he always wanted to know what she thought.

In the evenings she would meet Roberto at the restaurant. Normally she wouldn't go until after the rush, around nine. But tonight she went early because Giorgio was trying out a new chef, the fourth this month, and he wanted Roberto, his friends, and Jamie to taste the food because he, himself, was on a strict, no-salt diet for his blood pressure.

The restaurant was in the center of town, a ten-minute exhaust-fumes-filled tuk-tuk ride along the sea from the condo and hidden in a maze of side streets packed with fish stalls, noodle shacks, massage shops and farang pubs. The restaurant was full, but a table was always kept on reserve for the ex-pat contingent: the same prime outside location, no matter what time of day. Roberto was already settled in a seat when Jamie arrived. She had already met most of them: Saipan Dan was there, from Scotland. Before retiring to Hua Hin, he taught school and ran a restaurant in Saipan for twenty years. There was Harry, an ex-security officer from Zurich with horrible teeth. A heavy Buddha charm hid the quadruple bypass scar on his chest, and a cigarette dangled persistently from his lips. He was a hell of a golfer. There was a guy from Liverpool who ran a wine shop, and Stefano, an ex-taxi driver, tailor, and tax evader from Napoli who also sang operetta at the Sofitel lounge. They were all in their mid-to-late-fifties, here to escape something—a wife, debt, hassles, or responsibilities; the kids they had somewhere, grown and perhaps forgotten. They came here to live out their lives in peace, with relatively little means and perhaps a mistress. Thailand was a place men came and never left.

She took the seat between Roberto and Stefano, and just as she did, Giorgio came up behind her and slid a large platter of grilled eggplant, *asparagus, marinated bell peppers, olives, and bruschetta onto their table. Jamie's eyes went large at the plate. "And here we are at the equator," someone said. Giorgio dribbled on some olive oil from the bottle he carried around and then sipped from his wine glass he kept on their table, awaiting their critique. Roberto put spoonfuls of the antipasti on her plate, sampled the eggplant, and conferred with Giorgio in that gesticulating Italian, their voices rising to a crescendo before Giorgio stomped off to attend to another customer.*

Jamie watched him go. "He doesn't like the chef, I take it."

Stefano filled their wine glasses and gave Roberto a knowing look. Stefano, aka Zio, was like an uncle to Roberto. ItalSteele had rented Giorgio the Hua Hin apartment as a perk when he'd first arrived to open the factory in Bangkok. Roberto and he would often spend their weekends here when Roberto was growing up. Stefano introduced Roberto to golf, though he himself was a horrible golfer, and a cheat, according to Giorgio, who refused now to play the game he once loved. Stefano raised his wine glass. "To Giorgio, may he rest in peace."

They toasted, drank. Giorgio was back with a pad and pencil asking Jamie how she liked the roasted peppers. It occurred to her that she hadn't tried the peppers, so she picked up her fork and took a bite. "Bellissimo."

"Buonissimo," Roberto corrected her.

She looked at him. Nine years with this man and she still couldn't get it right. But then she reminded herself that she no longer had to. After everything, he was still here beside her, loving her. She had only to look in his eyes and see that, she had only to let herself dissolve…here, now, inside the range of foreign topics and tongues floating around the table: Italian, Thai, Scottish English; the financial state of the world; the tough slope of the new course at Black Mountain; the finer points of Islay vs. Speyside malts. Roberto looked relaxed even while impassioned in debate. He draped his arm about her chair, the touch of his fingers on her moist back sending a tingle through her body. No translations. She preferred to sip warm wine and watch her husband come to life in the world from which he came. She felt at peace in the self-absorption of it, cocooned here inside her husband's peace.

After a mysteriously long absence, Roberto went to the kitchen to find out what was going on with his father and their entrees. He and Giorgio returned minutes later carrying them at Roberto's insistence, for Giorgio had been refusing to serve the dishes, in a fury about the chef who had apparently overcooked the pasta, bought the branzino from the wrong stall, and burnt the Australian filet.

Jamie culled her branzino, slipping the knife through the spine as her husband had taught her. Roberto watched her take a bite—succulent, her expression said. When he then tasted his own filet, he dropped his fork, waved his hands together in prayer, and told his papa that he was going crazy; the food was excellent. Giorgio pressed two fingers into his neck, checking his pulse. He then grumbled and popped a couple of pills he had stored in a bottle in his pocket, and then hurried off again. Stefano, who had the pasta, let loose some frustration. "What is wrong with your papa?" He wiped his forehead with his napkin, for even though the ceiling fan was twirling, the air sat heavy and unmoving. "He never returns my calls or meets me for coffee anymore." He continued on about how Giorgio had grown isolated, bitter, and harsh. How he was always complaining about his health, Hua Hin, the traffic, the tourists. No chef would work with him. In fact, the last chef didn't leave because he went back to his wife but because he couldn't work with Mussolini!

Roberto sighed. His father had always been a perfectionist. But his demeanor of late, even for him, was getting out of control.

"He has changed," Stefano insisted loudly, and the other men at the table grunted or spoke out in agreement.

Jamie watched Roberto closely here. His face showed that he did not disagree, though he was lost in thought now, somewhere inside the cavern of his father's brooding and sadness, perhaps walking along the trails they had once walked together, from Italy to Bangkok to Vietnam to Australia to

Malaysia, back to Bangkok, and then Hua Hin. They had reached the end of the earth here, and now there was nowhere left to go.

"Alas, it's good his son is here," Stefano said. Then he rose, abruptly, and broke into the most stunning operetta. It took Jamie a minute to understand the raw beauty of what was going on, as it did the rest of the restaurant's spellbound clientele, and when she did her eyes filled, for it felt as if her skin were breaking open, the chords of all humanity reaching down into her soul.

When he was done he sat back down, and the conversation went on as if it had never stopped.

** 1989 **

Four o'clock on a Friday. Jamie's officemate and boss, a short, bald ex-Marine, played out his last hand of computer solitaire, shut off his machine, and stood up from his spit-clean, paperless desk. "You're done for the day, Waterson," he wheezed, wiping his brow.

Jamie glanced up from her five-inch thick binder. "Just want to finish this section."

"See you Monday then," he said, shuffling out with his empty briefcase, his belly before the rest of him.

Jamie remained hunched over Volume II of the Army Corp's Civil Engineering Standards manual until she was sure he was gone. Then she slouched back in her stiff metal chair and closed her bleary, burning eyes. She'd been reading that volume all day for the past five days, and Volume I before that, all while her boss played solitaire on his computer. After just two weeks she was going bonkers with boredom.

Her first post-college job wasn't as lofty as she'd planned. It had been two years since the surgery, two years of living with her mom and Gary and their disintegrating marriage. At least that's how Jamie saw it even if her mom refused to. Gary, retired now, lurked around the house drinking from a bottle of beer and spent weekends on his boat, alone, not sailing. Jamie spent the days in the tiny spare room off her mother's garage recovering from daily zaps of radiation and weekly catheters of chemo, while her mother's dogs yapped away somewhere. At night she'd hear her mother's car pull into to the garage after another long, exhausting, yet exhilarating taping of *One-to-One*. On each episode her mother would interview community leaders about the new learning programs going on in the district. Jamie had been to a taping once downtown. Her mother had always been manic about showing off her daughters, especially now, with Jamie in her headscarf. Mostly Jamie watched the show's reruns with her mother late at night and on some obscure local channel.

But her treatments had been over for six months now, her cancer in remission. If the disease didn't return within five years, she would be "clean," the doctors told her, sending her on her way. With twenty grand in student loans waiting to be paid, she went straight to BCC. But BCC rescinded their offer because their insurance wouldn't cover her. McDonnell Douglas had no more open positions, even in the mailroom. Neither did Hughes or Boeing or the variety of private firms she approached. When they did have an opening, they would stumble at her response to the question, "What have you been doing the past two years since graduation?" "Recovering from cancer," even put delicately, elicited a variety of responses, none of which were, "You're hired."

So she flew to D.C. and moved in with Betty. The decision came spontaneously while they were talking on the phone, lost in yet another long, purposeless conversation, when Jamie mentioned, not so offhandedly, about someone knocking on her bedroom door the previous night at one a.m., and that whoever it was had tried to turn the knob and get in.

"Do you think it was Gary?"

"He's been drinking more. And I've had this sense…Anyway, I started keeping the door locked… Thank God."

"That's not right. You should tell Mom."

"It's fucked up, and there's not way I can tell Mom."

"Go to Dad's."

"I can't," Jamie had said after some delay. She wasn't yet ready to talk about the fight she had had with her father. And Betty wasn't apparently ready to ask. "Then come here."

And so it was decided.

Jamie was on a plane to D.C. the next week. The week after that she was interviewing with the Army Corps of Engineers per some ad she'd found in the Washington Post, and lying about her health history. She told them that she'd spent the past two years backpacking around Europe, studying comparative civil engineering methods for a paper she planned to publish. However well-acted her response was, the Corps didn't seem to care. They only wanted a body to fill this green metal desk that looked retrofitted from a war tanker.

She flipped to the next tab just as her phone rang.

It was Betty. "Is he gone?"

"It's three o'clock. Who leaves their job at three o'clock?"

"A government employee."

"Thanks." Jamie laid her head on the desk. "What time's the movie?"

"Seven." She cleared her throat. "And I'm bringing a friend."

Jamie sat up.

"Actually I've never met him. He's a friend of my boss." She paused. "He's here to intern with Senator Carver."

"Carver?"

"He doesn't know anyone, Jamie."

"But Carver's a Republican, Betty."

"You're never going to get over Jim if you don't meet someone else."

"I don't want to meet anyone else."

"You can't be a hermit the rest of your life."

"Why not?" Jamie said, suddenly craving the isolation of her mother's.

They agreed to meet at quarter to seven outside the theater and hung up. Jamie closed her book and put it on the shelf with the others. Other than her fingerprints on these manuals, not one piece of forensic evidence could expose this office that she shared with her boss as either his or hers, and if neither of them came back on Monday no one would know they had even worked here. They were the sole occupants of this basement floor. Others were to be assigned down here her boss had assured her when she was hired. Banished others, she realized, after a day of watching him play solitaire on his computer. It was hard for her to imagine once being BCC's top pick, and the drive that that accomplishment had required of her. Because she really didn't care that she had nothing to do but read these ACCE standards, as her boss had sardonically suggested on her first day. He seemed surprised when, in fact, that's exactly what she did, for she only wanted to do what she was told, get her measly paycheck, and go unnoticed.

Red Line to Metro Station, Orange Line to DuPont Circle, a misty five blocks to the art-house theater and still Jamie managed to be early. Betty, of course, was late. Her sister's incessant tardiness used to infuriate Jamie, but since the cancer she'd lost all urgency for things, including infuriation, even as it began to rain and she realized she had no umbrella. She watched the puddles form and felt her hair, still growing back, begin to frizz. It was chin length now, and she regretted listening to Betty that morning about wearing it down. She was twisting it up in a clip just as a figure protected by an umbrella and a stylish hat came running towards her shimmering in a self-possession that Jamie was still getting used to.

"What did you do?" Betty was frowning at Jamie's hair. Jamie was frowning at Betty's new briefcase. "Forty bucks at Eastern Market," Betty chagrined, forgetting about the hair. "I talked the guy down from seventy."

A handsome man in a London Fog coat climbed out of a cab and Betty waived him over. Neil. He was smiling easily at them as he approached, as if it was a warm spring day and they were all old friends. His eyes lingered on Jamie for a moment, before passing to Betty, then back to Jamie. "Are you guys twins?"

"Sure," Jamie said, heading inside.

"Irish twins." She heard her sister say as an apology behind her, shaking Neil's confused hand.

Inside, Betty lingered purposefully behind so that Neil could get to the theater door in time to open it for Jamie, who flew in without breaking her pace. There was an in-sync sense about it that threw her off balance, or perhaps it was the sudden darkness, the musty, packed in heat that made her reach for her missing ponytail.

No three seats together.

"I can sit by myself."

"You sit with Neil," Betty said.

"You girls sit together," he said.

"You don't mind sitting alone?"

"I think I can handle it."

"Then take that seat." Betty pointed and Neil moved towards it. "Actually take that one, it's much better." Betty was about to change her mind again, but Jamie dragged her to the second row. They stumbled over a disgruntled couple with their jumbo tub of popcorn, de-layered themselves of coats, gloves, and scarves, and sat down.

It took a minute for the air to settle, for Jamie to realize that the movie had started, that the static on the screen was actually a close up of speeding gravel. The camera panned out slowly: wheels, chrome, car, and, finally, a very young, cool, and self-possessed James Spader driving with the top down, one hand on the wheel, his long blond hair flitting about.

"He's handsome," Betty leaned over and whispered.

Jamie's brows rose in a most definite yes.

"I mean Neil."

"Oh."

"Mark says he's a really nice guy."

Mark, Betty's new boss at the Smithsonian, had given her these sought after preview tickets. Since he'd promoted her to a senior associate, he'd been calling Betty at home, and his name popped up in every other sentence she spoke. Jamie couldn't fathom how her sister's heart survived so many men and relationships; Jamie had barely survived one. "Go for it."

"I meant for you," Betty said with a huff, though Jamie had stopped hearing her. Her mind had pierced through the screen and settled itself on the other side, where Betty and Jamie no longer existed. Two other sisters did though, the older one ethereal and good, the younger one seductive and base, in her first scene she's having sex with her sister's husband in her sister's house, and Jamie pulled back from the screen here to be grossed out for a minute. She could simply not imagine, let alone fathom sleeping with someone Betty had. For wasn't that one step removed from… She snapped her mind shut.

"You OK?" A tightening ran down Jamie's throat and into her chest, and she tried to breathe evenly. The feeling wasn't unfamiliar. She'd been plagued with claustrophobia-induced hot flashes since her treatments…and all these wet woolly mounds around her weren't helping. She envisioned herself hurtling over moviegoers towards the exit sign, popcorn and cokes splaying in her wake. No man would ever be shared between them, if for no other reason then pride, for if you were attracted to the same man your sister was then it meant that you were no better than her, and you so wanted to be better than her…Jamie stretched the neck of her black sweater until it snapped, and Betty pulled all the items off Jamie's lap and bundled them on her own. It helped, and she blinked slowly a few times at the screen, trying to refocus on James Spader, who seemed entirely unfocused now, and well, perhaps he might be the exception to the shared man rule, given the way that Betty just shifted in her seat and Jamie couldn't stop sucking on her lips. This handsome man who'd rolled his way into town and into all of their lives, and there was something strange about him, illusive. The beads of sweat dried on Jamie's brow and she began to breathe evenly. This man who spends his days lying on the floor of a temporarily rented house before the only furniture, a TV/VCR, watching videotapes of women talking about their first sexual experience. He's got a box full of these tapes, those he made himself—strangers, friends—all of them women talking about their first sexual experience. He is impotent, he languidly admits, and this is his way of touching them. Jamie thought that maybe she'd been touched, for his affliction came off as seductive rather than perverse, and deeply intimate. And so too for the sisters, as each would eventually make her way onto one of those tapes…

"You ready?" Betty was nudging her.

Jamie released her gaze from the screen, which had gone grainy with static, as if the reel had finished but the projector was still running. Or that was the effect the director wanted to achieve anyway— Soderbergh. Jamie made a mental note of his name.

She caught up with Neil and Betty in the lobby where the three of them proceeded to stand for a minute avoiding each other's eyes and adjusting to this new, strange, post-*Sex, Lies and Videotape* intimacy. They finally managed to cobble a decision together: alcohol. Neil hailed them a cab, and Betty directed the driver to the Tune Inn.

They took the parkway. The Potomac streamed by on their right and nobody spoke. The movie was like a fourth passenger, sitting squeezed between them in the slippery, concave back seat. When Jamie's leg brushed against Neil's she felt a spark, the kind of spark that made you think anything could happen. She looked at Betty, who was gleaming: *I told you so.*

The Tune Inn was an institutional dive on the Hill, stumbling distance from Betty and Jamie's flat. They liked it because food was cheap, shots were half off, and they were barely making rent. The bar was packed when they got there, neighborhood drunks and young preppies all shoved into a small, smoky space with a pool table and jukebox.

Van Morrison's 'Brown Eyed Girl' was playing as Jamie and Betty squeezed up to the bar and ordered Michelob Lights. Then they turned around to face Neil, who was forced by the crowd to stand uncomfortably close.

"So Senator Carver?" Betty tilted her head at Jamie. "Can we be seen with him?"

"If he buys us a round of tequila shots, I'll make an exception."

Neil narrowed his eyes and asked where they were from.

"Southern California."

"Hawk territory."

"Doves by birth," Betty made sure to correct him. "Our older brother was born the day Kennedy was elected President."

"And took it as a sign from God."

"Does he work on the Hill?"

"He's at the Kennedy School of Government…" Betty started, and Jamie finished, "…Preparing for the presidency or something."

Neil waved the bartender over and asked Betty about her work, tipping his beer towards her after she'd answered, "It's refreshing to meet someone who doesn't work on the Hill."

"You should come by the museum while you're in town. Next week we're doing a special on seamstresses from the Edwardian era. Sweatshops and stuff." Betty then rambled on about her job for a short while with a genuine enthusiasm that made Jamie proud and a touch envious.

"It sounds like you really like what you're doing."

"Two years have gone by fast. Mark and I have been talking about taking the exhibit to the Met in New York."

"New York?"

Betty beamed, but then quickly turned to Jamie, who'd been perfectly content listening. "Tell Neil what you do."

"I manage a bowling alley," she said without delay.

Betty flashed her an annoying smile, then turned to Neil. "My sister's in the army…" She paused, as always, stumbling over the rest.

"…Corps of Engineers," Jamie smiled blandly.

"Jamie designs bridges," Betty clarified. "Like the Golden Gate."

"Well, not exactly." Jamie regretted ever using the bridge analogy with her sister. She really didn't *do* anything. She sat in a dungeon and read.

Their shots arrived, golden and fitted with lime wedges. Jamie raised hers. "To Videotape Guy," she said. "He makes fucked-up look good."

Betty clinked Jamie's glass with hers. "Real good." They downed their shots; Betty sucked her lime, Jamie her beer, and both held back a cringe as the tequila singed their throats.

Neil slid his empty shot glass on the bar. "So you like perverted?"

Jamie put down her glass and pulled an imaginary video camera up to her eye: "Tell me about your first sexual encounter."

Betty choked on her lime.

Jamie held the camera firm. She didn't know what made her do it. The tequila maybe—suddenly nothing felt the same.

"I'm still a virgin," Neil said playfully.

"That's what I thought." Jamie made a mental note. Guy was quick.

She turned the camera on Betty.

"I'll need another shot for that." Betty waved the bartender over.

They did more shots. Then Neil turned the camera on Jamie.

"I took advantage of a friend who had a crush on me. I just wanted it over with."

"Jesus, Jamie," Betty said, and it occurred to Jamie that they'd never had this discussion.

"I practically threw him out when it was over."

No one spoke.

"I'm kidding," Jamie lied, at Betty's alarmed expression. "And I suppose you were in love."

Betty blushed so hard that Jamie for the first time wondered. "Of course you were in love." *High-school Rich, duh.*

"Perhaps you don't know as much as you think."

"Oh really," Jamie said, studying Betty sidelong. "Please enlighten me then."

"I'm not sure I want to hear this," Neil said.

"Because you're a virgin?" Jamie asked.

"Yes," he said, loosing his straight face, and Jamie was thinking that he might be getting cuter by the minute.

"Good," Betty announced. "Because I'd prefer not to talk about it." She lifted her refilled shot glass. "Are we going to do this or what?"

They may have grimaced this time, alcohol having officially replaced the imaginary camera they'd been using for this conversation. "It all comes down to sex," Jamie said. "It's basic, instinctive. It's the one thing we can't hide from." It felt good, the tequila dulling her senses. "Like the sisters in the movie. They're so different, yet in those moments talking about sex on camera, they're the same." She paused to chase her shot with beer. "You know…exposed."

"Maybe that's why they were able to reconcile at the end," Neil added casually.

"Yes!" Jamie heard her voice too loud, the way it got when she was drunk. But Neil didn't seem to mind. He was getting her.

Betty's eyes, on the other hand, were crossing slightly. "Because of sex?"

"Because they had set ideas about who the other was, and when they revealed their own intimate sexuality on those tapes, those notions collapsed. It was just them that were left, raw and starting over."

Betty's eyes tried to focus. Finally she just blurted out, "Requests?" and pushed her way over to the jukebox. They watched her dissolve into the crowd. Or Jamie watched Neil watch Betty dissolve. After a moment Jamie could see her sister again, tapping on the hued glass, the colorful albums illuminating her face. Her beauty had grown deeper still, Jamie couldn't deny, as if each year that passed her sister shed another layer…of hair, which was now waves of silk down her back, of her face, which was more carved and etched, of her eyes, a purer blue. Slim from running six miles a day, she fit sleekly into a tailored black blazer and fitted chords, Jamie's fitted chords, for they could share even pants now.

"Mark didn't mention that you guys were lunatics." Neil stepped in closer.

"I'll take that as a compliment." Jamie would have stepped back, if only she could.

"He also wasn't clear on his relationship with Betty."

"He's her boss."

Neil glanced at the jukebox. Betty was discussing selections with probably the best looking guy in the bar. "Does she have a boy-friend?"

"I think right now work's her boyfriend, if you know what I mean."

"And you?"

"Me what?"

"Where's your boyfriend?"

"I don't believe in relationships."

"Really."

"Really."

"So then what do you believe in?"

She looked at her beer. "Building bridges, of course."

He tried to read her seriousness. "Do you ever have fun?"

"I try not to."

"Are you trying not to now?"

She didn't have an answer.

"Do you ever smile?"

That surprised her. She smiled.

After closing the bar down, they stumbled back to Betty and Jamie's apartment. It was a basement flat south of the Capitol that they'd make-shifted from one bedroom to two by converting the small den. Betty switched on the stereo while Jamie went and found a half open bottle of white wine in the fridge. R.E.M. was playing when she returned with full glasses. She handed Betty a glass and the two of them danced around in the middle of their tiny living room, while Neil slouched on the couch perusing the album cover. When the tequila caught up with them, they all stretched out on the carpet and discussed critically important things they wouldn't remember the next day. It didn't occur to either Jamie or Betty when or if Neil would leave until Betty all at once stood up and announced she was going to bed; and her absence left a gaping hole, like the couch was suddenly missing.

Neil remained stretched out on his back, Jamie on her stomach trying to calm her racing heart. It had been a almost two years since

Jim, but still, there was no mistaking the hollow, aching desire. What happened afterwards didn't matter. Right now she needed her body pressed up against his; she needed to lie in his arms. Neil switched albums to Lou Reed, and they listened for a time, before all at once Jamie stood and went to her bedroom doorway. "You can sleep with me if you want."

He looked at her.

"We don't have to do anything. I mean…I know you're a virgin."

He stood up.

She shut the door behind them.

He took off his shoes and jeans and stretched out on her bed in his sweater, boxers and tube socks. She lay down next to him in her jeans and tank, and their sides collapsed into each other. Her chin found an innocent spot on his shoulder. He turned on his side, and she searched his eyes, green like the sea, and felt her heart breaking all over again. Perhaps there was life ahead of her. Perhaps Neil would be part of that life.

But he never made a move. They lay there like buddies and didn't even kiss. Maybe he wanted to take it slow she rationalized thirty minutes later. Maybe he was a gentleman. Maybe they needed to get to know each other better. Maybe he was gay and didn't know it! Maybe…but by three a.m. Jamie's throat began to tighten, her body felt on fire, and she was sweating through her clothes. Desperate for air, she crawled over Neil to get to the window, opened it wide, and leaned far out into the frozen night.

"I was hot," she said to a staring Neil when she finally crawled back to her side of the bed.

"Better?" he asked.

"I had cancer." The words came quickly and before she could stop them. "It's nothing, really." She bit her lip. "It was two years ago. And I'm fine now."

He didn't say anything.

"Colon cancer. Of all places," she sensed herself rambling. "Why couldn't it have been in my arm or leg or something?"

When he didn't laugh, she did, nervously. "They got it all out in the surgery…though it seemed to have attached itself to a lymph node…had to do some radiation and chemotherapy." She couldn't make herself stop. "I'm fine now, it seems. Or we'll know in three more years."

"Jesus," he said.

"I don't know why I just told you that." She paused. "It's nothing, really."

"You said that already."

"Right," she said, turning on her stomach.

He sat up against the wall. "Did you lose your hair?"

She frowned. Hair seemed to be the first thing that came to everybody's mind, as if hair was what defined you. And what's ironic was that Jamie did once believe that her red, medusa-like-hair defined her, in some way anyway. "It used to be as long as Betty's." Now what defined her was a constellation of radiation tattoos on her belly and hips, those she was now showing him because he had settled on his side wanting to know more; the tiny scar in the shape of a half moon below her collarbone where they'd stored, temporarily, a chemo catheter; the worm-like creature crawling down her pelvis that the surgeon had been so proud of later. She went on about it all banally, abstractly, as if it were just something anyone might have had to slog through, like high school. It actually felt good to talk about it. The cancer was the easy part. It was fascinating almost, on the edge of reason, like a David Lynch movie. It was the Jim part that crippled her, the fact that he had conveniently met someone else just as she was starting her second round of treatments. But she didn't mention Jim to Neil. She closed her eyes, exhausted. Suddenly all she wanted to do was sleep.

Jamie fully expected Neil to be gone when she awoke the next morning, but he wasn't. He lay there curled up in his boxers like a baby as she crept from the room and shut the door behind her. She went and got the Advil and some water and brought them to Betty, on the couch with the *Washington Post*, her face as gray as the mug she was holding. She took the pills, tilting her head in the direction of Jamie's room. *Situation not good*, Jamie's face responded, and as Betty started to ask more, Neil stumbled out, dressed, his sweater tied around his waist. On his way out, Jamie assumed, disappointed but also relieved. If it was going to be over, she wanted it over now.

"Coffee?" Betty said.

"Absolutely." Neil smiled.

Jamie didn't move and Betty gave her a look that said go fetch the man some coffee. She rubbed at the mascara under her eyes while searching for a good mug in the high cabinet. As she poured, each waking moment brought a new memory of the things she'd told him. She was mortified by the time she returned to the living room, where Neil had already made himself at home on the couch with the sports page.

Jamie, puzzled, excused herself and went off to the bathroom. She washed her face and brushed her teeth and then stood staring in the mirror. *Is Neil still here because he pities me or is he actually interested? And if he is not interested, would she settle for a little pity?* The morning trudged on: bagels, the video store, a Redskins game. Betty did laundry and other Sunday afternoon tasks. By six Jamie still hadn't been able to give her sister one of those communicatory glances where a strategy is conveyed. She had none, which is when Betty suggested pasta with fresh zucchini for dinner.

Neil accompanied Betty to Eastern Market while Jamie took a shower. She wasn't sure what was going on with Neil, and she needed to clear her head; but when she stood under the scorching water all she could think about was Jim, until tears joined the streams running down her face.

Still, she felt better afterwards, and she even put on some makeup before joining them in the kitchen, where Neil was slicing zucchini, and Betty was pouring canned tomatoes into a pan. Jamie got busy cutting the bread. Neil seemed really interested in Betty's recipe, and kept probing about the variety of cookbooks Betty kept on the shelves; he loved to cook. I'm more of a setting-the-table-kind-of-person, interjected Jamie, getting down glasses and plates. After Betty put the water on to boil, she made a move to step away as if to leave the two of them alone, but Jamie's eyes pleaded for her to stay because Betty was the one keeping the conversation going. Somehow the questions kept being redirected back to her. The hole her absence made was bottomless, apparently, a reality suddenly sifting its way into Jamie's consciousness and she paused what she was doing to gaze out the window. Night had fallen…and with it the hard cold realization that Neil's looks, his gestures, his smile—they were all for Betty…it had only taken Jamie this long to figure it out, and she looked back at Neil now looking at Betty. So much for pity, Jamie thought; the reason Neil was still here was for Betty, and the way he just looked at her.

Her first instinct was to turn a switch and be gone, and it took everything in her power to stay put because she knew that leaving wouldn't be fair. Betty was not interested in Neil, Jamie could tell this just by the depth and curvature of her laugh lines. Plus, this scene was not easy for Betty either, Jamie knew. Putting up with her younger sister's sudden and morbid appearance in D.C. was no joyous boost to Betty's new found, high-spirited life, and it all just got really depressing suddenly, even Betty sensed it, because when the phone rang, she practically flew to the living room to answer it. "Mark," she mouthed, taking her plate and the phone with her to her room, unable to hide her relief, at least from Jamie. Neil still seemed to be waiting to make his move. It was humiliating, watching Neil spend thirty minutes finishing the dishes so methodically and expectantly; Jamie finally went and sat in front of the TV. "I should probably get going," Neil said, coming in from the kitchen. "OK," Jamie said. They could hear the din of Betty on the phone in her room. "I'll wait to say goodbye to Betty though," he added, taking a seat on the couch. Thirty more minutes passed until he said it again, "I should probably get going." "OK," Jamie said. The light under Betty's door switched off.

"I'll tell her you said goodbye if you want to just go. Who knows how long she'll be on that phone."

Neil stood up, hesitated, "Well," he said. "OK."

Jamie walked him to the door.

Neil struggled with what to say, something nice but not leading, meaningful but not intimate. "We should do this again," he said finally.

"Yeah."

"Maybe next weekend."

"Sure."

"Tell Betty I'll call."

He left.

She shut the door and leaned up against it, flushed with the realization that life can, in fact, sink lower. You think things can't get worse, but then they do. Perhaps the ceiling is going to fall in next, you fix your eyes on it and wonder. Of course it doesn't, so you go to bed, where you cry for hours and pray for sleep to take you, like the night before, and the night before that, your sadness like a worn Teddy Bear you've become too attached to. And just when you are sure you won't ever fall asleep again, the alarm goes off and you are blinking into a new day, the day that keeps coming whether you want it to or not. But apparently there is a breaking point, a last straw, because this morning something is different. Angry, pissed, determination is throttling inside you, not new but resurrected. Fuck them, the notion rips through you while shoving on your work heels, you are not going to sit in a dungeon and do nothing. Up, dressed, and gone before Betty wakes because you can't bear to see the hope in her eyes; you don't want to lose focus. You seethe your way to work, where you pretend to read in your dungeon while waiting for the floor above yours to come alive with busy, purpose driven people. Then you march upstairs and into the office of your boss's boss with that imaginary camera you've got attached to you now. You tell this rather pleasant looking bespectacled man that you want a real assignment…that you're smart, a quick study, a relentless worker, and you deserve a chance. He examines you a long hard moment, admiring your boldness, you think, either that or he's wondering what the hell you've been waiting for because he wastes no time in pulling you out of the dungeon and assigning you to a real project. A bridge of all things, and on this bridge you work like there is no tomorrow because there isn't. There's just you and that camera. Through it you see them, but you don't ever let them see you.

C H A P T E R   7

UNFORGIVEN

October, 2003

Two months had passed. Betty still hadn't sent Jamie the e-mail asking her to be at the birth. Each time she'd gone to click the send button she'd find herself rewriting it. Plus things had been getting better between her and Dave, and she didn't want to jinx that. Then yesterday Nick came home from pre-k with a drawing he'd made of the Roman Coliseum. "Nick has a sense for spaces and objects," the teacher had written on an attached note. Betty wasn't surprised. He also had a sense for numbers; at four he was already beating her at poker. "Your aunt should see this," Betty said to Nick without thinking. "Maybe you'll be an architect, or an engineer like her."

"I want to send it to her as a present!" Nick exclaimed with a glee that pierced Betty's heart, not to mention her ears. And before she could even tell him that she didn't know Jamie's address in Thailand, Nick had folded his drawing into a tiny square and sealed it inside an envelope he'd retrieved from somewhere. He bound the envelope with extra tape for the long journey, and then wrote her name on the front with an "I love you" on the back. He was all excited about it. "You have to send it now, Mom!" he said, off again, toward the basement stairs.

Betty went upstairs to get a real envelope. She'd print her e-mail to Jamie and send it with Nick's drawing, she'd decided. But when she'd printed the letter out, she was astonished to see that it had grown to five pages, and she wasn't even sure what it said anymore. She sat back, spaced out for a minute, then picked up the phone and called her mother. She would have Jamie's address in Thailand.

"I'm worried about you, dear," her mother started the conversation.

Betty put her mom on speaker, moved to the rocking chair, and got busy knitting, something she always found herself doing when she spoke to her mother.

"Are you taking care of yourself?"

Betty reached for a new spool of yarn.

"You sound distracted."

"Sorry," Betty said after a delay. "I'm just finishing this blanket."

"Should we talk later?"

"No!" She could feel her mother ready to hang up. "Now's fine. It's just . . . a new fabric and I'm not used to it."

"Your sewing? Now?"

"I'm knitting . . . and why not now?"

"Shouldn't you be resting?"

"It's just a little side project I've got going. And for me this is resting; it takes my mind off of everything else." Betty thought about running the business idea by her mom. Debbie had been over again that day, bringing more fabric samples from her distributor contact in Mexico. They'd discussed putting together a business plan, getting an investor. Why couldn't she just ask her mother for help? She had, after all, directed the Chamber of Commerce at some point in her career. Betty tried to recollect when . . . sometime after One-to-One and before her Council position. Anyway, she knew something about small, community businesses.

Her mother sighed. "Promise me you won't tell Steven, Betty. Please! But I'm thinking about not re-running when my Council term is up next year. My busy schedule and public life are hard on Richard. You know this isn't exactly his world. And," she reflected for a moment before going on, "taking on this job has been a huge challenge for me. It was different than anything I'd ever done before in my life. And to always be in the public eye is stressful. A piece of bad press just kills me…you know how I am with confrontation. I just want to wake up in his arms in the morning and not have to go any-where."

Betty didn't react. She still didn't believe this Richard guy was entirely real, and she'd heard this exhaustion plea from her mother before.

"But my constituents rely on me. I don't like to disappoint people. You know I'm a people pleaser."

Betty smiled.

"But anyway, I don't want to talk about me. I wish I could come out there and take care of you."

Betty closed her eyes and set down her knitting. "What do you think about Mary Jamie for the baby's name?" Her voice cracked a bit. It was the first time Betty had said the name out loud. Betty barely remembered her maternal grandmother, who was an alcoholic and died when Betty was just a baby. Her mother rarely talked about her.

There was a noticeable silence.

"I wanted to honor your mother, Mom, the woman who adopted you."

She sighed, a bit put upon. "I guess I don't know what to think."

"I just thought it would be nice to maintain the female chain in our family. I want my daughter to be part of something bigger than just you and me."

More silence. Then her voice changed, growing deeper and grainy. "She was a strict mother." She paused, and then added quickly, "But a good woman. You know she was a nurse."

"I know."

"I just don't think she knew what to do with me."

The line went still. Betty didn't move or breathe or do anything. She wanted to hold onto this moment—there were so few of them. After she hung up, she realized she'd forgotten to get Jamie's address. And then she was *knitting again and so determined to finish the blanket that she never called her mother back. When she was done she stitched on the new My Mary label she and Debbie had designed for their company. "For whatever it's worth," she heard herself say, looking at the finished product. She took the blanket downstairs to the basement to store it with the others.*

She had to pause halfway down the stairs to deal with a cramp that hit her with more force than usual. She held the base of her protruding belly and breathed in and out. Six months in the womb and already Mary had taken charge. Betty had had to adjust her eating and sleeping habits to accommodate her daughter's distaste for chocolate and the pirouettes she liked to do at three a.m. Maybe she'll be a ballerina like Jamie had been once... or something else entirely, like a painter or a poet...or maybe she'd run for office like Betty's mother...or be like me. But here Betty drew a blank, because she had no idea what "being like me" meant. She stood there massaging her pelvis, listening to the din of her kids on PlayStation below, and came up with nothing. The cramp released and Betty continued down the stairs.

She stood at the bottom step for a moment and took in the scene that was exactly as she'd imagined: Clay at the controls, Sam barking unwanted advice, and Nick on the carpet sucking his thumb, riveted by the action.

She'd been temporarily storing her baby clothes in neat piles along one of the walls, but now it looked like someone had taken a running dive into them; in fact the whole room was a disaster. "Nick..." Betty sighed and began putting away the toys scattered about, reminding the boys they needed to clean their rooms after the game. "It's freezing down here." She went and shut a window that someone had propped open. "Aren't you guys cold?" Again they didn't answer, so she just went over and wormed her way in next to Clay on the couch and encircled her legs around Nick. She needed to sit down. That cramp had sucked the life out of her. She ran her hand mindlessly through her youngest son's golden locks while observing her middle son, who didn't seem to notice she was there. His hair had grown even lighter, almost platinum now, and strength had begun to define the pale, soft features that still seemed so foreign to her. He sat with his elbows on his knees holding the controls, cool and focused. For Clay this wasn't a game. On weekends he'd start at six a.m. When he grew up he wanted to "shoot people," something she used to worry about. Now she glanced out the window above their heads and noticed the leaves piling up in the yard, the end of autumn.

She couldn't believe how quickly time had passed, only a few more months to get in shape for the birth, a thought which forced her off the couch and to the wall, which she squatted against. Thirty seconds, two minutes, five minutes before the burning got too much and she slid down to her butt. Getting stronger, she told herself, tucking in one leg and reaching for the toe of the other.

Rohan suffered a set back. "You suck," Sam said, taking the controls from Clay.

"Excuse me?" Betty faced her oldest son sternly.

"Sorry." He had a glint in his eye.

Betty moved over to her pile of baby clothes and began refolding them. They were all in various shades of earthy pinks, and she reminded herself that it was time to start weaving in some blues or purples. She examined a cotton candy colored bonnet she'd knitted a while ago. It really was beautiful, and with that she let loose the excitement growing inside her about this business, about this baby, about Dave's promotion. She looked at her boys, thinking, I can do this, be a mother and still pursue this dream. She had to do it, for Mary. Her boys were troublesome at times, but still, she never worried about what they would become, or whether they would love her. She just wanted them to be healthy and happy. But daughters were different. Betty wanted Mary to respect her as a mother, a woman. She felt more and more desperate about it.

She got up, went and got the phone, and brought it back to Clay, who was still absorbed in the action. She touched his head. "Why don't you call your aunt? Ask when she's going to come for a visit. Ask her what she thinks of Mary Jamie as a baby name."

He looked at the phone, then back at the TV. "Why should I call? You're the one that wants to talk to her."

She narrowed her eyes at him and didn't answer.

"But what if it's a boy, Mommy?" Nick said.

"I'm pretty sure it's a girl. I can tell by the way I'm carrying the baby."

"You can?"

"I could tell that each of you would be boys, and I also knew that Clay would be obstinate, Sam would sleep late, and you, Nick, would suck your thumb." He popped his thumb out of his mouth then, unsure whether to believe her. "My maternal instincts have rarely been wrong."

Clay grabbed the controls back from Sam, whose Forces of Sauron had succumbed to a crevice in the cracking earth.

"Mary?" Sam quipped, sulking back in his chair, defeated again. "Yuck."

"It was my grandmother's name," Betty said defensively. "Your great-grandmother."

"It still sucks," Sam said.

"Sam!" Dave was on the stairs. He must have just gotten home from work, and Betty wondered how long he'd been standing there. "Please don't speak to your mother like that." He came and stood behind the boys at the couch. Betty still had to adjust to the sight of his short hair—the missing ponytail he'd had since she'd known him—and the Home Depot vest he liked to wear around the house, as if he was sending her a message. Apparently he, too, had given in to PlayStation. He, who had once been so idealistic about how they would raise their kids, now folded his arms over his chest and watched.

"Hey Dave," Betty said, upbeat. "What do you think about a cedar closet for all these baby clothes?" She knew she shouldn't ask, but she couldn't help herself. If she and Debbie were going to do this business, they had to do it now. In one month Betty's sabbatical would begin, which would cover six months of income. After that she'd have to either go back to work at the museum or refinance the house and take out more equity. She was hoping Jamie would help her with the business plan. "Dave?" she said. It just occurred to her that he hadn't responded to her question, that his eyes were more glazed than the kids'.

"Sam, did you do your homework?" He spoke absently, and so got no response, which didn't really matter because he was already headed back upstairs. "I'm going to work in the shed on the birthing tub." He paused at the top and added, sardonically, "Unless, that is, anybody needs me."

"I need you," Betty said. "To make dinner..."

"I've got my GMAT class tonight."

She'd completely forgotten. "Oh right." Be careful what you wish for. Last month Home Depot singled Dave out and promoted him to site manager. With his knowledge of woods, craftsmanship, and the natural way he dealt with customers, he had a promising future they had told him. They increased his salary and put his name in for the MBA-in-training program. He'd have to apply, and it would depend on his GMAT scores, but if all went well, they'd pay for his night school and rotate him through the various departments of procurement, marketing, and corporate strategy while he went to business school at night. They were opening new stores in Georgetown and Capitol Hill as well as in other cities throughout the country, not to mention Europe.

The promotion had lit a spark under Dave, it seemed. He'd grown focused, more intent. In the mornings he got up at five a.m., worked on the birthing tub for an hour, and then hit the gym before work. Two nights a week he was at the community school taking a GMAT prep class. He'd lost weight, and Betty was still getting used to that new haircut. The distance between them was dissipating, she told herself. He seemed happier.

"Daddy's not eating dinner with us again?" Sam asked.

"Daddy has his class tonight."

"Why is Daddy always in such a bad mood?" Clay asked, manning the controls again, and she frowned at her rather pragmatic middle son. What she refused to see, he wouldn't. "He's not in a bad mood, honey. He's just busy. We're all busy. In fact you should get busy finishing your homework."

"I don't have any homework."

"What about you, Sam?"

She was back at her piles now, sifting through them. She found the envelope Nick had only minutes ago made for Jamie, buried in a bootie.

She pulled it out, held it before Nick with a tilted head. "How did this get here?" He smiled at her, that silly expression. She shook her head and took the sticky, crinkled envelope upstairs, where she would hand write her request to Jamie simply and directly, call back her mother, and mail this thing once and for all.

But when Betty got to the office, she froze. Dave was at her computer. "I thought you were working on the tub?"

"You didn't tell me you and Debbie were in business together."

Her mouth fell open. "We're not in business together." She walked up behind him to see that her e-mail was open. Mark, her ex-boss and longtime friend, had responded to her e-mail requesting that they get together off the clock. Mark knew a ton about fabric and the business of design, and she and Debbie wanted to pick his brain. "We're just discussing the idea," she added, thinking about that letter to Jamie that Betty had left open. Her mind scanned through it for anything revealing.

"Then what was all that about devoting your sabbatical to your kids? Isn't this why I went back to work?"

Her face flushed red. There were those other e-mails she'd sent. She'd never erased them. A fire burned through her; she couldn't believe that he'd actually gone through her e-mails. Every time she was ready to believe in him, he'd do something unforgivable. And then she'd have to sit back and face the fact, all over again, that she had too.

✱✱ 1992 ✱✱

There's something I need to tell you girls, their mother started out the conversation. "I've hired a detective to search for my birth-parents." The line they were all on went silent. Their mother was not the kind of person who would willingly subject herself to a poten-tially harsh or ugly reality: the reasons people give up a child. But alas, thus she officially commenced her soul-searching mission after turning fifty-five, after Gary moved permanently onto the boat, and after the Learning Channel canceled *One-to-One*. She delivered the news about her and Gary's separation as if it might come as a shock to her daughters or even a disappointment, a deathly tone assumed as she went on to explain the reasons she'd joined AA for children of alcoholics, for reconnecting with the Immaculate Heart Community, for requesting that her children fly out next weekend on a mission to reconnect with her.

And so here Jamie and Betty were, driving out of LAX in their rental, an emergency trip of sorts.

"Shit, that was close," Jamie swerved the car, causing Betty to search her purse in a sudden panic. For a moment she couldn't remember if she'd packed it. She unzipped the inside pocket and felt the antique, unaffordable ring that she and Dave had picked out together. She was dying to put it on. To tell someone she was engaged. But then, technically, she wasn't engaged, and she sighed quietly and closed her eyes. She'd told Dave she needed to think, that she was distracted by this trip to California and wasn't... She blinked her eyes open, in fact she didn't know what she wasn't. A sigh no one heard, and she glanced over at Jamie, the speedometer, back at Jamie. Ever since Dave had moved in, her sister had been distant and cold, and, it seemed to Betty, purposefully pulling all-nighters at the office. She'd worked the entire flight here and they'd barely spoken. Betty cracked open the window. "We should call Vivi and let her know what time on Sunday."

Jamie glanced in the rearview for cops and didn't respond.

"It's weird." Betty paused, trying to imagine it. "That Dad sees Masa more than me."

"Is Masa still modeling?"

"She lives with some big producer in Hollywood now...paints portraits for stars like Angelica Houston, Dad was proud to tell me. Apparently, he goes out and takes care of her German Shepherds while she's working in her studio."

"Angelica Houston? Really?"

"Whatever."

"Trust me, Betty. It's better this way. Vivi takes care of him, and those Shepherds give him something to do. His practice has dwindled; he's only got a few clients keeping him going."

Betty shrugged, unconvinced.

"What's your problem?"

"Nothing."

"You're the one who moved to D.C., Betty."

Why did she move to D.C.? Betty suddenly asked herself, as the 405 bled into the 101, and an ache settled in her chest upon sight of the Pacific. She missed Southern California, had been idly considering returning, especially after getting rejected for that transfer to the Met in New York. She'd been at the museum five years now; she'd restored garments for the most prestigious exhibits, but she was desperate to move on. And then she met Dave and became possessed with the idea of settling down, of helping Dave become the man he wanted to be.

His passion had always been woodshop. As a teen he was a semipro skateboarder and carved all his own boards. But law school had been a dream of Dave's Yale Law parents. He'd compromised by going to George Washington University, an escape more than anything else. He quit after the first semester, and then worked odd construction jobs to pay the rent. He was smart and well read, but he refused to sell out to his parents' money. Most of his jobs were out in the suburbs of Bethesda or Virginia, where, as a hobby, he started collecting scraps and natural materials from old barns and making coffee tables out of them, all kinds of odd shapes and sizes. He sold them at Eastern Market on the weekends, a craft market where he and Betty met. She'd had her eye on a smaller piece that he ended up giving her for nothing after they'd gotten to talking and he mentioned he was a Big Brother and she told him that she had once been a Big Sister. He wanted to do good things, he told her. Betty wanted to do good things too.

It was Betty who convinced him to turn his hobby into a business. He had been hesitant about the idea, didn't want to compromise his craft for money. But Betty kept prodding and nudging until at last she just blurted out, "Go after your dream!" By the look on Dave's face, it was apparent that he'd never heard words like that before. He told her how beautiful she was, and she had felt beautiful in that moment, so beautiful, not to mention needed and so many other things she couldn't explain. Just that she was bursting inside. Why couldn't she just burst? "This is ridiculous," she blurted out so suddenly that Jamie let up on the gas. "If Gary wants to leave, why doesn't Mom just let him?"

If there was a response, Betty didn't hear it over the car's sudden reacceleration, over her tormenting visions. "I can still see the smile on his face as he carried Mom in his arms out the door of our house while Dad watched on." She turned at Jamie, who still hadn't spoken. "I can't believe you don't remember this."

Jamie shrugged. She seemed elsewhere, and Betty faced forward again. "And I thought, wow, he's saving her life because that's what she told me, that he was literally saving her life." Her face twisted in disgust. "Why did he smile at me? As if I knew him already? Did I? Had I already been brainwashed? She does it even now that Gary's moved onto the boat with his beers and who knows what else. She still puts him up on a pedestal to me. Why! Why! Is anything she says the truth?"

"It's all the truth, Betty. She believes he's beyond reproach… that all men are beyond reproach."

"And what's this crap about finding her birthparents? It's all dramatics. I don't even think she really wants to find them."

"She's searching, Betty, that's all she's doing."

"Well, I'm not going to let her get away with it."

Jamie flashed her a doubtful look. "Get away with what?"

Betty didn't respond. She'd gotten her sister's attention. With a satisfied huff she got out the directions. "Where the hell is this place?"

They spotted the sign for Montecito just in time to miss the exit. Backtracking, they found the off-ramp and took it inland, down a dark stretch of road and finally into the tiny town whose shops were mostly closed by seven p.m. The sign on the theater kiosk was missing a few letters. "You won't like it," Jamie said, about the movie currently showing.

"You've seen it? With who?"

Jamie didn't respond, didn't need to, for Betty knew she'd seen it by herself. "Well, thanks for inviting me," she mumbled. Jamie's consolation was to point out the Mexican dive on the corner, because when it came to tequila, she and her sister were always on the same page. Starving, Betty considered it, and Jamie was thirsty, Betty could tell. But they could only sigh, communally, already way late, and opted for the liquor store instead. They bought pretzels and beers, which they immediately popped open in the car. Betty directed Jamie a few turns up an incline that grew steeper and narrower and more gravelly. It leveled off before a small, barely-lit sign that read Immaculate Heart Community Center for Spiritual Renewal. "We're here," Betty announced, swigging her beer.

"And so is she," Jamie said, pulling up and parking next to her mother's white Audi.

"Yeah, but where's everybody else." There was only one other car in the park, and it wasn't the black Mercedes they knew so well, their brother's trademark.

Jamie switched off the engine and they sat finishing their beers, not sure what to expect about the place their mother had rarely talked about. It had once been a boarding school run by nuns, and her adoptive parents had sent her here for a time when she was a child. Now it was some kind of retreat center for faith searchers, or something. Betty sort of cringed at the thought of spending two whole nights here: a series of low buildings situated around a courtyard with shuttered windows and a shingled roof, and a statue of St. Jude on the front lawn; it looked so isolated and lonely. A dull yellow light over the front door cast shadows on the surrounding forest. Things croaked and chirped from walkways leading into blackness as they waited for someone to answer their ring. Somewhere behind them in the distance, they could hear the ocean.

A large woman dressed in plain clothes with a friendly, quiet smile welcomed them inside. She knew their mother from the past, she said softly, knowingly, shuffling them through the dark parlors. They passed an inner courtyard, where the leaves swirled all around in little bursts of wind, then down an arched corridor. She showed them where their mother's room was, then led them just beyond it and opened a wood door, no key, lowered her eyes, and went on her unobtrusive way.

For a moment they just stood there feeling the depressing quiet.

"We have to share the same bed?" Jamie let out a disparaging sigh.

Betty dropped her bag and went over and tested it: lumpy, squeaky, Jesus above the headboard; and on the nightstand was a Bible and a marketing brochure that Betty grabbed. "Cool, horseback riding," she said rather mockingly, after a minute of flipping through it. As a kid Jamie had had a thing for horses—horse posters, horse dolls, horse stuffed animals. It never really made sense with the rest of her, but Jamie made no comment, she was busy spreading out her engineering drawings on the tiny antique desk, leaving Betty to stare blankly at her studious profile. Her sister had been so determined lately, so driven and single-minded. Towards what, Betty had no idea. *The New Jersey Light Rail Transit System?* "Give it a rest," Betty said.

"I've got three plans due by Monday, a plane to catch on Tuesday, and here I am…,"

"…Pursuing your spiritual path," Betty held up the brochure and met her sister's dead expression with her own. "It's in the mission statement."

Even Jamie had to smile.

They knocked once on her door, softly, before letting themselves in. She was sitting up on her bed reading her daily meditation book, the accompanying meditation candle glowing on the side table. She looked up at them, sleepy-eyed. Betty hadn't seen her since Christmas, six months ago. She looked smaller, if that was possible, caved and drawn. "My girls are here!" She got up from the bed to give them hugs and didn't let go for a while. After they finally extracted themselves, she looked kind of embarrassed and unsure. "I miss my babies."

They'd missed dinner. "In-N-Out Burger?"

Their mom gaped at Betty's remark, as if she herself didn't have a serious weakness for the place. She then led them arm-in-arm to the communal kitchen, where everything was dark and put away and silent. They found some turkey, bread, and cheese in the refrigerator. Betty and Jamie stood at the counter munching on various combinations of the three until their mother asked them to come sit at the table with her, and they reluctantly moved everything over.

"Diana saved my life," their mother said, referring to the woman who had shown Betty and Jamie to their room. "I don't know what I would have done without her during this crisis."

"Diana?" Betty said, shoving a piece of bread in her mouth.

"Diana taught for me when I was a principal in South Central. She came to me after her husband had left her with two babies and no money. I got her a job as a teaching assistant in the art program and then got her going on her credential; she's a wonderful artist. When I left to go work on One-to-One, I brought her with me, but we lost touch when I went to the Learning Channel. I hadn't seen her in almost five years." She paused, redoing the math. "Five years I had that show. Can you believe it?"

"Maybe it's better this way, Mom."

"Yeah, Mom, maybe it's time to move on."

She didn't seem to like either of those suggestions. She would dictate her own emotional recovery, thank you. "Anyway, Diana called me a few months ago out of the blue. The show had just gone kaput, and I was really down. It was almost as if an angel had been sent to me from God."

Betty blinked and smiled.

"Speaking of God," Jamie said. "When is your number one son coming?"

Her eyes lit up at just the thought of Steven. "Well, he called and promised to be here first thing tomorrow."

Betty shoved some turkey into her mouth, noticing her mother trying with everything she had not to see or smell the food. "Want some, Mom?" Betty offered, somewhat maliciously.

"Oh, I'm not hungry, dear. You know I can't eat." She waited a moment, then, "Can't you tell?" She made a gesture to indicate that something physical had changed.

"Your hair is shorter?" Betty offered.

"I've lost fifteen pounds, dears." *Dears* came out strangled, and then she went into a little coughing fit.

They waited for her to finish. "You look good, Mom," Jamie said, going on to say that weight loss in general was good, that we all carry around too much weight. Betty bit her lip because, as Jamie knew, their mother didn't want to hear that. She wanted their concern, their worry; she wanted them to take care of her. She dropped her head forward like a rag doll, reached out, and squeezed their hands. "I'm just so grateful for you girls. It means so much to me, you coming all the way out here to be with me."

"We know, Mom," Jamie said, caving finally like she always does, adorning her soft, empathetic tone, the one she reserved for their mother.

Betty thought of that beer in her room.

Her mother must have thought of something too, because at once she was up and putting the plastic back over the turkey. "You girls must be so tired."

"It's seven, Mom." Betty grabbed a last slice of cheese before her mother put it away.

"Being on East Coast time and all."

"*Unforgiven* is showing at nine," Betty said, nodding expectantly at Jamie.

Their mother looked stricken. "Unforgiven?"

"That Clint Eastwood movie," Jamie responded. "And Betty's just joking."

"Oh," she smiled as if she got the joke. "Of course, dear." She was wiping down the counter now, weighty with misery suddenly, as if that joke stole the last bit of life from her.

"Are you going to be alright, Mom?"

She put on a smile. No.

They walked her back to her room.

"Breakfast is at eight," she reminded them. And our first session with Father Patrick is at ten. He's a wonderful man...I've known Father Patrick since I was first studying to become a teacher." She went still for a moment. "He was there for me during the divorce with your father," she said gravely. "And you Jamie, you remember how Father Patrick helped you...during that awful time..."

"Goodnight, Mom," Jamie said, singsong, like their father did when he wanted to hide how he was really feeling.

"Goodnight, girls," their mother said, after some hesitation.

"I'm serious about that movie, Jamie," Betty whisper-shouted back in their room.

"She doesn't look good."

Betty popped open another beer.

"I'm worried about her."

"Oh, please." She took a swig.

"Why are you being so…"

"Just this once…" Betty didn't let her finish. She took a deep breath, "Maybe I need her."

"For what? You've never needed her. By the age of six you were already separating our laundry into colors and whites." Jamie was on her bed now, sifting through her drawings.

"You're so busy with work these days, avoiding me and Dave like we were…" her mind shot somewhere. When it came back she said, "What do you know what's going on with me anyway?"

Jamie clicked her mechanical pencil and got to work.

Betty considered shoving on her ring and announcing her engagement right then. If the news didn't pierce her sister's stone cold heart, then at least the ring might wipe that smug look off her face. But like the hundred other times Betty had considered sharing her secret that morning with Jamie, her gut told her this moment was wrong. Instead she went in search of a phone to call Dave. But there was no phone, not one she could find anyway, so she surrendered and went back to their room. She felt thirteen again, trapped with someone who despised her. She grabbed her beer and lay on her bed. There was no TV. She refrained from pulling out the *Bride* magazine she had in her bag and pulled out *People* instead. She flipped through it, willing herself to be open-minded about this place, this retreat, maybe learning something about her mother. And perhaps Betty did need this solitary time to "reflect" about Dave, about how if she married him it meant staying in D.C. because Dave, born and bred in the east, had a serious aversion to California. But would they make a home there? Would their kids grow up there? Certainly marrying Dave was the change she'd been seeking, everything she'd been seeking. Yet she couldn't see it, picture it. So she closed her eyes and envisioned her wedding dress—white, off the shoulder, chiffon maybe—until she drifted off to sleep.

They were woken by howls in the night. Lying under a quilt that seemed made of sand paper, they conferred upon what animals might be making that noise, what kind of feast they might be celebrating in that savage, bloodcurdling way. Jamie finally got Betty to go over to the window to check it out, but she saw nothing and came back to bed. They were just starting to drift off again when something scratched on the door, and they both jolted upright. It turned into a soft knock, and it took a moment before they could process, then sigh, collectively.

She was teary, couldn't sleep, and didn't want to be alone. Could someone sleep with her? Certainly, once upon a time, Betty would have been the one to go, though to this day she couldn't remember when that time would have been. Or perhaps it had always been Jamie that went and soothed their mother. She left with her now, leaving Betty tossing and turning in bed, trying not to feel jealous.

When she woke up, Jamie was back, working, her breakfast a cup of coffee she'd snuck from the kitchen. Famished, Betty threw on her running clothes, washed her face, brushed her teeth, and went down to the kitchen. Her mother was already there with Diana and two gray haired ladies, sisters apparently, also seeking spiritual renewal. "This is my lovely daughter," her mother introduced Betty, who sat down so that Diana could serve her poached eggs on toast, which everyone else was eating. "I was thinking about going for a run this morning? Are there any good paths?"

"Dear," her mom frowned. "This isn't the place for that."

Blinking calmly back, "How about a walk?"

"I'm meeting with Father Patrick alone this morning. But you go on." And with that came silence. There was to be no talking during meals.

After breakfast Betty wandered around the grounds, no less lonely in the morning light. But at least she could feel the sun, the ocean, pushing through the mist. There were acres of beautiful forest, and not far down one of the paths Betty stumbled on an old adobe church. It was tiny, and she had to duck under the little arched door to get inside, where there were only three pews, and an altar that came up to her waist. Apparently it was built for a smaller people, a time when civilization took up less space. She spoke just to hear her voice, which sounded hollow against the cracked stucco and left her feeling immense, like she was inside one of the dollhouses her mother used to collect, disconnected and apart and not wanted. She wondered if that was how her mother had felt those times she'd boarded here as a child. She never spoke of it except to say how lonely she'd been. Betty wished she knew more about her mother's mother. Not her birthmother, the stranger her mother claimed to be searching for, but the woman who adopted her. It didn't seem right to wonder about her mother's birthmother.

Steven arrived just before the session with Father Patrick at ten, frantic and distracted and happy to see them. The goatee, Bermuda shorts, and Birkenstocks that Betty had found so incongruous years ago were now simply a part of him, engrained now in Betty's mind as the look of a man with money and nothing to do.

Father Patrick had arranged plastic chairs in a semicircle in the private garden underneath a weeping willow. Betty and Jamie wore sunglasses just in case the cloud cover broke. The Santa Ana was blowing in from the north, making little swirls of half dead leaves and leaving everything feeling parched and abandoned. Father Patrick began the session by telling them why their mother had asked them here. That she wanted to connect with them and her faith. He then nodded at her to go on. She stared down at the stack of index cards she held in her hands and took a deep breath. "Well, as you all know, this change in Gary's and my relationship has really awakened me. In the private letter I wrote each of you, I told you that I've joined Al Anon and begun my path down the Twelve Steps." She paused to hand out a card to each of them. Written on it in their mother's perfect cursive was the definition of each step.

"But you don't drink, Mom," Jamie jumped right in.

"Al Anon is a program for addicts dear. It can be any kind of addiction."

"But what are you addicted to, Mom?" Betty said.

"This program has given me a means of self-discovery," she went on, not hearing them. "A means of helping me understand my own addictive behaviors. That I am, in fact, powerless over my addictions."

"But what is this addiction again, Mom?" Betty needed to know. "I'm not quite clear on that."

Her mom cleared her throat. "I'm at Step 5, admitting the exact nature of my wrongs."

"What have you done wrong?" asked Jamie.

"Well," she said, fuddled because this was not on one of her cards. "I left your father and you kids the way I did."

Jamie waived a hand in the air. "That? Hell, I'm impressed that you stuck it out as long as you did."

Steven almost fell over.

Their mom looked confused. "Anyway," she went on, albeit flustered and reading from her note card. "I need to make amends to the people I've hurt, which is why I've asked you all here."

Jamie, "You haven't hurt us, Mom."

Betty, back on the addiction, "You're addicted to Gary?"

"I'm trying to control Gary, and who Gary is."

"So you admit Gary's an alcoholic."

"I never told you kids, but my parents were alcoholics."

Jamie, "You told us."

Mom sighed.

"You spent the evenings dancing on that Hollywood Hill near your house to escape them. You told us, Mom."

"Anyway. You know that Gary and I have been in counseling for a while now. A lot of things are coming out in our sessions." She paused here to look at each of them. "I'm really learning a lot, about myself and about my need to please people."

"But what about Gary?" Why Betty felt the need to push the Gary issue she wasn't sure. Maybe because nobody else was.

"Gary has been depressed for a long time, dear. That's what's causing the problems in our intimacy. Not his drinking. He has no drinking problem, dear." She glanced at Father Patrick for help, but he remained quiet and unobtrusive. "We're working towards Gary moving back into the house," their mom added.

No response.

"He's agreed to work at this."

"You've been saying that for years, Mom," nobody said.

Father Patrick asked Steven, "Is there anything you'd like to add?"

"I think my sisters are addressing the appropriate concerns."

Betty waited for him to go on, they all did. But his face remained closed and empty.

"Jamie?" Father Patrick addressed her with familiarity, but she was already shaking her head no. He turned to the group, "Then I think now is a good time…"

"I still don't think you're addressing the problem, Mom," Betty interrupted him. "It's like Gary's all good and you're all bad. To me it seems like you're still trying to fix it, to control it. To make us all like him." That sort of slipped out, but it didn't matter. Her mother was looking past her now.

"Why don't we just sit in silence for a while," Father Patrick said, noticing their mother sinking into her chair. He reached out with his hands, indicating it was time to hold them in silence.

Betty glared unconscionably at Steven. The brother she'd always looked up to now had his chin on his chest as if he were contemplating his growing belly. She had wanted him to say something thoughtful and smart, to reflect some ironic light on this dreary moment. He sat there looking almost serious, which Betty couldn't fathom, but then Betty didn't really know what was going on with Steven these days. He hadn't been to D.C. since Senator Gordon, his mentor and champion the past five years, was forced to rescind his candidacy for president due to that picture of the woman on his lap. They say he would have won. Steven hadn't really worked since, but he didn't need to, of course. The investments he'd made with that real estate firm he'd worked for before going to campaign for Gordon had paid off big. She really didn't know what he did other than flying around the country being inaccessible and making plans on where to fly next. But he was here, and he'd even showed up relatively on time, which should have been the first sign of something wrong.

"I'm about ready to slit my wrists," Jamie leaned in and whispered to Betty at some point. That got a chuckle out of Steven, which Betty found unnerving. Their mom laughed too, even though she hadn't heard what was said.

Finally and at last Father Patrick broke the silence in order to give them their assignment for the afternoon, which was to write down what feelings they wanted to express to their mother. Isn't that what I just did? Betty thought but didn't say. That evening their mother would reach out to them one-to-one. Someone groaned. Steven left to make some calls from his car phone. Betty found a cement bench under a tree and contemplated her wedding dress, this time the skirt balled, no train, and the veil was mesh and iolite. It was frightening how many times she could change her mind in a day. "Mom snores," Jamie said, sitting down next to her. "Loudly," she added, glancing at Betty's card over her shoulder. "What are you writing?"

"I don't know. You?"

Jamie looked at her own card. "Nothing. I have nothing."

"I just want her to confess that Gary's an alcoholic."

"Why do you feel the need to push her?"

"Isn't that why we're here?"

"You're just going to break her."

"So?"

"So who's gonna carry her out the door this time when you do?"

"I have the feeling she'd want that to be you."

Jamie ignored Betty, contemplating her own notecard: "Step 5: So God's going to remove our defects of character? Just because we admit what they are?" When she looked up Betty was already headed down a narrow, wooded path. "It's ridiculous," Jamie called after her, then got up and followed. The path curved around into a flat ravine, where they came upon that stable Betty had read about in the brochure. Three tired-looking mares stood tied to a wood railing. Neither of them had ridden since they were kids, and for Betty that meant the family excursions to Tijuana and a donkey. But before Betty had the chance to confer with her sister about whether this was a good idea, Jamie had hopped up on a pale yellow horse like an eight-year old equestrian, even though she'd never taken a riding lesson in her life. "Hey, Charmer," her sister cooed, stroking her mane.

Betty managed to clamber her way up onto the gray one, Sutter. The horse hand, a woman with a smoky voice and long straggly hair, tightened their stirrups. The horses could walk the trail in their sleep, she said. Betty and Jamie didn't need a guide as long as they knew how to ride. Of course they knew how to ride, Jamie assured her, and off they went, in a painfully slow, disappointing gait.

Sutter led the way through the brush, along a narrow dirt trail that dipped and sloped through spotted clusters of willow and pine and the odd cactus. They tracked single file along the dried remains of some riverbed. Palms peppered the hills in the distance. The horses seemed utterly bored. Every once in a while, Betty would dig in her heels and Sutter would trot and her butt would hurt. They reached an opening in the brush and caught their first glimpse of the ocean, and even their horses paused to snort in the gorgeous view and salt air.

"I've been wondering," Betty said. "If I died now, where would I be buried?"

Jamie's horse, Charmer, ignited into a trot, as if inspired by Betty's question. "I want my ashes spread in the ocean," Jamie called back.

Sutter stayed firmly in place and peed. "I can't be buried in D.C.," Betty yelled ahead to Jamie. "But then where? California? Next to the grandmother our mother has seemingly forgotten completely? That doesn't seem right either." She kicked Sutter, done peeing now, to get going. It took some time and a bunch of futile kicks before she finally did, albeit slowly. "Do you ever wonder about fate?" Betty asked when they caught up. "If we weren't meant for another life?"

"I believe in choices, not fate," Jamie responded, struggling to get Charmer to stay at a walk. "And by the way, I have some news." But just as she spoke, Charmer took off trotting again, taking the news with her.

Betty kicked Sutter to follow suit, she wanted to know the news, but apparently Sutter wanted no such thing. "What news?" Betty called after her anyway.

"I'm going to Berkeley," Jamie yelled back.

"You mean, Bay Area Berkeley?"

"You've got to give her a good kick, Betty!"

"I did!"

"Harder!"

"OK!" And with that Sutter lurched forward, if reluctantly.

"A job?" Betty wanted to know when she'd caught up again.

"School." Jamie ducked her head under a branch. "Their Graduate School of Engineering."

Betty ducked too. "I didn't even know you'd applied."

"I didn't think I'd get in."

"When do you go?"

"School starts in September."

Betty thought of more questions to ask. She and Jamie had been living together most of their lives, but they were going to have to part at some point. Apparently her sister already knew that. Betty wondered what she herself was waiting for, because she still couldn't say it: Dave proposed. No, the words wouldn't come to her lips, and then it didn't matter because Charmer started trotting again, determined to get somewhere apparently, as determined as Sutter was not. With difficulty Jamie got Charmer to slow down just enough so that Betty could hear her sister say: "But I'm sure you and Dave will be glad to get rid of me."

The words came like a slap in the face, and whatever congratulatory remarks Betty was going to say dried up. "It's only a matter of time until you meet someone too." It came out sounding petty, but nevertheless it felt good to say it.

"What does that have to do with anything?"

Betty leaned over and petted Sutter's mane.

"Well, soon you won't have to worry about it," Jamie retorted. "Soon I'll be gone for good." And with that, Jamie's horse took off again. This time Betty didn't even bother trying to catch up, and they'd reached the end of the ravine anyway. The trail sign said turn back. Betty yelled ahead at Jamie, wondering if she'd missed the sign. Then she turned Sutter around, swiftly and naturally, too naturally in fact, which is when it occurred to Betty that this is what the poor old beast had wanted all along—to go home. Betty could feel the animal's loins ready to burst forth with the anticipation of it. She pulled tight on the reigns, waiting for Jamie, who was struggling to get Charmer turned around. "She's not going for it," she yelled.

Betty felt Sutter grow skittish beneath her; then suddenly Charmer bucked and hurtled forward in that same, determined direction, taking Jamie with her. In a flash they were gone. Sutter shifted sideways, backwards and snorted loudly, then sprinted in the opposite direction, like a racehorse towards home. It took a moment for Betty to realize what was happening, and then she yanked back on the reigns with everything she had, which was like putting a hand up to stop a ten-ton truck. It was all she could do just to hang on, as she and Sutter blazed down the trail like lightning, a curdling scream coming from somewhere…her, when she saw a flash of herself slamming against a cactus and tumbling down the rocky slope when the trail narrowed up ahead. Just get it over with, she thought, starting to slip off. She didn't try to hang on; she hit the ground hard and fast and slid for a good ten feet in the dirt. Sutter never looked back.

A hawk circled above. A burning sensation ran the length of her side. She heard someone crying in the distance. When she realized she was still in one piece, that there were no broken bones, she let herself cry harder as the shock of what happened hit her. Then she wiped her face and pushed herself up. She had no idea where she was. She waited for Jamie and Charmer for a while, and then she started walking in the direction from where she came.

She'd walked a mile, she guessed. The sun was bearing down on her. No sign of civilization. She was thirsty. After a while she began wondering if she was walking in the right direction; perhaps the stable was the other way. She stopped and sat down on a rock to think, but all she heard were horses' hooves pounding the dirt—her head throbbing, she figured—until she realized that they actually were horses' hooves. In fact it was Sutter racing towards her, Betty's grandmother riding her with a stick. She brought her to a skidding stop, not her grandmother but the horse hand. "I thought you said you could ride," the woman said, pissed.

She rode Betty back to the stable, and then turned Sutter back around to go find Jamie and Charmer. It hadn't occurred to Betty that her sister wouldn't already be here waiting for her. It hadn't occurred to Betty that something could have happened to them. Her wounds began stinging in the painful reality of it. Dust, salt, and tears had dried on her face, her jeans were torn at the leg, and her elbow was bleeding. She glanced at her watch when a half hour went by. It hurt too much to sit.

Just as she began to panic, Sutter came trotting back with Jamie riding her (the horse hand rode Charmer), her face more amused than frightened, for apparently Charmer had commandeered Jamie a couple miles further to another stable across the park. The horse hand, still miffed, dismounted Charmer and mentioned that she had recently purchased the mare from that other stable. Charmer must have gotten confused when Jamie tried to turn her around at the ravine. The mare's instincts were to go home, to a home no longer her home, and Sutter must have gotten spooked. She had her own home to get back to.

That might have been information they should have known beforehand, Betty wanted to say. But she kept her mouth politely shut. She was too mortified from having fallen off Sutter, by being scolded like a third grader, by having Jamie see her like this.

They went back to the retreat center. Betty cleaned up what were ultimately small scrapes and made Jamie promise not to tell their mom or Steven what had happened. She didn't want to make a big deal about it. "Here are my girls," their mom announced to the group, as Betty and Jamie rushed in late for dinner. She was peering at them, envying their sisterly closeness and, as usual, missing the real battle going on between them and their flushed faces. On either side of Steven sat the two gray-haired sisters, and his expression said, thanks guys, where the hell were you? Diana was serving their mom's favorite: hamburger patties with A1 sauce, coleslaw, and potato chips. Their mom put a hand out to her friend. "Diana and I are kind of like sisters, aren't we Diana."

Diana said, "We are."

Then her mom put her other hand out for Betty. "And we sisters are so lucky to have each other."

And Betty said, "We are."

By seven the house lights were out, and they were back in their rooms waiting for their mother's soft knock. Jamie was back at work, and Betty was going nuts. Her leg was on fire. She read the mission statement again about deepening your spiritual life through quiet reflection and communal prayer. Well, she'd tried to reflect, she'd tried to contribute in a communal manner. "I'm getting Steven," she said, standing up, "and we're getting out."

Jamie smirked and kept working, but when Betty grabbed the keys, her jacket, her purse, and ripped open the door, Jamie didn't hesitate. "I thought you'd already seen it," Betty sneered. Jamie grabbed her sweater. "I'll see it again."

Their mom wasn't in her room. They went to Steven's down the hall and opened his door without knocking…and there she was, having a seriously one-sided conversation with her son. Steven leaped up from his chair at the sight of them, like he'd been waiting his whole life for them to show up instead of the other way around. He saw their jackets and purses, grabbed his wallet, and said, "I'm buying."

"But where are you going?" their mom cried.

"Out," Jamie said. "And you're coming with us."

"I don't think we're allowed to go out." Even to her it sounded silly. "Well, besides, you always go out…"

"We can make the seven o'clock showing if we hurry," Betty told Steven.

"We're supposed to be…" her voice faded off. Then she just looked scared.

"Look, Mom, whatever we're supposed to be doing/discussing, we can do it over a movie and drinks. Same damn thing, no?"

They were all looking at her, and she was about to appeal again, but something made her pause. Maybe it was the vision of herself as a kid, alone in her boarding school room, Jesus hanging over her head. "Okay," she agreed, standing up. "But we shouldn't stay out too late."

They all climbed into Steven's Mercedes, and he peeled out of the lot, spewing a cloud of dust and gravel that could not have gone unnoticed.

* * *

Wyoming, 1889, is where the movie started. The sun folded over the horizon while cowboy Bill and his motley crew made their way across the dusty, barren valley. They were going to avenge the mutilation of a whore. Bill, a legend throughout the valley, had once been a mean bastard of a cowboy himself, a man who killed women and children for no reason. But now, thanks to his wife who had changed him, he was just a poor old pig farmer with a kind heart and two kids. And though his wife had died of smallpox, Bill was going to stay true to his promise about no killing. Even now he was only on this crusade to help out an old friend. He still insisted he was a changed man.

Jamie nudged Steven, who was snoring.

Betty thought about change. Moving to D.C. had changed her, had given her a confidence she'd not had before. But she'd reached some sort of ceiling; she wanted another change, and she thought leaving

D.C. would be that change. It was a city of transients, after all, and she stifled a pang of jealously, because soon her sister would become one of those transients. She'd leave and Betty would stay, for Dave would be Betty's change now, maybe they'd help change each other.

Their mom passed Betty the popcorn, and Betty passed it to Steven, who passed it to Jamie, who didn't want any. The bag came back to their mom, exasperated because she didn't want to eat junk food. She munched away anyway, while on screen Bill started killing again, slowly and clumsily at first, then easily and precisely. By the time their mom had finished the bag, Bill had gunned down every last man in that saloon, finally giving into who he was—a killer. Even the sheriff couldn't change from the bad sheriff he was into the good sheriff he now wanted to be; he got what he deserved in the end. Something or someone can't make you change. Now Betty knew why Jamie had warned her about the movie: there wasn't much hope in it.

Their mom, anxious to get back, was up the minute the credits came on, while Jamie, Betty, and Steven stayed conferring about that Mexican dive on the corner…as if there was any question. Their mom, a hostage now, didn't have a choice, and they corralled her into a booth whose table was sticky from beer and kept her distracted from her surroundings: dark, musty, trickling with sodden locals. A waiter slapped down some chips and salsa, and Jamie ordered a pitcher of margaritas on the rocks, plus a strawberry daiquiri for their mother. "Light on the rum," she added, wiping the table down with the napkins she had Betty go snatch from somewhere.

When the drinks came, Betty put up her glass, because when it came down to it, she just wanted her sister to be happy. "To Jamie, for getting into Berkeley."

Jamie blinked at Betty tentatively, and then she put up her glass too, as did Steven and their mom.

"I assumed everybody knew but me," Betty added.

"It's a conspiracy," Steven said.

"Oh, that's good," their mom said after sipping her drink.

"Steven pulled some strings with my application," Jamie told Betty.

"The next time I need a city built, you owe me, Jamie," said Steven dryly.

They finished the first round and ordered another. Their mom wanted to pass, but Jamie told her that if she was going to be in AA she might as well drink. Mom cackled at that, but luckily the mariachis were having a go around the tables now and no one heard. The rum was making their mother relax, and the tequila was dimming Betty's memory of slamming against the dirt, and the whore's cut-up face as she watched Bill ride off without her. When the second round came, their mother raised her glass. "To forgiving," she said. "I hope one day my children will forgive me."

"Oh, for God's sake, Mom," Jamie brought her glass back down. "We can't forgive you for who you are."

Actually, I could, Betty didn't say in the dead silent aftermath.

"What I mean is, there's nothing to forgive, Mom."

Oh but there is so much to forgive. So much I will never forgive.

"To the *Unforgiven* then," Steven said, and Betty caught in Jamie's eyes that touch of hatred she harbored for Betty there. It was always there, and Betty wondered if her sister would ever be able to forgive Betty for all that she'd done wrong, for what she was about to do wrong, in her sister's eyes because Betty did believe in people, like Dave, that they could change, she lived in the hope of that, it's who she was. She and Dave were going to grow and change together. And before Betty could think, she pulled out the ring from her purse and slipped it on. "I have an announcement to make," she said. "Dave and I are engaged."

There it was.

A loud silence pounded between her ears even though they were all saying stuff to her. Betty's mind must have been on delay or something…it took her a minute to catch up with their reactions, especially because they weren't reacting at all how she'd expected. Jamie, for instance, grabbed Betty's ring hand and screamed with delight, which queued her mother to scream, both of them now screaming together. Steven gave her a big hug, then exhaled back in his chair and mumbled something about the pressure being off him and Kate. Jamie ran to the bar and ordered a bottle of champagne from the bartender, who remarked snidely about having to check the "cellar." It was as if they were genuinely happy for her (except the bartender), and Betty was stunned. But why was Jamie reacting like this? She seemed to despise Dave so. Perhaps Betty had read her wrong, or perhaps Jamie knew that Betty would need her support now more than ever. Or maybe it didn't matter and maybe Jamie knew that too, and Betty's eyes filled with tears reflecting their warmth and love and the knowledge that, above all the crap, they would always have this. This was what counted. That indefinable this.

When the DJ began playing "Celebrate," Jamie and Betty got up to dance, like they'd done a million times before in their living room or dorm room or the room they shared as kids, whether they loved each other or hated each other or just wanted to pass the time. No one else was dancing but they didn't care. They dragged their mom out of her chair, and then Steven, who brought his drink and rolled his eyes. They danced around in a circled haze, their mother fast-dancing as if an invisible man were leading her in some kind of frantic two-step around the floor. They quickly corralled her in the center of their dancing cir-cle. She looked so unscripted, so unconfined by the rules, so free and happy that they just let her stay there, in the middle of them all.

CHAPTER 8

VERTIGO

October, 2003

Their departure date came and went. Giorgio's fatigue and irrationality manifested in headaches and shortness of breath and the need for Roberto to stay on to run the restaurant until his father was better. But he hadn't gotten better, and this week he was in Bangkok so that his doctor could do a workup of tests.

"I didn't know you could do that." Roberto had just returned from the complex's tiny afterthought of a gym, drenched in sweat. He stood at the bedroom doorway, guzzling a bottle of water, watching her. Two years ago she would have been embarrassed for him to see her like this, to know that her life could sustain itself on yoga and reading and long walks by the shore. But he didn't laugh when he found her now standing on her head. He just looked into her eyes, upside down.

She lowered her legs to the floor, resting in child's pose. Sweat poured off her body. Her heart settled, she sat up, and wiped her face with the towel he held out for her. They passed the bottle of water back and forth.

"I'm starving," she gasped, after polishing off the last drop.

"I know." He started undressing. "Come on, let's take a shower. Then I'll make lunch." His eyes got that gleam simply thinking of lunch. He'd

gone early that morning to the outdoor market and come back with two pounds of half-moving squid, Thai chili peppers, cilantro, limes, and lemongrass. "You're going to die when you eat the squid," he said, getting into the shower.

She stripped off her wet yoga clothes and stepped in after him, waiting for her turn at the dribbling spout. And then, of course, they got sidetracked, shut the bedroom door, and pushed the two beds back together to make love. And with Giorgio in Bangkok, they no longer had to worry about holding in whatever it was that wanted to reveal itself in the depth of their desire. Roberto always made sure to please her, and today they'd been rather aggressive with their freedom. When they were done they laughed because they would have to take another shower. She got up to go to the bathroom.

"Jamie, what's that?"

She looked at him, then at her feet, where there was a trail of blood from the bed to where she stood. "Oh God," she sort of laughed and ran to the toilet. She sat with a wad of toilet paper in her hand in full view of his pale worried face. He looked like he was frozen in the middle of a crime scene, blood on his penis and on the sheets. "It's my period," she said. She hadn't had a real period in almost a decade. The only blood he'd seen come out of her was from some spotting she had every so often, which had grown more substantial in the past months. It was erratic since she'd gone off her hormones. "I must have gotten a small version of one."

"That's a lot of blood, Jamie."

"I know...calm down. I went off my Prempro, and so, I think, naturally the spotting will get a bit stronger."

"You went off your Prempro?" He was referring to the tiny pink pill she'd been consuming every day for the past decade to compensate for the effects of her premature menopause. The ones she let him think for so long were birth control pills. "Why?"

"I don't know." She pictured herself the moment the inspiration came to her, here in this bathroom, staring into the mirror, her face flushed and *glowing, her hair a tangled mess. She had simply thrown the plastic round pill case into the trash and then gone to the patio and let Roberto feed her mango.*

"I feel fine, I feel great in fact." In one month not one hot flash, no errant hair on her upper lip, and her juices flowed as naturally during sex as she could ever remember. But this…she looked down into the toilet. She hadn't expected feeling twelve again. "I think I need a tampon."

"Do you want me to go to the store?" He came and rinsed himself at the sink.

She arranged a stack of toilet paper into her underwear. "I'm fine. We can go later."

"Hold on." On a sudden thought, he ran out of the room, and returned a minute later with a box of Maxi Pads.

She stared at the box. "Where'd you get that?"

"Under my father's bathroom sink, hidden in back. I stumbled upon them a long time ago."

She raised an eyebrow at him. "Perhaps he's not so depressed."

"I think they're from the dark ages."

She took a pad and arranged it onto her underwear.

"Are you sure you should be doing this?" He was looking away. "Going off your hormones?"

"I don't know," she sighed, a decade worth of them. "I just want to know what it feels like to be me."

After she finally convinced him she was fine, they got dressed and went to the kitchen, where he spent a while at the sink cleaning the squid. The space was tiny and stifling, so she took her wine glass outside to the "Coffee Shop," where she could talk to him through the open kitchen window that faced the shore behind her. The breeze felt nice here, like her body was breathing, not her lungs. After the squid was clean, he sliced the garlic and lemongrass and chilies, and then fried it all in olive oil and lime, flipping the mixture up in the air a few times. He transferred the squid to plates, which they took with their wine out onto the back terrace overlooking the sea.

The day was gray and hazy, which they preferred. A balmy breeze tossed the tall palms and blew his napkin away. He watched her intently as she took her first bite. Of course the squid was lovely, she said. And the view and this wine and being with him, and watching him cook with such ease and quiet. It all had a sublime effect on her, and after that they barely spoke, devouring the squid and the wine and enjoying the time alone. When they were finished, they sat back and he smoked a Toscano, and he asked her if she was happy here.

She smiled lazily at him. She really didn't know. "Of course I'm happy here."

He examined her for a moment. "I want you to be happy here like I'm happy here."

She rose and took her glass to the ledge and stared down at the pool shimmering in the wind by the sea. She didn't tell him that that was not possible, only because she was not him.

Later that afternoon they got the awaited call from Giorgio. Roberto spoke in Italian, his face stony and unreadable. After he hung up, she stared at him, waiting. "What is it?" she finally demanded.

"Emphysema."

Her faced opened with shock.

"The doctor did a CAT scan."

She didn't know what to say.

"He's going to Italy."

Now she was confused.

"The treatment is dry air. He doesn't want to go of course. I assured him it was only temporary. He's leaving on the next plane."

"It's all those cigars," she mumbled finally.

"He smoked a pack of cigarettes a day when I was a kid…but then so did my grandmother, and she lived until she was ninety."

"How did he sound?"

"How do you think he sounded?" It came out harsher than he'd intended.

"How long will he be gone?"

"Don't tell me you're going to miss him."

In fact, she was. "Are you OK?"

"He said Rimini is too humid. He's going to the house in Ferrara." He shook his head. "He hates the house in Ferrara."

His face looked paler and his hands shook slightly, and Jamie knew that the hatred Roberto was talking about wasn't so much Giorgio's as it was his own, for Ferrara, for Giorgio's estranged wife, for his half siblings and their children, for that part of his father's life from which he'd been excluded. For Roberto had never been to Ferrara, though he went with Giorgio to Italy every summer, his father would drop him off in Rimini with his sister, the woman Jamie met that one time, the woman Roberto referred to as Zia.

"You said he has no choice but to go."

"I know."

"What are you going to do about the restaurant?"

"He needs to have something to come back to."

"What if he doesn't come back, Roberto?" she said, and then, more delicately, "I mean, maybe it's time he went home."

He looked up at her ever so slowly, from so far a distance. When he did at last speak his words were steely and even. "Italy will suffocate him."

Jamie didn't think so. She thought that perhaps Giorgio had been wanting to go back all along; that perhaps, nearer the end of one's life, guilt takes over. And Giorgio was too afraid to tell his son this directly, yet it was there, hidden beneath those words, "The past is always better than the present." She'd read in one of his books recently that a man spends his entire life trying to find his way back into the house in which he was raised. Perhaps that's what Giorgio was doing now.

But if Giorgio wasn't coming back, it meant that she and Roberto were really staying. There was no choice for either of them now, and she went to the balcony railing and looked down into the sea. She pictured Giorgio in Ferrara, sitting on a veranda in the house in which he was born, in which his children were born, the house from which he'd fled long ago, looking out at the fig and olive trees and feigning that grim face because his wife wouldn't leave him be and his grandchildren were crawling all over him. But she knew he was secretly happy, because somewhere in the world of his dreams, his son was living on in his stead. His beloved son, the only person who knew him for who he was and would always be. She turned back to this person now, who was relighting that stick of death, as if to honor his father, as if to say, fuck everybody else, I'm doing what I want. I'm doing what feels right, inside, to me.

"I'll help you with the restaurant," she said.

He opened his mouth and let the smoke fall out. "You don't have to."

"I do."

He looked at her.

"And you need me."

She was all he needed. He'd told her this more than once, but she'd never believed him. He was someone who didn't need anybody, she'd thought. Though now, in his eyes, she could see that she'd been wrong.

The reality sent a shudder through her. She looked back over the railing for Giorgio, but his vision had morphed into Roberto in old age. To which house would he eventually return? And would he face that alone, without her? Who would care for him? She turned back around, struck by some foreboding. Certainly she would die before him. She wasn't sure why this idea struck her with such urgency now—it's not like she ever thought the cancer would come back. Perhaps it was the flow of blood, the hormones, or the lack of them, but all this contemplation was making her woozy, out of body. She turned back to the ledge and stared down into whatever it was, a sense, just steps away, that she'd been through all this before. Vertigo, that's what it felt like. She closed her eyes in the warm breeze and let the familiarity rush through her core. It was something she did often after the cancer, stand near a ledge and feel the wave of what could only be death, if one could feel death. Only this time she had to step back quickly because it didn't feel like death at all. It felt like giving herself to someone. In fact, it felt like life.

** 1994 **

Jamie peered out her tall window through the dense morning fog. A piece of suspended metal poked out from the mist, but there was no sign of the bay. So then perhaps it wasn't there she told herself, looking down at the pregnancy meter she'd been holding. "This is really stupid," she said to Betty who'd been waiting with her on the phone.

"I can't believe it's been two months since your period and you're just doing this now."

It had been more than two months, but Jamie didn't tell her sister that. She pulled at her turtleneck, burning up. "Did you have hot flashes?"

"Who the hell is this guy anyway?" her sister wanted to know again, and again Jamie couldn't respond. She didn't have an answer. She'd been mentioning him to Betty, albeit carefully, over the phone in recent weeks. She hadn't explained the depth of their relationship because she didn't entirely know herself. She certainly hadn't told Betty that she was in love. Saying it out loud made it real, and Jamie had had painful experiences with real. She looked back out the window at the bridge, which had disappeared. "You know I'm leaving for Russia next month."

"Well, maybe you're not!"

A foghorn blared in her imagination. A ship had lost its way. "I'd get an abortion."

"Oh, Jamie, don't say that."

"What's wrong with saying that?"

This time Betty didn't answer, and they waited the final two minutes in silence with Sam, Betty's newborn, gurgling and suckling in the background. When at last a dark pink plus sign came through, Jamie told Betty, "Negative. Blue."

There was a long silence in which Jamie could sense her sister's disappointment. She listened to her swing Sam from her breast over her shoulder and sooth him there. One would never know Sam was Betty's first child given the confidence and ease in which her sister's maternal experiences unfolded. "I guess you're just lovesick," her sister finally resigned, patting Sam on the back. There was a tiny burp, they hung up, and another hot flash struck Jamie. It ignited in her core and spread quickly to her externals. She threw down the phone and climbed out the living room window onto the thin balcony, constructed for decoration more than use. It's where she often found herself these days, perched here on the top of Nob Hill taking relief in the cold, wet, and whipping wind, sliding her gaze up and down the pastel Victorian slopes until they fell off into the bay, and by then, like clockwork, the heat flaming inside her would be gone, almost as quickly as it had come. As it had now, and she crawled back inside, threw on her raincoat, grabbed her briefcase, and sprinted to the bus stop at Clay Street.

It was drizzling, and she'd forgotten her umbrella. Distracted with what this might mean for her hair, she didn't see him at first. They always arrived at the same time, two minutes before the 8:05, and today would be no different, his tall, graceful frame growing out of the mist.

"*Fa freddo*," he said, stepping up and covering her with his umbrella.

She blinked up at him.

"It's cold," he translated, touching her cheek.

It always took a moment for her to adjust to his presence. But today she couldn't let it consume her, for she needed to tell him about Russia. One year. She had planned on telling him tonight.

Though would she, should she, be telling him something else?

It began to rain harder. Three minutes late, the rush hour bus lurched to a stop, burped and sighed. The door swung open. They squeezed in and grabbed the high handles just in time to keep themselves righted as the bus began its free-fall into the financial district.

Their sides collided, their eyes spoke: tonight they'd meet at the wine bar, and she'd tell him about Russia—Ukraine, actually—about being sent over with a team to dismantle missile silos from the Cold War. He'd be impressed, certainly; he'd like the James Bondness of it, plus she'd already told him that travel was what she'd always wanted. New experiences, her career, everything she'd worked so hard for… He brushed her cheek with his hand as the bus stopped at Bush, and she looked down at the umbrella he'd slid into her hand, thinking, he should be happy for her, right? When she looked up he was gone. Two stops later she was gone too.

* * *

A cricket match was in progress on the television behind the bar, softly lit, and draped in dark velvet. Jamie loved coming here with him, of another time, with all its foreign wines and dark, malty beers; it reminded her of all the places she'd never been. "Cricket world champs," he was saying, switching to an Australian accent, as he could do with any accent. In this case he was referring to Melbourne, where he'd spent a period of his youth, and she imagined this place now, with its deep blue sea on which they might sail someday. "You couldn't pay me to go back there."

Her image snapped shut. "Why not?"

"It's an isolated, racist country, and that's all you need to know." Then he switched the topic back to cricket. Half his peers at CS Partners were Indian, and some of them had gone to Dubai for the World Cup.

She made the mistake of comparing cricket to baseball.

He insisted that cricket was vastly superior to baseball and then began to explain why. Like the fact that there are no field positions, like first base or left field or shortstop. The coach strategically places his players on the field based on the batsman and bowlers.

"You mean pitchers."

"I mean bowlers," and he enjoyed her muddled expression.

They watched the match for a while, drinking from glasses of Barbera, he continuing his attempts to explain the game she was not getting. But she kept trying to…she was ready to try all night.

The waiter delivered a cheese plate.

Roberto held out a piece for her, not to taste, to smell.

"Feet?" she said, after deliberating a moment.

His eyes were like chocolate in the soft orange light, and in them she could see she'd gotten it right. He looked proud, not of her getting it right, but because the cheese smelled like feet and it was Italian. His father was Italian, the little she knew, and that his mother had died hours after he was born. He fed the cheese to her. She glanced back at the TV if only to collect herself from the intensity of his gaze, but the teams had taken a tea break, he informed her. She thought he might be insane. No. A tea break wasn't insane; this was simply India, a part of the world to which she'd not been exposed…and he might love her. She lost the sense of herself in that look, in all those places she would someday go, and smiled back at him. His hair was silky and brown, like the Andaman, his skin golden, like the Mediterranean. She would not have believed he was part Thai had he not told her. By the time they finished their wine and stepped out onto the streets still wet with rain, she realized she'd forgotten to tell him anything.

They walked arm-in-arm to the bus stop at the intersection of Montgomery and Sacramento. It was clumsy to walk in this way, especially given all the work she had lugged home in her bag, the Russian language book, tips on local etiquette and customs…and yet it felt unnatural not to walk in this way. Only when the bus didn't come and they began scaling the hill on foot did they separate and resort to holding hands. When their thighs started burning they took turns pushing each other up. Then they tried walking backwards. At the corner of Mason, the street leveled off in repose, and they sat on a low wall to catch their breath. Across from them was the peach sandstone mansion that appeared in the movie he'd made her watch. They waited, imagined. But no seductive, gray-suited blond came or went.

Roberto had minored in film at Stanford, and when she mentioned that the only Hitchcock movie she'd seen was *The Birds* he didn't hide his alarm. *Vertigo* became their first date. That was four months ago when they were still just strangers riding the same bus, the same bus that appeared now out of nowhere. They waved and it pulled over, unexpectedly, perhaps the driver was bored, for it was empty inside, and obnoxiously bright. They made their way to the back and fell into seats just as it lurched into motion, preparing for that impossible climb. Roberto turned around to watch the mansion fade into the mist. Jamie unbuttoned her coat, leaned over him, and cracked open the window.

"You OK?" He eyed her sweaty brow and fanned her with his coat. Cool air swept her neck and blew her hair back, and she closed her eyes.

"Better?"

She nodded.

"You didn't eat anything. Maybe you're hungry."

"Maybe," she said, feeling full.

He studied her a moment, then announced in one of his Italian outbursts that he was going to make her pasta *aglio e olio*! As if that were the answer to everything. "You a gotta eata the pasta." He shook pinched fingers before his chin.

The bus dropped them at Hyde, and they walked the four blocks to her Victorian apartment building. At Jackson, the cable car came at them from the opposite direction, the conductor clanging so wildly on the bell that she dropped her things. Roberto bent down to help her, staring skeptically at the book, *Russian for Business*. She pulled it from his hands, mumbled something about working with Russians on an assignment, and stuffed it back in her bag. Curdling screams made them spin around just in time to catch the tourist-laden cable car turn sharply down Washington, as if it had just driven off the side of a cliff.

Inside Jamie's first floor flat, she changed into jeans and a t-shirt before joining him in the kitchen, where she immediately became useless. She never knew what to do, so she poured herself some wine and took a seat on the stool and watched. He set a pot of water on the stove to boil, chopped garlic and hot peppers, and began frying them in olive oil, a wooden spoon in his hand, a dish-towel tucked in the pocket of his jeans. He never commented on the Top Ramen lining her cupboards. One day he simply brought over sharp knives, a string of garlic bulbs, and a curiously large bag of colorful peppers, Thai chilies, he informed her, from one of his recent trips. Sometimes they talked as he cooked, but tonight she just stared at his focused profile and wondered what he would say if she told him she was pregnant. Her head told her he'd support her decision to have an abortion; her heart told her he wouldn't. But then she'd never gotten his thoughts right. In fact he often acted in ways that completely surprised her. He cursed in Italian, for instance, cooked in Thai, read novels in French. He pretended to disdain America, yet studied American history obsessively. He had a collection of the teeniest tiniest little Buddha statues and a rosary, but assured her he was not religious. He had an accent ready for every language, and he could spot a nationality at the drop of a hat. He knew things and had been places she didn't even know existed.

His skin was sensuous and soft, his lashes dark and full, like his hair, that silky luscious brown; yet his features seemed chiseled out of some rare Roman stone. She began imagining what their baby might look like, the languages he or she would speak, the places he or she might grow up in, and without really thinking she blurted out the question, "Where's your home?"

He was shaking the garlic around in the pan over the fire, and for a moment she wondered if he'd heard her. "I mean if you had to have one, of all the places you've lived."

He still didn't speak.

"Your father's Italian, you were born in Thailand, you spent summers in Italy, but went to Jesuit school in Malaysia…"

"Australia."

"Right."

"I went to middle school in Malaysia."

"Anyway. You know what I mean. Which place feels to you like home?"

"I will never have a home!" He banged down the pan, and she jolted backwards, almost falling off the stool. The force of his words, the desperation in his voice, startled her senseless, and seeing her alarm he softened his tone, though what he said next came out just as even and definitive. "I need to know that I can leave whenever I want." It was just that simple, his expression said, and then he checked on the pasta.

She picked up her glass, took a sip and said, in a barely audible tone, "Me too."

The pasta was done. He drained the spaghetti, mixed it in the frying pan with the olive oil, garlic and chili pepper, and then transferred it into a bowl on the kitchen table in front of her. She got out some forks and napkins and sliced some bread. He served them both. It was a simple dish, he shrugged, intently watching her taste it. We made it at home all the time he went on to say, and something stung the back of her eyes…So he did have a home. The sting became a burn, and she fanned at her open mouth, which was on fire. The dish was spicy as all hell…and not simple at all.

* * *

Jamie didn't have a regular OB/GYN, having stopped seeing doctors when her treatments ended six years ago. She'd go in for the disturbing colonoscopy every other year, but was always clean. Other than that she would ride out a bad flu, suffer through a bladder infection, and use the Today Sponge for birth control. She couldn't deal with the doctor's skeptical look upon sight of the checked *cancer* box on her medical history form. Only when they came upon her scar during the exam was she taken seriously…as if she would lie about something like that. Then proceeded the inquisition in which she would be required to recount all the horrid details of an illness that to her was ancient history, especially when the purpose of her visit was related to something else.

The gynecologist was in Marin. Friday morning, borrowing Roberto's Fiat for what she told him was a routine physical check-up, Jamie set off across the Golden Gate Bridge fraught with Friday morning traffic. As she inched along the orange suspension in a blinding fog, she reassured herself that the pregnancy test was wrong. But when she reached the other side, and the sky was all at once clear and blue, as if a whole other world had opened up, she felt deep in her heart for one spectacularly hopeful moment that the test was right.

Warmth lingered on her sweater, as if to nurture that thought as she entered the clinic lobby, what was also nurturing a variety of waiting women in various stages of maternity. Even the receptionist was pregnant, with a fresh daisy tucked behind her ear. She smiled genuinely and passed Jamie the clipboard. With the scalding Pete's coffee she'd brought for protection, Jamie sat in her vinyl chair and flew through the questions, drawing a straight line through the 'no' column until she got to that dreaded box, and she brought the cup to her nose. Part of her always wanted to mark "no" here too. It felt wrong to mark "yes" when she was perfectly healthy now. Anyway, she handed in the clipboard, then sat flipping through a *Mommy and Me* magazine wondering: *Is this me?*

A nurse measured her weight, one-twenty, height, five-eight, and blood pressure 120/80. As instructed Jamie used the adjoining bathroom to pee into a cup. She removed her clothes and organized the paper gown onto her body. Then she sat on the examination table between the cold stirrups poking out from either side of her, staring at the collage of baby pictures on the wall directly in front of her. Again she tried to imagine the child she and Roberto might have, a redheaded Californian her, a brown-haired Cosmopolite him, then a freckled freak with a cleft chin, which is when the doctor stepped in.

Alarmingly tall with thick silvery hair, he looked like he'd just stepped off his yacht. Am I in the right place, said his fleeting eyes. The nurse handed him Jamie's chart, which he studied. Jamie sat motionless, eight years back and waiting for the inevitable pause followed by the inevitable interrogation. When it came she gave him her seasoned responses, unflinchingly, like they were discussing the weather. Yes colon cancer was an unusual disease in a woman so young. Yes she was lucky or unlucky depending on how you looked at it. But thankfully this particular doctor didn't belabor the subject. He just took a cotton swab of her cervix for the Pap smear she hadn't had in five years and felt around her belly and breasts. She told him about her nausea and hot flashes. Severe? If putting her head in the freezer defined severe, then yes. Then the nurse took her blood. He'd call her in a couple days with the results. When she asked him if she was pregnant, he said, like he hadn't just said it, that he'd call her in a couple days with the results.

She didn't feel like going back to work, so she wound Roberto's car around the cliffs of Highway One, trying to shake off the desperate urge to call Betty. Her sister wouldn't listen to Jamie's logic.

She wouldn't accept an abortion, the same abortion that Jamie was beginning to wonder about herself.

And suddenly everything was foggy again, so foggy that she didn't see the congestion ahead of her until she was upon it and had to slam on the brakes. Crawling by the exit for Muir Woods, an image from *Vertigo* struck her and she veered the car in that direction. She parked in the visitors' lot and stepped out into the misty cold unaware that she was cradling her chest, that she wore no coat. She walked numbly, hypnotically towards the tall groaning beasts, until she came upon one, fallen, and paused. On its side the redwood was twice her height, and she stared at it for a time. It didn't seem of this earth.

And maybe it wasn't.

On the trail now, she passed tourists in small clusters gaping up. At what, one might wonder, for the trees simply disappeared into grayness. She noted how crowded the place was, and very unlike the scene from the movie, when Scottie and Madeleine wandered around in the pockets of mist, isolated and alone and falling in love with the people neither of them was. She stood before the oldest living redwood for a while, she and a hundred other people; it's roots rising over their heads and disappearing into the clouds. For what she was waiting she didn't know…for something to move maybe. Wind howled off the bay and not even the leaves would rustle. She finally gave up, fought the wind back to her car, and wondered if she was going nuts. How could she let this man come between her and her career? She'd never wanted a baby before.

She drove back down Highway One to the overlook at Muir Beach, where she could stand on the low cliff and watch the sea crash on the rocks that reminded her of home. She spotted a tree on a plateau of lush grass nearby. It was under a tree like this that Scottie vowed to Madeleine to find the key to the spells that tormented her, the ones in which she believed she was another woman, a woman long dead of suicide, a woman named Carlotta. "I'm afraid," Madeleine told him, in his arms, begging him to stay with her, and into her ear he whispered, "All the time."

The doctor called Jamie at work the following Monday. "Your blood work shows a hormone deficiency," he said, not hesitating. "Well, in fact, no hormone activity at all."

There was a pause before she frowned, and tried to think of the right question.

"It could be a result of your chemo treatment." Papers shuffled. "Here on your chart it says that they moved the ovaries during your surgery as a precaution for radiation treatment," he went on. "But for some reason your ovaries are not releasing eggs, and so you're estrogen deficient."

More silence as she attempted to digest what he was saying.

"So I'm not pregnant," she said finally.

He cleared his throat. "You're experiencing symptoms of menopause."

A joke, that's what she wanted to say, something sarcastic, but no words came.

"There's no reason you need to suffer with the hot flashes. There are options."

A life sentence.

"Like hormone therapy."

She wrapped the phone chord around her wrist. "So I can't get pregnant."

He refused, it seemed, to answer.

"You mean, like never?"

She heard his frustration. "There are other ways to conceive," he said quickly, awkwardly. "When you're ready, if you're ready, we can talk about that."

"Right," she said after a moment of processing, when it became clear he didn't want to talk about anything of the sort. But then neither did Jamie. In fact alternative means of conception was the last thing she had ever expected herself to be concerned about, a child had never been on her list of priorities, and why should that change now?

"Have your pharmacy call us for a prescription of Prempro."

There was a pause.

"Hormone replacements." Then he answered a few questions she couldn't ask, mostly about side affects, which he said were limited. Risks of breast and uterine cancer didn't sound so limited. "OK," she said anyway and hung up. What else was she going to say?

"He's wrong, Jamie!" Betty blurted out into the phone. "That doctor doesn't know what he's talking about." Jamie could hear Sam cackling in the background like he thought this was all such a gas. He was a happy baby. In fact Jamie couldn't remember if she'd ever even heard him cry, and over the din of his elation, Betty was well onto her second supporting example, a woman she knew who had lymphoma, whose doctor told her she couldn't reproduce, and here she now was, mother of two.

Jamie didn't feel like arguing. She sat perched on the back of her living room couch gazing out at the piddling rain. The water accumulating on her roof and dripping onto her balcony railing should have bothered her. Tin, tin, tin. "I don't want children anyway."

"But you said yourself you felt something."

"Well, I was wrong." She went to the TV and picked up the video lying on top of it. They'd watched it again last night. It wasn't the same tree. She read the back cover while her sister rambled on. What Scottie didn't know was that Madeleine, the troubled woman he'd fallen in love with, wasn't, in fact, Madeleine, but somebody else pretending to be Madeline. "Have you seen *Vertigo?*" Jamie said idly, changing the subject.

"The movie," she added when her sister didn't respond.

There was a sigh.

"It's classic Hitchcock, Betty," Jamie said in a preaching voice, reading the tag line off the back cover. "You've never heard of him?"

"I've heard of him," Betty said defensively.

"Well, you should see the movie."

"What's it about?"

"A woman who pretends to be someone else, twice really, to please the man she loves."

"Sounds like Mom," Betty said in that voice Jamie hated. And now she regretted having picked up the phone in the first place. She had known it was Betty all along, she could tell by the way it rang. "I've gotta go…"

"What are you going to tell Roberto? Because you don't even know for sure…"

"Do you want a signed affidavit from my doctor?"

"Why do you always have to be so dramatic, so finite? Like this is it?"

"Because this is it."

"It's like you want him to leave."

Jamie hung up on her mid-sentence, afraid of her own seething words, which at their worst could be ruthlessly cutting. Why had she ever listened to her sister in the first place? Let her fill her head with all this maternal instinct stuff when it wasn't in her heart. When what she really had was no instinct at all. She'd had the hot flashes occasionally since her treatments ended, but in the past six months they'd grown steady, and her period had been spotty at best. So if she'd had any instinct at all, she would have sensed this coming.

The rest of the week was miserable. The rain wouldn't let up, and Betty didn't call her, and Jamie didn't call Betty. But worst of all she knew she had to tell Roberto something, if not everything. Luckily he'd been out of the town on business, and didn't show up at her place until Saturday morning after his soccer game in the Marina. Cold and muddy, he came over to the couch, bent down and kissed her. "I missed you," he said, pausing to take in her scent before heading for the shower, turning when she didn't naturally follow.

"I already took one," she said.

After he'd cleaned up, he came back and began managing the difficult process of reading his pink Italian sports paper while rubbing her head which rested on his lap. "Let's go see it," she said, speaking for the first time in twenty minutes.

He kept reading, intently.

"The church bell tower from *Vertigo*."

He turned the page.

"I want to go to the top."

He looked at her over his paper. "What, so you can jump off?" He was kidding. She was not. "It would be a nice drive." She stood up. "We could have lunch in Saratoga." She tried to suppress the sudden urgency. "What else are we going to do today in this miserable weather?"

"Cuddle," he said simply, and she dropped her shoulders and settled back into her spot. He resumed rubbing her head and absorbing his paper, and she didn't mean for it to happen, but a tear trickled from her eye and hit his bare leg. He brushed it with his finger and stared at it for long, confused moment. Then he fixed his gaze intently on her, and she looked away. "Maybe I just need to get outside."

They took the 101 south. The roads were wet but traffic was light. For a while they followed the windsurfers skirting along the bay, until the bay evaporated into cloud, literally, they could feel its dark heavy weight above them now, hitting Mountain View, a monotonous series of low-rise office spaces. RAPID had its headquarters there, and Roberto was still getting used to the fact that this would soon be his commute, that their companies had just merged. A spark ignited in him as they passed the big bold sign, and he went on about how their new joint pitch would redefine technology in the new world. They were already talking about an IPO.

The horizon turned brown and green and bland, and she wondered if that new world included places like Russia. For the first time, Jamie tried to imagine what the country she'd be spending a year in would be like. She hadn't really cared before. It was a place far away and different, and that's all she had ever needed to know. Now she pictured a land cold and gray, a land of nerve agents, sulfur mustards, and chlorine hazards, those listed in the waiver she'd signed, a land no different than here or anywhere. The work would be grueling, but she'd never had a problem with grueling if that's what it took to reach her goals, goals she couldn't remember suddenly.

An hour later, that same dense cloud tracking them, they exited the highway and ascended a narrow winding road. At the end of a sleepy town, before a view of Santa Clara Valley, stood a small, reconstructed mission: a grassy square framed by low adobe buildings, the church and monastery in a far corner, the saloon, livery stable, and jail in another. What struck her, when she got out of the car, was the silence. There didn't seem to be anyone else around but them. And perhaps some ghosts. They wandered around under cracked archways whose ceilings were made of old wood beams and from which cast iron candelabras hung perilously. A decrepit sign on the wall read, "Building not reinforced for earthquakes." They fled the archway and stumbled inside the church, which was a chaotic display of color and slanted, fuzzy light streaming through stained glass high windows. Outside again, they found themselves in a beautiful, secret-feeling garden, where they sat on a bench even though they weren't tired and pretended not to notice the clouds swirling and swaying overhead. They went to the tiny gift shop, where Roberto spent a half hour perusing the prints and photos depicting the lives of the Mutsun Indians that once lived here. He bought a book about the history of California missions, seemingly happy to have come, and it made her wonder why he had resisted at first.

The bell tower stood at the end of the monastery next to an old cemetery that was overcrowded with wood crosses tilting in all directions. The tower was much smaller than the one in the movie, they agreed, after some examination. Not high enough to die from a fall, Jamie noted, and based on the positioning of the tower next to the roof, Madeline would have landed on the dirt, not the red tiles. And with that thought, came thunder. It slapped hard, and the rain that had been hovering above them all day at last poured down.

Jamie sprinted to the tower door. It was made of old wood and adorned with a life-sized carving of Jesus on the cross…and locked with a massive chain. She tried to open it anyway, and then stood staring at it while the rain came down harder, as if that were possible. "What are you doing!" Roberto called out to her, having taken cover under a nearby archway. Jamie stepped back from the door and looked up at the bells, three of them she counted through the sheets of rain, not one like in the movie. And there didn't seem to be internal stairs or any means for someone to get up to the top as Madeline had done. There was something wrong, something about those bells, as if they never rang at all.

Come on! He was getting pissed now.

She envisioned that massive redwood from the other day and wondered about all the people that tree had known before her. She thought of the Mutsun Indians Roberto had been so intrigued by, the four thousand of them crammed into that earth over there. Roberto would have appreciated all those layers in that million-year old tree. He seemed obsessed about the origins of people and places, probably because his own origins were so vast and varied. Just the other day he'd taken out his atlas so that he could explain to her why Sicilians were barbarians; apparently his paternal great grandfather was Sicilian. "See," he was trailing his finger across the route from the Middle East and then back from Europe, and either way you had to pass through Sicily. It was constantly being conquered, a melting pot of nationalities. His face was illuminated. And that wasn't the first time he'd lugged out that hundred pound book and searched for an answer in its geography. There was always an answer, he'd say. It was why he liked technology, why he never got impatient or frustrated setting up some new device, like the VCR or the stereo system he'd helped her select. If you were patient, researched the instructions, you could always find the answer. She wondered how he would find the answer to her infertility, and if he couldn't, if he would allow his own history to end with him.

She turned to ask him but he had already fled.

"What were you doing?" he wanted to know, when she got to the car where he'd been waiting with the heater on.

"I don't know," she said, shivering, water dripping off her nose. It was hard to tell if she was crying.

The rain turned into a drizzle.

They gave up on Saratoga for lunch and opted for Dona Esther's Mexican because it was right there on the edge of the mission, and it was one of those lonely, empty dives where they could sit at the bar and order tequila straight up and nobody would blink (though because of the drive back they kept it to watered down margaritas). Sensing her distance, he pulled out the mission guidebook and pointed out little facts that might bring her back, like the original bell tower, it turns out, was burnt down in a fire. Hitchcock built a replica for the film.

"How could he love her when she didn't exist?" was Jamie's response. She was talking about Scottie's love for the Madeline-who-wasn't-really-Madeline.

Roberto sat back, closed the book, and thought for a moment. "To him she did exist," he offered eventually. "Even if it was only in his mind, she existed." He polished off his drink.

Jamie, already done with hers, wanted another, needed another. But he wanted to beat traffic home, so they left but got caught in it anyway. Roberto cursed in Italian under his breath every so often when someone didn't move out of his way. Jamie fell in and out of sleep. Dusk had fallen by the time they squeezed into a spot around the corner from her apartment. He turned off the engine and they sat for a minute. Cable car lines hummed beneath them. The sky was a purplish gray. He asked her why she'd been so quiet on the ride home. She said she was tired. He wanted to ask more, she could tell, sensing something wrong. But in the end he couldn't.

After they made love that night and he lay tracing her scar lightly with his hands, he told her, as if he already knew what lay absent beneath the layers of hardened flesh he felt there, even though she had yet to say anything, that he did not want children. And perhaps she had vaguely heard him say that then, but what she heard more strongly were Betty's words: *Why tell him anything? Because you don't even know for sure.*

CHAPTER 9

Breaking the Waves

November, 2003

Steven was in town. No heads-up before this morning's barrage of e-mails, then the voice mails: he was meeting with Senator so-and-so on the Hill…be at Betty's place by five; next call he said he'd be there by six; the next one was of him cussing because Sarah had fucked up his schedule. At six he called and said he was ten minutes away. Yeah, right. Next call it was seven and he was outside on her doorstep. "Who's Sarah?" Betty said, giving him a hug.

He wore a custom made Armani suit and tie, his goatee was trimmed, and he sported a limited edition Batman watch. His rental car was a Lexus. Normally he stayed at the Four Seasons in Georgetown, but more recently he'd insisted on staying with Betty and the kids in Bethesda. He'd been making an effort to visit more lately, even if it was for just the night and part of a business trip. Presumably his lobbying business was going well. At least he'd broken off from McDonald's after four years. They were just one of his many clients now, those he was having difficulty managing because few people could stand to work for him, and for a moment Betty relished back to the days her brother didn't have to work, seemingly, a façade apparently, one that had crumbled. He'd gone through a plethora of hires. But Sarah, who'd contacted him through the alumni network at the Kennedy School, was a sharp shooter, he'd said, all pumped; a political science major from U.C. Irvine.

She sent him downstairs to get settled in the guestroom, and after a half hour went down to see what he wanted for dinner. He was still unpacking, meticulously laying out all of his clothes and toiletries onto the bed, his cell phone glued to his ear, which he held out to Betty. "Here, talk to Sarah." Betty made a gesture—she didn't want to talk to Sarah, she didn't know Sarah. But it was too late; he'd put Sarah on speaker. "Sarah, I'm here with my sister, Betty."

"Hi Betty."

"Hi Sarah."

"Betty's just getting ready to order from Tortilla Flats. I'm thinking the queso dip sounds good…what about you Sarah?" His voice curled up in that flirtatious way, and he winked at Betty, who was backing out of the room. When he saw that she was really leaving he cried, "Wait," and put Sarah on hold so that he could give Betty his food order, which took a while. She went upstairs and placed it over the phone. By the time she was done, Steven had changed into his Raider sweats and was wrestling with the boys in the living room. It was their ritual: three on one; her kids had been waiting for this all day.

Betty grabbed an alcohol-free beer from the fridge, fell onto the couch, and watched them tumble about the carpet. For a while she sat lulled by their antics, exhausted really. Her sabbatical had finally started, and she still couldn't quite believe it. All that productivity planning, and she wasn't sure she had accomplished anything that day. She'd barely sewed a stitch in a week. Her mind was numb, her feet hurt. She massaged them, watching her brother, who seemed bigger than her three boys put together. Still, he insisted on double orders of guacamole, not to mention that queso—for the boys he had said, and she put up no fight…he was buying, after all. And she was glad he was here; she needed a sibling in her midst, and he needed family around him after breaking up with Kate, his girlfriend of five years. Betty had loved Kate, and was still hoping for their reconciliation. She so wished for her brother to have a wife and kids—a family. He loved his nephews so. He'd gone through two girlfriends since Kate. He had big bags under his eyes and looked like he hadn't slept in weeks. No doubt she'd be lying in her bed tonight listening to him rant on his cell phone at three a.m. But that was just Steven...and she never worried about Steven. "Sometimes I wish we all lived closer together." Her own words, released with a misty sigh, took her by surprise.

Steven rolled over on his side, Nick clinging to his neck, Sam and Clay falling off only to jump right back on. "Yeah, but then you'd have to deal with Mom."

"See, that's just it. In doses she's fine. It's those weeklong visits that are painful...more for her than for me."

He grunted. Someone just pummeled him.

"I want the kids to have grandparents."

"They're putting up a new Home Depot in Irvine. I'm helping them get the zoning rights for the land."

"Really?"

"If it goes through they'll owe me big."

"So you could get Dave a job there?" She paused, picturing California, bright, sunny, her kids at the beach. "And California is a stronger market for natural baby clothes...this business idea Debbie and I are developing." She'd left him an opening, hoping he would bite. She'd yet to approach anyone in her family about it.

"You could help me out with Mom's re-election campaign, though hopefully she'll run uncontested. That district loves her." Steven was pinning Clay's arms with one hand, Sam's with the other.

"Doesn't Mom want to retire?"

"Mom will never retire."

"I'm just saying..." Betty let her voice trail off. She forgot she wasn't supposed to say anything.

"She can't retire. We're just getting going. In two years Wiseman's seat will be up, and she could run for the State Assembly. Come on Betty, don't you know what this means?"

"She's turning seventy, Steven. She's engaged to Richard..."

"Fuck Richard." The kids' eyes went wide. "Sorry," Steven barely added, and they continued their tackling maneuvers. "Does the guy even have a job?" he managed, back on the bottom of the pile. "Gee, I wonder what he's in this relationship for. And besides, Mom can't retire, her district needs her. Just like you'll never retire, Betty. In fact when Dave goes to work in Irvine, you could work for me."

Betty swigged her beer and cringed at this mound of a stranger before her, buried underneath her children. She needed the missing alcohol at this moment. She wanted to ask him why he didn't run for office. Why, instead, he pushed their mother with a sort of fury. Did he really have that little faith in himself? Or was he just lazy? But Betty didn't have the energy to confront Steven right now. She'd been feeling lazy herself and less confident about her own abilities after seeing Dave's reaction to her and Debbie's plan. Did she really have the guts, stamina, and smarts she'd need to pitch the idea to investors? She hadn't been feeling well all day, and now she felt worse. She'd been unusually drained entering her third trimester, cramping more than she was used to. Debbie wanted Betty to gain more weight. She was also nagging Betty about that third birthing participant. She wanted to get to know them, answer any questions they might have. Betty's mom was hesitant to commit. Dave's mom had offered to come out, but Betty had been stalling her response. For a moment she pictured Steven in that tub and giggled. Even a loud cry didn't erase the silly thought or make her move. Even Nick crying in front of her a minute later triggered no adrenaline within her. He was her youngest, her most aggressive. At four years old, he was built like a football player. She wiped his tears, kissed him where it hurt, and he ran back for more.

At last she forced herself up and into the kitchen to call Dave on his cell. She wanted him to pick up the food on his way home from work. She *left a message on his voice mail, slightly frustrated not to get him directly, and hung up. She was still getting used to her husband's unavailability. She was the one home now. She was the primary caregiver now. "Your father needs to remember to turn on his phone," she said to Mary, walking to the back window off the den, surprised by the sight of the rain pouring down in the lamplight, even though she'd seen the weather report. "Especially with only eight weeks to go." She was excited about the birth and admittedly a bit nervous, as well. "I told your father a million times about replacing the tires on the GTI." She didn't realize she was talking out loud. These days, it seemed, Mary was the only one listening.*

She checked the clock. Where was Dave anyway? He got off work at five and it was now seven. Massaging an ache in her lower back, she picked up the phone and called Home Depot. Yes, Dave had been there today…left at five…his usual shift. Maybe he went for a drink with a friend, Betty thought. But Dave didn't have any friends that weren't their friends. Then she remembered. He was chattering at her this morning about a variety of things, one of which was his GMAT prep class tonight, the class he'd been going to every Tuesday and Thursday night for the past month. Where was her mind? She was a bad listener; that's what he always told her and he was right.

Relieved and slightly guilt ridden, she caressed her belly, soothing her daughter and herself at once, until a loud bang startled her. "That didn't sound good, Mary." Someone was screaming and it wasn't one of her boys. She ran into the living room to find Steven lying in agony on the couch. Clay and Sam were pointing at Nick, who was sucking his thumb in a corner under a table. "What happened!" she tried not to yell.

Steven couldn't speak because he was biting his tongue in fury, one hand over his eye. Clay explained, quite calmly, that Nick had punched Uncle Steven in the face. "My eye," came strangling out of her brother then, followed by a variety of expletives that reminded Betty of her childhood. He bit his tongue again, letting go only to ask in a forced calm for an ice pack. She went to the kitchen and brought one back. He held it to his eye, wincing.

His terror both alarmed and amused her. She pulled off the pack and examined his eye as demanded. "It doesn't look so bad, Steven."

"He could have damaged my fucking retina."

She was about to laugh but then saw his mouth clench under its wrath. She feigned concern. "You need to breathe Steven."

He took some deep, huffing breaths, then made an attempt to open his eye, yelling out "fuck," and scrunching it shut. "Do I need to go to emergency?"

She bit her lip: No. "I'll call urgent care and see what they suggest," she said, getting up.

In fact she couldn't imagine spending hours with her moaning brother at urgent care for no urgent reason. But she could at least pretend to call. She pulled Nick from under the table and told him that it was an accident. Poor kid was horrified and Steven's behavior wasn't making him feel any better. She carried him to the kitchen, Clay and Sam following reluctantly. They wanted to watch the movie they'd rented, but she asked them to give their uncle a little space. Sam switched on the tiny TV they kept in the den and the boys immediately fell into a trance before it. Betty picked up the phone in a pretext of calling urgent care, and then stood there with the receiver in her hand, entranced too. Until she realized they were all watching the D-Day scene from Saving Private Ryan *and ordered Sam to change the channel!*

At some point she heard the clock ticking over the cartoon din and it occurred to her that it was time to do something. Only she wasn't sure what to do. Then the phone rang in her hand and she got a very vivid and real premonition, swelled in the relief of it, until she answered it and heard Debbie's voice.

She was just checking in. She'd been worried when she saw Betty that morning. Her blood pressure was high. Was she resting? Sure, she was resting. She'd seen Dave at the Martsons, Debbie mentioned then. The Marstons were good friends of theirs. Their son was Nick's buddy. Sandy ran with Debbie and Betty on Thursday mornings, and her husband worked for The Post. *He and Dave hung out sometimes and smoked pot. Betty acted nonchalant; when exactly had Debbie seen Dave at the Marstons? A half hour ago, according to Debbie, when Dave was supposedly in his GMAT prep class. A shudder ran through Betty as she hung up the phone; a sickness settled in her core. Her limbs felt apart from her as they began moving, slowly at first, towards the back sliding glass doors, then faster, shoving on boots and grabbing a rain slicker, which she held over her head as she maneuvered outside around puddles of brown leaves in the yard towards Dave's workshop, the one he'd resurrected to make the birthing tub. It was pitch black, and he'd left the door ajar, which immediately incensed her because they agreed to keep it locked so that the boys wouldn't ravage the place or step on an errant nail. But the door was off its hinge, she noticed, so of course it couldn't be locked. She had to kick it, with all the force of hatred she harbored for this beaten down old burden of a house that Dave loved and she, going on five years now, had tried to convince herself to love. Inside was a cluttered mess and reeked of veneer shavings and turpentine, the smells of a past life. She had promised herself she wouldn't snoop; Dave said he'd wanted the finished product to be a surprise. Now she no longer cared. Now she wondered if tonight's wasn't the only GMAT class he'd missed. She looked around only to find a few crude sketches on the drawing table, but no tub frame. He didn't like to constrain his craft with written plans, she'd heard him say a million times—he wanted his pieces to build themselves. She used to revel in those words. "God!" she cried out suddenly. Then she stood there, stunned by the sound of her own voice, a deranged stranger's voice, so apart from her and yet so her. She was apart from herself. Herself and her were two different beings. The universe became eerily still with this knowledge, as if all the waves of the world had suddenly stopped crashing and Betty had this moment and this moment only to step out of them. Is this how it happens, she wondered with a sudden abandon, just like that? Is this when the cycle stops?*

She went back to the house, told Sam (back watching Saving Private Ryan*) that he was in charge because she was going to go pick up the food. As she was headed for the door, Steven broke from his snore to say, "You're leaving?" childlike.*

"*Urgent care said to give it a couple more hours,*" she lied. "*So I'm going to go pick up the food. I'll be right back,*" she went over and assured him, not so sure herself. And perhaps he sensed this, for he grabbed her wrist and asked if she could sit with him for a minute. "*Steven…*" she released a curt, burdened sigh. "*Please?*" he cooed, and she sat down. He lay flat out on his back, calmer now. She examined his eye again while he blinked helplessly up at her. Pink with a slight swelling. She sat there until his breathing became less irregular, less panicky, and then the doorbell rang and it was she who panicked. They weren't expecting anyone.

"*That's probably Sarah.*" Steven said as if it were the most natural of things for her to show up here.

"*Sarah?*"

"*Didn't I tell you?*"

"*No, Steven,*" she said, wearily, "*You didn't tell me.*"

"*She came with me.*"

"*She's going to stay here?*"

"*You don't mind, do you?*"

Of course she minded. He was supposed to be getting back together with Kate.

Betty stood up. This was how her brother introduced her to his girl-friends. She went and answered the door and met Sarah, nice, fine, plain… whatever, Betty no longer cared, and perhaps it shone on her face because the woman smiled sympathetically at her. Betty smiled sympathetically back, then she handed over the ice pack and nodded in the direction of Steven over on the couch; he was her problem now. Betty was tired of playing mother to needy men. When was it that she had become such a sucker for needy men!

The door slammed on her way out.

✳✳ 1996 ✳✳

To Betty a phone ringing was the sound of opportunity. It would never occur to her not to answer it, to break her link in the chain of existence. That would be like turning down fate. Even nestled on the living room couch breastfeeding Clay, she didn't hesitate to get herself up and through the score of unopened moving boxes in order to get to the kitchen, cradling her baby at her breast.

Of course the receiver wasn't where it should have been on the wall base next to the fridge. She searched underneath the *Washington Post* strewn across the kitchen table; on top of the microwave where Dave sometimes left it; in the adjacent half bath. There was no toilet paper on the roll, she noticed, as the phone rang a third time. She checked under the sink for what reason she didn't know. Toilet paper? She had no idea where anything was. The movement caused Clay to bite down on her already tender nipple. She gasped. No teeth, but shit, that hurt.

"Sorry sweetie." She brushed her hand across his clenched forehead and gazed into his hazel green eyes. He had blond hair and white skin and didn't look anything like any of them. A mystery, like the ear, Betty heard a little voice in her head say. Only with the birth of Clay had she begun to be curious about her mother's natural parents. What genes they were passing down and leaving to her kids unknowingly. Their mother ended the search for her birthparents a few years back, rather abruptly Betty recalled. She never told them why, and Betty hadn't cared then. But now more and more she found herself wanting to know. She put her finger out and Clay grabbed it just as the answering machine clicked on and reminded her of the task at hand: finding the phone. Mark, her old boss at the museum, began leaving a message. She gave up on locating the receiver, leaned back against the wall and listened. She knew why he was calling, and her heart sank before he even said it. Had Betty thought more about his offer? He'd gotten a verbal commitment on seed capital from that philanthropist who had just joined the Smithsonian's board, Gilbert somebody, Betty hadn't pretended to know his name. Anyway, the deal for Fashion.com was a go, and now Mark needed Betty's formal answer on the COO position he'd offered her. She felt honored, she'd told Mark a month ago, stalling because of course her answer was no. She was secretly hoping that the seed capital wouldn't come through and that that would be the end of it. Why hadn't she just told him no a month ago?

The line went dead.

Clay released her nipple and started crying. She stared at him, a knot tightening in her stomach, a kind of homesickness she didn't recognize. She'd never experienced postpartum depression with Sam, nor had she felt the stress other mothers described upon the arrival of their second child. Clay was already sleeping a good portion of the night, and Sam was thriving in his new, part-time daycare regimen. She couldn't think of one thing to complain about. Motherhood came naturally to her. She didn't feel blessed by her children, she felt entitled. This was who she was. Still, she was having these little pangs of loneliness. Her maternity leave was up; next Monday she would return to work and she felt torn, especially since now she'd have to commute from Bethesda. Part of her wanted to stay home with her kids, forever; the same dreamy part of her that wanted to take Mark's offer, but the reality was that she had no choice about either. Her family needed her salary and benefits from the museum, now more than ever, since they'd just made this big investment in Dave's furniture business.

Betty wasn't sure which came first, finding this old farmhouse with the attached industrial-sized shed, or the plan for the business that would burst forth from it. Betty had been eight months pregnant with Clay, when she, Dave, Sam, and Dave's parents had been driving back from Baltimore and, spotting the For Sale sign, stopped in. It took only a minute before Dave looked at her and she nodded in agreement. Or had it been the other way around? She couldn't remember. Just that she'd been working at the museum for a decade, something needed to change, and if it wasn't going to be her job then she'd settle for this.

She lay Clay over her shoulder and idly ran the fingers of her free hand along the scuffs and scrapes of the maple kitchen table, thinking how timing was really everything. Dave had made this table just before Sam was born. They hadn't planned on getting pregnant so soon, and they just fell into this mode of Dave being the primary at-home caretaker. He'd carved a few pieces here and there and in-between since, but for the most part his furniture business was put on hold. Betty got pregnant with Clay a year later. Another surprise. Then they stumbled upon this old farmhouse and everything fell into place. They were able to gather all Dave's unfinished pieces from various storage facilities, including friends' garages, and he was now able to give them the finishing touches they deserved in preparation for the expo next week. Dave seemed really happy, and even his parents were being supportive. They put Dave's law school money towards the down payment, and Dave's dad helped him refurbish the shed into a professional woodshop. Finally she and Dave had an actual plan.

Now Mark has to drop this incredible offer at her feet, an offer six months ago she would have jumped at.

She set Clay in his rocker, and they both immediately fell under the spell of its monotonous motion. Her mind drifted across the country to Silicon Valley, the place to be, Mark had emoted, and she envisioned herself in the middle of a team crowded over a design table, waving hands and giving orders, collaborating about fabrics she could almost feel in her hands. She envisioned Dave's furniture store somewhere in the Haight or the Presidio…she'd have to ask Jamie what might be the best location. After work she'd meet her sister for a beer at the top of one of those hills, on weekends they'd stroll through the Marina with the kids. Jamie would be there if something happened, if Betty needed her to take Sam or Clay in a lurch. They'd be a real family.

She found the phone in the master bathroom upstairs and took it with her down the hall into her sewing room, where the hardwood creaked beneath the weight of her and the sun poured in the through the clapboard windows. From them she could watch the flowers bloom and the leaves sway, Sam kicking around a soccer ball with his dad playing hooky from his work in the shed. She walked over to the windows now and ran a hand along the iolite curtains she'd sewn just before Clay was born, fluttering in a spring breeze. Jamie wanted a set for her apartment in San Francisco…in fact you should sell them, her sister had said, as if Betty hadn't already had that thought…a million times. "Someday."

Two squirrels chased each other up a tree and onto their roof, and Betty reminded herself to tell Dave to trim those branches… plus the grass, it occurred to her staring at it now, hadn't been mowed, a sigh, the ceiling needed plastering, and if that wallpaper didn't come down soon… She sat in the rocker and made a list, then considered the chair itself, and why Dave hadn't moved it to the shed so that he could refinish it for the show. Next week was the Furniture Expo on the Mall, and they were banking on some serious orders. Of course Dave was dreading it, for he hated selling himself, and as if to make that point, just then a loud, persistent clanging noise came up through the pipes from the basement. She dulled her eyes, and then went downstairs to find Dave in the basement immersed in the boiler. He had the whole thing practically pulled apart. "What are you doing?" she yelled over the clanging.

"Winter's coming."

"It's April."

The clanging stopped. "Do you want heat or not?"

"Well, yes but…"

"Can you hand me that wrench?"

She huffed, inwardly, and handed it to him. "I thought you were going to refinish the rocker for the show?"

"What rocker?"

"The one upstairs in the nursery."

He stopped what he was doing to look at her, hurt. "I made that for you when Clay was born."

"And it's beautiful. And you can make me another one."

"When? After I fix the leak in the roof and paint the sewing room?"

"Can't we get someone else to do that?"

"With what!" He sighed and fell back against the wall, apologetic. "Sorry."

"That's OK. I know you're stressed, and it probably doesn't help having me around nagging all the time. It's weird being home together like this, no?"

"Look Betty. About the expo next week…"

"Where's Eddie?" She glanced around for Dave's "little brother," which always left her with a little pang of guilt, for she'd lost track of what had happened with her little sister. But not Dave. When Betty first met Dave, Eddie was eight. Now he was applying for junior college, thanks to Dave's unending encouragement and support. He never gave up on the kid, never judged him, even with the set backs, like that time he got the DUI or when he was accused of stealing from the register at the restaurant where he was a busboy. It was Betty who had insisted Dave pay Eddie to help him get ready for the expo. Dave didn't want to spend the money, but it was for a good cause after all, and it gave Eddie a head start on putting some money away for college.

"He didn't show today or yesterday. I think his mom my have fallen off the wagon again. I need to get over there and check it out."

Betty let out a curt sigh that she immediately regretted.

"There'll be other expos, Betty."

She stared at him, confused. "What do you mean?"

"I mean I don't think I'll be ready."

She waved him off, stifling a flutter of panic in her chest. "Oh, you'll be fine. The kitchen table's ready. And most of the coffee tables, no?" She paused to think of more, not realizing how hard she'd been squeezing the phone receiver in her hand until it rang and startled them both.

"Hey," Jamie said when Betty answered.

"You'll do fine, Dave," Betty palmed the phone and said, backing away from him.

"When are you coming?" Betty wanted to know, at the top of the basement stairs now.

"Next week. I'll fly through on my way back to San Francisco."

"You've gotta meet Clay. He's adorable. And this hair of his…"

"I couldn't believe the photos!"

"Dave's mom insists that it's her German ancestry."

"Or it's the milkman. Remember how we used to always say that?"

They both tried to laugh, but it didn't feel right. There was an awkward silence.

"How's the farm?" Jamie finally asked.

"It's not a farm."

"Whatever you want to call it."

"It's only a forty minute drive to D.C."

"You don't have chickens or anything do you?"

"Mark called me again about that offer."

"Oh?"

"He got the seed capital. Of course he would get the seed capital."

"Bummer."

"Is it?"

Jamie's silence said everything.

"It's just…you know…fun to imagine," Betty added.

"It would be kind of cool," Jamie offered, playing along.

"We could be neighbors."

"I could come over for dinner."

"We could meet for drinks or lunch."

"I could babysit."

"Exactly."

"And Dave knows you're considering joining a company with your ex-boyfriend?"

"OK fine, ruin my fun." Betty paused. "And you know it's not like that with Mark."

Jamie didn't say anything.

"Anyway, we're working our asses off over here getting ready for the expo. That's our focus right now."

"OK."

"You know his stuff is really good."

"I know."

Betty paced down the hall to her bathroom. "We're happy here."

"I know."

"We love D.C."

But you're not in D.C., her sister didn't say, but that's what Betty heard her say. "Anyway. Sorry." There it was again, that word. Betty hated when she said it.

Both of them could sense the mood falling sour, which it was doing more and more ever since Jamie returned from Russia and moved in with Roberto, just as Betty and Dave decided to buy this house. Still, neither of them was willing to hang up. So they changed the subject to movies, which is when it occurred to Betty, as her sister rattled on about this or that Indie film she'd seen either with Roberto or alone in some obscure part of the world where she'd been holed up on a project for work, that she hadn't seen a movie since Clay was born. So she changed the subject to their mother because there was always something to be concerned about there. An hour later Betty and Jamie hung up, and even still it was hard saying goodbye. It wasn't kinship but something else that made them hang on, what made all their phone conversations of late longer, like they were searching for that comfortable place between them that had gotten lost. Or, for Betty, to avoid feeling what was to come after hanging up, what she felt now, less confident about her choices than she had an hour ago.

In the mirror she examined her pores and sagging skin. All the weight she had lost after Clay's birth had left her looking gaunt. She chalked it up to high metabolism, abundant energy, an inability to sit still, what had started with Sam's birth and grew worse after Clay's. She must have sewn him twenty burping blankies, it occurred to her, heading to her bedroom now, where she threw on jeans and a blouse because suddenly her adrenaline was surging. She had to get out of here. Being home with Dave wasn't productive. Perhaps with her out of the house, he wouldn't get so distracted. He only needed a few more pieces to make a good showing next week; there would NOT be other expos, what the hell was he thinking?

The clock said noon, hours before she had to pick up Sam from day-care at the museum. She checked the paper for a movie, but there was only one that really worked both time and location-wise, and she thought she'd heard of it. She dashed on some makeup and gave her hair some life with a blow-dryer, then rattled something off to Dave about getting a head start on her in-box before picking up Sam. Dave would not have cared about her going to a movie, that's not why she didn't tell him about it. She didn't tell him about it because she was afraid he'd want to come with her.

She prepared a diaper bag, stuffed Clay in his car seat, and bolted out of Bethesda. Clay was asleep by the time she hit the Beltway and slobbering by the time she cruised over the Fourteenth Street Bridge. The Capitol rotunda rose up to meet her nostalgia head on, and she rolled down the window to feel the rush. At thirty-two, mother of two, she was surprised to find that she felt exactly the same as when she first drove into this city of monuments ten years ago: things just beginning, everything attainable.

Was it bad to want so much, even now?

The movie was showing at a campus theater that she'd been to once with Mark back when they were still seeing each other. *Fargo* was playing in the main theater, but the ticket-taker directed Betty to a smaller room upstairs where foreign movie posters plastered the walls and the carpet smelled like a frat party. She had Clay nestled in his sling, his warmth against her womb as she peeked through the window of the door and saw the movie's caption displayed on the screen: "Love has no boundaries." Great, she thought, throwing a blanket over Clay's head and heading in, a porno flick.

She found a cold metal seat on the aisle. There were some old couches in front that looked like they'd been pulled out of a garbage dump. One guy was already asleep on one. A handful of other single viewers were sprinkled throughout, a few couples. She should be home helping Dave, she thought, but then reminded herself that every time she tried to help him things only got more muddled. Clay's arm sprung out from the sling and whipped back behind his ear. He winced as if he was having a bad dream, and his mouth curved into a sad, silent wail. Betty felt her breast, unbuttoned her maternity blouse, and lifted Clay's head to her leaking nipple. The two of them twisted around and settled into a rhythm while before her the sea thrashed against rocks on a land cold and oceans away. Scenes from a small wedding unfolded: happy faces, celebrating faces, faces of people deeply in love. But then the groom returned to his job on an oilrig out at sea, only to return a week later, paralyzed and on life support due to a freak accident. Besse, the simple-minded, God-faring bride who wasn't right in the head to begin with, was so beyond herself with grief that she began offering her body to other men. She was underneath one of them now, a sloppy old drunk, on a dirt road behind some bar, with her legs spread, head turned, and eyes deadened. She was doing this for her husband, who told her that her having sex with other men, then coming to him afterwards and describing it, was the only way he would stay alive.

Naive, blindly believing Besse.

Betty looked down. Clay had let go her nipple. His head was hooked over the sling and his mouth lay open in a gluttonous, blissful sleep. She wiped his chin with the blanket, afraid to look back up, for the movie was descending beyond logical comprehension. Certainly that poor girl was headed towards some barbaric, pointless end. Six months ago she had been a blushing bride, now she was a whore, an outcast in the isolated, pious town, all because she believed in, not what she was doing necessarily, but in her husband, and it was destroying her. Well, this was a mistake, Betty thought, taking one last look at Clay, his head still bent in slumber. She packed up their things and left.

Her car clock said three. She drove southeast from Georgetown towards downtown, the nagging uncertainty Dave had planted inside her about there being other expos was now a thrashing kind of panic, the kind that comes with responsibility, all of her family's resting solely on her shoulders. She wanted so badly for the feeling to go away, to forget about Mark, about Fashion.com, because she needed to believe in her husband, now more than ever, and with that thought she swerved the car into the left turn lane, the entrance for the National Gallery, where Mark had been heading up the modern design department for the past six years. She pulled into the underground employee parking lot, one building over from where she worked, and sat there in the car for a moment collecting herself: things were good. This furniture business was right. She'd go tell Mark her answer right now and put Fashion.com behind her. A quick diaper change, Clay back in his sling but not as happy about it this time, he was squirming against her belly as she headed to the elevators. With her employee pass she was able to take shortcuts through the underground tunnels and passageways that connected the museums, where she had gone from her building to his so many times before; it all felt so familiar. Until she got closer and the sensation grew stronger that everything was, in fact, very unfamiliar. She was unfamiliar, for she couldn't get Besse out of her mind, and what could have possibly happened to her.

His door was open, he was at the window strategizing with someone on the phone, his lawyer, she quickly surmised. Mark was going through an ugly divorce and child custody battle. He'd often sought out Betty's advice on the matter, or if nothing else to just vent, so when he turned and saw her at the door, he almost looked relieved; he waved her into a chair where she waited for him to finish. He'd gained weight, she noticed, and lost more hair, though she still found him handsome, if only in an absent-minded-professor kind of way. She was no longer attracted to him sexually, which she still found odd, given that that's what their relationship had been about. But unexpectedly, ever since they'd broken up and sex was no longer between them they'd become great friends. They'd gone to each other's weddings, knew each other's spouses, shared pictures of each other's kids. Every few months or so they'd have lunch, there was still that connection. And in a way, Mark would always be her mentor.

"Sorry," he said, getting off the phone and coming over. She stood so that he could get a look at Clay.

"Oh my God, that hair."

"I know."

They hugged, awkwardly with Clay between them but it still felt good, and she found herself clinging for perhaps a second too long because he pulled back and searched her eyes.

She searched his, as if knowing what he was going to say.

"She's fighting for full custody."

"No!"

"Can you believe it?"

"She can't be serious, Mark."

"She's punishing me for going to the Valley…for pursing my dream. She wants me to be miserable. As if everyone should be miserable like her." He was shaking his head, but then he quickly cleared his throat and stepped back. "Why didn't you tell me you were coming in? I would have cleared my schedule." He looked at his watch. "As it is," he moved some things around on his desk looking for something, and when she opened her mouth to speak he stopped her. "Don't give me an answer right now, Betty. I don't want your answer until you've met Gil, the investor. Until you've had time to really understand the opportunity."

"Ah," he said, finding what he was looking for. He passed her the business plan. "You know I can't do this without you, Betty. You're the only one I trust to get shit done."

She smiled, she knew. "I guess it wouldn't hurt to meet this guy…Gil, you said?"

He picked up the phone and called his assistant to set something up. "I told him all about you. You'll love Gil. And I know he'll love you, they'll be no problems there. Then he talked more in depth about the concept, told her to study the business plan, and then set a time for them to get back together again after she and Gil had met privately. They talked about timing, hypothetically of course, if she were to take the job. He was hoping she could be out there in a couple months.

"You know my sister lives there with her boyfriend. She's just back from Russia and…"

"We'll need to work out a contract," he said. "Pay will be a little less, but a big potential upside if things work out."

"…And the rest of my family is just an hour flight away."

Clay popped opened his eyes and let out a meek little wail. Mark leaned in and let Clay grab his finger. Betty looked at Clay, and then back up at Mark. "I still need to work some things out…" her voice shook and she paused.

He grabbed her hand, which was sweating. "They have great schools out there, Betty. And Dave being an outdoors guy, he'll love it there." He looked into her eyes, which had misted over. She wondered if he knew that she was dreaming, living in a dream in this very moment, and they stood like that for a long time, it seemed. She didn't want the dream to end. But then the phone started ringing and his assistant came in with some urgent messages and life continued on its forward motion and Mark's eyes darted about looking for what came next. So did hers. They were alike that way.

"You should go," Betty said.

He met her eyes again, holding them steady. "I need you to keep me in line, Betty. We'll be a team again. And you won't regret it."

Her voice was too shaky to respond, and he closed the door after her.

She stood there stunned for a timeless minute. Had she really just let that happen?

Somehow she made it back through the maze of tunnels to her office, which was mostly empty because it was now quarter to six. She lay Clay on the couch and let him wriggle free from his sling at last. He was so happy to be free, all wondrous smiles as if to say, are we really going to California, Mommy? Meanwhile, Betty was trying to figure out how to call Mark back, how she might say something like, April fools, or simply ask him why he hadn't considered asking her what the hell she was thinking uprooting her family and moving across the country for a job with little security.

She picked up the phone; she needed someone to tell her what to do.

Her sister answered after the first ring, which Betty wasn't prepared for. She thought she'd have some time to at least think of what to say. "I saw this movie today," she stalled, shuffling some papers around on her desk as if that might get her thoughts organized. "A foreign film with Emily…somebody." She briefly described it.

"Emily Watson and you mean *Breaking the Waves*."

"You've seen it?" *Of course her sister had seen it.*

"Lars von Trier's the director. He's totally fucked up."

Betty couldn't fathom a response; fucked up didn't quite do the movie justice.

"I can't believe you went and saw it. If I'd known I would have advised against it."

"What happened in the end?"

"She got beaten to a bloody pulp," Jamie said. "That's what happened. Did you miss it?"

"I was getting nauseous."

"She died so that her husband could live."

"What does that mean?"

"He recovered, miraculously. Even started walking again. It was a miracle."

"And they expect me to believe that?"

"It's so hard to believe that you're kind of left believing. Great movie."

Believing what? Betty was so confused. "But you don't believe in miracles."

"No, but you do."

"Not like that. I don't believe that someone has to endure so much suffering to make a miracle, like life was some kind of tradeoff."

"Isn't it?"

Betty didn't answer. To her there were just the things you were handed, and then there was fate. "What if I said I was seriously thinking of taking Mark's offer in Silicon Valley?"

"I'd say what happened?"

"Nothing happened," she said defensively. "You know, you'd baby-sit, we'd be neighbors, all that."

"I thought we were just daydreaming."

"Maybe we weren't. I mean I don't know, Jamie, you're right, maybe something did happen, like maybe something clicked inside of me. Maybe this opportunity is my fate and I shouldn't let it slip away. I've always wanted to move back to California. I mean, Dave and I could do it, don't you think? Dave could build furniture there just as well as he can here." She went on and on, her excitement swelling like a wave, cresting, a seagull crying for help. She was out of breath by the time she fell silent.

"I may not be here, Betty."

The wave crashed.

"What does that mean?"

"Delphiant's buying RAPID and transferring Roberto to New York, and well, I'm going to move with him."

The silence grew awkward.

"What about your job?"

"They'll transfer me. I travel so much it doesn't matter where I'm based."

How easy life was, when one had no kids, Betty thought.

"But then you weren't seriously going to do this, were you?"

Betty couldn't respond. She felt like she was sinking.

"You know, the furniture business? That expo next week?"

"Of course not," Betty paused. "I was just, I don't know…"

"Betty is everything OK?"

No, she didn't say, making an excuse about Clay starting to futz and getting off. In fact, Clay was thoroughly entrance by her desk light. She sat there staring at him staring at it, stunned and slightly numb, until her gaze naturally settled on the tall pile in her in-box. Her heart sank as she took in her surroundings, which looked exactly as they had three months ago when she'd left and would certainly be that way when she returned in a week. It always would.

Her phone rang. It was Dave wondering where she was. Betty didn't know where she was momentarily. I'm here at the office, she said to him. *Isn't that where she always was?* "I'm sorry about snapping earlier," he said. "You know I can't do this expo without you." She cringed at those words knowing what would follow, a huge point of him thanking her for being the woman that she was. And the man he was not, Betty bit her lip, hard. She couldn't help herself. Hadn't Mark just essentially told her the same thing? That he needed Betty to fill the gaps of the man he wasn't. And perhaps this was what marriage was about, what relationships were about, but she couldn't help feeling used, as if someone were sucking her life's energy, her ONLY life's energy. He'd refinished the rocker, Dave was telling her now, sheepishly, sure to emphasize "for her" at the end of his sentence. For the expo, she reminded him, thankful that he couldn't see the disappointment in her eyes, disappointment not in Dave but in herself for not having the energy or strength to carry her family all the way to Silicon Valley on her own shoulders, for succumbing to the belief that we were all a little like Besse, that we all wanted to believe in our husbands because it was easier than believing in ourselves. She told herself now what Dave had told her earlier: there would be other expos. This she would make sure because she was going to help him be the success she still believed he could be. Despite his faults, she loved Dave…and when it came down to it, Betty had no one else. Not even Jamie anymore, really.

She glanced at Mark's business plan one more time before throwing it in the trash and then swiveling her chair around to face the window. Dusk was settling on the Mall. A soccer game was fin-ishing up on the grass. The joggers were out. An angelic little scene that Betty had witnessed time and again though all it really meant was that it was time to pick up Sam from day-care. Working for the government meant exceptional benefits, including subsidized day-care right here in Betty's building. It was this job that had sustained her family, it had always been.

She swiveled her chair back around. Sometimes she wished they'd just fire her.

PRIMARY COLORS

November, 2003

November 3rd was her dad's birthday. On November 5th Jamie picked up the phone and called him. It always took her a few days to get the courage to hear the words that always ended their conversations, "Will I see you soon?" followed by some quote: "Tomorrow, and tomorrow, and tomorrow, Creeps in this petty pace from day to day…" or something like that. She hadn't spoken to him since she'd left California.

It always took her father a while to process where she was. Today was no different, though he did seem relatively coherent. He said that they'd gotten Vivi's diabetes under control, that they'd been busy with their grandkids. He meant Masa's and Kit's kids, whom he didn't distinguish from his own. It gave Jamie relief, knowing her father had a close family around him. And even though it was someone else's family, she wouldn't allow herself to feel jealous. She knew she had no right, no claim to the man she'd abandoned long ago.

He'd been reading a lot, gotten engrossed in many books that he'd some-how misplaced and therefore couldn't finish. He talked emphatically about an article he'd read in the New Yorker *comparing Lawrence Olivier to*

Orson Welles and their respective takes of Shakespeare in film. She relished all this, her father's love for the theater, movies, books, especially now that she'd been reading more herself. They seemed to connect in these fictional worlds, and she wondered why his passion for theater and literature hadn't had a greater influence on her life choices. Then he digressed about a book he'd read called Anger, and whatever connection had passed between them abruptly ended. Apparently this particular book was helping him deal with the anger he still harbored about Jamie's mother leaving him…his father too…everyone for that matter. And as he spoke he got angry. He promised to send it to her, as if it could help her with her anger, when and if he could find it that is. His bitterness at the world seeped through her skin, and she hung up feeling depressed and guilty.

Was she angry? Just asking the question brought it all back. Forget the yoga and the Buddha and the Zen lifestyle, one phone call with her father and it was back. Yes, she was angry. The reality sent a wave of nausea through her, one that left a residue she couldn't shake, even later that afternoon in the steaming hot kitchen of Giorgio's restaurant, where she stood over a pile of garlic cloves. After nine years together, Roberto finally showed her how to properly wield a knife and mince a piece of garlic. It wasn't easy for him. The kitchen had always been his domain. But November was high season, and with Giorgio gone, in addition to being the chef, Roberto was now working overtime managing the restaurant staff as well: One hostess, two waiters, an assistant chef, and a dishwasher—all Thais, all cheap labor, all smiles, but all lazy. You get what you pay for. "Mai pen lai" was a Thai saying meaning, "Don't worry about it."

Thais don't take things too seriously.

Italians worry about everything, particularly their food.

Roberto, a mixture of both.

She'd been at it for two weeks now and still chopped one clove to Roberto's ten. So her prep started early in the morning, which she didn't mind, the concentration required for dicing and slicing as meditative as her yoga. She found the long workdays reminiscent of times past, when *everything was a milestone with a deadline and the client always came first. Running a restaurant was not much different. Except her face was puffy and blotched, her fingers were chafed and tired, and her breasts ached, but still, it felt good. After all, she'd been contributing to the GDP since she was fifteen up until two years ago, and it felt natural to get her hands dirty, to become immediately engrossed. Sure this new job was only garlic, but at least it gave her a sense of achievement each time she got the skin to peal from its clove in one whole piece.*

She and Roberto would prep the kitchen from nine to eleven a.m., when the restaurant opened for lunch. They'd serve lunch until two, take a break from three to four, and then prep again from four to six, when the restaurant reopened for dinner. By eleven, the restaurant now closed and scoured clean, they'd both be so exhausted that it would be all they could do to drag themselves back to the apartment, spent but exhilarated.

But today, after that discussion with her father, Jamie was feeling absent. She was standing at her station watching Roberto chop through a leek at warp speed. That muscle in his jaw was twitching. Perhaps that's how she'd always think of him: focused and intent. That scowl on his face could so easily turn into a smile…or indignation. She thought back to the other day when she'd made some sarcastic remark about a book he was reading, Founding Brothers. *She'd only ever heard him mock America, the country that had given him opportunity, and now here he was, studying its history.*

"I'm reading the book because it's interesting, Jamie." It was a familiar scolding. Her non-American husband knew more about American history than she did. Then there was world history, of course, which he drank in like water, sustenance, his only hope at understanding. What he wanted to understand, Jamie wasn't exactly sure. Where we'd all come from perhaps, or why we were all here, as if one could understand that. "Aren't you curious," he might say to her, "to know how the pandemics of the 1800s transformed our existence? She often didn't respond. She was curious, but only about why he was so desperate. Otherwise, she couldn't muster the same passion, especially about politicians; to her they had become so inherently disappointing…she couldn't remember the last

time she was inspired by one, as her parents had been by Kennedy, for instance. Clinton had lied about Monica and a million other things. Her brother used to inspire her. He spoke so eloquently in front of a group, so purposefully and down-to-earth, even the surfers and potheads at their high school looked up to him as class president. But even he had sold out: now he lobbied for fast food and other retail chain organizations. She'd become disenchanted with Kenneth, her boss at CADnet and longtime mentor. "We're not lying, just spinning the truth," he had rationalized to her just before the company went bankrupt. The only person left was Jamie's city councilwoman mother. But Jamie had never been sure if her mother's public life wasn't anything more than an addiction, an unending search for validation, attention, and love.

"Che cosa fai," Roberto said then, Mussolini-like, as if he'd read her thoughts and was trying to relieve her of them.

She'd wondered how long she'd been standing there idle. "Focus," she told herself, slicing again, chopping and chopping, watching her blade slide closer and closer to her left thumb like he'd showed her, until it cut right through and she dropped the knife and stared at her thumb bewildered at the sight of oozing blood. She sucked on it, hoping he wouldn't notice, but no use, he was upon her in a moment. "Let me see. Let me see."

"I'm fine. I'm fine."

"Let me see. Let me see." He was yelling now. His fear always took the course of anger, like the whole world of responsibility rested on his shoulders: his father's spiral, his mother's ghost, his aunt's oppression, Jamie, and the children he'd refused. And he didn't want it. He didn't want any of it.

He dragged her over to the sink.

"I'm sorry," she kept saying over and over.

He wrapped it up tightly with gauze. It wasn't deep, but she felt light-headed and he helped her sit down. His face was as white as hers…and as vulnerable. He pulled up a chair and sat down next to her, searching her face.

* * *

That night after they returned from the restaurant, Jamie went straight to the shower and stood naked under the dribbling spout. She wanted to be alone, but also…she started feeling around her breasts, which were still hard and sore and achy. It had been getting worse recently, and there was one particular lump that worried her. She examined it, though she never quite knew how. It was nothing she'd ever felt before. Even her reaction, the slight panic, felt foreign, for she'd never once had the slightest fear that the cancer would come back. She's not sure why, perhaps surviving something like that leaves you with a sense of invincibility. Tragic death had its turn and now couldn't touch her—so she scoffed when people warned her about drinking water from foreign taps, or walking dark streets alone at night, and if the plane took a sudden dive she might even laugh. For how could she die, after all that? So she took a lot of breaths presently and told herself that this lump was a reaction to something she ate, that the swelling would go down, that tomorrow there would be no lump, if that's even what it was.

"What were you doing in there?" he wanted to know, after she'd slipped on shorts and a tank and joined him on the terrace. She didn't answer, and he didn't ask again because he sensed she was in one of her moods. He poured her a small glass of grappa from the bottle he'd set on the table as she fell into the worn whicker chair next to his with her book closed on her lap. He put his feet up and lit a cigar and they absorbed the stillness for a moment, the soft orange lamplight, and the sounds of the sea settling in for the night.

He passed her a letter. "This came for you today."

She stared at it for an interminable moment, then leaned her head back, and closed her eyes.

"Aren't you going to open it?"

A warm breeze fluttered the curtains behind her. She opened her eyes, then the envelope. A smaller envelope thickly bound in tape fell onto her lap. Her heart went immediately to her throat; she knew it was Nick's. It took her a while to break into the envelope and unfold the drawing, which she showed to Roberto, who said, "Not bad," and handed it back.

"Not bad?" she gasped. "It's amazing."

"Eh, it's the Coliseum," he shrugged, Italian style. "Of course it's amazing."

She took Betty's note to the balcony railing and read it. Afterwards she stood for a time staring down over the ledge at the illuminated pool there at the edge of the sea, and she felt what had become a familiar feeling lately, life, in the form of her sister's pregnancy, as if it might be her own as they had planned for it to be. "Mary Jamie," the note said. She was going to call the baby Mary Jamie. She lifted her gaze to the horizon, where the blue lights of fishing boats danced under a big, bold moon.

She went inside and got her cell phone. Pick up the phone and be connected; life was much simpler than her thoughts. But after dialing Betty's number and hearing the first ring, she hung up and went back outside. This was the first time her sister had ever asked Jamie for something.

"How's your finger?"

She'd been clutching the book and the letter beneath her breasts.

"Jamie?"

She came over and sat on his footstool. He examined the cut. It was fine. He held the cigar out for her. She took a long puff, and they both watched the ghost of smoke fall from her mouth, morph in the air, and then dissolve. But then she handed the cigar back. It hadn't tasted right, and it was a time before she recovered, before she cleared her throat and said, "She's having a home birth."

He examined her, and then said, simply, "She's nuts."

She wanted to agree with him. But something else kicked in, something primal, her primary colors. "She's just being Betty."

"She's being irresponsible." He took a puff from his cigar.

"She wants me to be there."

He leaned his head back and let the smoke out. "Go."

She met his gaze and tried to see beyond it, to a life that was, in fact, that simple.

** 1998 **

Jamie heard a car pull up in front of her mother's house. A door slammed, Sam yelled at Clay, Clay yelled at Betty, and Betty yelled at Dave. Jamie had to bite her lip to keep from smiling as she went outside to greet them. Sam, five now, flung his backpack from the car, then the rest of him, and Clay, sweaty and flushed, was bent sideways trying to extract himself from the car seat. After retrieving their suitcases, both kids proceeded to let them roll down the driveway on their own so that they could be free to leap into Jamie's arms, what was impossible with the stuffed packs on their skinny backs, and then off into the house in search of Blue and Rocky, their mother's poodles.

Meanwhile, Betty and Dave were standing over the open trunk. "What do you want me to do, honey?"

"Of all bags to leave behind," Betty moaned.

Dave slammed the trunk closed. "I'll go back and get it."

As if there had been any question. Betty followed him around to the driver's side. "Remember, Dave, I'm going out tonight, so you need to be back to watch the kids…"

"You're going out?"

"I told you this, Dave."

"You didn't tell me."

She held her tongue for a moment. Then calmly, "I'll just be gone for a few hours."

"That's what you said last night."

"That was work, Dave."

"Fine, it's just that you promised Clay…."

"Don't tell me what I promised him. I know what I promised him. God, don't treat me like that!"

Dave started the engine and took off.

"Having a good trip?" Jamie said, and Betty spun around, "Hey, gal." Her voice was hoarse, and she looked exhausted, not to mention pregnant, but her cheer remained resolute. She stole a glance at the thin gold band on Jamie's wedding finger, and then, without comment, rolled her suitcase into their mother's living room, where Chanel No. 5 lingered in the air and fresh cut roses adorned every side table. The only thing missing was their mother, and, of course, a warm homey smell emanating from the kitchen. "I have no idea where she is," Jamie said, referring to the woman of honor, the reason why they were all here, presumably. *Waterson for City Council*. The poster stood propped on an easel, front and center in the living room, and they stood before it a moment, scratching their heads.

"I hate that picture," Betty offered finally.

"She looks stiff."

"I told her to use the other one."

"The one with the cleavage."

"She never listens to me…"

The kitchen door to the garage sprang open. "Here I am." Their mother, dressed in her gardening motif—blue overalls and sandals that revealed her perfect little feet—was stringing along her freshly groomed yap dogs, which the boys came scrambling over to terrorize. There was a third one now. "He's only got three legs," Clay said flatly, and their mother made some tight-lipped motion, as if it was a secret they were all keeping from the dog. "Angel is her name." Their mom scooped up the little hyperactive ball of fur. "Because she is an angel really, she shouldn't have survived. A policeman found her in a dumpster left for dead. Of course, after she was all fixed up and had nowhere to go, he brought her straight to me."

Betty opened the fridge. "Do you have any tortillas, Mom?"

Their mom set down Angel, perplexed. "You're hungry?"

Jamie got down some pretzels from the cupboard.

"But I've got nothing to eat. I haven't had a minute to go to the store. And I've just had the kitchen cleaned." It all came out curtly and exactly the opposite of how she had wanted to express herself—motherly. She sighed, that manic weightiness about her, the kind that always left a slight dread in Jamie's chest. "I've just got too much going on. Of course it's exciting and I'm getting all this attention…you wouldn't believe how many people have come forward. You saw the campaign poster?"

"Umm," Betty said, biting into a pretzel, her face warning Jamie—stale.

"And?"

Luckily Betty's mouth was full. "It's great, Mom!" Jamie offered, a bit too urgently. "Oh, and Steven's trying to get a hold of you, Mom…something about the Deputy Mayor coming to the event?"

"Well," she played coy though she was practically beaming. "I wouldn't know anything about that. Your brother did say he had a surprise for me…"

"It's not Steven's doing, it's Kate's," Betty reminded her. "Kate's the one who works for the Deputy Mayor, not Steven, Mom. Give credit where credit's due." She turned to Jamie. "What else did Steven say?" She seemed desperate to know, and so Jamie tried to remember the call she preferred to forget. Steven had been driving in his Mercedes on the 405, on speaker, chowing down a Big Mac, going on about why a photo op with the Deputy Mayor and the family was critical for her campaign. "Do you think she really wants to run, Steven?" Jamie had said, still unable to imagine her mother in such an important political position. "Oh, you know, she eats this shit up," was her brother's response, then he got another call and hung up, leaving Jamie with the feeling that the burger was sitting on the bottom of her stomach and not his.

Their mom lit up suddenly. "Oh I can't wait to show you…" She ran to her car and retrieved something from the trunk. "I bought them on sale at Robinsons," she said, returning with a shopping bag. "They're for the boys to wear to the event tomorrow night."

Betty swallowed—her pretzel, her laugh—and said, matter-of-factly, "The boys won't wear dress shirts, Mom."

There was a pause.

"I'm just giving you a heads up."

Their mom folded the shirts back up. "Fine, whatever, I can take them back."

"You can try, of course…I just don't want you to be disappointed."

"No, that's fine."

"I'm just saying…"

"What are you saying?" Jamie interrupted her, suddenly wanting to know why her sister consistently felt the need to poke holes in their mother's bubble. But the gaze Betty returned said that she had her own opinion about that, and then, slowly turning back to their mother, she changed the subject. "What I'm saying is that Steven's going to propose to Kate this weekend while were all here. It's imminent, don't you think?"

Their mom, who had put the bag aside, was now before the open fridge pulling things out. "There's some cottage cheese…and some canned peaches…and I think I've got some crackers…"

Reaching past her, Jamie pulled out a Corona and handed it to Betty. "When it comes to Steven, imminent means one thing only: highly unlikely."

Betty popped open the beer and took a guilty pregnant sip before handing it back to Jamie. They went back and forth on the subject of their brother for another minute, then turned to their mom and asked what she thought.

"Mom?"

Their mother blinked back at them.

"Are you OK?"

No answer.

"Maybe you should rest before we go out tonight, Mom."

Still nothing.

"The premier of *Primary Colors*, Mom." Betty reminded her. "Don't tell me you've forgotten."

"Of course I haven't forgotten," their mother at last responded. "I've really been looking forward to it."Though her weary smile said something else. "I think I will go rest though…my back's been sort of…well, anyway, what time are we leaving again?"

"Six, Mom," Betty replied dully, as if she'd not already told her mother this a hundred times. "We're meeting Kate at the theater."

An uncertain smile, and then their mother headed for the stairs, taking her daily meditation book with her. She paused before the campaign poster, tilting her head as if it was suddenly too heavy to carry upright. Then she continued on, ascended the steps slowly; gone was the bounce she'd arrived with not twenty minutes earlier, and Jamie, watching her, thought how much she and Betty were like bulls in their mother's china shop. It was always the same: she wanted them to visit, but once they were here, their presence seemed to suck the life from her.

In the guestroom now, Betty going through her clothing options for this evening, Jamie lying on the bed with the beer. "So how far along are you," she asked, examining the belly poking out of Betty's tank. Jamie was still sort of surprised by her sister's third pregnancy when she and Dave were barely getting by financially with the two. Apparently, Betty had been surprised too. "Twenty weeks," she responded, an afterthought to the blouse she was holding up for approval. Jamie shook her head no. "More importantly," Betty added, dropping the blouse and picking up another one, "is that a new custom furniture store is opening up on Capitol Hill. Dave approached them about his work, and they seem really interested." Her back was to Jamie, which was a good thing because Jamie choked on her beer. It came out her nose and she had to run to the bathroom sink, coughing.

She glared into the mirror—incomprehension, disbelief—certainly it was Betty who had approached the store, not Dave, and certainly, like all his other opportunities, nothing was going to come of it. She grabbed tissues, blew her nose, and came back sipping from a glass of water. "Sorry," she managed, "The hiccups...I've got the hiccups." There was some silence, a knowing silence, and then Betty went on, manically, saying that her job at the Smithsonian was changing again now that her boss had moved on and she'd been handed his responsibilities, though the promotion and title had not been forthcoming because of the museum's funding cutbacks, but soon though, soon, and she was working crazy hours, and... The rambling died off mid-sentence; Betty dropped whatever clothing item she was holding and sat down.

An earthquake? Or was her sister shaking. Either way, Jamie couldn't help herself. "Why doesn't Dave just go to work *for* them?" She spoke as delicately as she could. "You know. Like a job."

Betty looked at her with alarm. Then she grabbed another blouse from her suitcase and stood back up. "Look," she said, exhaling. "Dave can't work nine-to-five. OK?" She avoided Jamie's eyes avoiding hers. "It's something I learned a long time ago—he needs to do something he's passionate about." She took a jittery breath. "Otherwise he can't..."

Silence.

"Can't what?"

"He thinks he's selling out."

More silence. "So what, I'm selling out?"

"I didn't say that."

"Because I've got stock options?"

"I didn't say anything like that..."

Jamie narrowed her eyes, and Betty said, "Anyway, I don't want to talk about me. Let's talk about you. Where's Roberto again?"

Jamie hesitated; she didn't want to talk about "me" either. "On a plane back from Singapore."

"Will you guys continue to travel so much? You know, now that you're married."

"Why should that change anything? We're together when we're together. So that when we're apart we can be apart." There was an undertone of defensiveness in her voice she didn't like. Even Betty noticed it.

"Anyway, in fact no, I won't be traveling so much, but it's because of CADnet and not any silly vow."

"Right, CADnet, and about that." Betty turned at her. "What the hell? I can't believe you left BCC."

Jamie shrugged.

"I mean, didn't you just make Partner or something?"

"Or something…whatever, I just did." It came out harsh and perhaps revealed how little Jamie knew anymore of what was driving her decisions, why she'd left her lucrative position at BCC to go work for a brilliant crazy person for half the salary. Was Betty right? Was it the travel? Had being away from Roberto at last gotten to her? Or was it her boss Kenneth, the intellectual challenge, his brilliance? She'd been mesmerized by his passion, his vision, the same vision that often made no practical sense; not to mention the fact that this IPO was happening too fast. Her design department was barely hanging on to meet less scalable requirements, not to mention her serious doubts about the product's viability. She'd tried to convey this to him, but she could never quite do so with the same conviction and keen insight he could counter with. In fact, she was starting to wonder what was wrong with her…if she'd follow Kenneth, or any individual with that kind of passion for that matter, off the side of a cliff.

Or, was it simply money. Didn't it really all come down to that? Because there sat a singular moment in her mind upon which her future became crystalized, and she thought back to it now. Two or three years ago, she couldn't remember exactly when, but at her mother's request she'd been in attendance at yet another of her events held in her honor for yet another good deed or service she'd performed for the city of L.A. Towards the end of her mother's acceptance speech, she made Jamie stand up before three hundred people, plates of rubber chicken, and watered down drinks so that she could praise her daughter as a cancer survivor, an inspiration to herself and to others. Jamie's faced flushed now, recalling the moment, and not from nostalgia, but from sheer anger at her mother for using her like that. For Jamie had done nothing inspirational. In fact, the way she saw it, there were only two ways these cancer things could go. You died. Or you survived, miraculously (or not so miraculously). Perhaps you wrote a book, but writing a book would mean that her ordeal was particularly noteworthy and Jamie didn't believe that. She didn't believe she could help people. What she did believe, however, was that if she became wildly rich, she'd never have to worry about anything ever again.

"Jamie." Betty was staring at her.

"Oh sorry, Computer Aided Design Software, that's what we do—one that enables engineers to work in distributed environments via the Internet."

"Just what we need, another dot.com millionaire." It was Dave, at the bedroom doorway, appearing out of nowhere, as he liked to do. He was holding Betty's make-up bag.

Jamie flashed him a tight-lipped smile. And then something struck her, the realization that perhaps it was *this* driving her decisions, everything she was doing was being done for just *this* reason: Betty. The woman smiling blindly at the bag her husband with the chip on his shoulder just set on the bed; the woman now rummaging nervously through the bag and rambling on without breaths or pauses about how "the kids need to eat, Dave…I thought you could make them pasta…but remember that Sam prefers his plain with butter and Clay likes his with sauce but no cheese…only my mom won't have the sauce—or the pasta for that matter—so you're going to have to go to the store; and Ralphs not Vons because…" She paused, not finding what she was looking for in the bag, apparently. "Oh, here it is," she gaped up at them in relief, or at Jamie anyway. She'd not looked at Dave, not once in the entire time he'd been in the room. He, on the other hand, had been gazing at his wife both fondly and absently. One last bat of the eyes and he headed out of the room, leaving Jamie with a sour taste of patronization in her mouth, however oblivious her sister remained towards it, more bedeviled was she by their mother's morbid entrance. Robe, slippers, it was back pain, she claimed, and she simply couldn't go out tonight.

"What!" Betty dropped her bag and yelped so loud that Jamie bit her lip, secretly relieved, for the night would be easier without having to deal with her mother and Betty at each other's throats, however polite they pretended to be about it.

"But you made such a huge point of me inviting Kate, and she's…" Betty stopped herself. Their mom shuffled over and rested her head on Jamie's arm, too short to reach the shoulder. "You don't need me to have fun."

"But will you be alright Mom?" Jamie asked.

"It's just good to know that my girls are here."

Betty ripped open her sewing kit and began fixing a loose thread on her shirt. The room went quiet, and Jamie wondered why Betty wanted their mother to go with them so desperately when the woman clearly only got on her nerves.

"Well, I guess you guys will be heading out then." Their mother stepped back. "You don't want to be late."

"Mom," Betty said. "It's five."

"But there'll be traffic, dear."

"Uh huh." She bit off a piece of thread with her teeth.

Their mom continued stepping back, slowly from the room, gazing at one daughter and then the other, until something occurred to her and she paused. "You girls look beautiful."

"We haven't even gotten ready yet, Mom."

"You girls always look so beautiful."

Jamie reached out and softened one of her mother's curls.

"Oh it's a mess, dear." She brought a hand to it.

"You look young, Mom."

Betty took her bag to the bathroom; their mother, still blushing from the compliment, left; and Jamie went to go change for the show, which took all of about five minutes. Waiting for Betty, she went through some designs in preparation for her conference call tomorrow morning with Kenneth and the IPO lawyers. After a while, fed up, she went and let herself into the bathroom where she found Betty still wrapped in a towel, examining Jamie's bottle of face moisturizer.

"It'll take years off your skin," Jamie said.

"How much was it?"

"You don't want to know."

"Like what, fifty bucks?"

Jamie's eyes widened at something, and it wasn't the moisturizer.

"A hundred bucks?"

She gasped.

"What? What is it?"

That all too familiar sound of a vintage sports car pulling into the drive, that's what—and Jamie waited for Betty's gaze of recognition to meet hers in the mirror. "What's he doing here!" she said at last. Jamie didn't respond. She watched her sister's eyes narrow, expand, and then bulge. "I knew she was faking it!"

"Those Coronas were his."

"She knew he was coming over all along!"

"I'm not going out there." Jamie sat down on the toilet seat lid. Betty snorted at that, but then saw that her sister was serious and began hastily putting on her make-up. "We'll wait for him to leave."

Thirty minutes went by, even Betty couldn't pretend to primp any longer. "We have to leave. We're going to be late!"

The first person they saw as they headed for the front door was Dave, in the living room, chatting up Gary as if they were the best of friends. Their mother, dressed in jeans and a sexy blouse now, was handing them Coronas and bustling around pretending as if it was all such a surprise. Jamie thought that Betty's water was going to burst at the sight of her boys strutting around in their new dress shirts, but for Jamie the worst was seeing Gary in those pressed jeans, and thinking back to the night that he'd tried to get into her room. She'd only seen him once since then, at Betty's wedding, and only because their mother had no doubt bribed him into being her escort. When he saw Jamie now, his blue eyes sparkled and, to Jamie's quiet horror, he came sauntering right over. It made her feel dirty just looking at him, knowing what he'd been doing to their mother all these years, keeping her on just a long enough string so that she'd continue paying the mortgage on his boat. Ugh, she thought she was going to throw up at the thought of his slimy lips on her cheek. Luckily, the dogs intervened. They were careening in from the patio, on a barking frenzy, slipping on the stone tiles across the living room headed for Gary, as if he was their lord and master.

The sisters were screaming this to each other in the car now, having practically fled from the house. "He was acting as if he lived there." Her eyes were wide at Jamie. "You don't think they're back together?"

Jamie didn't respond, she was trying to keep pace with the flying L.A. traffic.

"You realize that he's in my wedding pictures." Betty held the door handle. "You realize that don't you?"

"Why do you think I didn't have a wedding."

Betty went quiet, they both did, in their own thoughts, those predominately consisting of the need for a stiff drink, so they were no less than ecstatic to find that this particular Santa Monica theater establishment was one of those new, swank places that came with a high-end bar. Kate, dressed in a double-breasted blazer and slacks, pearls, and no engagement ring, was waiting for them out front. With a perky, delighted smile, she asked them what was so funny. Betty and Jamie looked at each other. *Had they been laughing?*

Steven, who'd agreed, too readily Jamie thought, to take their mom's unused ticket, pulled up to valet just then, mysteriously on time. Kate went to go meet him, while Jamie and Betty got distracted watching Emma Thompson stride inside the theater with an unknown escort. Flashes went off. Forgetting about their cocktail, Jamie and Betty followed Emma to the concession stand, amazed that a woman so beautiful and famous ate buttered popcorn too. They bought two tubs of what Emma got, plus a Big Gulp as preordered by their brother via phone.

The buzz level grew ten decibels, and Betty nudged Jamie. Travolta was making his way through the theater wearing black on black, including sunglasses. He went right up to where Kate and Steven, dressed in an elegant, oversized black suit, were having an intense discussion, perhaps even an argument. Travolta gave Kate a big hug. Apparently, she'd worked as a consultant on the set and knew him personally. They chatted for a brief minute. Travolta was more handsome in real life, Jamie and Betty both agreed, and much shorter. After he went inside, Betty and Jamie walked over and handed Kate her popcorn and Steven his Big Gulp, which he proceeded to suck down, barely even saying hello. Kate told Betty that they should go ahead, that she and Steven would be there in a minute.

"What's his problem?" Betty whisper shouted as they struggled to find four seats together.

Jamie kept her thoughts silent, because what she'd failed to mention to Betty was one other thing her brother had told her on the phone that morning, which was that, like all the others, his relationship with Kate had run its course. With that depressing thought the movie started, and the conundrum of her brother, their mother, everyone and anyone, became replaced by the more spellbinding conundrum unfolding onscreen: Travolta's transformation into presidential primary candidate Bill Clinton, aka Jack Stanton. His impersonation was so realistic that even his cleft chin seemed like Clinton's, even though Clinton didn't have a cleft chin. But what became even more gripping was watching this Southern charmer slip and slide his way into the presidency. Jamie, expecting this to be a yawning political drama, was overwhelmed by her own conflicting emotions—inspiration, anger, pride, hatred, respect, more hatred, and then the worst, sheer and utter disappointment—she became a wreck. It wasn't so much the lie Stanton told, but how easily he told it; as though he actually believed he didn't impregnate the underage daughter of a friend. They were an hour into the movie at that point, and no Steven. No Kate.

That's pretty much how the movie ended, with Stanton disappointing the people closest to him, like his wife, his campaign manager, the father of the girl, the same people now standing and clapping wildly as he went up and accepted the presidential nomination. Even the audience in the theater was standing up and clapping. Jamie wasn't exactly sure if the applause was for Stanton or the movie. She and Betty stayed seated. Jamie had tears in her eyes. Betty was pissed.

* * *

At six-thirty the next morning, Jamie's alarm went off for her conference call. The dogs went into a tizzy, first spinning in circles, then scratching and panting at the sliding glass doors. Jamie glanced over at Sam, with whom she'd shared their mother's L-shaped living room couch last night, the entirety of which he spent twisting and turning and talking in his sleep. Of course he was sleeping peacefully now in the midst of this racket.

Jamie got up and opened the doors to let the dogs out. A crisp ocean breeze chilled her bones, and she quickly shut the door. In the kitchen she poured herself some weak coffee from the pot her mother had already made, and then she went into the office garage, sat down at the corner desk, and opened her laptop. Images haunted her, as they always did when she sat in this tiny, closed off space, while she waited for her machine to boot up and she sipped her coffee, like the day when this room was home, that year of hibernation while undergoing radiation and chemo treatments. Ironically, when push came to shove, her mom was the only person who could take care of Jamie the way Jamie needed to be taken care of: to be left alone, unbothered, with no coddling. Her dad, whom she'd fought horribly with at the time, had wanted to treat her in just the opposite manner, and she squeezed the bridge of her nose, which had started stinging. She was thinking of that day her father arrived at her mother's doorstep with a box of adult diapers, as if that might be a means of reconciliation. Radiation treatments to her pelvis had made her incontinent. "Dad!" she recoiled. "I don't need these!" He limped back up her mother's drive to his car quoting, "Me thinks she does protest too much." Another time he brought over some brochures for the Wellness Program. "I thought you might want to share your feelings with others who..." She threw the brochures in the trash. And then there was the time that he just came by to tell her how proud he was of her. She could still see the look on his face as he'd poked his head inside her mother's front door, searching for the woman who bore his children. Jamie's eyes welled at the thought. He'd just been trying to help, but she'd been so stubborn.

Single-minded, stubborn, blind—it was all the same, Jamie thought, pushing back tears and dialing into the conference call. She refused to give up on making these designs scalable. But seriously, how many all-nighters can one pull in a lifetime? If you worked hard enough, you could figure it out. Who had told her that!

"Aunt Jamie, there you are!" Sam had stuck his head in the door, just as Kenneth initiated the call, and everyone's name chimed in with a bell.

She muted the phone, hoping Kenneth, in all his pontificating glory, would quickly forget about her, and she wouldn't have to say anything. "I thought you were half dead," she said, mimicking Sam's deep sleep breathing.

Betty stumbled in behind him holding a mug. "This coffee sucks," she said, taking a seat in a chair in the corner and pulling Sam up on her lap.

"What the hell is everybody already doing up?"

"Were on East Coast time and you're not working again, are you?"

"I'm on a conference call, muted," Jamie said drearily, holding up her cell.

"Steven broke up with Kate," Betty proceeded to tell her.

"What!"

"Kate called me last night, and then I called him."

Even Jamie, who'd half known about it, couldn't quite believe it. "Who breaks up with someone at the movies?"

"You know what he said to me?"

"Hold on." Jamie unmuted the phone. A lawyer had asked her a question, which she proceeded to answer, jotting down some notes.

When Kenneth continued she muted the phone again and motioned for Betty to continue.

"He said that he wanted to marry someone like Emma Thompson."

"The actress?"

"Her character in the movie. Jack Stanton's wife."

"You mean Hillary?"

"No, I think he meant Emma's version of Hillary."

"Or a Hillary-like version of Emma."

"Whatever," Betty said, looking tired suddenly. "A woman who'll be his…"—she made quotes with her fingers—"'wing person,' someone with the balls to 'kick his ass' if need be, to make the 'hard calls,' and when the chips are down, 'lie' if she had to. His exact words."

"He saw the movie?"

"He went in after Kate left. He looked for us, so he says, but couldn't find us."

Jamie put up her hand and unmuted the phone. "I don't think that's feasible, Mike." She held her tongue for a moment. "No Kenneth. Not exactly." She muted the phone again shaking her head, at Kenneth, at Steven, she wasn't sure anymore.

"He says that we should be happy for him." Betty finished, narrowing her eyes, not at their brother but at their mom, who had just poked her head inside the room. She was showered and already dressed for the event that night, and Jamie forgot how tasteful her mother could look in a tailored black pantsuit and a string of earthy beads. She was bustling with energy, still on a high from last night, presumably, on her way over to the reception hall to drop off the centerpieces, she told them. And shouldn't Betty get going on those thank you cards she'd asked her to write? Oh, and their father called for Jamie. "It's seven a.m." Jamie repeated, because it didn't appear anyone was listening. "And I'm on a conference call."

I told your father you'd call back, her mom mouthed apologetically, as Jamie unmuted the phone to make a comment about the new specifications she was quickly pulling up on her computer. Betty scooted Sam from the room as their mother set down some papers Gary had left with her the previous night. "Don't mind me, dear."

Jamie paused what she was typing, muted the phone and eyed them.

Betty eyed them too. "I thought you said the divorce was final, Mom."

Jamie went still.

"I never said that," their mother spun around.

"Did you know he was coming over last night?"

"I did not know he was coming last night." She said each word slowly and deliberately, so there would be no mistake. "He comes to get his mail. He has a key."

"He has a key?"

"He comes to get his mail?"

She glanced from one to the other. "Well, he can't get it on the boat."

Jamie, eyes fixed on her mom, unmuted the phone and told the lawyer that he'd have it by tomorrow. She almost wished her mother had the courage to tell them that her relationship with Gary was none of their business—Jamie wished that it *was* none of her business, or that she wouldn't feel the need to judge people so unforgivingly, that she could be more like her mother that way. She watched her mom move a stack of papers from one side of her computer to the other. "There are financial reasons…he's on my health plan. Plus…" She hesitated, and then gazed down at Angel now scratching at her shin with her missing paw. "He's agreed to move back in for the duration of the campaign."

Jamie put down the phone. The conference call was over.

"Gary and I…" she sighed and patted the dog's bristly head. "We've been through a lot together."

"He left you, Mom." Betty said, turning at Jamie, whose heart immediately started pounding, because according to her sister's expression it was now Jamie's turn to say something. All the dogs had gathered now, waiting for it too, presumably. Dog treats, their mother, looking like the wind had been knocked out of her, stumbled backwards to retrieve some from the bin she kept right there, and placed one down before each of them. They all watched as they sniffed and scooted and spun into their respective floor pillows. It took a while, and then, with a wistful smile, their mother left.

"Why did you do that?" Jamie whispered at Betty. "Couldn't you have waited until after the event?"

"Why didn't you say something to her!"

Jamie sighed. "What's the point? I just don't see the point."

"How about just being honest. There's no point in that?" Their eyes met, briefly, and then Betty fled the room.

Jamie followed her, through the living room and all the way to the bathroom where she shut the door so no one could hear them. "Why don't *you* be honest?"

Betty pulled her hair back and turned on the hot water. "About what?"

"You know what."

She smeared her face with cleansing cream. "I don't know what you're talking about."

Blood was pounding between Jamie's ears. "Don't tell me he didn't try something on you."

Betty wet a rag and began wiping off the cream, methodically, hopefully, the same way Jamie had watched her do it a millions times. "He never touched me." Betty met her eyes in the mirror, at last. "But I won't tell you he didn't try."

Silence.

"And you didn't tell me."

"You didn't tell me you were getting married."

"That's not nearly the same thing."

"Isn't it?"

"No, it's…," Jamie gave up and sighed. So this is what it came down to, wondering if not including Betty in her elopement was something she would regret for the rest of her life. Why hadn't she? Certainly she had wanted to, as much as she had wanted to keep breathing. "I'll tell you why I didn't say anything," Jamie said to the person in the mirror, for sometimes she wondered if there was really only one of them. "It's the same reason you didn't tell me about Gary—if you don't tell people it's not real."

Betty paused what she was doing.

"And when it's not real it doesn't hurt so much when everything gets all fucked up."

Betty, after absorbing her sister's words, "Am I fucked up? Are things all fucked up?"

"No," Jamie quickly assured her, and then, dropping her shoulders, "Oh I don't know Betty. When do we know?" Of course no answer came, just a silence so heavy it made Jamie long for her husband, wishing he were here in this moment, that she hadn't lied to Betty—Roberto wasn't flying back from Singapore, he was at home in New York. In fact he had offered to come with Jamie to California, but she had assured him that he would not want to be here, not for this; it was totally unnecessary, and he would be miserable. She glanced at Betty staring at that bottle of moisturizer again, and realized that that wasn't the point.

"Here," Jamie said, picking up the bottle. "Take it."

CHAPTER 11

SHReK

November, 2003

Betty took a detour to the Marstons' on her way back from getting dinner at Tortilla Flats. She had to see for herself if Dave was there getting high instead of where he said he'd be, at his GMAT class, contributing to the future of their family. The visions began now: herself back at the Smithsonian, going over the fundraising projections; her boss lamenting about more budget cuts; the hour on her desk clock approaching six, the cut-off time to pick up Mary from daycare before getting fined, again; putting in for that transfer to the Met, just for fun, again; being looked over for that transfer to the Met, for reasons she didn't know, again. Her future felt like a stone sitting in the pit of her stomach. No, she insisted, spotting their rusted GTI in the Marston's driveway, pulling up behind it and flinging open the car door. She sat there, panting, imagining the confrontation, and then she quickly slammed it shut again. "No! We're not going to live like that anymore, Mary." She pounded the steering wheel for emphasis. Then she sped off towards the Beltway, her mind on one thought: a night she didn't regret. She had never regretted sleeping with Gil, (if that's what they had done, she was drunk and didn't entirely remember) she admitted to herself now, just as a cramp struck her pelvis. She felt it down to her toes. Betty let up on the gas and breathed out through her teeth. She'd been selfish, even childish, in her desire for change, for something more, something better. She knew Gil wasn't her future, but now he was part of that change, and so perhaps that's just what change was, selfish and childish, and there was nothing she could do about it.

The cramp wouldn't go away so she pulled over just before the Beltway entrance. Betty's mind went back to that morning, to the message she'd found waiting for her on her cell phone from Gil. He was in town, wanted to do lunch, no pressure, no obligation. They'd both agreed to forget that night, to call it what it was—a momentary lapse in judgment. They'd go on being the flirtatious acquaintances they'd always been. Or more apropos, they would simply stay away from each other, which they did, and so Gil didn't know she was pregnant. But maybe it was time he did, she decided, getting out her cell phone, dialing, then hanging up and closing her eyes because the rain was pouring down harder. She heard the drumming in her heart all around her. That premonition came to her again, just before the phone rang in her hand. She stared at it before answering: it was Jamie. She picked up. No, it was Sam. Uncle Steven wanted her to make sure she got an extra order of tortilla chips.

Tortilla chips. Is this what got her going again? Perhaps, but even still, her excursion to Tortilla Flats had taken longer than she'd expected. When she returned home, over an hour later, Steven was snoring on the couch, Sarah was playing poker with Nick, and the older boys were nowhere to be found. Assuming they were in the basement, she set out the food bags on a picnic blanket in front of Steven and the TV, found Nick his taco, slipped Shrek into the DVD, and then went downstairs to get Sam and Clay.

She called out a few times, but even before she got there she sensed something wrong. It was too still: no cartoon gibberish, no PlayStation antics. When she got to the bottom, she glanced about, afraid they were going to jump out and yell, "boo." Then she heard whimpering and caught Sam's feet wriggling out from behind the couch. She ran over to find Clay holding his older brother in a chokehold; Sam's face was beat red and streaming tears. Clay saw Betty, but he didn't let go. Betty had to go yank him off. Sam gagged, coughed, and spat before taking a lunge at Clay. "Stop it!" she yelled, interceding. They circled around her taking jabs at each other. Then Clay reached down and grabbed an errant baseball off the floor and chucked it hard and fast at Sam. But Betty's protruding stomach got in the way. She grabbed her belly and doubled over as a burning sensation swept through her pelvis. The room spun, her ears thudded. The boys stood there, stricken and white.

"It was Sam's fault," Clay screamed.

Sam denied this of course, and the two stood on either side of their mother's balled up figure and screamed back and forth. Betty took some long, slow breaths, put up her hand. I am OK I am OK I am OK I am OK, she said in her head. She crawled up off the floor and onto the couch. Sam sat down next to her, put his hand on her belly, and asked if Clay killed the baby. Everyone was still crying.

"I didn't mean it," Clay said, meekly this time. "You know about my temper, Mommy," he stammered defensively and she put an arm around him. "I know," she said, realizing how scared he was. She wiped away his tears and then her own, reminding them that babies were tough and made to absorb accidents. She smiled then, lightening her tone. Didn't they remember when Sam accidentally head-butted Betty when she was pregnant with Nick? Or when Sam flipped off the top bunk when he was sleeping? They all laughed at that. And didn't they remember Clay running smack into that cab door in New York? The boys laughed again, but Betty's heart dropped as all the visions came flashing before her; the nine lives of her family almost up.

The queso dip was almost gone by the time they got upstairs. Nick and Steven were side by side munching their way through it like nothing had ever happened between them. Betty dug in, starved. But the queso was spicier than usual, and she immediately regretted having eaten it. She left the boys, Steven, and Sarah engrossed in ogre antics for the kitchen to escape the food smell and sipped from her unfinished alcohol free beer, hoping the carbonation would help. It didn't. Suddenly nothing felt right. She went to the bathroom and threw up.

She woke up on the bathroom floor, clammy and disoriented and with no idea of how long she'd been there. She heard her kids singing along to "I'm a Believer," which worried her because it meant she'd been lying on this floor for a long time. She heard a phone ringing, but this time made no move to get it. The caller left no message, and so she knew it was her sister because of course her sister would leave no message. Jamie had this idea that Betty would know what she wanted to say anyway, so there was no need for a mes-sage. Her thoughts were cutting in and out. She was trying to decipher the non-message, but all she got was an image of herself in the hospital. Mary was in her arms, hours old and already beautiful. Her hair was red. Now Betty was handing Mary over to Jamie. Mary was Jamie's daughter now, and Jamie was looking at Betty as if she was seeing her, really seeing her, for the first time. It was all Betty could think about now, as she became one with this cold bathroom floor. That look, and getting it back. She wanted her sis-ter to believe in her again. She closed her eyes, and drops fell off her cheeks and onto the linoleum. She tried calling out for them, but her voice made no sound, it seemed, though she heard herself calling out for Clay, screaming at him to stop running, and then everything went fluorescent, Clay receding into that cold hollow tube. "It's all my fault, It's all my fault," Jamie was say-ing over and over, which is when Betty tried to rise from the floor, using every ounce of fortitude she could muster because she had to tell Jamie that she'd been wrong. She couldn't have done it. She couldn't have carried a child inside of her body for nine months only to give it away after it was born, even if it was to her sister, her other half, the person she'd do anything for.

She felt dizzy, like she was falling. Luckily she was already lying down.

✳✳ Fall, 2000 ✳✳

Betty squeezed Clay's knee. "Are you excited?"

"No," he said, as the train rolled into the underground plat-form. She observed his sullen, obstinate profile for a moment and then tousled his stick strait hair, which he hated. Sam jumped up.

"There she is." And there she was, waving and running alongside the train. Her hair was loose and much longer now; her jean jacket was half off her shoulders. Friday at five and her sister wasn't buried in an office somewhere. Betty still couldn't believe it.

This trip was Jamie's treat for Sam's seventh birthday, though it had been Betty who had planted the suggestion with her sister. She desperately needed a weekend away and some special time with her older boys. Nick was one now, but he'd been born colicky, and between dealing with him at night and working all day, she'd barely read the older boys a bedtime story, let alone done a drop-off or a pick-up at school recently; and weekends were a blur of practices, school fundraisers, play dates, not to mention the endless array of half-finished home improvement projects that Dave kept himself busy with. He'd been feeling low about that distributor not panning out, and she was trying to accommodate that, but in reality she didn't have the time.

"We're here!" Betty announced, as the three of them spilled out onto the platform.

"You're getting big," Jamie grunted as she failed in her attempt to pick Sam up, his bony limbs knocking with her bony limbs. She gave up and waved at Clay, who had lingered behind, hands in pockets, waiting to be noticed. Then everybody took a hand and they jostled their way to the escalator while Jamie reviewed the itinerary: tonight they'd keep it simple, see a movie maybe; tomorrow, the Natural History Museum, Central Park, *The Lion King*.

"Oh, shoot," Betty interrupted, letting go of Clay's hand to dig out her cell. "I forgot to remind Dave to pick up Nick's new medicine." She dialed as the escalator ascended, stopping too suddenly when she got off so that Clay rolled his suitcase into her Achilles tendon. "Ouch!" she said curtly.

His face flushed. "I didn't do anything."

Betty put a hand up for quiet and left Dave a detailed voicemail. The next thing she knew Jamie was tapping her on the shoulder and pointing at Clay now sprinting through the crowded terminal.

"Clay! What did I tell you!" Betty called after him. The three of them ran to keep up, but it was hard with all the baggage. Soon Betty lost sight of Clay in a sea of dark clothing. She stopped and deftly scanned the room, catching that distinctive flash of white behind a Dunkin Donuts trashcan. "Stay here," she ordered Sam and Jamie before running in Clay's direction with a look on her face that said *don't fuck with me, I'm a mom*. When she got to the trashcan, he'd already relocated to the convenience store. She found him casually perusing the ten-foot-long candy counter with a look of "mission accomplished" on his face.

She knelt down beside him, caught her breath, and then calmly, careful not to raise her voice, she asked him why he took off when she'd specifically asked him to be a "helper." Clay was so sensitive that all it took was one-decibel change, the slightest hint of condescension in her voice, and his mood would take off running. "Because I hate you, Mommy," he responded so that everyone around them could hear, even Jamie and Sam, who'd managed to drag the luggage over. Clay refused to take Betty's hand, but Jamie convinced him to take hers, and she was able to lead them out from the maze of Madison Square Garden and into the world of steel and cement.

"I should have warned you about that right off," Betty said, after they'd all shoved into the back seat of a cab.

"Does he do that a lot?"

"Clay's going through something with me right now." She spoke more to Clay, gazing out the window now, than to Jamie, who feigned alarm and asked, "What did you do to him?" It got a smirk from Clay. "I'm just kidding," Jamie added, and Betty flashed her sister a skeptical smile, unable to ignore the familiar implication, and then settled her gaze on her obstinate son. She knew Clay didn't hate her, and that if this were a battle, she would win because he couldn't make her stop loving him. No matter how much he wanted to lose her, Betty knew that he wanted her to find him more.

The cab dropped them off at Jamie's loft on Twentieth Street. On the tenth floor, the elevator opened up to the sight of Roberto at the kitchen island…"Stay clear," he told them, as the deep fryer sizzled and spattered. "What is that?" Betty cinched her nose, and Jamie smiled apologetically for her husband's penchant for odd smelling foods. Fish cakes, Roberto announced, and that his maid Theum used to make them for him when he was a kid. Betty wandered over to the stove and dipped a finger into the *nam pla*, and shit that was hot. She waved at her mouth.

"What part of *stay clear* do you not understand?"

Betty smiled, frowned, and then smiled again, sucking on her lips and never able to tell if her sister's husband was kidding or serious. Anyway, where could she stay clear? The apartment offered no delineated lines anywhere; the kitchen simply bled into the living room, dining room, office, and bedroom, where Jamie had gone with the kids to store their luggage. Betty didn't know quite what to do, so she just stood there, until Roberto directed her into a stool at the island, poured her a Thai beer and told her to relax, which she immediately did, thinking it kind of nice being told what to do for a change.

Meanwhile, Jamie gave the boys a tour of the place by slipping off her shoes and showing them how to run and slide in their socks on the factory stained hard wood floors.

Betty watched them, picking at the boiled peanuts and dried sardines in the ceramic bowls before her. The blended aroma of garlic, oil, and chili pepper made Betty feel at home even though this wasn't anything like her home.

She swiveled around on her stool. Jamie and the boys were at the foosball table now, which sat in one corner by the walled windows that faced the building across the street. Their antics grew loud, as Jamie proved no match for them, which is when Roberto marched over touting his legacy at the International School in Malaysia. After shooing Jamie away, he proceeded to win four games in rapid succession, roll, thwack, no pouting kids.

Afterwards they all sat around the kitchen island and ate the fish cakes, which the boys didn't like, although Clay made an effort to say that they were "really good." Sam asked for ketchup to dip them into. Roberto cursed in some unknown language and threw a dishtowel at him, which sent Sam, and then Clay giggling back to the foosball table. *Shrek* starts at seven at Union Square, Jamie took this opportunity to remind them, and that they still had time. But as she stood up her cell phone rang, and she frowned at the number. "Work," she said, turning it off.

"I thought CADnet was done," Betty said, as Roberto poured her more beer.

"It is, mostly." She glanced over at the boys. "There's still some fallout from the bankruptcy filing."

"Fallout?"

"I can't even go into it."

"You have to tell me now." She couldn't help herself. For once she wasn't the only person in the room whose career had fallen short, and she couldn't help feeling vindicated. Even Fashion.com, Mark's company, had folded. She wasn't proud of herself for feeling this way. Gil, after all, had lost his entire investment. "So?" she probed, when her sister hadn't responded.

Jamie looked at Roberto. "They're saying we lied about our earnings."

"Who are *they*?"

"The shareholders."

"Did you?"

"Of course not. We just, well, managed things poorly. We anticipated huge growth and overspent, mostly on real estate, office space, and top-of-the-line equipment. Then the market went away just like that, and we couldn't cover our debts. Essentially we went bankrupt."

"But isn't that what happened to everyone else? Mark's company had the same issue."

"They say that we knew we were overleveraged, yet on the analyst calls, we reported everything to be fine." Her tone changed. "Meanwhile, of course, our CEO and CFO were selling stock… minor details."

"And you?"

"Not one share."

"Well, at least it's over."

"They've filed a class action law suit."

"What does that mean?"

"I don't know exactly. Lots of legal proceedings and paperwork I suppose."

"You're not going to jail or anything are you?" She kind of laughed, nervously.

"She's not going to jail," Roberto said.

"So what does this mean for you?"

"As part of the management team, I have insurance. So they can't go after my assets, or Roberto's."

"Thank God."

"Not that my assets are worth anything now."

"But did you know they were selling stock?"

"No," Jamie said, sinking in her chair, "but I'm just as guilty—I drank the Kool-Aid like everyone else."

"Tell your sister to give herself a break," Roberto said, clearing their plates. The two of them held a soft, undecipherable look, and Betty felt a twinge of jealously. She no longer had insight into her sister's dark soul, Roberto did. The change had already been happening, but it wasn't until the dot.com fallout that Betty noticed it distinctly. Jamie rarely visited anymore, and Betty now had her own, wildly different problems, so she'd let slide the persistency she'd always maintained regarding Jamie. They talked by phone only once a month.

"I had no idea." Betty fiddled with her glass.

"I told you on the phone, Betty."

Yes, she recalled, Jamie did. She just wanted to hear it again, in person. "I guess I didn't really hear."

"Anyway let's not talk about it," Jamie said, getting up and helping Roberto with the dishes. "I'd like to focus on the kids this weekend and not on the fact that I've ruined my career."

"Maybe you and I should start our own business." Betty hesitated. "I've been thinking about a clothing business." She spoke idly, eyeing the boys, secretly keen on her sister's reaction, which, when Betty stole a glance at her, was glazed over. And who could blame her? Betty had been talking about leaving the Smithsonian for so long that it had simply become a part of her, imbedded, an accepted reality, a conversation Jamie and she repeatedly had that always ended with her mumbling, "Anyway, someday," as it did now. At this point, thankfully, a foosball dribbled its way over. Jamie rolled it back at the boys, who were getting too boisterous, Betty's instinct told her. Only she didn't feel like dealing with them right now—she felt stuck to her seat. The next thing she knew the Tolomeo lamp was crashing to the floor from an errant ball. *Shit*, it's not that her instincts weren't right, it's that she was always one second too late.

Betty and Jamie untangled the boys, now in full brawl, while Roberto vacuumed up the splinters of glass, a vein splitting his forehead.

"Time to go see Shrek," he ordered, stretching out on the couch with the TV remote. He sighed ceremoniously with relief as they waved goodbye to him from the elevator, carrying light jackets. "Don't hurry home," he added, and Jamie flashed him a look of utter incomprehension. She always made out to Betty like Roberto completely unnerved her, when the opposite was so obvious. Suddenly Betty wondered why Jamie felt the need to hide the deep feelings she had for her husband, why it was they couldn't discuss their respective marriages, openly, intimately. Was it that they were afraid to find out how perfectly happy the other was? Ha! Betty chortled inwardly, as they were making their way across Twentieth Street, when she decided that it was finally time to try for a real conversation about it, if not for Jamie then for herself, because it was she who needed to get some things off her chest, about Dave.

"Roberto would make a great father," Betty said, starting off as casually as she could.

Jamie took Clay's hand in her own.

"Both you guys, in fact, would be great parents."

They walked a little further.

"Have you thought about kids?"

It wasn't until they reached the light at Fifth Avenue that Jamie responded, "We've talked a little…well, not really. He doesn't like to talk about it." She looked so relieved to let it out that Betty kicked herself for not asking sooner.

"I've discussed in vitro with my gynecologist…"

"Really?"

"Yeah."

"Wow." Betty frowned, and then thought hard to catch up. She and her sister had not spoken about Jamie's fertility challenges since Jamie had first discovered them, or at least "challenges" was how Betty thought of them; her sister, however, was leaning forward now, looking at her. "So you believe me now?"

Betty recoiled, ever so slightly. "Believe what?"

"That I'm infertile." She spoke as if she'd been waiting six years for this moment. "You said that doctor was an idiot. Don't pretend you don't remember."

Which is exactly what Betty did, for why did her sister have to hold onto every word Betty ever said? For Betty, the past was the past, and it was the future where her mind preferred to remain, where all challenges worked themselves out naturally and people got the good they deserved. It was the place her mind was now, swimming through all those little embryos. "Though something about in vitro…it seems unnatural. What if you get five fetuses? Then you have to…you know…" She mumbled the rest…"get rid of some." There was a pause. "Is that morally right?" And then, when her sister didn't respond. "Well, I'm not saying it's not right of course, just that if it were me…"

"It doesn't matter anyway," Jamie said. "The doctor said there's a strong chance I won't be able to carry the baby to term. He suggested a surrogate."

"What does Roberto think about that?"

"He doesn't."

Betty stayed silent. Her mind was chewing on that surrogate option.

"To be honest I haven't exactly brought it up yet."

"What about adoption?"

"He avoids that subject too, though I get the feeling he's not going to want to adopt."

"Adoption seems more natural than in vitro." Even Betty had dreams of adopting one day; their mother was adopted; it was just the right thing to do.

"Mostly he says things like, 'Why would I want a kid, Jamie, when I have you?'"

"Oh, certainly he wants a kid." Then her stomach knotted around a fact that she still refused to process: Dave getting that vasectomy without telling her. She still couldn't look at him. "Why wouldn't Roberto want to adopt?" It came out harshly.

"I don't know!"

"Sorry."

Jamie sighed. "I don't understand it either. I don't know if he really doesn't want a kid, or just doesn't want a kid the hard way, or if I'm just doing this because I've got no career currently, or..." She went silent for a moment. "He and I," she stammered, "we've never needed much else."

Betty didn't respond. None of this was making any sense to her. Did it need to be this complicated? Did there need to be this much thought involved? She watched Jamie race the boys across the street and up the next block. Lingering behind, she felt lost and small amongst the towering buildings, and, far off, the two tall shadows stretching into the night. "Sam," she yelled instinctively. Up the street she saw Clay sprinting for Broadway. "Make sure Clay stops at that light!" She watched Jamie catch his hand and hold him back just as a bus whooshed by so close that the hairs on his head blew back.

"Clay," Betty ran up to them breathless. "I told you to wait. It's dangerous here. Cars do not stop!" She repeated the speech to Sam, but her sons remained oblivious. When the light flashed green, the kids dragged Jamie across the street and into Union Square Park. Betty found them chasing each other through the tunnels of the concrete jungle gym. At least in here they were safe, insulated by trees, and she could relax for a moment. She followed their shadows circling down the slide one after the other. She always enjoyed watching her sister playing with her kids. She glanced at her watch. "Time to go, guys," she yelled. "We're going to miss the opening song."

Sam sprinted out of the jungle gym at that. He already had the album and new the opening song by heart. "I'm a Believer," he sang it through the park, up three flights of escalators, waiting in line at the concession stand. He only stopped when Clay accidentally side-swiped an overweight woman, spilling some of her oversized pop-corn. She mumbled something about discipline and Betty pulled Clay into her side. "Welcome to my world," she mouthed to Jamie, who slapped money onto the greasy counter and reminded Betty that her sister could be this woman in ten years. Betty, horrified, pushed the money back. "Please don't say that. Please don't ever say that again."

The airless theater was crammed with children. They fumbled into seats near the front and Sam immediately flipped over his pop-corn. Jamie went and bought him another one. Now he had both a Shrek and Donkey action figure, which put Clay out of sorts. Then Sam had to go to the bathroom, and Betty took him. By the time they got back they'd missed the song. When Sam finished whining about that, Betty settled into her seat and dozed.

Clay's cackling kept her half awake. Every time Donkey bonked into something or said something ironic, Clay would laugh and look at Betty to share the adult, subtle humor. It was times like these with her son that she was confident his rebellion would pass. She just had to keep believing in him, and then in herself as a mother. At one point he laughed so hard he looked over at Betty with pure, unadorned awe, and it occurred to Betty that her sister had no idea what she was missing out on; otherwise she wouldn't consider missing out on it. Sam's favorite song ended the movie, and Betty hummed along.

The Scottish ogre left them all in high, hungry spirits. Jamie suggested the Coffee Shop, a place where they could get martinis and kids meals. They shared two plates of French fries and ham-burgers between the four of them, until the kids started sinking slowly into their seats, and they headed back to the loft carrying them on their backs.

"You're lucky to live in New York," Sam said, choking Jamie's neck.

"Can we see the Big Apple tomorrow, Mommy?" Clay asked, letting loose his excitement. But she mistakenly laughed, they all did. "There is no Big Apple, stupid," Sam said. That's when Jamie and Betty dropped the kids from their backs, trying not to laugh further, but letting little martini giggles slip out here and there. Betty sensed Clay's embarrassment, but she made light of it, hoping it would go away. She took his hand and they kept walking.

"Why don't you have kids, Aunt Jamie?" Sam asked.

"Because I'm married to an ogre, Sam."

Sam frowned. "Uncle Roberto's an ogre?"

"Not everyone has kids, Sam."

"But you're not a mom if you don't have kids."

"Not everyone wants to be a mom, Sam."

He mulled that over a moment. "But you have to be a mom. You're married."

Jamie laughed. "You don't *have* to be anything, Sam. Life isn't a fairytale, that's what *Shrek* was trying to tell us: there isn't one way it's supposed to work."

He squinted at his mom. "I don't get it."

"Look at it this way," Jamie said, picking him up as if she could still throw him over her shoulder. "If I had kids of my own, then how would I harass you?"

Hers was a point Betty had noted before: once Jamie had kids of her own this would all change. Today Jamie was theirs and theirs alone, and a selfish part of Betty wanted it to remain that way. "It will happen when it happens," Betty said offhandedly.

Jamie set Sam down. "What is that supposed to mean?" And from the stone expression on her sister's face, Betty knew she'd said something wrong. Sam wedged between them and grabbed their hands, making them swing him back and forth as they walked on. From Betty's other hand, she dragged Clay, who had decided to be Gumby, which he did when he sulked, presumably still hurt over the Big Apple debacle. She felt like she was slogging waist deep in mud. After a few minutes she paused to rest her arms. "All I'm saying is that if you're meant to have a kid, you'll have one."

"How? A miracle?" Jamie increased her pace.

Betty began to say what she meant, but then she didn't know what she meant. Why not a miracle?

"I told you six years ago that I was infertile, and you refused to believe me, made me refuse to believe it. So…and now…," her voice shook uncontrollably, and she looked away. When she could speak again her tone cut bitterly, "For you it might be fate, nature, pop pop pop, no birth control, let's just see if it happens…"

"That's not what I…" She increased her stride to meet her sister's.

"For someone like me it's a choice. I, he, we…someone's got to make a decision. Do we want to have kids, or do we want to face what happens if we don't. It's different."

It hadn't come out right. "You're not getting what I'm saying." Betty paused to gather her thoughts, but Jamie had already pulled away emotionally.

Then something else stopped Betty in her tracks, some kind of commotion up ahead. It grew piercing…screaming, and horns were honking. She finally focused on what was happening around her, which was that Jamie was screaming, and Clay was splayed out on the street next to a taxi. There was a moment where everything went white. The world fell silent, and she was above it, looking down on something happening to someone else. She felt his hand in hers, but when she looked down it wasn't there.

Betty snapped into gear. She ran and fell beside Clay, checked his legs, arms and torso, his face and head, while repeatedly telling him he was all right…there didn't seem to be any blood. He opened his eyes wide, stunned and disoriented. When he saw his mother's face he started crying. He reached his arms out for her. "Don't move him," someone said. The taxi driver was ranting at Jamie who stood frozen in front of him, sheet white. "He just ran out without looking," another woman said. "You should be more careful with your son, lady."

"It was my fault," Jamie said, kneeling next to Betty. "It was my fault."

"Jamie!" Betty shouted, her heart in her throat. "Stop it. He's alright."

But tears were streaming down her sister's face. "My fault."

"He ran into the door," a man wearing a suit finally offered, bringing some sense to the situation. "I was getting out of the cab and he ran right into the door and knocked himself backwards. I saw him hit his head against the cement." Betty felt the back of Clay's skull. A large bump had swelled there. Thank god the skin hadn't broken. "You need to get that looked at," the man added, before walking off. "How helpful," Betty said, watching him disappear into the crowd of fleeing pedestrians.

Jamie jumped in front of a taxi to hail it, Betty picked up Clay, and they all stuffed in. Betty pulled Sam out from behind Jamie's shoulder so that he could see that his younger brother was alive and breathing. Jamie held up three fingers. "How many?" "Three," Sam replied. "Not you, ding dong." She turned back to Clay. "How old are you?" "Four," Clay responded, and Jamie looked at Betty with relief, but Betty couldn't look back. She was spiraling in her own world of dread, anger, and guilt.

Clay's tears had dried by the time they pulled up in front of NYU's Emergency Center. He couldn't remember what had happened. "That's normal," said the pretty, blond, triage nurse as she interviewed Betty in a small room just behind the reception. Betty filled out paperwork while the nurse poked around Clay's body with an instrument, and took his blood pressure and pulse. Clay blushed at all this sudden attention. The nurse asked important, concerned questions, and acted like there was nothing she couldn't handle, which made Betty feel better. After examining Clay's head she concluded that he wasn't in immediate danger. They'd have to wait to see a doctor. Unfortunately there were ten cases ahead of theirs. Don't let him fall asleep, she instructed.

They sat in the waiting room. Jamie had her head between her knees, and Sam watched cartoons on a TV hanging in the corner. "Sorry," Jamie lifted her head. "I have a hard time with hospitals."

Betty told her to take Sam home, that it would be a long wait.

Roberto was already coming to get Sam, Jamie said, adding another "Sorry."

"Why do you keep saying that?"

"I wasn't paying attention," she said to the floor.

"Oh please. I'm his mother."

"Can't I just be sorry?"

"Are you alright? You look green."

"I need air." She stood up and weaved out the double doors, Sam with her.

Betty found a seat and pulled Clay into her lap. The wall clock said eleven. Her martini had worn off, her adrenaline was leveling, and reality had set in. She perused her surroundings: A baby was crawling around the linoleum floor in a saggy diaper; an emaciated woman was bent over her knees, drooling from her mouth; a belligerent couple sat across from them, reeking of alcohol. Betty put her hand to her mouth and smelled her breath. She hoped the nurse hadn't thought she was drunk. She definitely wasn't drunk. She couldn't hold on to her son 24/7. She bit the inside of her lip until it bled.

What would she tell Dave? He'd already accused her of being unfocused with Clay. He had not wanted her to take the boys to New York, saying they were too young and wouldn't appreciate it. They'd gotten into a horrible argument about it. It had been late, the boys were asleep, Dave was reading in bed, and she was packing for the trip. "I want the boys to have new experiences," she was saying.

"It's too much money. And they won't appreciate it."

"Why are you always so negative?"

"I'm realistic."

"You're a quitter. You quit everything. Even your kids."

He didn't respond.

"Remember when Sam wanted to do swim team last summer? You said he would just end up quitting like he always did, and plus it meant someone would have to get him to the pool by eight every morning, and who in reality was going to do that? Me? God forbid I ever be on time for anything. Isn't that what you said?" She paused. "Isn't it?"

"Whatever you say, honey."

"Well, *now* look at him. His wall has ribbons on it and he wants to be on the team again this summer."

"You're right, Betty. You're always right."

"God, don't take that tone with me." She slammed her suitcase shut, struggling to zip it closed. "Just because you're stuck in the funk of depression doesn't mean the rest of us have to be too." She went to the bathroom, turned on the faucet, and stormed back. "And how dare you get a vasectomy without my consent? Just because you don't want another child doesn't mean I don't! You can't make that kind of decision for me!"

"My body, my choice."

"Fuck you," she'd screamed, if only to wipe that look off his face. Had he always despised her this much?

"Mommy?" Betty jumped and turned. It was Clay, standing in the doorway, his face pale with fright. "Mommy, what's a vastomy?"

Betty was cringing now at that image, and wondering if Dave had been right. She's the one who wanted to come to New York. She was the one who was self-absorbed. She didn't deserve more kids.

Jamie and Sam returned, relatively refreshed and with Roberto, who had just arrived, slightly pale. Clay happily slid off his mother's lap so that Roberto could examine his head. He concluded, in a Scottish accent, that Clay's head looked like an orange on a toothpick. Then there were some *Austin Powers* monologues and a skit from *Saturday Night Live*. Roberto helped Clay—cackling now—hone his Scottish accent, and soon the two of them were repeating the phrase, "If it's not Scottish, it's crap," in unison, and people were staring.

"What is it with guys and Mike Myers?" Jamie pretended to fathom.

Betty didn't know. She didn't care to know, and she found herself staring absently at them. They didn't get it, not really anyway. They had no idea what Betty was going through. Tonight they would both go home and sleep. Betty, on the other hand, would spend the sleepless hours convincing herself that her child wasn't going to have brain damage. She'd lose a lifetime of sleep. The thought made her feel terribly alone and experience a state of mild panic. She wanted to be close with her sister, for the bind to be permanent and deeper than blood. She wanted her sister to lose sleep too, the kind of sleep you lose over a child because otherwise, she feared, they'd remain disconnected forever.

By the time the nurse called Clay's name, they'd waited two hours and Betty had vowed never to see *Austin Powers: International*

Man of Mystery. She left Betty and Clay in a curtained-off room with a bed and various machines and instruments. A young-looking intern with no facial hair arrived. He went through a chart of procedures so methodically that Betty wondered if he knew what he was doing. Then he announced that Clay looked fine, didn't think he needed an X-ray, took off somewhere and didn't come back for thirty minutes. When he did return, he went through the same methodical routine, as if for practice, concluding again that he didn't think Clay needed an X-ray. If he could drop the word "think," Betty would feel more assured. He vanished before she could ask a question, and another thirty minutes went by before a different nurse showed up with release papers. They needed an attendant's signature and then they could go. Betty relaxed her shoulders. It was over.

Then the attending doctor strode in, took one look at Clay's head, and ordered an X-ray. "If it's a skull fracture there's nothing we can do, but wouldn't you like to at least know?"—Like the desire to be released without an X-ray was her idea. "Of course," she said, confused.

They proceeded to X-ray. A technician took pictures and put them in a different room to wait for the results. This room had windows facing out onto the nurses station and the shades hadn't been drawn, so Betty could see the attending doctor standing before an X-ray onscreen. She could see the little skull and knew right away it was Clay's. He called another doctor over and pointed a finger at something in the X-ray. That doctor pulled over some others so that now a half-dozen people were ruminating over her baby's skull. Her heart began thudding against her chest cavity, blood rushed to her head, and her bowels moved. Then there was a big void, a period of blankness where she wept without crying. When she resurfaced from wherever she'd been, she found herself on the other side of all right, the place where everything was NOT all right. And she was alone.

She felt her body rush out the door and her voice demand to know what was going on. The doctors stared at her, the mom who had a martini and let her kid run into a cab. The attending physician led her back to the room where she'd abandoned Clay and drew the shades. She was shaking. Tears were streaming down her face, though she refused to cry. He told her that they'd seen a hairline fracture and needed to do a cat scan to check for internal bleeding. That's when she sobbed.

Clay tried to be brave. The nurse wanted to strap him to the gurney for his journey into the center of that big cold hollow tube, but Betty refused the straps, instead wrapping Clay tightly in a blanket. She sang "I'm a Believer" to calm him, suddenly the only song she could remember. They reminisced about Donkey and how he was always knocking into things and falling over and getting back up. They laughed about how he slept on his backside, with his hooves sticking up in the air, and all the while Betty couldn't stop the tears from streaming down her face. She loved him so much. Then the doctor led her into an adjacent room with a five-inch-thick metal door where she would be safe from the harmful rays. It made the most horrible sound when it shut, and she thought back to the times when her sister had described to her this exact same door over the phone. Betty was three thousand miles away then, back when her sister was getting radiation, and now this door would be lodged in her memory forever, this door would be Betty's burden.

She awoke from a dream. The attending doctor was telling her that everything was all right: no internal bleeding, they could go. Clay was going to have a bad headache, that's all, and Betty should wake him every few hours during the night. She signed the release forms and picked up Clay, who clung to her body with every limb. If only she could feel him. She shuffled down the busy corridor in a daze…numb…someone else.

Roberto had taken Sam home, but Jamie was still slouched in her chair, her head rolled back in sleep, her mouth slightly open. Sadness gripped Betty's chest at the sight of her sister, a woman who'd traveled the world building bridges, only to land up here, disconnected, in the depths of her own cancer hell. Back in the theater, at a tender moment between Shrek and the princess, Betty saw her sister wipe a tear from her eye. If Betty didn't deserve more children, certainly her sister did. That's when Betty made a decision, knowing she'd have to fight to make it happen.

KILL BILL VOL. 1

November, 2003

Betty's baby wasn't due until late January, but Jamie couldn't wait any longer. Her heart had raced home on autopilot after reading Betty's letter and hearing her husband say so simply, "Go."

Let it go.

Let the anger go.

It was like she'd been released from some heavy weight, and now her mind and body were free to catch up. She'd fly direct to L.A. and see her mother, fly to D.C. to spend Christmas with Betty and the boys, and then stay on until the baby was born. She'd rejoin Roberto in Thailand in February. Giorgio was staying on indefinitely in Ferrara with his family according to his abbreviated e-mails, and while this confirmed Jamie's suspicions, Roberto still anticipated his father's eventual return with utter certainty. But she had no bandwidth to contemplate that at present; nor could her husband, it seemed. There was too much desolation already in the air regarding her departure, for him because they would be apart, for her because she could no longer deny the physical change taking place within her. That hardness in her breast still hurt, terribly, and each morning, after her self-examination in the shower gave her the same answer, she'd stand lamenting at her naked body in the steamy mirror. She'd been so complacent all those years, popping a hormone drug with a label that clearly stated, "Risk of causing breast cancer." Then she would bend over the sink and put her head in her hands. It had never occurred to her how much she didn't want to die—even back when the threat was real—until this very moment.

It was because she'd gone off her hormones, she kept telling Roberto, who'd noticed the changes in her body. She told him she'd go back on the drug when she got to L.A. and saw a doctor and refilled her prescription. He seemed relieved though skeptical. He knew how much she hated doctors. Well, not doctors per se, but the whole damn concept that no one, not even "the experts," really knows anything…Like the famed L.A. oncologist Jamie's mother had finagled to take Jamie on as his patient; he'd assured Jamie that these new chemo drugs he was putting her on were significantly less invasive. She probably wouldn't even lose her hair, which she did. And as far as possible infertility? So improbable it wasn't even worthy of discussion.

Her flight to L.A. was out of Bangkok Sunday evening. Roberto put Stefano in charge of the restaurant for the weekend so that on the Friday before her departure, they could check into Bangkok's Oriental Hotel, the place where they'd said those vows that she'd once thought so silly, and drown their parting sorrows in a few days of old fashioned luxury. They didn't leave the air-conditioned parlors of the legendary resort except to lounge by the impeccably kept pool. In the evenings they sipped vermouth and smoked cigars in the bar. At night they ordered room service and watched bad TV huddled in bed as if the hours could be prolonged by motionlessness.

On Sunday at noon, with still twelve more hours before her flight, Jamie's persistent, low-grade nausea started to feel worse. She'd already dry-heaved twice into the toilet. That Thai chili pepper, she reassured him, retaking her fetal position on the canopy bed. In reality her heart was splintering as she lay there, lost in his determination. He was organizing and packing her suitcase. There was something comforting, if not comical, about the way he rolled her tank tops into little sausages so they'd stack better, the certain way his jaw clenched as he rearranged her half dozen sandals, his interrogation about identification, house keys, money. She was worried about leaving him alone. "It's only two months," he kept telling her. But she had a bad feeling, like this life was no longer about them.

She tried calling Betty to tell her she was coming, but was ultimately relieved when no one answered. She was too nervous to hear her own voice try to describe the past seven months, as if they hadn't completely changed her. She also didn't want Betty to sense her fear about what was happening to her physically. So Jamie left no message; some things between them couldn't be communicated in words. She resigned to just show up on Betty's doorstep and assume that things would be like they'd always been. That was one thing Jamie could always count on.

The other thing was her mother, which was why Jamie was stopping in L.A. Her mother would know what to do. She'd know people, the right doctors, as she had before. She'd get all busy about it, not allowing either of them time to think, and Jamie would blindly follow along. When her mother was in Glenda the Good Witch mode, she still held certain powers over her younger daughter; and when it was over, just like that her mother would ascend in her bubble, and Jamie would get on with her life. That was Jamie's idea anyway.

Roberto had been standing in the bathroom doorway watching her. She was sipping a Coke to settle her stomach while trying to transform the thirty-nine year old woman in the mirror for their day out together. She felt old. Nothing about her glowed. Her face was breaking out. She'd been retaining water and her feet were perpetually bloated. And horrified by her Medusa hair, she was trying to straighten it with a blow dryer now, her eyes filling at the futility. He seemed as lost as she. He looked like he wanted to say something but couldn't. He always looked that way.

The streets were hot and steamy at five when they set out from the hotel to go catch a movie at the Emporium. They agreed that a chaotic, blood-spattering Tarantino film would be a good distraction from inevitability. Dogs were lying around half dead from the heat, and the food stalls, selling unrecognizable meat, were crammed with families who looked liked they'd surfaced from nearby crevices and cardboard cubbyholes. Barefoot kids sidled up to Jamie with bracelets of garland. She had learned to refuse them, to smile and keep pace with Roberto expertly threading her through the chaotic maze. She didn't let go.

By the time they reached the SkyTrain her palm had melted to his and beads of sweat were trickling down her back. The SkyTrain was a sleek, new, civilized mode of transportation, a big step up from the tuk tuk. They boarded just before it zipped into motion, and everything instantly hummed of silence. It was her first view of the metropolis from above the frantic fray of families packed on zooming scooters. "Look there," he said, pointing out the window. "I used to go to school down that street, Soi 15."

She looked, but it was hard to navigate through the maze of freeways, skyscrapers, and jungle. Her husband's gleaming eyes would have to suffice. "There used to be klongs running along both sides of Sukhumvit Road."

"Klongs?"

"Canals," he clarified. "Kids used to take boats to school in those days."

"I don't see them."

"They're paved now." His voice faded for a moment. "It's sad," he went on. "Even our house was left abandoned. When the Thai government evicted the Americans after Vietnam, they let the infrastructure crumble, leaving the rest of us to suffer in the aftermath. My father and I moved to Malaysia, and when we came back to Thailand five years later even the movies were gone. The government put a ban on American imports."

"You went to the movies? Here?"

"Those they could get, anyway. Bed Knobs and Broomsticks, Fiddler on the Roof, The Sound of Music. . . My father was working all the time, so my aunt, when she visited from Italy during the winters, having nothing to do, would take me to movies. . . I was six, I think, when I saw Sleuth." A glow had overtaken his eyes. Top Secret!" he gasped suddenly. Val Kilmer's first movie. He went on to list some others, some she'd heard of, some not. ". . . and then, of course, the greatest comedy ever made. . ." he gave her a moment here to insert what that was, was horrified when she couldn't. The Adventure of Sherlock Holmes Smarter Brother. And GeneWilder may as well be the pope. "I went with some school friends." He was far away from her now. "My aunt was upset because I wouldn't let her go with us. We had been very close; she never had children of her own. But I was a teenager by then, and well, I couldn't wait to break free of her constant doting. Two years later I was in the States and she was back in Italy, and I'm still all she has." His mind went somewhere then. When it came back he was shaking his head. Jamie thought it was to clear his mind of the unsettling memories, but then she realized he was chuckling at some scene he'd suddenly remembered. "Brilliant movie."

She still wasn't exactly sure which movie he was talking about, what he was really talking about at all, and they fell silent. Then he opened his eyes at her and said, with an innocence and wonder that matched her own, "I mean who doesn't like movies?"

She thought that perhaps they didn't grow up so far from each other, after all.

The SkyTrain dropped them off inside the Emporium. They rode the escalator up a few levels to the theater: modern, slick, neon. Posters for Thai Warrior movies flanked the walls. Instead of popcorn they ordered shrimp chips. Their Coca Cola seemed laced with extra sugar. When he was a kid, ticketholders had assigned seat numbers, but today they could sit wherever they wanted, and they chose an empty row near the back.

The lights dimmed and a short film played about the Thai king's fifty-seven-year reign. Roberto stood up, as did the other theater patrons, and pulled Jamie out of her seat when she didn't immediately follow. It was disrespectful not to stand in honor of the king he said. Was he kidding? No, he was not kidding, and so she was mortified when her cell phone rang just at the climax of the Thai national anthem. She fumbled to switch it off. Then everyone sat down again, and the movie started. "Revenge is a dish best served cold" splayed on the black and white screen, the last words Jamie understood, for it quickly became apparent that the movie had been dubbed in Thai with no English subtitles. It was disconcerting, the Thai sounds so warped and incongruous coming from the American actors' mouths, and Roberto asked, apologetically, if Jamie wanted to leave. She blinked a few more times *at the screen, then waved him off, "Mi Pen Lai," because she hadn't seen a movie in forever, and already she felt at home in this lumpy velvet seat with her shrimp crisps and her cold nose. Her stomach had settled, her hair felt smooth, and her feet weren't swollen. Plus, when Uma Thurman, aka Black Mamba, struck the sultry Vernita, posing as a suburban housewife, with her knife from ten feet back, Jamie decided she didn't need a translation; Uma's eyes did the translation: she was pissed. Someone, apparently this Bill person, had done the worst thing that ever could be done to a person. He had killed her unborn baby.*

Jamie contracted in her seat as a dark sensation passed through her, what felt a little like guilt, not to mention shock at the sight of Uma's womb being cut open like that. A physical detachment seemed to occur, as if Jamie's soul had been cut open too, and then removed, allowing her to watch on unaffected, even with all the blood spraying, the arms and legs and torsos flying, for Uma had moved on to the next target on her revenge list: O-Ren. (Bill was at the bottom of the list, in caps, underlined.) But before Uma could kill O-Ren, she would have to kill the crazy eighty-eight warriors protecting O-Ren, not a small job, even with the Samurai sword, and when it was done O-Ren almost seemed like an afterthought, a simple swipe to the head, which went flying into the air in slow motion, hit the snow, and rolled to a stop.

So the movie ended.

For now, anyway.

Don't tell me there's more.

Kill Bill Vol. 2; it comes out next year. We'll have to wait until then to see how it ends, Roberto told her, whistling the theme song, which was also a whistle, on the way out.

They went back to the hotel where the airport shuttle was picking her up at nine thirty. Waiting, they fell asleep on the bed, fully dressed, including shoes. A heavy, deep sleep. Jamie was in labor, pushing and screaming and in unbearable pain. There were people around her that she couldn't make out, shadows of strangers. Betty was there, holding her leg, telling her to push, but something was odd about her sister: she couldn't hear Jamie nor respond to her desperate calls. Worst of all she looked frightened, and Betty never looked frightened. There was blood on Betty's hands and between Jamie's thighs where Betty held her focus. Over and over she commanded Jamie to push. Jamie felt something splitting apart inside her, and she reached down to feel the baby's head. She knew it was there, but just before her fingers brushed it, it retracted. When she looked up again, Uma was standing over her with that I've-never-been-so-pissed-off-in-my-life-look eating away at her tan face. Her yellow leather suit was soaked in blood, and she held the steel Samurai sword in the air with both hands. There was a distant scream, Uma brought down the sword, and in one swift maneuver sliced open Jamie's stomach, only it was no longer Jamie's stomach but Betty's, and Jamie was staring at the bloody sword in her own hands. She'd missed. The top of the baby's head was chopped off and blood was spraying all over. Jamie was shaking. "I didn't mean to do it," she said.

But Betty couldn't see what was happening. "Is it a girl? Is it a girl?" she kept asking.

"I didn't mean to do it," Jamie kept responding.

"Wake it up," Betty said, beaming with anticipation. "Just slap its bottom and wake it up."

But Jamie couldn't move; the yellow suit was a straight jacket.

"Jamie?" Someone said.

"It's dead," Jamie said.

"Who's dead?"

Jamie was shaking all over.

"Wake up, Jamie."

She tried but she couldn't scream. Only a strangled moan escaped her before Roberto came into view. Heart pounding. Wild eyes. She stared at him. "Something's happened."

** February, 2003 **

Jamie heard the elevator door push open, and she glanced at the clock: four p.m. He was home early; she'd yet to take a shower or even brush her teeth. She toggled her computer screen from the surrogacy article she'd been reading to her resume that she was supposedly updating. Technically, as far as the world knew, she was looking for a job. The CADnet lawsuits had settled over a year ago, she was free to move on, and while she'd had some offers, in reality she just couldn't imagine it. In reality she had yet to pick up a mechanical pencil. Everything she'd wanted so badly and for so long all seemed so manufactured suddenly.

She heard the fridge open and shut and the clap of his dress shoes in her direction. *I can do this.* She tried to rally, if not for herself then for Betty. Her sister had been pushing Jamie about this surrogacy for almost two years now, and then this morning Betty had announced on the phone the receipt of her test results from her OB/GYN. She'd be a high percentage donor, even at thirty-eight. Her tone was expectant and all business. She was ovulating on the thirteenth, and wanted to shoot for that cycle to have her eggs extracted.

"Are you sure about this, Betty?"

The hard silence meant yes.

"And Dave?" It was Dave who had answered the phone when Jamie had called. "That's my wife," he started off. "She's not only smart and beautiful; she doesn't stop giving." Jamie cringed at the undertone of patronization that always echoed when he spoke of his wife. She sensed something going on between the two of them but had yet to ask. She wasn't sure she wanted to know, she wasn't sure she wanted anything to change.

"Let's just do it," Betty said, for the umpteenth time.

They went on to waste another hour running through the possible timeframes. They tossed around a few baby names; they seemed to already know it would be a girl. Anyway they'd already gone through all this yesterday, and the day before that. It felt right, like breathing again, their daily discussions, as if their relationship hadn't lapsed after all.

He dropped his briefcase on the floor and fell onto the couch beside her.

She swiveled her chair around to face him. What Jamie had failed to mention to Betty was that Roberto remained frustratingly adamant about not wanting kids; that when Jamie had brought up "options" they'd fought about it; that Jamie went and slept in that hotel.

But like a runaway train, Jamie didn't know how to stop what was coming to a head.

He rested his head back against the brick.

She could smell the city and sweat mixed with his scent. His silky brown hair fell easily about his face, his suit draped from his limbs, and she felt the pull of all that, an aching need for him, and yet she wouldn't go over to him, couldn't, so she just let him sit there examining her with that hint of fascination in his eyes, this stranger he married.

"How was your day, dear," he began.

She smiled at his irony. As if she'd had a day.

He cocked his wrists together testing an imaginary club. "If I were you, I'd play golf."

She blinked at him. That idea of hers came back to mind, the one where she tells him that she and Betty will get a sperm donor if need be, that she's going to do this surrogacy with or without him. Once she took it that far, certainly he would give in. She felt certain that someone so adamantly against something must have some deep hidden desire for it.

"Speaking of which…" He abruptly stood up. "…I was looking into tickets today." He headed for the bedroom unbuttoning his shirt. "There are some good deals on Thai Air."

Her heart stopped.

She listened to his keys, money clip, cell phone, and Palm Pilot hit the dresser. The slipping on of jeans, a t-shirt, the care and thought he placed into hanging his suit.

"So are you ready to step away from the world…everything… this?" He was back before the open office, his hands braced against the doorframe above his head.

How further apart could their thoughts be?

He went off to the kitchen, his mind sifting through ideas.

She forced herself to follow him. He'd been talking about this for a while.

He extracted a parcel from the fridge, and she stepped back from the stench as he unwrapped it. He looked as relaxed and excited as she'd seen him in months. "So you told them?"

"Yep."

"What did they say?"

"There wasn't much to say. They want me to give them four weeks. So it looks like April that I'll go."

Her husband still spoke in the first person.

"Isn't it hot in Thailand then?"

"Jamie, it's always hot."

He'd been threatening this for so long…and yet…She wandered over to the tall windows by the couch and stood looking out. The woman on the fourth floor across the street was on her cell phone by the window, pregnant again.

"So?" he said, pots and pans banging.

"So what?"

"So what do you think?"

She sat on the arm of the couch. "I think you should do what you want to do."

"Not me. You! I want you to want this too."

She twirled her gold wedding band around her finger. "Me, you, I? Are we still supposed to be speaking in the first person?" It was her way of reminding him of their fight, the one he'd chosen to forget.

He pulled down one of his Thai cookbooks, examined it a few minutes. Then he came at her sharpening a knife. "All I know, Jamie, is that I need this. That I'll go fucking crazy if I don't breathe different air for a while."

She stared at the knife, at him, and said guiltily, "I know." CS Partners, RAPID, Delphiant…he'd ridden the technology wave all the way up and all the way down.

"Go," she blurted out. "I want you to go. You deserve it."

"But I want you to come too. You don't have to stay the whole time."

She didn't respond. That was a first, him asking her to come. They didn't ask things of each other, let alone force them upon each other. If she didn't want to go to Thailand, he wouldn't make her. If he didn't want a kid, she wouldn't make him have one. That had been their unspoken resolution. They would go on together, even when they were apart. This is how they'd operated. She sunk into the couch. When had her life become such a lie?

"Jamie, you're grimacing."

She lay down on her side, tucked her hands under her head, which hurt. "Do you think it's too late for me to become a ballet dancer?"

He was back at the cutting board now, slicing garlic. "Why are you all the way over there?" was his response. "Why don't you come over here, open a bottle of wine, put out some cheese…you know…*do* something."

But didn't he see, this was the problem. She couldn't seem to *do* anything, let alone get up from this couch. Even with the surrogacy, Jamie could feel herself simply going through the motions with Betty. A child had never been a physical reality for her, and with that thought everything went still. The world no longer made sound—even Roberto seemed on mute, slicing and dicing so patiently and contentedly at the kitchen island surrounded by four empty stools. Why four when it was only ever the two of them? How could he not wonder what this quiet would sound like fifteen years from now? Would they even be able to hear it? Their kids would be teenagers by then if they had them now. Their visions came to life in those stools; they were sweaty in their jerseys, their high tops untied, devouring a bag of potato chips and bantering about a lost game.

"What'd you shoot?"

"Eighteen."

"That's it?"

"Mom." He whined it.

"Just kidding." She winked at him.

Roberto then waved his wooden spoon at them because they were crossing the boundary of his cooking space; the kids were giving him grief about the anchovies he was stirring into the sauce. "That's gross, Dad." Roberto picked up an anchovy, wiggled it in the air, and then dropped it in his mouth with a look that only Jamie could possibly find endearing. "See what you've done? Our children are Neanderthals. *Tutti a letto!*" (He will only ever speak to them in Italian.)

She snapped her vision shut and reminded herself that she'd been spending too much time alone, at her computer, researching those surrogate links Betty kept sending her. She no longer checked the financial news or stock prices, barely the weather. Two years ago she checked them every hour and recalculated her net worth on Quicken. She didn't have visions of kids then; she had bigger clients to meet, deadlines to make, and milestones to achieve.

"Check this out." Roberto held up a baking sheet.

She forced herself from the couch and went over. It was a whole sea bass he'd picked up in Chinatown—head and tail still intact—gagging on a sprig of parsley and thyme. "Well, there you have it." She opened a bottle of Prosecco. He wrapped the fish in parchment paper, folding the ends over neatly, then placed it carefully in the oven and set the timer. She poured two glasses and took a sip from hers. He was on a stool now, waiting for her to meet his gaze. "What do you want, Jamie?"

A muscle in her leg began pulsating. It truly amazed her he could ask such a question, that he didn't know what she wanted without her having to say it.

"What's so funny?"

She relaxed her face, which had been twisted up, apparently.

What do you want, Jamie? At last, she thought, opening her mouth to tell him, but then something occurred to him and he jumped up from his stool and went to his briefcase in the office. He came back with two Italian movies on DVD that he'd purchased at the MOMA store. "They were having a Fellini special," he said, watching her.

She eyed them.

He slid one towards her. "You should watch it. Maybe you'll learn something about me."

She perused the bleak, black and white cover. "It's been nine years, Roberto. Why can't you just tell me about you?"

He sat back down, his body language saying that was a question he couldn't help her with. "I want you to come with me, Jamie."

"Weren't you asking me what *I* wanted?"

He sliced her a piece of cheese. "I thought this was what you wanted."

She picked up the other DVD.

"I got that one for your dad."

This cover was even bleaker than the last. *Isn't Italy supposed to be colorful?* Another of his homes she'd been alienated from…

but then she had liked it that way, had wanted it that way. She pretended to read the back flap while he got out plates, napkins, and forks, and then proceeded to burn his thumb removing the fish from the oven. He cursed in Italian, transferring the fish to a platter. She set aside the movie and fixed her eyes upon the poor dead beast, feeling its warmth and smell and Roberto settling into the seat beside her. He began dissecting the fish, culling back the skin, digging out the eye (and popping it into his mouth), extracting the meat, and serving their plates. "Watch out for the bones," he said, their gaze meeting briefly, before he dug out the other eye, for her.

The next day, while he was at work handing in his formal resignation, Jamie turned off all the lights, slipped one of those DVDs into her computer, and then called her father. Perhaps, in his own fumbling way, he could enlighten her about this famous Italian director, or enlighten her in general for that matter, which, in fact, for possibly the first time in his life, he went on and did; and it had nothing to do with Fellini or movies. He announced to Jamie on the phone right there that he was trying out for a part in the Long Beach Theater's summer stock performance of *King Lear,* as if he were twenty-five and not seventy. Jamie almost fell out of her chair. It was Vivi who encouraged him to do it. "She won't give up on me, it seems." He pretended to sound bothered, but it was clear he was pleased—and perhaps a bit embarrassed—to be so loved. Jamie's face flushed. She didn't know what to say about her aging, undone father taking such a bold step; it didn't compute. *"What, in ill thoughts again? Men must endure their going hence, even as their coming hither; RIPENESS IS ALL,"* her father quoted Edgar then. Her eyes welled, and she quickly got off the line.

* * *

Half the bottle of wine was gone when Roberto got home from work and she was still seated in the office before her computer. He poured himself a glass and brought it to meet hers. To moving on, he said, taking a seat on the couch. She said, "I new I was infertile, Roberto, before we were married." She held his eyes, which seemed to recede. "Those weren't birth control pills I was taking all along, they were hormone replacements."

He didn't look shocked or stunned.

"You never asked me what they were. I let myself assume you knew."

There was no expression there whatsoever.

"You'd seen the scar, you knew about the cancer, so I let you draw your own conclusions."

Only silence.

"Did you draw your own conclusions?"

"Jamie, I'm not having kids."

Her breathing stopped momentarily. How her husband could cut right to the heart of things. "I lied to you."

He turned away ever so slightly so that he wouldn't have to see her face.

A long, long time went by.

"I'm bleeding here, Roberto. Help me out a little."

"It doesn't matter now," is all he finally said.

"Of course it matters."

"No, Jamie. It doesn't."

The world went white for a moment.

"It's what you believed. What you let yourself believe. So it wasn't a lie."

No, she wasn't going to let him off this easy. "Part of this feels like punishment." She paused. "Are you punishing me?"

He looked at her like she was being ridiculous.

"Then what is it?"

"What's what?"

"You have to tell me why you don't want kids."

He sat down in his chair and gave her a look full of guilt, one she in no way recognized. It frightened her so much that all she wanted in that moment was to take everything back, to stop what was coming.

"Because I already have one."

That…to stop *that* from coming. There was a long, indefinite silence. Perhaps she'd not heard right.

He went on to explain in barely a whisper, making the most of brevity, this likely being the first he'd spoken of it to anyone. "I was with CS Partners. She was a friend. It was an accident."

She was still too stunned to speak.

"She wanted to get married, but I couldn't marry someone I didn't love."

A little gasp for air.

"I'd seen what happened to my dad. She didn't believe in abortion, so we agreed on adoption."

Silence.

At some point she swallowed and for whatever reason needed to know, "Boy or girl?"

There was a hesitation.

Another.

She waited.

"Boy."

Him? Her husband has a *him* out there? She couldn't imagine what her face looked like in this moment. "Do you know where…?"

"Of course not!"

She sucked on her lips. It took her a long time to get the courage. "Where is the woman now?"

"I don't know," he offered reluctantly. "Cincinnati…I think… Married, with kids of her own now."

Can you enter into marriage without divulging this kind of information? She would have asked this question, had she herself been honest. She should have wondered why he didn't get upset when she'd told him a year ago that she was infertile, pretending she'd just discovered it herself. "So you're punishing yourself then."

He didn't respond, which to her meant yes.

A vision of that dead fish flashed before her for some reason, its guts, innards. "All that time…I thought I was the one who'd lied."

He made no apology. It was his business.

"I guess we both lied."

Still nothing. His very specific, vacant look was one that she recognized. She had always thought it was about his missing mother, but, in fact, it had been a baby between them all along.

He noticed the movie frame frozen on her computer. "Did you like it?"

She pulled out the DVD and attempted to put it back in its case. But her hands were shaking and he did it for her.

"Are you crying?"

No, she was not crying, she assured him. She was remembering when she first found out about her infertility, how the symptoms made her think she was pregnant, how embarrassed she'd been, wondering if Roberto would want to marry her if he knew, or if he'd support her desire to have an abortion.

"Why are you crying?

She was trying to remember how the hell they got engaged in the first place, for neither of them was interested in forever; yet she had wanted him to propose to her. She remembered that distinctly, picturing the moment a number of times, particularly on that trip to Italy Roberto had taken her on, albeit reluctantly, to introduce her to the aunt that had partly raised him…Rimini, the small seaside town where Roberto stayed with his aunt every summer since he was born. She pictured that bike ride they'd taken on rickety cycles with baskets on the front handle bars, vibrating through the cobbled town square, passing underneath this famous director's mother's balcony, some guy named Fellini, then trailing along the sand, numbed by the sea air whipping at their faces. Marriage, something she'd never wanted for herself, was suddenly all she could think about. They were riding to the Tiberius Bridge, because Jamie had studied it in one of her engineering classes and was excited to see it at last. An antique print of it hung in their apartment, a romantic notion that had been a part of them even before they had met, apparently. She was struck again now with the knowledge that she wasn't always who she wanted or purported to be. She was sure he was going to propose to her on that bridge, and afterwards they would ride home to his aunt, announce the news, and break out the Prosecco. Perhaps they would marry in that quaint little relic of a church with all the stained windows…and perhaps she and his aunt would be great friends.

But none of it happened that way.

It was months later, in San Francisco, over plates of porcini risotto at Café Milano when she asked him, jokingly, when he was going to ask her to marry him. He responded by asking her when she was going to ask him. "Will you marry me?" she said. And he said, "Yes."

What else was he going to say?

Now here she was, wondering if the whole thing hadn't been a big mistake, wondering if she'd not asked him, would he have ever asked her.

"Why are you crying?" he asked again.

She took a moment to gather herself. "I don't know, Roberto, I guess…" She blinked up at him…"I'm trying to remember why you married me."

"Because you asked me to." It had become a joke between them, and she searched for the irony she'd always thought there, but she could no longer see it clearly.

They say that the Thais are the most elusive people on earth.

But he wasn't Thai, she reminded herself, or Italian, or American, or Malaysian or Australian. He was some kind of lunatic, a man all his own, the man presently heading straight for the tiny drawer he kept reserved for certain personal records and things and trinkets that she wasn't allowed to touch, pulling out a tiny scrap of paper. He marched back over and handed it to her.

The receipt from that dinner…all this time…she'd no idea he'd kept it.

CHAPTER 13
UNFAITHFUL

December, 2003

She remembered asking herself, for perhaps a flicker of a second when all this began with Gil, what, really, could be the worst that could happen? Dave might get hurt, her marriage could end, her kids would be taken away from her. No, her kids wouldn't be taken away from her. Dave would never do that. This miscarriage, though, hadn't been on the list…and if it was, would it have stopped her? Because it seemed that nothing could stop her. It had only been a month since she'd lost Mary, and she'd already gone back to work. Of course she could have her old job back, her boss had said, when she'd called right after. Of course he needed her. They all needed her. She'd make it different this time, she promised herself. She had plans…fresh ideas…Yes, she would bury herself in work.

She cleaned out the basement in preparation for their impending move back to the city. Six years' worth of commuting Betty had logged, and for what purpose? She was convinced that moving back to civilization was part of the answer, even if she didn't quite know the question. Yet another decision she'd made for the both of them. She'd spoken with realtors about putting their property up for sale. The My Mary clothes had been stuffed into a big black duffle bag and stored out of sight.

She organized a garage sale before they even had offers on the house. She hated that shed, and she couldn't wait to get rid of everything inside it. Dave's rocker sold for five hundred bucks; the kitchen table went for a grand. Word got out and even some collectors came. There was a bidding war on the credenza, then the bed frame. They made close to fifteen grand. She was holding the envelope of cash in her hands, staring down at it, when Dave came over and took a seat on the crate next to her.

"I was thinking," she said, handing him the envelope. "We could adopt. I've always wanted to adopt."

"I've been talking with my therapist, Betty, and…"

"I told you I won't go to therapy, Dave," she interrupted him with a burst of bitterness, irritation. She still felt deep in her heart that she'd done nothing wrong.

"I didn't ask you to."

"Oh," she said after a slight pause.

"What I wanted to say is that I'm not moving with you, Betty."

"Well, I can't stay here."

"I know."

It took her a while to focus on what he was saying, which was that he'd take care of the kids on weekends…his parents would help out with money…anything the kids might need…Dave would be there for them…it was she he needed space from. He was crying.

Betty had yet to shed a tear. She told him she understood, of course she understood. It was she, in fact, who'd made this happen. It was she who had wanted this to happen, for him to do something. Take a stand at last. And here he was, doing it. She should have been satisfied with herself. But in fact she could feel nothing. Her body was numb. The skin had melded back together, they'd removed the staples, the swelling had gone down, and what was once black and blue had turned a grayish yellow. Betty settled her palms habitually over her stomach. So this is how change happened: violently. "Something or someone can't make you change," her sister had told her once, but she was wrong.

Dave's parents had come and gone. Her dad and Vivi had come and gone. Friends had come and gone. And soon Dave would be gone.

But when her mother's number popped up on the caller id, Betty couldn't get herself to answer the phone. She knew Jamie had been at her mom's house since returning from Thailand, though Betty suppressed any desire to know or care why her sister hadn't come to visit Betty in D.C., or even gone back to New York for that matter. They still hadn't spoken, and now Betty couldn't imagine hearing her sister's voice. She felt so disconnected from her now. She wasn't there when Betty needed her the most. And Betty didn't think she could ever forgive her that.

Still, when the doorbell rang late one evening, a week before Christmas, Betty leaped for the door, heart pounding, and could barely breathe by the time she opened it. This was just the kind of thing her sister would do. And sure enough…tears rushed from her eyes, disappointment perhaps, then disbelief, and then some deep stirring in her womb as the tears streamed and streamed. It was her mother, or some other woman who looked like her mother, standing there on Betty's frozen doorstep in her flats and thin coat, no hat or gloves, her Christmas earrings on, her hair fuzzy with snow. Betty was bawling now because she couldn't believe her real mother would leave her dogs, her Hallmark Holiday decorated house, all her Christmas causes, not to mention her phantom fiancé, to board a packed plane and fly all the way cross country in a snow storm to face misery head on.

At least misery was what her mother had been expecting, apparently, given how surprised—and a touch delighted—she was by the scene that awaited her. It was the kids who'd spotted her at the door, even before Betty, and they went absolutely wild with excitement. After they'd all settled down and her mother got a chance to look around, she seemed mystified. Betty and the kids were in the midst of decorating the tree with all its twinkling lights. The house was aglow with candles, Christmas music was playing, and the scent of ginger hung in the air from the cookies Betty had baked earlier. They were all drinking eggnog.

Her mother blinked and swallowed and had to stifle her own emotions. She was all upset suddenly because she'd sent the kids their gifts by mail, and they wouldn't arrive for a few more days. She had nothing to give them. This trip was such a sudden decision after all. She came to help.

Betty didn't need help.

The next morning she was up and dressed for work at eight a.m. when her mom dragged herself in the kitchen for coffee in her robe and slippers. It was five a.m. her time; she looked exhausted and jetlagged. "What are you doing up, Mom?"

Her mother looked astonished by the question, but Betty didn't flinch, she'd been preparing for this ever since her mother's grand entrance. She wanted something emotional from Betty, Betty had sensed right off, and here she was at eight a.m., looking for it. Betty nodded towards the L.A. Times article laying on the table, the one her mother had sent her a week ago, a spread about her upcoming re-election campaign. Best to keep her mother distracted, and as Betty had predicted, her mother lit up when she saw the article about herself, but then her light just as quickly faded. "I look old, don't I?" It didn't seem to be a question.

"Oh, Mother please. You look great."

Her mother sank into her chair quickly scanning the article. "Who would have thought?" She paused. "Me." Another pause. "Presenting to the Congressional Subcommittee on Education." Her tone was unusually flat, and Betty waited for her to go on. Oddly she didn't. Something else was up, Betty surmised, something besides Betty. The holidays, no doubt; her mom usually got reflective and depressed during this time, especially if there was the threat that she'd be spending them without a man. Betty carefully asked her mom if she were spending Christmas with Richard this year, but her mother remained evasive. She was going to play Christmas by ear this year, she said. And besides, I'm here with you now. She squeezed Betty's arm.

Betty picked up the classifieds and a pen.

"Well, I think it's just great about your moving back to D.C., Betty," her mother's voice turned upbeat. "A change is exactly what you need." She went

to pour more coffee. Betty circled a house on Mass Ave—too expensive, but it couldn't hurt to look. She turned the page and circled a few more listings.With her growing absorption in the ads, she hadn't noticed the quiet falling over the room, her mother settling back into her seat as if for a good long chat. Dave had gone to drop the kids at school, and the empty space that remained felt awkward. Normally there was someone to run interference, at a minimum, Jamie.

Betty stood up. "I have to run into town to take care of a few things, Mom." She tucked the classifieds into her briefcase and stuffed the last bite of toast into her mouth.

"You're going to work today! But it's Christmas."

"Next week, Mom. Christmas is next week." She pretended to search her purse for something. "I've got some appointments to see some houses, Mom. I tried to reschedule, but it was just impossible. I should be back no later than five or so. Dave will pick up the kids from school and I'll get some takeout for dinner." She glanced quickly at her mother, who looked as if she'd just been popped with a pin.

Silence loomed.

Betty sighed inwardly. "I could drop you off at the National Gallery," she offered, as a consolation. "And then pick you up when I'm done."

Her mother, who loved the National Gallery, looked hurt at the suggestion. "I thought we could spend some time together. You and I."

Was that a slight tremble in her mother's voice? "Well...I guess...if you want to come see these houses with me..."

"Oh, I'd love to, dear." Her mother jumped up, went and rinsed the mugs, dried them, and put them away. "And I thought I'd watch the kids tonight so you and Dave could go out."

"Oh, Mom, that's not necessary."

"Certainly you two could use a night out."

"Mom, Dave's working tonight..."

"On a Friday?"

"Plus, I told you, Mom..." she bit her bottom lip. Betty had told her mother over the phone that she and Dave were "getting some space," but that

was all. Now she'd given her an opening, Betty could see, as her mother was about to speak…"And I don't really want to talk about it."

Her mother waited for Betty to go ahead and talk about it anyway, instead of saying something evasive, like, "Well, I'm sure you guys will work it out." Which, in fact, was what Betty wanted her mother to say…*It will all work out, Betty.*

"It's going to be difficult, Betty," her mother said, looking directly in Betty's eyes for once. "But I'm here for you, if and when you want to talk. I'm here to listen. You know I won't judge. That's not who I am."

Betty averted her eyes. "Anyway…"she waved her hand as if at a fly… "I thought you could take Sam to see that new animation movie tonight. He's dying to see it with you."

Normally her mother was adamant about Betty setting aside one-on-one time with her grandkids; it was the only way she could have their undivided attention. But now, apparently, it was Betty's undivided attention her mother wanted. She was about to bring it up again, but thankfully her cell phone rang, and her mother got all distraught trying to turn it on. Betty had to help her find the answer button. Then she spoke unnecessarily loud into it, pacing off as if that's what one did when they talked on a cell phone; or maybe she just didn't want Betty to hear her conversation.

When she came back she was frantically upbeat, which meant something was wrong.

"Who was that?"

Her mom gaped innocently at the question. Then, "Oh that was just Liza. She's house sitting the dogs this weekend while working on a briefing I'm presenting when I get back next week."

"You look pale, Mom. Is everything alright?"

"Oh, you know how Liza gets." She sighed, a bucket full of sadness. "She worries about me."

As if Betty didn't. Well, OK, maybe Betty didn't worry about her mother. What was there to worry about? "Seriously Mom is there something…"

"I'm not here to burden you with my problems, Betty."

Betty then waited for her mother to do just that. But, uncharacteristically, she stood up and went to go get ready.

If her mother's mood had been flat before, these skinny old row houses looming before the Capitol brought tears of joy to her eyes, especially after the sprawling suburbs of Los Angeles. The creaking wood floors, ceramic moldings, postage stamp yards, all had "so much potential!" She grew particularly possessed about the one on Ninth Street with the red front door and tilted hardwood. French doors opened onto an even crummier and smaller back yard. Roses here, geraniums there. Everything, suddenly, had so much potential.

Apparently her disease was infectious. Even Betty couldn't deny feeling charged. Over greasy burgers at Eastern Market her mother assured Betty not to worry about money, the mortgage, switching the kids' schools. The kids will adjust, she told her, and then, grabbing Betty's hand. "Do what you feel passionate about, Betty."

Betty stared at her mother sort of in shock. Those were the same words she herself had used over and over with Dave, her kids, Jamie. She couldn't shake the weird feeling it left her with as they wandered around the stalls underneath the veil of her mother's optimism, buying up necklaces and scarves for their friends that neither of them could afford, as if Betty were under some spell.

"I've always lived by what was in my heart." Her mother stopped walking at one point and pondered this idea as if for the first time. Then she sighed, her optimism leaving her, it seemed, because what she said next came out weighted and weary. "I suppose you kids know this about your mother."

"This," Betty understood, to be the ramifications of "living by one's heart."

Apparently it had taken its toll again. Her mother's manic energy all but evaporated at the thought. "I've finally found someone with whom I want to share my life, after all this time…and yet…I am still alone when I come home from work, Betty."

Betty let out a little gasp.

She and Dave had agreed to separate once they'd sold the house. But, honestly, she just couldn't imagine being alone like her mother. This couldn't be her fate. "But I thought Richard was moving in, Mom."

"Oh, I never said that, dear."

Betty's confusion was no surprise. Her mother's story often changed.

"I know it's hard to believe, Betty." She spoke mockingly. "That even at sixty-eight a woman can still grow and learn. For instance, I don't know that I can live full-time with a man; you know it's different at my age. I do like my alone time."

"But you just said…" Betty paused, and then she gave up. It wasn't long ago that her mother announced that she was ready to give everything up for Richard, and now, suddenly, she wanted her alone time? It wasn't long ago that her mother told Betty that she didn't want to run for re-election, and then the following month she sends Betty a newspaper article on just that.

"This engagement happened so fast. I think we just want to slow things down."

"Is this him or you talking, Mom?"

"Well, both of us dear. Or at least that's what I said in the letter I wrote him. You know Jamie was staying at my house for a while since returning from Thailand, and so Richard was giving me my space, I guess. But anyway, in the letter I told him how much he means to me, and if he needs space, well, then I'll give it to him. I know how hard it is for him, trying to assimilate into my high profile life." As she said this, she stumbled upon a painting of the Flag that thoroughly entranced her. Richard would love this, she insisted to the artist, whom she began to interrogate. Then there were some blue ceramic plates that she wanted to buy for Richard, a yard sign that said "God Bless America" that she wanted to buy for Richard. Soon Betty's arms were piled up, her mother making plans for Betty to ship the load home to her.

"Is this giving him space?"

Her mother flashed Betty a perturbed look. "Love isn't easy, Betty," is all she said.

Well, actually, she may have wanted to say more, but Betty wanted to get the hell out of there. The problem was that they still had three hours to fill before the kids got home.

A movie?

Why don't we just drive by the theater, Betty insisted, back in the car now. "Let's just see what's showing."

"Whatever you want to do, dear. This is your day. I'm here to hang with you, Betty."

Betty slowed up to the curb and deftly scanned the billboards. Her mother was freaking her out. Something was brewing…in her mother, herself…Betty wasn't sure, but she could feel it. Unfaithful. *Betty didn't even think. She bought the tickets and they hurried in, ten minutes late but still managing to buy the buttered popcorn and Sprite her mother so loved, just in time to catch the wind blowing Diane Lane into the arms of some wickedly handsome Frenchman. Betty seemed to blow right with her…before being struck. "Jesus," Betty said out loud.*

"What dear?"

What the hell was she thinking? Unfaithful?

But it was too late to leave.

Plus, Betty had already been swept back into the arms of her own Frenchman, only he wasn't French. So why not just stay and relive the moment, the guilt, the ecstasy, the tortuous rapture on the train ride home (or in Betty's case, the drive home), all those feelings she'd repressed throughout her pregnancy, the same ones that came screaming back after her miscarriage. There was no longer any use trying to bury them, and her body flushed now with this knowledge, and that there was no return from feelings like that.

Betty slouched far down in her seat, closed her eyes, and massaged her brow with her fingers. If the lights came on right now, would she be revealed as a liar and a cheat? Or a woman who followed her passions? And was her mother, seated next to her, sitting there wondering the same thing. Betty's eyes popped open on that last thought, only to see the Frenchman lying dead in a pool of his own blood.

And it wasn't just the Frenchman who died in that moment, presumably. Wasn't the husband, he who had inflicted his rage upon the Frenchman for sleeping with his wife, wasn't he dead now too? Hadn't all their lives ended?

Or were they just beginning?

Betty's eyes were burning holes through the screen trying to find out. Had it really been seven years since their flirtation began? When Betty had at last told Mark that she had to turn down the COO position at Fashion. com, he insisted that she meet with Gil, the investor, anyway. Betty agreed, thinking that it couldn't hurt to make a connection with a member of the Smithsonian's board. And a connection there was, an intense one, the minute he took her hand in his, locked his eyes on hers, and called her "Red." She lit-erally laughed, not to mention turned just that color from head to toe. Gil's head was huge and thick with black wavy hair, and if life were a color, then it was the color of his eyes. They glimmered of pure, unadorned life; he was so different from any man she'd ever known. An heir to a multi-billion dollar textile business in Georgia, his family was a big donor of the Smithsonian. His board position was more of a hobby than an occupation. Gil didn't really have an occupation. He was a big kid with no worries and a blank check. Of course his flirtatiousness caught her off guard, she'd forgotten how good it felt to flirt, to feel attractive, to be possessed. But Gil had a wife he loved and a daughter he adored, and she had her family, which was why it became so easy. They simply couldn't have each other. So they just wanted each other. A few e-mails, some phone calls, and then once a quarter he'd treat Betty to a fancy dinner in D.C. in the guise of museum business; they'd flirt, drink too much, and go their separate ways, he back to Atlanta, she back to Bethesda to have hungry sex with her husband.

Wanted and wanted and wanted.

In fact there had been times that she thought her relationship with Gil was helping her marriage.

Until that one night they went too far. And the bewitching thing was, she wasn't even sure how far, she was just that drunk. So, in her mind anyway, what she'd told Dave had been the truth: vasectomies aren't foolproof. But in her heart, in her body, in her soul...Betty knew the truth.

"I need Bourbon," her mother turned to her and said just as the lights came on. The movie had ended...if you could call it an ending. It was more like an unending. It was unclear whether Diane would be punished for her affair, whether anyone would be punished. Was simply knowing what you'd done punishment enough? Or had anyone done anything wrong to begin with? Betty refused to believe that losing Mary was her punishment, her ending; in fact there would be no ending, she instantly decided.

It was Richard who drank Bourbon, her mother revealed at the swank Asian bar with low lighting and tiny tables. Her mother rarely drank, so hers came with a heavy dose of Sprite and even then she had to choke it down so that she could then turn to Betty and say, "I want you to tell me how you lost your virginity...You know, like you would...well, like if we were girlfriends."

Betty almost swallowed her lemon garnish.

"Were you in love?"

The vodka burned in her throat.

Her mother was waiting.

"I thought I was." She tried to push the blood back down from her face. Her mind shot to High School Rich, as it always did when asked about her virginity because this was how she liked to play it out in her mind. Technically it wasn't Rich though, and she felt her lips part with the confession of it but then something caved inside, two decades worth of distance between when a mother should care to know this about her daughter, and when she actually did, and Betty shut her mouth then, thinking, sorry Mom, but you're twenty-six years too late.

"I've just never felt this way before...you know...physically," her mother, filling in the silence, flashed a conspirator's look at Betty, who proceeded to cross her eyes until her vision blurred. No, she didn't know, or didn't want to know, or relate in any kind of way like this with her mother.

"Before Richard I hadn't slept with anyone in fifteen years."

There was a pause and a very awkward silence. Betty wanted to glance behind her, for someone else to hear this. Then her mother belted out a deep, guttural laugh so earnest that Betty couldn't help but laugh with her.

"I am older than him, and I certainly don't have the experience he does in that department… But don't get me wrong," she quickly countered. "The sex is just wonderful, Betty. I mean… it's just…"

"I get it, Mom."

"He hasn't responded to my letter though, and that was a week ago. I was hoping you could give me some advice. Do you think I should call him?"

"He's your fiancé, Mom. I think you're allowed."

"Jamie says I shouldn't."

"Which is exactly why you should!" came bellowing out of nowhere, and Betty had to pause to collect herself. "Look, Mom, all I'm saying is that you should do what's in your heart," words said with no small amount of sarcasm.

There was an awkward silence.

"Well…" her mother's attempt to fill it. "Here we are, two girls talking about their sex life." She was gathering her courage, Betty could tell.

"Oh dear." Betty looked at her watch. "We've got to go, Mom."

"But I didn't get to hear about what's going on with you, Betty." And then very delicately, not one to probe with any real determination, "You said Dave was moving out…?"

The vodka was colliding in Betty's stomach. She didn't know anything anymore, except that she did not want to be having this conversation.

* * *

The next morning Betty was headed out for an early run when she found her mother seated at the kitchen table, a fresh pot of coffee on. When she saw Betty, she jumped up and quickly filled a cup for her. "I thought we could call your sister in New York before it gets too late and we get all busy with other stuff."

"I'm just going to go for a quick run, Mom." She stretched one quad, the other, and took off.

When she returned the kids were awake and her mom was helping Nick make pancakes. Her cell phone lay on the counter beside them. "Did you call Richard?" Betty was curious to know.

"I left a message on his machine." Her mom glanced at her phone then, so hard that even Betty thought it might ring.

"I take it he hasn't called back."

Well, you know, it's still early there. And he may not even be at his condo."

If not there, then where? Betty refrained from asking. She couldn't help herself. Over the course of the last year and a half since Richard came into her mother's life, just hearing his name infuriated Betty. It was two years ago that her mother made the announcement to her daughters: "I want passion and love in my life." She wanted a man, as if the decision itself was all it took to get one. Or a dating service anyway. There were some rejections, some dates, even a doctor, yes, a doctor, but he was flaky, and then there was Richard, a sexy Russian piano player who loved to ballroom dance. But it wasn't her mother meeting Richard through a dating service that incensed Betty, or that he was fifteen years her junior. What incensed Betty was that with the onslaught of Richard, her mother seemed to have completely forgotten about Gary. Of course, rationally, Betty knew forgetting about Gary was a good thing; but irrationally, all Betty could think about was the twenty-six years her mother wiped clean from her memory. The same twenty-six years Betty would never be able to wipe clean, the years her mother tried to push Betty to love Gary.

Her mother was holding her cell phone out for Betty to take. "Should we call Jamie now?"

Betty stared at the phone. Here she was on the cusp of forty—the same age her mother was when she left Betty's father—and instead of finding more distance from those twenty-six years, Betty seemed to be growing only more pissed about them.

Betty went to the basement stairs and called down for Sam to come up and get dressed for the game. She went to the laundry room to get his uniform. "I'm coaching at that tournament today, Mom, so if you can watch Nick and Clay, that would be great. But I'll understand if it's too much. Dave's around, he can watch them."

"But I wanted to go to Sam's game."

"You want to go to Sam's game," *Betty said after a serious pause, her tone deliberate, for she just wanted to be clear.*

"Of course I do, dear. He's my grandson, after all."

"Well, sure, Mom...I mean...we'll have to figure out how to get you there...You could drop me off at the tournament and then take my car, I guess. I can give you directions. A friend's taking Sam to the game."

"But I thought you were coaching Sam's game. Now I'm confused."

"Girls' volleyball, Mom. I coach girls' volleyball."

"You're coaching? Too?" *Her mom couldn't hide her exasperation, but Betty put her hand up like she didn't want to hear what her mother, or anyone for that matter, had to say about that. Yes, it was another thing on her plate.* "You know I love volleyball, Mom. You know it's my thing, that it makes me happy. Not that you ever came to one of my games..." *She paused, surprised and horrified by herself and avoiding what might possibly be her mother's expression.* "I'll be back about six, Mom." *She started gathering her things.* "Then I thought we could all go out to dinner or something."

"How about I cook dinner for us all tonight," *her mother's frown flipped into the most frantic of smiles.* "I'll get the kids to help me."

Betty couldn't imagine it and was about to say something but her mom put up her hand. "You can just sit and relax and let me do everything. I don't want you to lift a finger."

They'd been down this road before. Her mother didn't know where anything was. It would be a disaster.

"Let me do this for you, Betty. Please, let me do this for you."

It all came out so desperate that all Betty could manage was, "Fine." *Then she rushed out the door.*

When she came home that night—at seven—exhausted, she was surprised to find the dining table all set with the good plates and cloth napkins and lit candles. In the kitchen Betty found Clay and her mom flipping burgers on the griddle. "I figured we could use some good old fashioned grease," her mother said, and Betty literally had to bite her tongue to keep from laughing…or crying. Sam had made the mashed potatoes, Nick had set the table—with grandma's help of course—and there were little gifts on everyone's plate. They all sat down and had a lovely dinner, despite the amount of times her mother sought Betty's confirmation, "Hadn't everything come out wonderfully?"

"Thanks, Mom," Betty said after the kids had gone downstairs to watch a movie. "That was really nice. I mean it."

"Well, I just wanted to do something special for you, Betty. I know you don't need my help, but, well, I am your mother." She was clearing the plates and Betty watched her for a long moment. She was wearing a pink sweater and matching hoop earrings and the stretch jeans that were too big after losing all that weight stressing about Richard. Still, Betty had to admit, she looked younger and more couth than ever.

"Why don't you let me finish those, Mom?"

She wouldn't hear of it. So Betty poured herself another glass of wine and was about to head off to take a shower, but her mother quickly asked her what kind of wine and if she couldn't taste some. Her mother didn't like wine, Betty knew. Still, her mom sipped her glass and expressed great pleasure at the taste and took a seat at the table. Betty had no choice but to pour her mom a glass and take a seat too, because her mother had something she wanted off her chest, and if her mother wanted something, she usually got it. No doubt it was something about Richard. But then her mom pulled her cell phone out from her pocket and started dialing. "Let's call her now." Her voice sounded strange.

"Who?"

"Your sister."

"Mom," Betty gasped, in such a panic. "I'm too tired to call her right now."

She passed her the phone anyway. "Just call her, Betty."

Mist plagued Betty's eyes, and she had to look off.

"What is with you two?"

Nick appeared suddenly in a frenzied search for something. Betty cleared her throat with a silent thanks to God. "Kelzak's in the basement," she offered instinctively.

"Zurgane, not Kelzak," Nick said, poking his head under the couch. "The one Jamie got me." He tried to run off, but Betty blocked his passage and pulled him into her arms. "Love you Mommy," he said—their thing—and she let him go, albeit reluctantly. She was desperate for a buffer.

"Well?" her mother continued.

"Frankly, Mother, I have no idea what's going on between Jamie and me. I guess you'll have to ask her."

"But why don't you ask her," again with the phone and this time an alarm went off inside Betty. Something was wrong...something about Jamie...of course. Betty clenched her jaw. It was always about Jamie. She stood up and searched under the couch cushions. "What's going on, Mom? If there's something I need to know, tell me."

"Oh no!" Her mother's eyes widened. "I'm not going to say anything. I'm not going to get in the middle of this thing between you two. She can tell you directly herself."

Betty froze. "Is she sick?"

Her mother almost spit out her wine, but Betty couldn't help it. It had been almost twenty years since her sister's illness and it was still always the first thing that came to Betty's mind—is it back? Is the cancer back?

Her mother looked entirely blank, as if she'd completely lost track of her purpose. "I'm here now, dear, with you," she finally offered, as if it were a consolation, as if she'd much rather be someplace else. "You're the reason I came out here. I want to be here for you, Betty."

"Look, Mom," Betty said curtly. "It's not like you can just show up here and suddenly," she made quotes with her fingers, "be there for me. In fact,

Mom, in all honesty..." Betty took a deep breath. "You've never been there for me...as a mother."

There was a stunned silence. Her mother looked confused. Betty tried not to shake. She couldn't believe she'd finally said it. It felt good to say it... until she saw her mother's face turn ashen and her chest cave in as if she'd been punched. "But what do you mean, never been there?"

"I mean never. When I was a small girl, a teenager, a struggling woman, and finally a mother myself. All the times I needed a mother the most." Betty stood up and began picking up Nick's toys. She did not want to see the look on her mother's face.

"But I was there for you, Betty. I moved down the block after the divorce. I insisted on joint custody just like your father. How was it that I wasn't there?"

Betty looked back at her mother, shocked, for she could see by her expression that she had absolutely no idea. That she, in fact, thought she had been there for Betty. How distinct and apart their realities were.

"Look, Betty, I know what you're going through with Dave, but I don't think you should take it out on me."

"I'm not taking it out on you!" Betty gasped. Then she paused to gather herself and steady her tone. "And you have no idea what I'm going through with Dave. I am in no way like you. My situation has nothing in any way to do with yours."

"What do you mean 'mine'?"

"I can't have you making that comparison with Dad."

"I didn't make that comparison. I would never make that comparison."

No one spoke for a moment.

"I made some bad choices," her mother admitted. "But you're so much stronger than me, Betty. Whatever is going on with you and Dave, I know you're going to handle it a million times better than I did."

"But I'm not even talking about the divorce, Mom."

"Then what? What is it Betty!" Her mother looked distraught. "What was it that I did to you that was so awful?"

Betty blinked back, unable, in this moment, to think of one concrete thing. "Look, Mom. I don't want to go back over it. I just want to move past it." She paused as it came to her, one thing: "Forward. Let's just move forward."

"Forward?"

"Start fresh with our relationship. This, I'm willing to try."

"But can you really say all those…those things to me and then just expect me to move on? How do I move on from that?"

Betty found Kelzak jammed behind a spring. "I don't know, Mom." She tugged it free. "I guess you're just going to have to figure it out."

* * *

Betty wasn't surprised the next morning when she went down for coffee to find her mother there, all dressed and packed and ready to leave. She made some excuse about Liza calling during the night to tell her that Angel was sick. She'd changed her flight. A car was picking her up because she didn't want to be a burden. She seemed to leave just enough time available for Betty to apologize, but Betty had long stopped saying she was sorry. No more sorry. "I didn't mean to dump this on you now, Mom, but, well, you kind of pushed me," was all she said. Then she asked her mother if she was going to be all right. Betty got a big glossy smile in return. "It's OK, Betty. I'm going to be OK." On her way out the door now, "The kids all look great…you certainly don't need me, dear. You're such a strong girl, Betty."

"Mom…" Betty began, but her mother was busy getting herself into the backseat of the car. Just before shutting the door, she looked back. "Oh, and thank you, dear, for a wonderful time."

LA STRADA

November, 2003

Jamie immediately called Betty after that dream. It was the middle of the night her time. Sam answered. Said his mom was at the hospital having the baby and couldn't Jamie come over? As if she was just next door. It ripped her heart out not to be able to say "yes," she'd be right there, instead of " no," she was about to get on a plane from Bangkok and it would be more like a few days. She didn't say anything about the fact that it was too early for Betty to have the baby, something she internalized for sixteen hours, until she landed and called Betty again from the cab on the way to her mother's. Sarah, Steven's girlfriend, answered. Sarah, some stranger, told Jamie that Betty had lost the baby in her seventh month. Betty was fine, sedated now. They were still looking for Dave, but Steven was there, apparently. Sarah said he'd call Jamie later, but he never did.

When Jamie arrived at her mother's not much later, she found her dressed for a council meeting, wearing an apron and rubber gloves, darting about her house dusting. The dogs, also in need of dusting, were yapping about her heels. "I'm so sorry for all the dust," she kept saying. Her house was all torn up from construction, she then explained. The new den she was adding off the back for Richard was taking much longer than she'd originally planned, what with all the rains they'd been having. "Anyway," she concluded, "space is the problem. Once that's fixed, well, then, Richard can move in." She still couldn't say those last four words without her voice growing thin.

She led Jamie and her rolling suitcase to the guest room. "But I've got your room all clean and ready." There was a poinsettia in one corner, a doll-sized Christmas tree on the bedside table. Jamie dropped her suitcase and sat on the bed, which had already been turned down, a candy cane on the pillow. Jet-lagged, barely in shock yet, she had to force herself not to stretch out and let sleep wipe away all the aching thoughts swirling in her mind. Her mother motioned to a little box with a little bow next to the little tree. "I haven't been able to do much for the holidays this year," she sighed heavily. "This is just a little something..."

It was still November but Jamie didn't bring that up now. She studied her mother studying that box. She had that weighty manic look about her as she picked up Angel, who'd been scratching at the bed. "These dogs need baths."

"Have you spoken with her, Mom?"

"I've spoken to Dave a couple times, briefly..."

"She's not picking up my calls."

"I spoke with your dad. He and Vivi were there, and they said she was doing fine."

Fine. The word sat like a lump in Jamie's throat, which her mother must have sensed because she cleared her own and said, "Your sister is a very determined woman." She was gazing at the box Jamie couldn't get herself to open because she knew what was inside, Betty's tragedy, in the form of some sappy Hallmark trinket. It reminded Jamie that she needed to get to D.C. as soon as possible. Staying mad at Jamie was not in Betty's DNA. Jamie would just have to show up there. But first, and while it felt utterly selfish to bring it up now, Jamie didn't have a choice. As casually as she could, she mentioned needing a mammogram because, well, it was time, and she'd never had one and, well, particularly because, well, she'd felt lumps in her breasts.

Her mom grew still, her gaze weighing the burden, but only for a moment. Then her eyes quickly sharpened as she set down Angel, went to the phone, and got to work getting her daughter a hard-fought appointment with a radiologist for the following day.

Her mammogram was clean; so was her sonogram. She had a colonoscopy exam two days later at the doctor's urging. Jamie was supposed to have them every three years. It had been five. She had a CEA to test for cancer cells in the blood, then a bone density test. All returned negative, though she couldn't help see accusation in their eyes, the doctors, everyone; she'd done something terribly, terribly wrong to deserve something like this, confirmed by the fact that Betty still wouldn't return her calls. One doctor performed a pregnancy test. "There's really no chance you're pregnant of course," he said, adding when the test came out positive, "Of course these tests can be wrong." Jamie had had experience with false positives, she reminded herself, scoffing. Then the sonogram showed a ten-week fetus. "Well, in fact, I've read of a few cases like this," the doctor explained. "Children with premature ovarian failure who later begin producing eggs again. But it's very rare, and these women were in their twenties." Jamie was almost forty. Forty and pregnant apparently, the doctor said, looking at her sideways.

She didn't remember driving home. She wanted to feel idiotic for not recognizing the signs, those she'd so often heard Betty describe in all that glorious detail. She should have known all along that this was a life inside her; how quickly it could happen. If she could just feel something, anything, but even the pain in her breasts had gone numb. She couldn't fathom a logical ending to this…or even a beginning for that matter. How had this happened?

Her mother was upstairs in bed with the TV on when Jamie returned that afternoon. She'd not gone to work in a week. She tried. Each morning she'd get dressed, but then at some point, there she'd be, back in her robe and slippers.

Her mother smiled sleepily when Jamie came into her room and stood there in its center, the ocean at her back and said, "This is fucked up, Mom, but I'm pregnant."

Her mother's smile slowly waned.

"And I don't want any drama."

Then she just turned pale.

Jamie kept her eyes steady. "I don't even want to you say anything to anyone right now. I just need you to, like, find me an OB/GYN or something."

An indeterminate amount of time passed before her mother dragged her legs off the side of the bed. "Oh my God, you're serious."

Jamie's stony expression confirmed it.

"Was this…" she paused, gasped, stammered. "I didn't even know you guys wanted to have a baby…at this point in your life."

"Mom!" Jamie cried, and her mother froze in fright.

Jamie froze in fright. Only one, rather disturbing truth was flowing through her veins at the present moment, and it had nothing to do with Roberto; it was that one baby had been traded for another, that she had somehow made this happen.

Her mother tightened her robe and stood up, her hair all over the place. She reached for the phone, "We'll call Betty. She'll know what to do."

There was a time warp here, because what an odd thing for her mother to say. "Mom, she just had a miscarriage."

"Well, what do you want me to do?"

Jamie wouldn't let herself cry.

Her mother reached for the phone again.

"Mom!" She screamed it this time and it took a moment for the room to settle afterwards, before her mother, ever so calmly explained, "Zoe's daughter just had a baby. Can I at least get the name of her OB/GYN?"

Jamie dropped her shoulders. "Of course, yes, that would be helpful." Then she hurried past her mother into the bathroom to throw up.

Zoe, her mother's spiritual advisor and one of "The Girls," as her mother liked to call them collectively—these wacky, ageless women friends she had come to rely on over the years, particularly since Gary began disappearing from her life. Zoe, Diane, Nancy, and Liza, caring for their mother had become a group effort.

The next morning Jamie went to see the OB/GYN that Zoe recommended, while her mother went to see Nancy, her therapist. When Jamie returned from her appointment, Liza, her legal aide, was there. She was the brain behind her mother's operation, essentially, not to mention the looks and the sass. She'd brought some council papers over for her mother to sign, and her miniature poodles, Hansel and Gretel, to play with Angel and Blue. When her mother returned from seeing Nancy, she pretended to review the paperwork Liza had brought, while Liza took the dogs to the park to play. Diana, the woman who had devotedly served their mother since the girls had met her on that trip to Santa Barbara, the deliverer of all their mother's needed things, showed up with a platter of grape leaves and a proof of their mother's re-election campaign poster. Her mother could only stare at it blankly. It was that shot she'd always loved: her at fifty in a black gown and holding a long stemmed red rose. When she went back upstairs to lie down, Diana fixed a plate of grape leaves for Jamie and sat her down at the dining table. The din of construction hammered around them, the only thing that hadn't come to a halt this past week was that new den.

Jamie picked up a grape leaf. "Where IS Richard?" It occurred to her to ask.

Diana steadied her gaze and said evenly, "I have no idea."

Jamie set the grape leaf down. "I met him that once, when they got engaged. I couldn't help imagining him as an out-of-work actor that she'd hired to play the part of some blue-collar working stiff. Is this guy for real?"

"He's not from her world. I think that's what she likes about him."

"But what does he like about her? Certainly it's not being around when she needs him. Like now."

"I've tried to say this to her, but what your mother wants is what your mother wants…"

"What she wants is…" Jamie couldn't finish her sentence. So they held eyes, and Jamie tried to explain through them what she couldn't in words.

Diana smiled back, no explanation necessary.

Purgatory: the sonogram, a multitude of tests, the OB/GYN reading her the warnings and restrictions and risks, the very serious risks of not making it to full term, the dangers of an amnio at her age, the dangers of not having an amnio at her age (she was not having an amnio), and so came the percentages of Down's, autism, birth defects, etc. The list was staggering. They wouldn't know until the baby was born how this was all going to turn out.

Every morning Jamie would get a call from Roberto, late evening his time. Why hadn't she gone to D.C.? She'd told him that her mother was in a state of depression about Betty's miscarriage; plus Richard had gone missing and Steven, being Steven, was nowhere to be found. She told Roberto many things, except the truth. She wanted to tell him the truth. Each time they spoke she thought she might, but their conversations seemed weighed down by an unspeakable guilt.

Jamie exhaled deeply then, too deeply after being quiet too long.

"Do you want me to come there?"

"No!" she said too adamantly, and the line went silent. She couldn't deny her desire to have him and his world erased from her memory.

"What's going on, Jamie?"

He sensed her pulling away.

And she was; because she'd already had the conversation in her mind many times, and it always went like this: She'd blurt out, "I'm pregnant," and then not let him cobble together a thought before going on about all the risks of deformities, Down's syndrome, heart failure, etc. She didn't want him to settle, to be boxed in; this was not what their love had been about, and he'd been right all along to stand his ground, to be the person he was. So she'd make the risks sound direr than they were. She'd go on until she got him to say exactly what she wanted him to say, what she knew he'd say all along: "Jamie, I want you to have an abortion. I can't handle anything happening to you." "You mean you can't handle the uncertainty of having a special needs child," she would say. It never occurred to Jamie to have an abortion, which was the oddest thing of all. "Is that what you think of me?" he'd say after a pause. "Yes," she'd say, hanging up.

And this is how the imaginary conversation ended: with him hating her, and her hating him. It was the only way she could imagine leaving him. In reality, what she would tell him was that she would never be able to get over the lies they told each other.

* * *

Another week passed. The Girls made themselves scarce, and her mother shuffled around the house in her robe and slippers. Every morning Jamie would be woken by the shrill of her mother's phone, Richard, presumably, her mother told her, though Jamie found it hard to believe it was actually he calling. He'd still not shown his face, and sometimes she wondered if her mother—as Betty might have predicted—was outright lying about Richard still being in her life. Even that engagement ring she wore had belonged to her own mother. She'd had it reset. But if she was pretending, then she was a hell of an actress, Jamie decided. Through the ceiling she heard her mother's coos into the phone, the giggles, the contemplative silence. At night her mother would light a candle, do her yoga, and take a bath. Before she turned out the light, the phone would ring again.

Her mom saw her therapist every other day. At Nancy's urging, Jamie joined one of their sessions. It had not at all gone the way Jamie had expected. She expected her mom to go on about letting go of control, some step in the twelve-step program she was forever on. But no, this was about a specific gripe of Richard's: He didn't feel like he belonged in her world; she put her children before him; her children thought she was too good for him.

I've met him once, Mom.

I already said, Jamie, this is Richard's problem, not yours.

Apparently her mother and Richard were in couples' therapy, though Richard had yet to attend a session.

Her mom couldn't seem to snap out of her funk, and after that session Jamie realized that it was her presence here in her mother's life that was the problem. She was only weighing her mother down and a daily reminder of Richard's absence. It was time for Jamie to return home to New York and for her mother to get on a plane and go see Betty. Her mother needed a mission, and, oddly enough, it was her mother who came to Jamie with the idea of going to Betty's. She seemed almost shy about it. "I feel like my daughters finally need me, and I want to be there for them." There was a touch of sadness in her voice, a serious amount of regret. "Do you think Betty will be OK with me surprising her like that, and just before Christmas?"

Jamie smiled. "I think she'd love it, Mom."

Her mom almost fell over with relief then, and especially when Jamie told her that she, herself, was going home.

"Go dear. Go! You should be with Roberto now."

Jamie let her mother believe that Roberto would be in New York when she got there—it was just easier. And, as Jamie predicted, that very afternoon her mother came down the stairs, showered, dressed, her hair washed, her face bright, and she'd put on lipstick. The Girls were coming over. They were going to celebrate! Liza brought champagne and Hansel and Gretel; Diana brought Croatian dog treats; Nancy brought chewy toys; and Zoe brought candles. It was the holidays, after all. They were having a Christmas poodle party. Her mom set the dining table with red and green glittery fixings. The dogs sat in boosters on the chairs, sporting their paper party hats. Her mom made a special toast to her "sisters" for putting up with her craziness and always standing by her. No one meant more to her than them and, of course, her daughters.

Just like that Jamie was thirteen again, her time with her mother was up, and now she was being transferred back to her ever-waiting father. They'd meet, as always, at the Shell gas station in Long Beach Shores, half way between their two homes, where her dad would have her Porsche there waiting for her, all lubed and freshly waxed, no doubt. She'd driven the car to L.A. from New York eight months ago, before she had fled to Thailand and realized she could be someone else, for a time anyway, a time that now had to end. Now she would drive that car from L.A. back to New York, as if traveling back in time, erasing all the things that had happened since her last parting with Betty, until all that was left were the last words they'd spoken to each other.

The L.A. harbor glowed under a full moon, and while her mom drove silently on, Jamie thought of all the times she'd driven this route from her mom's to her dad's, from her dad's to her mom's. Going either way, it was always an escape; and now she tried to remember what had made her escape all the way to Thailand, and with such finality. Why had she sat hurtling through space and time on that plane thinking, this was it, I'm done with her. What, exactly, had Betty done that had infuriated Jamie so? For the first time, Jamie seriously tried to remember exactly what words exchanged between them. She had the feeling she wasn't remembering any of it right, but then why would she: How could you remember the truth when everything you've said were all lies to begin with?

* * *

Eight months earlier. They'd made their confessions, and still, Roberto wanted her to go to Thailand with him. But she'd insisted no, he needed a break from her. "I don't need a break from you, Jamie. I've never needed a break from you." "Well maybe I need a break from you," she'd responded. Another lie. "Do what you need to do," he'd said, the implication being that he was going to Thailand with or without her. "But you're not driving six thousand miles to L.A. alone," he'd added. "The idea is preposterous." "OK, fine," she'd said, waiting until his plane left for Thailand before hopping into her dusted-over Porsche, the last remnant of her dot.com failure, and heading west. She called her sister from her cell while speeding across the turnpike and told her that they'd have to postpone the surrogacy again. Another lie. There wasn't going to be a surrogacy, at least one where Roberto was going to be the father. He already had a kid, after all, a reality that Jamie had yet to internalize. The reason for the postponement, she'd told Betty, was that she was going to L.A. to help Dad prepare for Lear and, of course, upon hearing this news, Betty up and decided that when performance time came, she'd be there too.

Six weeks later, her dad in dress rehearsals, Jamie was sprawled in her spot on the grass before the amphitheater, enjoying the ocean breeze sifting through her hair. Until Lear entered stage left, that is, at which point she sat up and braced herself. *You'll remember everything you need to remember…*the hypnotic verse her father used to say to her on nights before exams. Act II, Scene ii. The gold crown sat crooked on his head, now beaded with sweat; that dark velvet cloche must have weighed a thousand pounds. "Meantime we shall express our darker purpose," he said at last, the Pacific a distant glimmer just beyond him. He hesitated again here. Gloucester and Goneril to his right, Edmund, Kent, and Regan to his left. They all waited.

"Come on, Dad." They'd rehearsed the scene just this morning. Cordelia gave him a few extra moments. Then he said the line, masterfully, just like all the times Jamie had heard him as a little girl; breathing a sigh of relief, she sat back and lifted her face to the flawless sun. Perhaps Betty had been right. Perhaps he could do it.

The last time their father acted the part of Lear was forty years ago. Yet he still knew the lines like he knew how to get from the kitchen to the bedroom of the house he'd lived in for about the same time. Jamie had never expected him to get the part. She couldn't fathom her father up on a stage, let alone in command of the lead performance, and since arriving she'd been operating in a perpetual state of angst, wondering what might happen to his weak and embittered soul if things didn't work out.

"I told you I could act," her father boasted later that night as Jamie read Scene II Act iv with him in the living room. Lear's two eldest daughters have betrayed him. Regan is refusing him his knights. "Those wicked creatures yet do look well-favored...And thou art twice her love," he read, teetering about in his tube socks.

"What need one?" Jamie read back.

Her father dropped his script to his side and positioned Jamie in the proper mark. "Here," he said, "three paces to the dining table."

"We're just reading, Dad."

"If you don't block, I won't know my cue."

Jamie sighed and paced the steps.

"Say the line again," he demanded.

"What need one?" Her vernacular was poor, but certain things he let slide; this, and the fact that she'd been camping out with him going on six weeks now after being virtually absent the past decade.

"O reason not the need! Our basest beggars are in the poorest thing superfluous." He stood still, overcome, seemingly, by his own abilities. He glanced at Jamie to see if she, too, saw the transformation. "You girls have not the faith in thee?"

She stared at the script. "That's not the line, Dad."

He gathered himself, went on. "Allow not nature more than nature needs..."

Of course she saw the transformation. In fact, only now could she finally understand what Shakespeare was saying, each of her father's lines like a breath, a bird flying free from its cage.

"Oh fool shall I go mad." He raised his arm, statuesque, but then his mind went blank.

"Exit Lear," she cued finally.

"Yes, of course." He limped off into the kitchen.

They re-worked the scene until Vivi popped in with Chinese chicken salads. Salads, salads, always salads, her dad grumbled. Vivi had recently been diagnosed with type-two diabetes. But even on a strict diet she was as vivacious as ever, selling used cars from her home computer and having the neighbors over for cocktails. Their dad didn't socialize or drink, but his and Vivi's relationship was becoming less of a wonder to Jamie…something in those late nights they spent on the couch in front of the Sid Caesar tapes Jamie had bought him last year, Vivi doubled over in a big meaty cackle, her father full of pride. He had made someone laugh. They made each other laugh. They laughed at each other.

Vivi was going to Masa's the following two days to babysit her grandkids, she reminded Jamie's dad over dinner. She'd be back in time for opening night. Of course he'd forgotten. A piece of chicken flew from his mouth as he moaned about how little he saw his own grandkids. Betty's coming out with Sam tomorrow, Jamie reminded him. He looked at Jamie, confused. Opening night, Dad, Jamie blinked back at him, while Vivi reached over and wiped his cheek.

When they were done with dinner her dad limp-walked Vivi back home. At least he wasn't alone. It was a solace Jamie allowed herself only momentarily, what with diabetes added to the list of Vivi's ailments and the fact that all five of Vivi's siblings were already dead—heart attacks, cancer, Parkinson's. No doubt this was the source of Vivi's free spirited take on life. Jamie, too, had laughed in the face of death once, or so she liked to imagine at times. If only she could have Vivi's spirit. Jamie's spirit seemed the opposite; she seemed to search out morbidity, something her husband apparently knew about her for why else would he give her this? She showed the DVD flap of *La Strada* to her dad when he returned, and he went still with recognition, as if it were some old family photo that had gone lost. Forget that it was already eleven p.m., he got the DVD player working, Jamie boiled water for tea, and they sat side by side on the worn tweed couch.

The movie was in Italian with English subtitles, and still her father turned up the volume to a distressing level. "Are you sure you want to watch this?" he asked with some foreboding. But he didn't hear her answer ("no") because he was already transfixed by the barren, colorless landscape, by the poor girl with the funny face and wide drooping eyes. Giulietta. He already knew her name.

A lonely seaside village was where the movie began, where Zampano, a circus strongman brute, purchased Giulietta (and the trumpet that accompanies her everywhere) from her destitute family. It was a place Jamie's father seemed to have already been, so said his sighs and mumbles as Zampano proceeded to unleash his brutality upon the poor girl. Jamie's father had never been able to put into words exactly what had happened to him as a child. Grunts were all Jamie ever got, ones not unlike these, and halfway through the movie Jamie wanted to put her hands to her ears, to pull the plug on the player, or simply flee to her room. But she couldn't. All she could do was ponder the fact that she was here watching this movie with her dad, and her husband wasn't here watching it with them, and that he could haunt her from five thousand miles away.

"Are you all right?" Her father was looking at her strangely. She refocused on the screen. "If I don't stay with you, who will?" Giulietta was saying to Zampano. Then she tumbled over on the ground, half mad from all of his beatings.

"I should warn you," her father said, his eyes a filmy gray. "Zampano leaves her on the side of the road."

This time Jamie grunted.

"She just won't leave him." And then after a moment, "It's alright." He looked at her. "I mean…I'll be alright."

"I know, Dad."

And they watched like that, from entirely different and similar places, until Zampano buried his face in the sand and cried at the news of Giulietta's death, the death he caused by leaving her mad and alone on the side of the road. She was the only person that ever loved him.

Jamie stood up.

Her dad sat staring at the blank screen.

Jamie retrieved the DVD from the player, shoved it back in its case as if trying to close back up Pandora's box. On her way to her room, she paused in the hall reflexively, standing still in order to confirm her father's retreat to bed versus stewing there alone. At last she did hear him heave up from the couch, a light switch off, and the stair banister creek from the pull of his weight. Giulietta's trumpet was playing from his lips until he reached the top step, bent his head down, and smiled knowingly in his daughter's direction.

Jamie's cue to flee to her room, the room she and Betty had shared as kids. Stripping off her jeans, she dove underneath the covers of one of the twin beds, poking her eyes out to stare into the face of Betty's gorilla poster. The carpet still had that musty smell from the quarters' games. Jamie pictured the masking tape Betty had used to split the floor. It might as well still be here, she thought, turning over and facing the wall. It was all so embarrassing really…childhood, life, Betty giving birth to Roberto's child, Roberto already having a child. It was still such an intangible concept, one that Jamie would have to make tangible once Betty arrived, for it seemed nothing was tangible unless her sister knew of it. Jamie's mind spiraled over the plethora of ways their conversation might go. In one of them, Jamie proposed her idea about the sperm donor; the idea that had only ever been a threat to get Roberto on-board suddenly, now, felt real. Roberto had gone to Thailand, with or without her, so then she would have this baby, with or without him. She barely slept, and when she awoke in the morning, her head was pounding and the phone was buzzing: Betty, hearing Jamie's thoughts cross-country no doubt. "Did you get my e-mail?"

Jamie squinted into the ray of sun slanting through the blinds. "What time is it?"

"I sent it yesterday. The invitation's attached. Did you see it?"

Her legs stretched like a cat's off the side of the bed.

"Steven's reserving a room at Walt's for the opening night party. You need to print out the invites and start passing them around."

"Are you sure you want to make a big deal of this, Betty?"

"We should invite Masa and Kit and their families…let's see, there's Aunt Rita, the shoe guy, then that mechanic…oh, and the hardware store guy…what's his name?"

Jamie thought her sister sounded weird, absurdly manic, and they weren't even discussing the surrogacy. In fact, in the few times that Jamie and Betty had talked these past six weeks, neither had so much as mentioned it. Something else was going on with her sister, Jamie was sure. If Betty was so "flogged with work," why did she insist on pulling Sam from school and dragging him all the way with her cross-country just for opening night?

"Don't you think this party's too much pressure on him?"

"Should we invite Mom?"

Jamie's foot swung up and hit the footboard. "Shit."

"Right, of course, bad idea. But if you think of anyone else, let me know. Sam is so excited. See you tomorrow." She hung up.

Jamie rolled from the bed onto the carpet and opened her laptop. These days her e-mails were mostly junk. Even her peers' requests for design advice had dwindled, except for one particularly determined ex-engineer of hers who wanted her to join his consulting firm. Steven cc'd her whenever he announced a new client win, which was often. It was sort of like being in touch. And her mother, who'd only discovered e-mail recently and was still trying to figure out how it all worked, insisted on forwarding Liza's dirty internet jokes. Jamie deleted them unopened; she'd warned her mother about viruses, to which Jamie got back a giggle. Her mother had recently become engaged, and, in her heightened state of romantic glee, she'd pretended that Jamie was making some girlish joke about STDs.

There were three new e-mails from Roberto. She'd been avoiding responding because this was the space she was giving him that he wouldn't admit to needing; the space that would force him to see the unbearable reality of a self-absorbed existence, their life without children. She knew she was hurting him, so, as painful as it was, she scanned quickly through his words. In the first e-mail he described the monkeys on the tenth fairway. His second e-mail said he'd been filling in as chef at his dad's restaurant. A dream of his, Jamie knew. In his third he said that he missed her terribly. He wanted to know when she was coming, which is when she slammed her laptop closed, filled with an emotion she couldn't explain.

She got dressed and marched upstairs to rouse her father out of bed, which took a while; her father's morning MO was sluggish and slow. This morning was worse. Jamie had to remind him ten times that Vivi was at Masa's. Then he couldn't stop reminiscing about the movie they'd seen last night, which Jamie was now kicking herself for showing him. She snuck in a caffeinated tea bag and fixed him an extra piece of peanut butter toast, which he hunched over, the Lear script unopened on the kitchen table. She poured Tuesday's pill tray into his hand, which shook more than usual, she noticed, as he downed the colorful variety of tablets in one gulp—for the first time wondering if she shouldn't be informed on what they were. They read a few scenes—all fine and good. He asked if Steven had called. No, Dad, Steven has not called. Vivi's coming by later? No, Dad, Vivi's at Masa's.

As they were about to leave for the theater, he couldn't find his wallet. He cussed and searched. Jamie went into the bathroom and turned on the faucet until he was done. When she came out her dad was sitting on a chair at the dining table, staring absently into the scattered mess he'd made.

The petite, manic woman director didn't hide her frustration at King Lear's tardiness. Jamie left him on stage and took her usual place out front to watch, but the minute she saw the sun beat down on her father's disgruntled forehead, something told her to go for a drive and come back. When she returned three hours later, the director pulled her aside and asked if everything was all right. Jamie glanced at her own feet and said everything was fine. When she peeked back up the woman's eyes were narrowed. He'd missed five cues today, and he'd been doing so well, she said, still awaiting an explanation. When she didn't get one, she sighed, huffed, and said, "Work with him on Act II Scene iv tonight."

Jamie stood at attention and assured the woman that she would. No way was her dad going to fail on her watch, she wanted to add, but the woman had already marched off.

Getting her dad into the Porsche was always an interesting accomplishment. His head brushed against the ceiling, his knees hit the dashboard. He fiddled with the air conditioning ducts. "Whoa, honey, slow down," was the first thing he always said, even before she took off.

Coasting in third gear, she asked how rehearsal had gone.

Cordelia wasn't blocking correctly.

Couldn't he improvise when that happened?

"You can't act without blocking," he replied, in a tone that said acting was his domain, not hers, and she wondered if he knew how often he'd told her that.

"Remember when I directed that play of yours?" he wistfully reflected. "What was the name of it?"

The Red Badge of Courage.

"The first thing I did was block out movements with the actors."

"We were twelve, Dad."

"And then that idiot kid pulled the curtain down right in the middle of the performance." He held his tongue with some bitterness.

"You did a great job with us, Dad."

He turned at her, blinked away the fog a few times. "I did, didn't I?"

Act II Scene iv. Betty tumbled into the house with Sam and wasted no time distracting their dad from the task at hand. He got all busy fumbling around the house trying to get them the things they might need   extra pillows, blankets, the blow up mattress—things that Betty had already gotten herself, no help needed. Then she wanted to take Sam to Johnny's Pizza, then Grandma's ice cream parlor on the pier, where their dad used to take Betty and Jamie when they were kids. "We don't have time for this," Jamie insisted, following them out the door. Then there was the park at the end of their street, not to mention the beach, their middle school, a stroll down Main Street. "What's with all the nostalgia?" Jamie wanted to know. Sam was getting older now, and Betty wanted him to see how she'd grown up, that's all. Sam really misses his grandfather Betty assured Jamie, who could only frown back after watching their dad limp around behind Sam all morning, he who remained polite but for the most part wanted nothing to do with his grandfather. It's important for Sam to have that grandfatherly influence…the one I never had, Betty made sure to add. She'd always felt so deprived by not having grandparents. To Jamie it seemed like passing the buck: it was easier to have Sam develop a relationship with their dad than having to accomplish that herself at this late and embittered age.

Act IV Scene iv. Her dad read stridently that night for the few minutes that Betty and Sam paused to hear it before slipping off somewhere ("be right back"), and their father fell into a chair and blubbered air out his lips.

"Dad," Jamie said.

He tipped back his chair to see down the hall.

It was only when Betty re-appeared a half-hour later that he re-energized.

"Pretend we're not here," Betty said, falling onto the couch with a magazine.

"Mommy said you get to wear a hat," Sam said, bounding in, freshly bathed and in his pajamas.

"A crown," Betty explained. "He's the king."

"Betty," Jamie interrupted her. "You're distracting him."

Betty bit her lip as their dad found his place again and continued. A few minutes later, when Betty ran off to plug her cell phone into the charger and their father lumbered off to help her, Jamie, watching him go, wondered, after all this time, if her father hadn't given up acting for his kids after all, but had simply just given it up.

She decided to give up as well, for the night anyway.

She sent her dad upstairs to get a good night's sleep. That's what he needed, Jamie decided, trying to remain upbeat as the house began to settle in for the night. She'd moved her things into her old room, what had once been Steven's room, now a makeshift office, so that Betty and Sam could have the twin beds. On east coast time, they'd passed out before Jamie could even say goodnight.

The next morning Jamie had her dad dressed, fed, rehearsed, and off to the theater early. But he kept nodding off on the way there. He hadn't trimmed his beard in the past two mornings, and tufts of hair were poking out his ears. He looked old, Jamie noticed; but then, he *was* old, she reminded herself, as her father snorted himself awake. He looked around disoriented. "You girls don't think I can do it, do you?"

It took a moment for his words to dig down into her soul. "Why do you always say that?" she gasped, guilty to the core. "Of course I know you can do it! I'm really excited for you!" Tears sprang to her eyes. She tried to push them back because he was right. She hated that he was right.

The car went piercingly silent.

Then everything about her dad seemed to soften and wake up. "Acting was always something I thought I could do," he said, blinking at her. "I always wanted to make you girls proud."

She wiped a tear from her eye, praying he'd not seen.

After dropping him off, she turned right around and drove home, her mind a swirl. She had promised to take Sam to the beach. Sam, nine now, was in need of some personal attention, as Betty had explained it to Jamie, she rarely got time alone with him anymore. So where was Betty now? Jamie vexed this inwardly after finding Sam waiting patiently in his swim trunks before the TV while his mother dropped off the invitations at the printer, went to Walt's to plan the menu for the opening night party, ran errands, visited some old high school friends…

Towels, toy shovels, a plastic bucket…Jamie and Sam took turns dragging the load on a boogie board three blocks to the beach. When they hit the sand, they started running, not so much because the sand was scorching as much as running towards oncoming waves was just what Jamie had instinctually done ever since she could remember. It was a wide stretch of sand, and with the wind against them, it took a while to reach the shore, where they immediately dropped to their knees and began digging a hole in the wet earth. Water rushed over them, filling their hole and fueling them with energy. They didn't stop digging. After ten minutes or so and not much progress, Jamie picked up one of the shovels and put her whole body into it, while Sam dug furiously with both hands. They dug as if it was all that mattered, until their arms and backs ached and they were breathless. At one point Sam chucked a bucket full of wet sand over his shoulder, pummeling Jamie in the chest. She fell down laughing until her eyes filled with water. Then she got up and went on digging.

When at last the hole was big enough and they'd packed a strong retaining wall, they climbed in and sat there. At some point Betty showed up. She stood over them shaking her head in her bathing suit, her breasts full, her face flushed as she announced lunch. They all went over to where she had spread out their towels and was passing out sandwiches.

"I hate mayo. I can't eat mayo," Sam whined, then jumped up and sprinted towards the water.

Jamie sniffed at her own sandwich, not a hint of mayo, her sister never forgot.

Betty searched inside her bag for sunscreen. "What do you think about Mom's engagement to Richard?"

Jamie finished her bite, swallowed. "I suppose she's happy."

"She's pretending to be happy," Betty said, frowning at her own sandwich, before setting it down.

"And what about you," Jamie wanted to know. "Are you pretending to be happy?" She didn't know why she'd said it. It just came out. And she certainly wasn't expecting that look on her sister's face, one of shock, embarrassment, and guilt.

"I'm pregnant."

A wave crashed in the distance.

Betty put a hand under her left breast like it hurt. "It was an accident."

Jamie looked out at the ocean, where she could see Sam hopping up and down over the whitewash.

"It's weird, I know."

"Not really."

"What do you mean, 'not really'?"

Jamie's heart was pounding through her chest. "I don't know. It was just something to say I guess."

Sam was running back towards them now.

"What about you guys?" Betty asked offhandedly, as if their plans for a surrogacy never existed.

What about Sam, Jamie didn't say. This gorgeous kid striding up to them now, dripping wet and full of wistful smiles. What happens to him? What is it about having a kid that only makes you want to have more? Like being a mother is never enough.

Betty handed Sam his towel as he came up, gasping for air and shivering with goose bumps. "Have you thought any more about adoption?"

"We've decided not to have kids." It only became a reality as Jamie said it.

Then Sam shook the towel and got sand all over everything.

* * *

Jamie didn't ask her father how the rehearsal had gone when she picked him up later. And when the phone rang that evening, while her father was napping on the couch, Jamie let Betty answer it. She had a feeling it would be the director, and by the look on Betty's face Jamie had been right. Good, she thought, let Miss Happiness deal with it. But the director spoke furiously loud and Jamie, hovering, could hear things like: "As I told your sister, things aren't progressing as I had thought, and I have to be honest with you. At this point I'm seriously considering using the understudy." Jamie fixed her *I-told-you-so* eyes on Betty, who remained undeterred; in fact she seemed amused, which only infuriated Jamie more. And then her sister did something unfathomable and completely unacceptable—she let strange words fall out of her mouth, lots of words about their father that Jamie could never quite muster, those closing with, "If there is anyone you can count on, it's our father. Please don't give up on him. Give it one more day. One more day."

The woman agreed, reluctantly. "If there's no improvement tomorrow, I'll do what I have to do."

Betty hung up, just a little too smug.

"What the hell are you doing?"

"Giving him one more day." She was practically giddy.

"One more day! Do you want to see him make a fool of himself? Is that what you want? End this thing now. Don't drag it out."

Sam came out of nowhere. "Aunt Jamie lets play hide and seek!"

"You're too old for hide and seek," Betty reminded him.

"But I'm bored."

"I'll take Sam to the park," Betty offered suddenly, as if that were the answer to everything. "Dad just needs some peace and quiet."

They both looked over at their dad then; he was sleeping on the couch with his arms folded over his chest like a dead man. Betty bit her lips and stifled a laugh. Jamie turned and faced her dead square. "I think we need to start talking about who's going to take care of him when the time comes."

"What do you mean?"

"What do you mean, what do I mean! What do you think I mean?"

Her face said she had no idea.

"He's old, Betty!"

"He's not old, Jamie."

Jamie had to blink a few times to calm down. "You have no imagination do you. You can't imagine what things might look like in the future."

Betty narrowed her eyes. "He'll be fine, Jamie. He can do it, you'll see tomorrow." She had this weirdly ironic, slightly taunting smile, as if even she was amused by her own perseverance—her signature trait, and one worth flaunting.

"*As flies to wanton boys are we to the gods; they kill us for their sport.*"

"What is that supposed to mean?"

"It means that for me, there's not going to be a tomorrow." Jamie turned and headed down the hall to her room.

Betty followed her. "Oh stop being so dramatic."

Jamie started packing her bag.

"You're not seriously leaving."

Jamie turned and fixed her sister a cold stare.

"You can't leave." She hesitated. "There's more I need to tell you, Jamie."

"It's too late, Betty. It's just too late."

Only now could she feel her sister start to panic, and Jamie stifled her guilt. Certainly there was so much more to Betty's pregnancy. Jamie knew of the vasectomy even if Betty hadn't told her. In fact Dave had told Jamie, rather proudly she recalled, probably the one decision the poor guy had made for himself since Betty came into his life. Jamie knew all along what her sister was doing by offering to be Jamie's surrogate; she was denying the end of her maternal self. She'd been using Jamie, clinging to some need of her own, while Jamie had been clinging to some closeness between them that no longer existed, perhaps never did. Anyway, as she'd said, it was too late—Not even tears could stream from her eyes as she calculated the time change, and when she needed to leave for the airport to make the night flight to Bangkok. She could no longer look at her sister. She had nothing left for her. Except—and here she paused what she was doing to let the cold, brutal thought reach down into her soul, into her sister's soul—this fourth pregnancy, it would be the one her sister would regret.

* * *

Jamie let out a little gasp as her mother descended the bridge into Long Beach, and the reality of that evil, hateful thought struck Jamie with its full force. All this time Jamie had been so angry with Betty, as if her sister had done something wrong, but, in fact, it was what Jamie had done wrong.

A minute passed.

The Shell ball spun into view, illuminating her Porsche, then her dad.

"Jamie dear, are you all right?"

Kill Bill Vol.2

October, 2004

"I think there's something wrong, Betty…and I need you to go over there and check it out."

The line went silent for a moment. This trip to New York was about Betty, not Jamie.

"You know I rarely ask you girls for anything."

You girls? Here they were, forty, forty-one and still one person.

"If I have time, Mom," was Betty's response though inside she was a definitive *No.* Betty was not going to be the one to cave, she assured herself, following the bellman into Gil's suite. An exquisite ensemble of marble, glass, and velvet, red roses on the dining table next to a bottle of Dom on ice. "Good luck, Red," said the note. She set it down smiling, like she was someone else. No. Not someone else. Her. She deserved this.

She poured herself a glass of champagne and took it with her outside onto the terrace overlooking Central Park, sure to not look down because everything below was but a silent image to her now, a tangled mess of people, cars, and cement. She kept her vision on the horizon far above the trees, whose leaves were full of color. The balcony was trimmed with dahlias and lilies, and Betty took a deep breath of their lush scent. After sixteen years with the Smithsonian, she had finally gotten that interview she'd always wanted with the Met in New York. Well, actually, Gil had gotten her that interview, and then lent her this ridiculously awesome penthouse suite for the weekend. They'd had dinner a few times this past year, but nothing had happened between them physically. She'd told Gil that she was working on her marriage and he had been respectful of that. She did let herself cry in his arms once, buckets of tears it seemed, and Gil drank them all in, enfolding her in his embrace and assuring Betty that he'd be there for her, whatever she needed, whenever she was ready. So many years had caught up with her in that one single moment, a lifetime of wanting to know what it might feel like to be taken care of, to be the child and someone else the parent.

Her family was resettled back in D.C. now, and Dave had yet to move out. After that confrontation with her mother, the consequences of Dave's leaving hit Betty with full force. If she separated from her husband now, Betty would someday have this same confrontation with one of her own children; being the "bad guy" in their breakup, being the liar and the cheat, was so unconscionable a thought that Betty started giving Dave a little hope here and there: gestures and cuddles—it was that simple—and he stayed.

But he'd never stop reminding her of her indiscretion, therapy only making him more insecure, it seemed. Often he'd call her a "liar" or a "cheat," insisting on knowing who *he* was, what *he* looked like, how old *he* was, if *he* was rich. It was a painful reminder of her childhood, and Betty decided that she would never tell Dave who *he* was, just that it was insignificant; *he* was insignificant. She wasn't even really sure what had happened that night with Gil, if they'd actually consummated their relationship, though she never told this to Dave. She'd let Dave think what he wanted, while she lived on with the shameful hope that he would do what any other man with a little pride might do—leave her. All this, so she wouldn't be the "bad guy." So she wouldn't be her mother.

She went back inside to refill her champagne glass. Then she wandered around the elegant rooms of the floor length suite drinking it all in, until her adrenaline slowed and she could begin to let go of her mother's phone call (perfectly timed to spoil Betty's arrival). She found the remote and stretched out on the massive bed. She should make some work calls, schedule a few coffee meetings, write down her selling points for those interviews tomorrow even though she didn't expect to get the job, wasn't even sure she wanted the job anymore. Plus, she was "working" on her marriage and couldn't take the job. She polished off her champagne, acknowledging at last the real purpose of this trip, which was, in fact, very simple. If she was going to be labeled a liar and a cheat, wasn't it time she at least reaped the benefits?

She scrolled through the On Demand movie menu a couple times. She'd seen most everything listed, and she didn't want to count how many late nights at the theater that amounted to the past year while she and Dave lived their separately married lives. All those nights she couldn't sleep, alone in her bed (Dave slept in the basement) in that house with the tilted floors that her mother had so loved.

Betty tossed the remote and went to the walk-in closet where the bellman had laid out her bags on stands. She stared at the black duffle for a long moment before moving it over by the foyer entrance. She'd give the bellman Jamie's address, have him messenger it over, and that would be the end of that. To the ceiling she said, "*It's the best I can do, Mother.*" And now, back to the buttery wood closet, where she searched for something to wear. Nothing seemed appealing, particularly the pea green suit she'd sewn over five years ago. She was frowning at it when her cell phone rang—not her mother again! Thankfully it was Gil. He'd made it, after all, though there was no real surprise there. And wear something sexy because he was taking her to dinner.

She hung up, grabbed her purse, and fled the hotel.

An hour later she was strutting down Fifth Avenue decked out in Prada.

Betty had never worn labels, but she hadn't picked up a needle in a year, and shades of pink made her cry. She shopped for clothes at Target now. Today, however, today she shopped without looking at the price tag. She didn't know what she was doing, just that she deserved this. She deserved to be happy.

Back in her room, she shed the new outfit and slipped on the silk robe someone had laid out on the bed in her absence. She sunk into the plush couch before a faux fire and let her gaze dissolve into the fresco-painted ceiling. It gave the illusion of a dome shape, and lost somewhere between reality and the façade, Betty fell asleep.

Gil was carrying her to the bed when she woke in a veil of sadness. Darkness had fallen, taking her with it, for she was crying now. He laid her down and held her for what could have been hours. She had a life's worth of unshed tears it seemed, but only for this stranger, oddly, this fixation. They made love, passionately and selfishly and with everything she had to give and take from him until she lay there spent and shaking and with nothing left but the satisfaction that *this is what it feels like to be ravaged.*

Afterwards Gil ordered room service and Betty took a hot bath in the marble tub with all its oils and scrubs. She lit a candle, poured salts in the water, and rested her head back on the silk pillow, hoping to dissolve; but after a few minutes she grew uncomfortable. The surgical scar on her pelvis kept peeking through the bubbles, horizontal where Jamie's was vertical, and Betty couldn't stop imagining their point of intersection: X marks the spot... She covered it with bubbles, then got out.

Wrapped in a robe, she padded over to the dining room where the butler had arranged a gourmet meal of burgers, fries, and more champagne on the long glass table. Gil was already there, eating his burger with a knife and fork and wearing that boyish grin of his. Betty ate a fry and examined him a minute. His dark, peppery hair was a disheveled mess. She still couldn't tell if he was attractive or not, and yet she seemed to desire him like no other, connected now forever, she presumed, because in her mind Mary would always be his. But Gil had no intention of leaving his wife, and Betty didn't want him to. She didn't want anything more from him than this, to devour burgers and each other one more time, to get dressed up and head out for a night on the town.

It was a nameless establishment downtown, tucked amongst storefronts locked down by iron gates. The steel door opened before Gil even knocked—a man with an earphone had been expecting them. They were passed to a gorgeous hostess who led them through a series of cave-like corridors into a semi-private nook. She settled them into low leather ottomans with drink menus and a pen-sized flashlight.

Betty ordered a Cosmo, Gil a scotch. She told him she didn't want to drink too much because of her interview tomorrow morning, where she should at least be presentable. He told her not to worry about the interview; that it was a done deal; the job was hers if she wanted it. All she had to do was say "yes." Betty narrowed her eyes, confused, then widened them in shock when she realized Gil was serious. Perhaps she hadn't made herself entirely clear to Gil: this job was no longer a reality for her; certainly New York was no reality, and yet in Gil's eyes she could see that he'd help her make it happen. A light went on inside her—had she been so stifled by reality that she forgot that there could be an alternative reality? Perhaps it was the vodka but her mind started swirling: was she really two people with two lives? Because that's what it felt like suddenly, after all those years of tugging, pulling, stretching, and tearing, was she finally, at long last, splitting in two?

After her second drink was gone and they'd sucked down slices of sashimi, Gil suggested they go downstairs, where *it* was happening. Whatever *it* was Betty didn't know or care, she just wanted to keep moving. They squeezed down the crowded stairs, which was more like a ladder, trying not to spill their freshened drinks. There was a soft orange glow in the brick walled space where heated, faceless bodies moved to what seemed like an unending wave of Reggae music. Something smelled like cinnamon. Betty half expected the bartender to send them back from where they came—with Gil she felt so aged and white—but only for a moment, and then they became invisible like everyone else. Their hips joined with other hips, their elbows brushed other elbows. "I thought I couldn't dance!" Gil yelled out to her, bumping hips with a woman with glittery, cocoa-colored skin. He got Betty to join hips on his other side and soon there was a long succession of hips hinging at the waist. It didn't seem like dancing, yet before long they'd danced themselves into a whole other location. She had to focus to keep up, but keep up she did, until her face broke into a wide smile. Gil's boyish curiosity, his way of not taking himself too seriously, was infectious. Before she knew it she was swept away in a sea of mocha and gold.

His name was Bola. He was here from Jamaica, playing bass in a jazz trio in Brooklyn. Gil, who played mandolin in a blue grass band in Atlanta, and Bola were discussing a jam session down the street. Gil was keen on going, and Bola made it known he was keen on Betty going. She didn't need convincing. There was something irresistible about Bola.

She wanted to sink into his skin.

She took a sip from her Cosmo and let the vodka numb the ache of her phantom limbs: her missing kids. Of all the missing that was yet to come because her kids had become her only chemical connection with the world, something she'd begun to sense more and more, and that it wasn't enough for her.

She wanted that chemical connection.

Even Gil was not enough.

The air was cool and sobering as they weaved their way down the middle of the empty street towards this strange address Bola had given them. Betty's heels stuck in the cobbled cracks, and she had to focus not to stumble. Gil chattered on about these kinds of random nights, where you didn't know what was going to happen. When you hadn't planned on things happening, they just did.

Their destination was a dilapidated little building with a wired glass door. Betty glanced behind her. The streets were empty but for them, it seemed. Gil spoke into the intercom and soon the door buzzed open. For a sober moment, she told herself not to go in, but then her mind began flashing those awful images: Dave in the GTI, stuck on the side of the road with a flat tire and a dead cell phone; Steven's stricken face as Sarah steered them through blinding rain trying to get Betty to the hospital; Clay asking her afterwards if he'd killed the baby. All the boys she'd had to placate, to coddle, to mother. Gil was holding the door open for her, his face hungry with anticipation. Anything could happen, that face was saying… Just open your heart, Betty, your mind.

* * *

She woke up the next morning not knowing where she was, for a moment anyway. In fact she'd made it back to Gil's suite, she soon realized, breathing a sigh of relief. Then she blinked a few times, trying to remember what had happened last night and at the same time hoping not to when Gil walked out of the closet with a mischievous grin. He was dressed in a suit and tie and heading to a meeting…and shouldn't Betty be heading off too? It was ten, and her interview was in an hour. He kissed her goodbye, told her there was breakfast, then left. She sat there for a minute, staring into a vision of last night, and then she slammed her eyes shut and pulled the covers back over her head. She woke sometime later and instinctively checked her cell phone for messages. Her heart sunk immediately, expectedly, at the three messages left by Nick wanting to know when she was coming home. These days he was always asking her when she was coming home, even if she was just going to the supermarket. This is when she noticed a phone number penned onto the palm of her hand. Sickened, she stumbled to the bathroom and tried to wash it off, but it remained there, faint and indelible. Avoiding her reflection in the mirror, she managed to get herself into the shower.

There was some white space.

At some point, dressed, she headed outside and began walking.

At some point she paused and blinked into the grey sky, unsure what time it was…and maybe she was cold, she wasn't sure. A red neon sign that said *Ziegfeld* caught her eye and she headed towards it, or her body did anyway. In front of the kiosk now, she stood staring at the display for an indefinite amount of time.

There would be a lot of blood.

She thought maybe she was immune to blood.

She bought a ticket and went inside, where, for a moment she thought she was seeing blood, the place dripping in it—the walls, the carpet, the curtains—the color and thickness of blood. In the main foyer now, underneath a massive, crystal chandelier, she squinted around at her surroundings, confused by the opulence, the grandeur, the ghosts passing by her in evening dress, and wondered if she'd entered a time warp, another dimension. Something on the walls drew her attention, faded photos of Ziegfeld girls. She examined them closely, searching their severely made-up faces, their pointy toes and draping dresses, as if looking for her mother. Then she stepped back suddenly, struck by an odd sensation that not long ago, days perhaps, her sister had stood here and searched for the exact same thing.

She bought nonpareils and entered the theater through one of the velvet draped doors, almost falling backwards so startled was she by the cavernous expanse of darkness, a sea of ghosts watching Uma Thurman being buried alive on that mammoth-sized screen. The place could probably seat a thousand people, and yet there were only a handful there, those looking to escape like Betty in the middle of a workday. It was the loneliest feeling in the world finding her way into one of those seats. But then she focused in on Uma and thought, things could be worse. She could be buried in a coffin six feet under. Uma was karate chopping the lid with her bare hand, methodically, deadly determined, failure not an option. Betty had no idea why Uma had been buried alive or why Bill's assassins were trying to kill her. She'd never seen Kill Bill Vol. 1. Anyway, an hour and a half later all the assassins were dead. One-by-one, Uma killed them, except for Bill, whom she saved for last. She'd just snuck into his desert house in preparation to finish him off only to come upon a girl living there, five-years-old—the age Uma's daughter would have been if Bill hadn't killed her. Betty let out a gasp at about the same time Uma did, when the realization hit them both because the girl *was* Uma's; Bill had kept her alive and raised her on his own. Someone chuckled and Betty glanced over her shoulder before realizing that it was she who was chuckling, and she shoved nonpareils into her mouth, blinking back tears because this was entirely ridiculous. Movies weren't an escape. She'd not escaped. Her life was playing out before her now, in fact, and in every other movie she'd seen too.

She hurried out of the theater.

She didn't need to see Bill get killed.

She needed to get her shit together.

She needed to stop watching movies late at night.

She needed therapy.

She needed her sister.

She sprinted back to her hotel and retrieved the duffle she'd yet to send. Back outside with it, she hailed a cab headed downtown. "Hurry!" she told the cabbie, as if suddenly she'd no time to waste, like Uma, whose hand kept springing up from the dirt in a vision before Betty. Uma had fought her way out of that box and clawed her way through that earth because giving up wasn't an option. And that's how Betty felt in this moment, as the cab sped down Fifth Avenue. Giving up on her sister wasn't an option because it meant giving up on herself. And that's exactly what she'd been doing, and not just since Mary, but a long, long time ago. Make a right on Nineteenth, right on Sixth, right on Twentieth she told the driver…pull over at the gray brick building next to the bakery. She couldn't tell him the address, but she knew how to get there.

She rang the buzzer repeatedly. It would be the first time they'd seen each other since *King Lear*—one year, four months, ten days to be exact. That night Jamie had abruptly left for Thailand, and their Dad had proceeded to steal the show. Betty had been right about their dad—that he could do it—and Jamie hadn't been there to see it. But Betty had been because Betty was a believer. Somewhere along the way she'd forgotten that.

Finally the door clicked open. There was no greeting from the intercom, but Betty could hear the baby wailing. The wails grew louder as the elevator ascended, a piercing shrill as the door slid open and Betty entered, biting her lip. For a moment she wondered if she was on the wrong floor. Dirty dishes were stacked in the stainless steel sink. Half filled baby bottles and spilt powdered formula littered the slate kitchen countertops. Wipes and burping cloths were draped over the designer Italian furniture. The Diaper Genie looked busted, and Betty remembered that Jamie never could work hers. There was a dirty diaper on the floor.

"Jesus," Betty sighed. She picked it up, put it in a plastic bag, and threw it in the trash. The wails were bouncing off the brick walls now, and Betty was beginning to wonder if it was, in fact, a baby in there, versus an alien. As boisterous as her boys were, they had been silent criers…if they had cried at all…Betty didn't remember. What she did remember was that they were all beautiful, perfect babies. Her babies.

She found Jamie in her open office, struggling to get on Francesca's diaper. Betty set down her black duffle and watched, clamping down on her lip to keep from smiling or crying or both. When Jamie was done she turned and held out the finished product: dark silky skin and hair, eyes shaped like almonds, it was an alien, a gorgeous little angel alien. "Three months and I still can't get it right."

"That's because you've got it on backwards, silly." Betty pulled Francesca into her arms and into a natural swaying bob while Jamie fell back on the sofa. "I shouldn't be doing this. I'm not a mother. I wasn't meant to be a mother. I never really wanted to be a mother."

"And look," Betty said flatly. "Here you are one." She felt her sister's absent gaze as Betty, still bobbing, took in her surroundings. "Where's your changing table?"

"I don't have one."

"You don't have one!"

"I ordered one, but it hasn't come."

"What have you been doing for three months?"

"This." She pointed at the changing pad on the designer foldout couch, now permanently folded out.

Betty laid Francesca there, slid off the sagging diaper, and expertly slapped on a new one. The scent of sour milk and baby flesh. Home. She balanced Francesca over her shoulder with one hand while rummaging through her duffle with the other. Baby onezies, throws, booties, and bonnets, all hand made, in hemps or organic pima blends, with My Mary labels stitched on everything. For Francesca she selected the pink hooded burrito wrap, folded her up in it snugly, and then laid the girl back on her shoulder and rubbed her back. "Mom said you'd hired help?"

Jamie was rummaging through the duffle now. "What the hell's all this?" She held out a baby bib.

Betty stared at the bib for a long moment, the little bear stitched on the front, the pink bow, one of her favorites, and tears sprang to her eyes. "I'm fucked up, Jamie. I'm so fucked up."

"No shit…is that Prada?"

The tears spilled as she laughed because only her sister would know without knowing anything at all, and still love her. She wiped her face with her free hand, which is when it hit her. "You cut your hair. That's what's different."

"I've gained weight." Jamie caressed the fabric of a burping blanket, shaking her head. "This stuff is amazing."

Betty stood there with Francesca in her arms watching her sister extract more and more of Betty and everything that had gone missing in her life from that bag. It took a while, and it was amazing how much there actually was.

"You should start a business."

Where the hell were you eight months ago? "Anyway…" she hid her face in the girl's fleshless neck. Smiling inwardly, selfishly as she contemplated the resurrection of My Mary…it was never too late…or better late than never…one of those phrases was struggling its way to Betty's surface. She cleared her throat. "That nanny?"

Jamie looked at her oddly.

"Mom said you had a nanny."

"I borrow the neighbor's nanny sometimes, but otherwise…I can't do strangers in my house."

Betty didn't bother responding. "I can't stand that idle chatter that's required."

She dulled her eyes.

"What?"

Betty shook her head, wondering for the first time if motherhood wasn't as natural as she thought. She started looking around then, this time with a keener eye. Forget about the changing table. Her mother had been right: something felt off. With Francesca's head bobbing over her shoulder, Betty sniffed her way down the hall to the master bedroom, where she opened a few tall closets, searched the medicine cabinets in the bathroom, then cruised back up the hall, past Jamie and into the main living area. A stroller sat parked on the Persian rug, and toys were piled up on the coffee table where once only a stack of silver coasters had lived. When she returned to the office, Jamie hadn't moved and Francesca was giggling. "Where is he?" Betty said.

"He's not here."

"He's not here right now or not here here."

"The second one you said."

Betty processed that for a minute. "But Mom said you guys were together, he was here, all was well, he was enjoying being a father…"

"Mom still thinks Richard's going to move in, Betty. I tell her what she wants to hear."

There was a moment of heavy silence. "And the birth?" Betty went dark at the image of her sister giving birth alone. Of course she would suffer it alone. Of course!

"It's OK, Betty. It was OK."

Her legs felt weak. She sat down. "Does he even know?"

"He never wanted a baby." Jamie looked directly at her sister. "I wasn't completely honest about that."

"Does. He. Know."

Jamie sucked on her lips. Her eyes welled.

Betty let out a long slow exhale. "You and I. We don't tell each other things."

"I know."

"Real things." She thought hard for a moment. "Why is that?"

"We grew up together. Maybe we didn't need to."

"We thought we didn't need to."

They blinked at each other, then at Francesca resting on Betty's thighs now, her little face curious. "Those ocean blue eyes are yours," Jamie said.

Betty gazed into them, the meeting of two seas. "She thinks I'm you."

"So did Sam," Jamie said, from somewhere in the past. "I remember, when he was a baby, I would hold him and he would just sit there staring at me thinking, 'Should I be scared or is she home?'"

Francesca let out a funny slurping noise then, and Betty and Jamie shared a look, their look, never changing, still alive and determined to penetrate through all the bullshit. "I'm sorry," Jamie said, her voice trembling.

"It's not your fault."

"I wasn't there."

"You were there, Jamie. You were always there."

"I made it happen."

"So much has happened. There are so many things I need to tell you."

"I dreamt that you had a miscarriage. It was awful. I can't get it out of my mind. There was so much blood. And then…" she put her head in her hands. "I can't…"

"Don't."

"I knew right then that I was pregnant."

"I knew too. It's weird for me to say that, but I knew." Betty held up Francesca then, who seemed to be discovering her tongue. Betty's bracelet—Hallmark's version of the Tiffany Heart bracelet—slid up her arm. Jamie noticed it, and so held up her own arm to model the exact same bracelet. "Mom," is all she needed to say.

"Mother's Day."

"Mine came in a heart-shaped box."

"So did mine."

Jamie read the inscription. "Sisters."

"Mom's got one too."

"It's her way of connecting you to me."

"And me to you."

"And then her to us. She knows something's wrong."

"I confronted her."

"She told me."

"I was so angry."

"I know."

"She came after the miscarriage. I was shocked actually, that she'd made such an effort at a time when…well, it was Christmas. And you know how Mom gets on Christmas."

Jamie knew.

"What's sad is that I was actually trying to make a connection with her." She drew a deep breath and unwrapped Francesca from her blanket. "I told her that she was never there for me as a mother. I thought I would feel better, but it only made me feel worse." She paused to look down at Francesca, who'd just let out a fantastic giggle. Betty had been sea-sawing her skinny golden legs and clearly she liked it.

"At least you've opened the dialogue now. There's still time."

"Still time," Betty repeated the words. "Lot's of time."

"Nothing but time."

They fell silent.

"Jamie."

"Yes." She closed her eyes. "I know."

"You need to tell him."

She breathed out, what was left. "He's never going to forgive me."

"He loves you. It's time to stop punishing yourself for what happened to me and just accept that."

Betty kissed the baby's soft belly. It felt warm and right. When she looked back up she'd forgotten what she was going to say. The baby started to fuss and Jamie jangled her Hallmark bracelet over the girl's face with a weary familiarity. Francesca reached out her tiny fist to grab the shiny silver heart, but it remained elusive. "I still can't fathom it," Jamie said.

"Mom?"

"Mother's Day."

Francesca tooted, they laughed, and Betty said, "Get used to it."

The Red Shoes

2007

Phantom Richard had become a joke between them. Until their mother died of heartbreak, then he became real. Though according to Diana who called Jamie with the news, their mother's heart had stopped beating, and she died in her sleep. When she didn't show up for the weekly coffee with The Girls, Diana got worried and drove right over. She let herself in with the key their mom kept under the heart shaped fichus pot. The poodles still had their Fourth of July bows on. They were yapping and sliding about in their own pee puddles and the house smelled like, well, the end. And it was.

"It wasn't heartbreak," Betty insisted after the shock wore off, the blubbery, angry mess. "She wasn't in love with Richard as much as her idea of being in love with him, of having that kind of relation-ship."

"She caught the two of them together, Betty. That wasn't real?"

"That's exactly what I'm talking about: if they were so in love, why would he go and do something like that."

She must have heard herself then, or Jamie's hard silence, because she went on in a rambling panic. "Clay has the flu. I'm in final negotiations with Nordstrom's for a deal that could put My Mary on the map. I've taken this big step, this big risk…and just when I need my mother the most…" her voice cracked. It took her a while to compose herself. "I'm just not ready to process," she blurted out, and what did sisters have to talk about if they weren't processing their mothers. They hung up.

Jamie put herself and Francesca on the five p.m. flight to LAX. They landed on the coast at eight thirty, and the taxi dropped them at her mother's around nine, where they could see candles flickering through the front windows. The door fell open when Jamie put her key in the lock, and she was struck by a scent embedded in her memory, a bouquet of roses, kelp, and half dead dog. It weighed heavy in the air and on Jamie's heart, and for a moment she couldn't breathe.

Then came the scraping and hyperactive panting of Angel and Blue, the dogs who's future Jamie had yet to even think about. Francesca giggled as Blue began licking her toe, and Jamie scooped up Angel and buried her face in her fur. From this dog her mother had rescued, Jamie drew in a deep breath of courage, before proceeding into the living room where The Girls were nestled around the couches in front of a blazing fire in the middle of July.

For a moment there was nothing to say. The Girls looked at Jamie and Jamie looked at the eight-by-ten photo of her mother they'd propped up on the coffee table—black gown, red rose, desperate smile. Her prayer candle flickered next to it. There was also her daily meditation book and a Bible, each opened to an earmarked page.

This spiritual moment, this reading, or sharing, or whatever The Girls were doing was a scene Jamie had witnessed many times in this house, her mother's sanctuary on the cliffs of the Pacific. As usual Jamie couldn't sit down with them, in fact her butt was burning from the fire she'd almost backed into. Her daughter, however, was already nestled between Diana and Zoe, entranced. She'd become terribly attached to her grandmother this past year as they'd spent more time with her, and so when Jamie told Francesca about the death, her response was, "Grandma's not dead. Grandma's just lonely. Grandma's just sad. Grandma just needs to cry on my shoulder, Mommy." Perhaps they'd been spending too much time with Grandma this past year. "She's dead," Jamie proceeded to assure her daughter. "This is not one of Grandma's fairytales, Francesca."

Francesca had barely spoken to Jamie since.

Before their mother discovered Richard's affair, she'd been on a high, which was odd, because in a big upset she'd lost her bid for re-election to the City Council. Their mother hadn't been unemployed since Jamie was a baby, and the thought of her retired from public office and idle was no less than frightening to her daughters. Yet she got over it rather quickly, the girls thought, because according to their mother there was no idleness, there was Richard. Losing the election had forced them to take their relationship to a new level, because now she had the time to devote to it!

Things happen for a reason, she reminded them.

She'd taken up oil painting and resurrected her leotards for the dance classes she'd enrolled in at the Y. She planned trips for her and Richard—a cruise around the Adriatic, island hopping in Hawaii, a spiritual retreat in Sedona—although there was some dispute between Betty and Jamie about whether these trips ever actually materialized. She and Richard cooked together. They watched movies, Westerns or classics from their era. They bummed around. He'd supervised the remodel of her kitchen and master bathroom, and though she and Richard still didn't live together, "We've really settled into this nice little place."

Harrumph.

Then, six months ago, Jamie got a call from her mother, who was hysterical after having discovered Richard was having an affair.

Jamie and Francesca were on the next plane. She was in bed crying when they got there, one of The Girls watching over her because she couldn't be alone. Francesca took this to heart: she slept with her, bathed with her, watched TV with her. Not that Jamie's mother watched TV as much as just lie there staring at it. When it came time to return to New York, Francesca threw a fit. "Why doesn't Grandma live with us?" she demanded to know. "Why doesn't Papa live with us? And Nonno Giorgio and Zia! Aunt Betty and Nick..." she stopped to count on her fingers.

"Sam and Clay," Jamie added.

"Sam and Clay!" she was bawling now.

"And don't forget Papa Tom."

"And Grandma Vivi! And Uncle Steven! Why don't we all live together?"

Jamie, who had been biting her lip, said. "I don't know. It's been so long that I've completely forgotten what caused such a radical disbursement of beings."

"*Un regalo!*" Francesca hollered, startling Jamie back to the present. Her daughter stood perched on a chair at the dining table, her pink mouth open, pointing at a large white box with a gold velvet ribbon tied around it. Jamie went still while her mother's presence passed through her, for Jamie didn't have to examine the package to know that it was her mother's handiwork, the way the bow curled a certain way. She let out a weary breath and went over. "For my children" was written on an envelope taped to the box in her mother's perfect cursive. She had left instructions not to open the letter or the box until all of her children were present. "She was going to give it to you kids at her seventieth birthday." Diana stepped up beside Jamie and said, "But, well, here we are, a few weeks short of that."

"*E qui!*" Francesca slid off the chair. "*E nascosta*, Mamma."

"Is that Italian?" Zoe asked.

"Something like that," Jamie offered, watching Francesca clomp up the stairs with her suitcase, the dogs on her heals, to her mother's bedroom. "She thinks my mother's hiding somewhere," Jamie paused to swallow back tears, knowing that she should follow her daughter up to the scene of her mother's last breath. "I'm afraid I'm not handling this very well…with my daughter…you see," her voice faltered. "These tragic moments, the ability to deal with them tragically…well, they're what I need my mother for." Jamie didn't know what she was saying, just that suddenly she was desperate for Betty to arrive.

Diana placed a hand on Jamie's shoulder. "She looked peaceful when I found her."

Peaceful was not a word Jamie would use to describe her mother. "I just spoke with her last week. She said she was doing better. She didn't like taking the pills, but she said they were helping with the depression."

"You know she hired a detective to find her birth father," Diana said.

Jamie looked at Diana, confused, and suddenly jetlagged. "A long time ago." Yes, Jamie knew.

Diana eyed the box. "She had something to share with you I'm pretty sure. But I don't now more than that."

Jamie stared at the box again, waiting for some profound thought or emotion to hit her. The Girls gathered their things and left and still Jamie stood staring at that box waiting for something, even anger would do. She'd need Betty for that, she finally decided, and she went to the foot of the stairs. Her intention was to go up, but then it hit her, as it often did at the oddest of times, that her daughter would face life without a sister. Jamie's mother had too, a concept Jamie could not, for the life of her, make sense of presently. She finally just called for Francesca to come down, which she wouldn't, busy, Jamie could hear, rummaging through her ballerina suitcase, sliding the proper clothes into the proper drawers, placing her hairbrush and shampoo into their designated spots on the bathroom sink, just like her grandmother had shown her. This was all really happening Jamie reminded herself, crawling into the guestroom bed and falling asleep to the sound of her daughter and the dogs snoring in the room above her.

The next morning she threw Angel, Blue, and Francesca into her mom's Audi. The lease must have come up recently, this was a new model, a sporty convertible, and Jamie put the top down, which the dogs loved, basking in the wind as she sped up the 405 to LAX. They found Betty and Nick standing at baggage claim over-saddled with luggage. Francesca ran to Nick and they clung to each other as Betty and Jamie watched on. Then Nick took Francesca's hand like she belonged to him and led her out the doors that slid open automatically. It was a magical moment, however fleeting, when their hair became bursts of red in the sun.

Betty talked to Debbie on her cell phone most of the ride back. They had a conference call scheduled the next day with Nordstrom's, who was considering My Mary's infant line for their stores across the northwest. After Debbie she called Dave, who had taken Sam and Clay until Betty could make arrangements to fly them out for the funeral. She didn't even pause entering their mom's house, rather, followed Nick who was following Francesca over to where the box was, for Francesca had already told them all about it in the car. And as Nick went to rip the thing open, Francesca grabbed his arm and reminded him again that they weren't allowed to open the box until Uncle Steven was here. Then she added something in Italian, and the two of them scrambled off.

"What did she say?" Betty watched her go.

"She thinks her grandmother is hiding in this house somewhere."

"Was that Italian?"

"We were with her father last month. This is her way of punishing me."

"But I thought he speaks to her in Thai."

"Giorgio. Giorgio speaks to her in Italian."

"And you?"

"Gibberish, apparently." Jamie unstuck the envelope from the box and passed it to Betty "It seems I've taken everyone away from her."

Betty blinked at her, then the envelope, resigning after a moment, "This is so Mom."

Jamie shook the box. It was clunky. There was more than one thing inside.

"Maybe it's the Mary Janes?"

"It's not the Mary Janes."

"How do you know?"

"Because she gave them to Francesca on our last visit."

There was some hesitation.

"She started giving a lot of things away, Betty."

"Did she say anything about the antique rocker?" A moment of silence passed. Then Betty cleared her throat and shrugged as if it didn't really matter. "When is Steven getting here so we can get this over with?"

"He said he was on his way over four hours ago. He had a meeting downtown he couldn't get out of."

They held a look: their brother's ill-fitted responses to family crises left them equally flabbergasted, then just hungry. Or at least Betty was, heading to the kitchen now. The woman was in a perpetual state of starvation. "Something's different," she said, opening the fridge.

"It's the Santa Ana winds. They make everything barren and lonely."

"No beer," Betty said, "I could really go for a beer."

"Richard drinks bourbon."

"Right. I feel like I should know that." And then, "Did she redo the cabinets?"

"Hello. She's redone everything."

"Oh right. For Richard."

"Phantom Richard."

There was a pause.

"We're going to need to buy some alcohol."

Jamie moved her sister aside and began searching the refrigerator's contents as if they might tell her something, the old jars of pickles and relish, a smorgasbord of crusted mustards, that bottle of Asti Spumante no one wanted to drink. Behind an open can of Sprite stained with lipstick was a box of Velveeta cheese that Jamie screwed her face up at. She pulled it out and searched the label for warning signs—like DEATH. Betty, holding a box of Wheat Thins she'd found in a high cabinet, reached past Jamie for the remnants of some stale slices of bread. "She never has tortillas," she lamented, putting two crumpled pieces in the toaster while Jamie got out the liquid margarine. When the toast was done, Betty held the bottle upside down over a slice, and they watched the liquid make its way to the spout, which took a while. When the margarine did finally escape, it spattered on the toast like a bird turd dropping. "Maybe she finally starved herself to death," Betty said, and threw the piece of toast in the trash.

Without really deciding upon this path, the two of them ventured upstairs. Francesca and Nick followed, as did the dogs. The noise of their group ascending on the hollow hardwood was thunderous and disturbing, especially with their mother's awards staring at them from every inch of the stairway wall: her Woman of the Year award, her Honorary Mayor gavel, a humungous photo of her crouched in the midst of hundreds of colorful school kids, none of whom were her own…"Is this it?" Betty paused in front a painting of their mother. "The self-portrait she'd been going on about?"

"She didn't like how it turned out."

Betty moved in closer.

"Then again, is it possible to like how you turn out?"

Betty, not listening, "At last, Mom and I agree on something."

Streams of sun-filtered dust poured over them when they reached the top. Francesca and Nick ran and searched under the bed, and, finding nothing, began jumping on top of it. The dogs barked. Rose petals fell from the vase on the side table and settled around a tiny heart-shaped frame inscribed with one word, *love*.

Betty, who had disappeared inside their mother's newly restored closets, stumbled out now with her mouth agape and headed into the master bath with its new Jacuzzi tub, rain shower, and his-and-her sinks. "Do you think he really ever planned to move in?" she came out and said.

"I'm so tired of trying to figure it out." Jamie was at her mother's dresser, studying the framed photos she kept there—a shrine of sorts—to the men in her life. A wedding photo with their dad, another with Gary, then one of her and Richard, not one photo but two separate ones, side-by-side, both in formal dress and posing before the same background; it was as if no one was there to snap the photo of them together. There was she and Steven behind a podium at her Woman of the Year ceremony. "Who's this?" Betty picked up a framed picture of a man neither of them recognized. The photo was in black and white and seemed old, touched up.

"He's handsome."

"He's young." Betty set down the frame.

He has Clay's platinum hair, Jamie didn't say, because her sister had gone pale suddenly, stepping backwards, as if she'd seen a ghost.

"What's wrong?"

She shook her head, nothing, then turned and went to the walled windows that looked out on the Pacific. Jamie followed her there. The sun was beginning its breathtaking descent behind

Catalina Island. "I've always had a bad feeling for this house..." Betty said with a jittery breath, "Bad memories I suppose, I don't know."

They stared out for a time, at a container ship crawling by.

"Dave met someone else," she said finally.

There was a pause.

Jamie turned and looked at her. "But it's what you wanted."

She shrugged.

"To be free."

"I'm alone."

"Give it some time. You'll get really good at it."

The ship was gone.

"I'm so sleepy suddenly," Betty yawned.

Jamie yawned.

They laughed at each other yawning...until a loud bang snapped them back to attention. It was followed by a long silence, then cackles, followed by rubber tearing across hardwood. The kids had found the three-wheeler.

"We should just open it," Betty said, heading downstairs. "We don't need Steven."

"Don't you dare," Jamie warned, following her sister down until they both stopped dead in the middle of the room because the box was no longer on the table.

"Nick!" Betty was already detouring to the guestroom. "I probably should have mentioned this to you before."

"Mentioned what?" Jamie said, on her sister's heels.

"Nick's on suspension from school."

"Suspension? But he's only, what, seven?"

"He got caught stealing. It wasn't the first time."

The dogs were pawing at the bed when they got there. Underneath it Nick and Francesca were hiding with the box. Betty dragged

Nick out by his feet, Jamie did the same with Francesca, clutching the box, and they sat the kids on the bed.

"I was just kidding guys," Betty said. "I wasn't going to open it."

"I just don't see the point of fighting who Mom is anymore Betty, especially since she's…" Jamie was going to say dead. Instead, she sat down and put an arm around her daughter, "Somewhere not exactly here."

"I'm not fighting who she is…" Betty paused in frustration… Then she softened her voice and told Nick, "I've gotta go do some work for my meeting tomorrow. Behave for your aunt. I'll be in the office if you need me."

A bit later, after Jamie had Francesca hide the box where neither Betty nor Nick could find it, Diana showed up with an accordion folder of funeral plans. Her face was a red puffy mess. She pulled out the picture their mother had already selected for the local newspaper. She did not want an obituary, mind you, but an announcement celebrating her life. Betty and Jamie looked at the picture, each other, and then at Diana, who gave them the same look back. Father Patrick was to preside over the funeral to be held at the Immaculate Heart of Mary Church. Jamie would write a poem and read it out loud, Betty would conduct the slide presentation, and Steven would lead the crowd in a prayer. Her grandchildren would sing a song, with Sam, the eldest, leading on the piano. After that there would be a party here at the house, where candles would burn, mariachis would play, and one of her adopted Mexican families would serve enchiladas. She wanted it to be festive. She wanted dancing. Liza, who managed their mother's accounts, would be by tomorrow to discuss their mother's estate. "What estate?" Jamie blurted out, having had the opportunity to review her mother's finances recently. "We'll need to sell the house in order to pay off the mortgage. What's left might cover the mariachis. Our mother didn't save. She spent every hard working penny she earned on living!"

Betty turned white.

"What?" Jamie asked her. "What is it?"

"Mom told me she was going to invest in My Mary."

"She told me she was going to sell the house and move to Italy with Richard."

No one said much after that.

By the time Diana left with the kids for an overnight (in order to give Jamie and Betty private time with their brother), it was early evening, and still no sign of Steven. "Who dances at a funeral?" Betty said, dialing Steven on his cell. "Where the hell are you?" started the conversation. She pursed her lips while he answered. "He's been held up," Betty mouthed to Jamie, who leaned into the phone so that he'd be sure to hear, "In other words he can't handle the emotional trauma."

Betty was shaking her head at something he was saying.

"Ask him about Mom's birthfather," Jamie demanded then, and Betty looked at her, confused, "What birthfather?"

"Just ask him."

She did. Silence followed. Then Betty's mouth fell open.

"What?"

"Oh my God," Betty said into the phone.

"Put him on speaker!"

Steven went on to say that their mom wasn't searching for her birthfather, but that he'd been searching for her.

Jamie gasped.

"Not the father, the son I mean," Steven corrected himself.

Jamie looked at Betty, who looked at her.

"Apparently he's an actor or something. In the movies."

There was a pause.

"The son?"

"No, the father."

Another pause.

"He's not Cary Grant is he? I mean, because that would be pretty cool."This was Jamie's question. Betty wanted to know, with an attempt at nonchalance, if he happened to leave them anything.

Steven instructed them to go get the box, they'd open it now, and perhaps they'd all find out.

"Francesca's not going to go for it," was Jamie's response, and Betty gave her this look, like, are you my sister, or an imposter? "We can read him the letter over the phone, Jamie. It'll be the same thing as if we were all together."

Jamie sucked on her lips.

"Don't you want to know?"

"Fine." Jamie ran to get the box. Only it wasn't in the coat closet where Francesca said she'd hidden it, and Jamie stood there for a minute, stumped. Then she ran back. "Tell Steven we'll call him back."

They called Diane's; Jamie spoke to Francesca: not that closet the other one, duh. Jamie went to the guestroom closet. Remaining calm when it wasn't there, she searched under the bed, then the bathroom, the den, the office, the garage, and of course any closet she could find. Betty was helping her look now. "I think her idea of a closet and mine are entirely different."

It wasn't until they'd finished scouring the upstairs and found nothing that Jamie felt the rumblings of panic.

"The kids probably buried it out back or something," Betty offered.

"Next to generations of dead dogs, great." Jamie was searching her mother's medicine cabinets.

"Well it's not going to be in there." Betty was crouching down reaching for something under the bed, not *the* box but another box, their mother's keepsake box, where she kept all her most precious photos and letters. Betty was pondering out loud the effort involved in this slide show her mother had requested, as there weren't many photos in the box because their mother never kept a picture around of her that wasn't, well, perfect. She would need to scan them into her mother's computer and overlay the music for the slide show. Where would she find that Barbra Streisand song her mother had requested?

Meanwhile, preparing for her grave dig out back, Jamie snuck one of her mother's sleeping pills under her tongue, then went downstairs and washed it down with a glass of Richard's Jim Beam, the only bottle of liquor her non-drinking mother had in the house. She ventured outside and started poking around the garden, pausing every so often to gaze out at her mother's starry night for inspiration. The ocean was out there somewhere in the backdrop of her rose garden, what used to be her mother's sanctuary. Now it just seemed like a burial ground for the dead. With that thought Jamie gave up her search, for the night anyway, and took her glass with her into the den, Richard's den, another space their mother had created and he'd not filled. She rummaged through her mother's classic DVD collection, sectioned and alphabetized. But when she opened the DVD player, she found a movie already loaded…and upon sight of the title the hairs stood up on the back of her neck.

She glanced behind her, a ghostly sensation. Then she closed the drive, pressed play, and was immediately gone, absorbed, as if this story of a dancer who dances in a ballet called *The Red Shoes* were some kind of hypnotic trigger. Jamie never understood if it was the red shoes that possessed the dancer, or the dancer who possessed the red shoes, whatever the case, the poor girl couldn't take them off, she couldn't stop dancing, and neither the ballet nor the story ended happily. Jamie had been haunted by the movie as a child, back when she still practiced ballet, back when she lived in the shadow of a mother who had dreams of being a dancer. After her first viewing, Jamie sat for days on her father's easy chair staring off into the empty space where the dancer had went. And yet Jamie couldn't wait to see the movie again, and when it did at last show up in the TV Guide, she excitedly told her mother about it so that they could, as mutual dance aficionados, watch it together. But her mother never did watch the movie with her in the dozens of times that Jamie proceeded to see it. And it wasn't until much later that Jamie began to understand why, for her mother would never watch a movie with so little hope. *The Wizard of Oz* was one thing, but *The Red Shoes* was the ultimate in dark tragedy.

So why would her mother choose to watch it now?

Disturbed by this question, Jamie slumped into Richard's over-sized faux leather couch and watched the girl in the red shoes dance tirelessly on. She must have fallen asleep at some point though, because when she roused it was morning and she was covered with a blanket. Wrapped in it, she went and found her sister in her mother's office at the computer, where she'd been up all night working on the slide presentation. Her eyes were bloodshot but undaunted. With a hoarse voice she clicked Jamie through her progress, proud, weepy, nervous, uncertain. There were a few things she still needed to change she assured Jamie with some sniffles, but she'd get to that after the call with Nordstrom's. First she was going to make the carrot cake their mother particularly loved, for the service. Then she had to call Dave to coordinate the older boys' flight. She'd need to figure out what song Sam would play on the piano. "What?" she stopped suddenly, for Jamie had been leaning against the counter with her arms crossed, examining her with no small amount of concern. "What's wrong?" Now Betty was concerned.

"You," Jamie responded, wondering how it was two sisters could be so different. "You're tireless."

Betty dropped her shoulders. "I'm tired."

"It's as if you're still trying to prove something to her."

Betty exhaled, deeply.

"What are you trying to prove? She's dead."

A noise came out of Betty's throat. She was trying to speak…

"What I'm saying is that it's admirable, Betty. I've always admired you for that." Jamie took a defeated breath and set her gaze out the window. "I'm not sure when I gave up on Mom, when I began to want her to be only the mother she was instead of the mother I wanted her to be, or when the two of those things merged together. I was almost relieved when she got engaged to Richard. Real or not, he made her happy, and Mom desperately needed to be happy. So I let her go on pretending. In my whole life I never confronted her. But if I had, I don't know, maybe she'd have woken up. Maybe she never would have caught Richard in bed with someone else. Maybe her heart wouldn't have broken. Maybe she'd still be alive."

"I can't let it go," Betty said. "The things I said to her."

"Maybe we should both let go."

Betty was crying now. "I blamed Mom for everything."

Jamie put a hand on her sister's shoulder. "It's what mothers are for. Even she would say that." It got a laugh out of her, if only for a moment, and Jamie wondered if this was as close as they might get to holding each other, to feeling each other's tears, to letting Glenda slip out from under their skin, to accepting that it wasn't her keeping them together but them keeping them together. Jamie sighed. "I wrote that one silly poem in junior high that won that silly little prize and it seems she'll never forget it. She had this idea in her head that I'm creative."

"She told me I'd make a good homemaker."

"Maybe she got us backwards."

"So you're the homemaker now?"

There was an awkward pause. Then they both fell over laughing. "Don't look at me like that," Jamie cried.

"I'm not looking at you like anything."

Tears were streaming down their cheeks.

Betty pulled herself together. "Seriously, Jamie, just go be with him."

Jamie stopped laughing.

"You know you want to."

I know, she didn't need to say, and Betty left to go make her Nordstrom's call. Meanwhile, Jamie found her way to the dining table with a napkin and pen to write that poem. But Betty's determined voice kept seeping through the walls, distracting her. Jamie didn't think that she'd ever heard her sister sound so decisive before, so sure of herself and who she was. Could she at last be on her way somewhere, as she'd always dreamed and wanted? Jamie truly hoped so, with everything she had, even as frightening and sad as this reality was because wherever Betty was headed, once again it was somewhere far and away from where Jamie was headed, into the den with her coffee to finish watching *The Red Shoes*.

Would it always be this way with them?

A short time later, Jamie, engrossed in the film, noticed Betty right behind her and jumped off the couch. "You scared the shit out of me!" she gasped, and Betty, nonplussed, said that Nordstrom's wanted three orders of terry-hooded towel wraps by September. She was trying to look burdened, as opposed to ecstatic and ready to burst. West Coast…Seattle…perhaps she and the kids would stay the rest of the summer here…She paused to take a deep jittery breath. Then she grabbed a chocolate chip cookie from the batch she'd made sometime during the night. "What's this?" she said to the TV, falling exhaustively into the couch.

"*The Red Shoes*." Jamie said, still hard at thought. "I just can't figure out why Mom was watching it."

"Why wouldn't she?"

"Have you ever seen it?"

"No."

"Well, if you had you'd know why."

"Just tell me."

Jamie motioned her head at the screen. "That girl's going to leap off the balcony and get run over by a train."

Betty sort of laughed, but then saw that Jamie was serious and grew concerned. "But why?"

"Because she has to choose between the man she loves and the passion that drives her— dancing *The Red Shoes*. Her career or him, she can't make the choice."

Is there a choice? The question, which sat heavy in the air, was never asked nor answered.

"Anyway, she can't dance forever."

Betty yawned.

Jamie grabbed the remote and froze the frame. She'd noticed something rather alarming. The leading man, the composer, the object of the dancer's undying love, looked just like the man in the picture on their mother's dresser. In fact it was the man in the picture! Jamie gasped. "Shit, it's Mom's dad."

"What?"

"Maurice Goring, the actor. It's him, the guy in the picture, Betty." Jamie thought for a moment. "And there's the answer, why Mom was watching this movie."

Betty gave him a closer look. "Well…maybe…"

"And you know what? I bet those are the Red Shoes in that box."

Betty laughed. "Now look who's not living in reality."

Why Jamie was so sure of this, she had no idea.

"Well, if we had the box, maybe we'd know."

Jamie unfroze the frame and they continued watching with keener eyes, searching for a resemblance, pondering the irony. "Here it comes," Jamie warned, when at last the dancer had come to her terrifying realization, and Jamie turned at her sister, who was, to Jamie's profound disbelief, asleep. A blissful, peaceful sleep, and Jamie watched her for a few moments wondering how it was that she always slept so peacefully, especially at times like this. She became so distracted by this notion that it took a while for the white box with the gold velvet bow to come into her vision, sitting just beyond her sister on the floor, tucked half under the coffee table and partly camouflaged by an afghan. It took another minute for the box to become a conscious reality, and then everything screamed— the music, the people, the train—all of them were screaming, for the girl had made her last and final *grand jete*, and now she was lying crumpled in the arms of her lover, their mother's father, silent. All was silent, as the red shoes were removed from her bruised and battered feet and snatched up by the hands of that creepy little shoemaker. Everything faded to black but him. He was making the red shoes dance on with his hands now, like two little puppets, before he laid the shoes on the ground and stepped back into the darkness. Then the shoes themselves went dark. And the movie ended.

THE END

ACKNOWLEDGEMENTS

Thank you to everyone who read portions or all of this manuscript in various stages, drafts, and forms. Your feedback and persistent encouragement has been immeasurable, especially given the many years it took me to complete this novel. My siblings and parents, an eclectic group of friends, all of whom, for whatever reason, refuse to give up on me, and above all my husband—my muse, my life, and without whom this novel could not have been written.

ABOUT THE AUTHOR

Jackie Townsend, a native of Southern California, spends a lot of her time in places not her own. As the youngest of four children, she carries a strong sense of family with her to these places, often foreign, and writes about belonging (or not belonging), loss, and love. She lives in New York with her husband. *Reel Life* is her first book.

Read an excerpt of Jackie's upcoming novel, *Hurray for the Bride and Groom*, at jackietownsend.com

www.ingramcontent.com/pod-product-compliance
Lightning Source LLC
Chambersburg PA
CBHW051600100726
47898CB00001B/168